"Mallon's characters look forward to the future with hope, expecting it to bring a better life. His prose has the lucid, conventional quality of vintage mid-century American fiction; it tells a straightforward story, untouched by modernist games, with narrative and perspective."

—Wendy Smith, *Newsday*

"Mallon has so meticulously re-created a time and place that even trivial data has the force of nothing less than truth...Mallon's complicated meditation on the trials of private and public identity is beautifully fashioned."

—*Publishers Weekly*

"One of the most difficult things for a writer to achieve in a work of historical fiction...is a believable sense of the times...For a good example of how it's done, see Thomas Mallon's *Dewey Defeats Truman*."

—Roger K. Miller, *The Cleveland Plain Dealer*

"Historical novels often lose sight of the fiction for all the history, but Mr. Mallon keeps a tight rein on period detail...The best writers can make almost anything...jump off the page, and in *Dewey Defeats Truman* Mr. Mallon achieves this and more."

—Marc Carnegie, *The Wall Street Journal*

"Thomas Mallon is a smart, inventive, prolific writer...What interests him is not history per se but the ways in which large events touch and alter the lives of ordinary, unknown people."

—Jonathan Yardley, *The Washington Post*

"[Mallon] treats everyone in Owosso, no matter how foolish, with such profound gentleness and understanding that there are no modest lives in this modest community, and by the end of the book its inhabitants practically glow with hope and humanity."

—Daniel Akst, *L.A. Weekly*

"...A jubilant new novel...[*Dewey Defeats Truman*] isn't a contemporary novel. Every buoyantly alive sentence is suffused with an emotion from an era long gone: joy."

—Adrienne Miller, *GQ*

DEWEY

DEFEATS

TRUMAN

A Novel

THOMAS MALLON

Picador USA ❧ New York

Picador® is a U.S. registered trademark and is used by St. Martin's Press under license from Pan Books Limited.

Library of Congress Cataloging-in-Publication Data

Mallon, Thomas, 1951–
    Dewey defeats Truman / by Thomas Mallon. — 1st Picador USA ed.
        p.   cm.
    ISBN 0-312-18086-1
    1. Man-woman relationships Michigan —Owosso—Fiction. 2. Dewey, Thomas E. (Thomas Edmund), 1902–1971—Fiction. 3. Truman, Harry S., 1884–1972—Fiction. 4. Presidents—United States—Election —Fiction.   5. Owosso (Mich.)—Fiction. I. Title.
[PS3563.A43157   D48 1998]
813'.54—dc21   97-33390
                                                    CIP

First published in the USA by Pantheon Books, a division of Random House

First Picador USA Edition: January 1998

10   9   8   7   6   5   4   3   2   1

For Helen Harrelson

DEWEY

DEFEATS

TRUMAN

O N E

June 24

IT WAS AT MOMENTS LIKE THESE THAT BILLY GRIMES FELT
humiliated to be riding his old Columbia instead of one of
the English racers he'd coveted for years, ever since they
showed up in magazines during the war. At seventeen, what
he really required was a car, but that was another story, and
right now his only course of action was to press the button
on the metal box beneath the crossbar and sound the bell—
somebody's cornball idea of a built-in horn. Jeez, he might as
well have one of those jinglers on a kid's tricycle.

"Yeah, yeah," said the guy in the hat with the press card,
who was in the way, crossing the street and trying to keep his
cup of lemonade from spilling. "I see ya, kid. I see ya." He
could also see the folded newspapers in the Columbia's big
wire basket, the Owosso *Argus-Press* for June 24, 1948. OUR
TOM'S NIGHT IN PHILLY, proclaimed the rubber-banded
stalks.

Billy wanted to ask him how much Eddie Regan's kid sister had charged for the drink: more than the six cents she

was getting last week before the reporters showed up, and would be getting again once they left town? This was the sort of situation Billy watched. No business was too small, so long as it was your own and had a good idea behind it. This paper route could never belong to anyone but the Campbell brothers at the *Argus,* and Billy still made two cents a paper, same as he had four long years ago at the age of thirteen, the first time reporters camped out in front of old Mrs. Dewey's house a block back, the first time "Owosso's favorite son" got the Republican nomination for President. The guy in the hat (who, if he were anybody important, would be attached to a radio microphone instead of a pad and pencil) had probably come out to Michigan then, too. He didn't look all that pleased about returning. Probably a Democrat. All the reporters were, according to Billy's father, and they weren't happy about Dewey, a sure loser last time (had anybody expected him to knock off FDR?) being a sure winner this one.

Billy threw an *Argus* onto the second step of 403 West Oliver, a perfect hit, and rounded the corner to Adams. As nice as the sound of folded newsprint hitting painted wood might be, and despite its meaning two more cents toward a used Ford, Billy had to wonder if anything in his world would ever really change, or if four years from now he'd be twenty-one and still pitching papers from his seat on the Columbia as Owosso's favorite son started running for his second term. How much had changed in the *past* four years, after all? Each morning Mrs. Hazel Grimes still sent Mr. Robert Grimes off with a sandwich and a kiss to his desk at Cadwallader-Lord Insurance; and Billy was still living on Pine Street with two older sisters who'd never gone off to the war the way everybody else's brothers had.

One more year. Then he would be out of Owosso High and *not* on his way to Ann Arbor or MSC. All his friends were now deciding to be college men, as if the world offered no other choice. Billy only needed to get out of school and launch the right scheme, something that would work better than the ones he'd already tried. Each summer he found a new one, whether it was peddling weed killer he'd made in the basement or running a raft up and down the Shiawassee River, its painted sail advertising Christian's department store. Last summer he'd tried to get Gus Farnham, an old barnstormer who had flown in the First World War, to split the profits on fifteen-minute joy rides they could give local kids in Gus's old biplane. Gus would do the flying while Billy spread the word and sold the tickets. His father's colleague Max Barber would have provided the insurance, if old Gus hadn't shown up drunk at Cadwallader-Lord the morning they all met to discuss the plan.

Billy sometimes wondered if he wasn't jinxed—which was why he held on to the paper route year after year. But his faith in himself (what Dale Carnegie preached in his amazing book) always reasserted itself and made him believe that one day he would be another Charlie Wilson running General Motors. Or at least enough of a success to carry Margaret Feller over the town line like it was a threshold. Before he was through he'd set the two of them up in some place on Park Avenue in New York City. He had known Margaret forever, and been "seeing her" (his mother's phrase) since '46, contenting himself with a date every other Saturday night and kisses that were directed to her cheek (roughly 75 percent of the time), her lips (most of the remaining 25 percent) and twice—only twice—to her luscious neck. About everything else, he had been dreaming almost since Dewey had run for President the first time.

Maybe tonight, as the town got all worked up, and Our Tom had his night in Philly, Billy Grimes would have *his* dream of Margaret Feller. He was hoping for cymbals and confetti and dancing down Main Street, the kind of stuff that would whip everyone, including Margaret, into a frenzy— even if all of it was over some New York governor nobody but the old-timers could remember. After all, Tom Dewey had gotten out of Owosso thirty years ago. He might have done it by way of Ann Arbor, but Billy was still happy to feel his fortunes connected to this rackets-busting Man of Destiny. The point was *he had gotten out.*

Oh, for crying out loud, there she was, Jane Herrick and her green garden hose, standing there like a sour statue, watering her grass. She might be the mother of his best friend, Tim, but Billy was determined to avoid having to say hello to her. He flipped an *Argus* to the house across the street from hers, watching its flight as if he really needed to concentrate. Mrs. Herrick didn't even take the paper anymore. After her husband's early death ten years ago, and Tim's older brother, Arnie, getting killed in Belgium in '44, she didn't, as far as Billy could tell, take an interest in anything. "She's angry at life," his mother would say sympathetically.

It was now safe to look back over his shoulder. She wouldn't notice him glancing up toward Tim's open window for some sign that his friend sat behind the blue curtains fluttering over the sill. No, thought Billy, he wasn't there. He was bound to be lying on a bank of the Shiawassee, along one of the stretches below town, the ones where no one had ever been around to see the advertising sail on the raft. He'd be there with a book, even though it was a perfect summer day. Tim Herrick was the best first baseman in Owosso, and whenever he and Billy managed to sneak a couple of beers behind the Indian Trails bus terminal, Tim could turn into a wild man of joy, whooping and hollering as if he were possessed. But most days he was too serious for his own good, too ready to ask crazy questions that ought to be left to philosophers. When the Russians pushed Masaryk out a window last winter, Tim had asked Billy, as they rode to school in his car (the '36 Chevy that had belonged to Arnie), if he, Billy, sometimes wondered "if it meant nothing at all." Billy had thought he was talking about whatever the Russians hoped to accomplish by "defenestrating" the Czech foreign minister, but no, it turned out Tim meant *life itself,* the whole thing. Living with his morose mother was having a bad effect on him. "Herrick," he'd told him, "you're too damned deep and depressed. You need a tonic."

It was time to dismount. If the paper didn't hit the top step of Horace Sinclair's porch, right in the middle of the space under the overhang—God forbid a drop of water got on it—the old Spanish-American War cavalryman would have a holy fit. Calculating things on a time/labor basis, Billy figured he lost a half cent a day climbing off the bike to hand carry the paper to the porch: that was more than five dollars in five years. By rights, fat-assed old Mr. Sinclair— who, Billy's grandmother insisted, had been thin and handsome when he charged up San Juan Hill, or the one next to it—ought to be paying extra for the custom service, but Billy never even got a Christmas tip.

"Thank you, Grimes," said Horace Sinclair, sipping his glass of iced tea and not looking up from his copy of *Ivanhoe.*

He and "the late Mrs. Sinclair," as he still referred to his dead wife (a nice woman; *she* used to tip Billy) had always been great readers.

"It's a pleasure, sir." (Dale Carnegie couldn't have done better.) Billy got back on the Columbia after wiping his forehead and taking an envious look at the pitcher of tea. A few more houses to hit and that was it. He turned down Oak, deciding that the shade of its trees was better than any sip of tea the old man might have offered. Racing back west on Williams, depositing two more papers on porches and four more cents in his bank account, he reached a point where he could see through a couple of yards to the back of the two-story Comstock Apartments on Oliver, the ones where a number of his female teachers had lived over the years, and where he sometimes saw Anne Macmurray, the dishy girl from Abner's Bookstore, going in and out. If they all looked like her in Ann Arbor, where she'd gotten her diploma a year ago, Billy might be convinced to reconsider his plans; but most of the college-bound girls he knew were plain Janes. Margaret Feller was another exception; his biggest fear was that she'd insist on a college man for herself and send him a Dear John letter a semester after she left Owosso.

No, it wouldn't happen that way. By that time he'd have launched his scheme in a place bigger than this, and she'd be desperate to hear of its success. He too would be a GONE GOOSE, as the bedsheet hanging from the upper story of an ardent Republican house put it. The painted bird above the two words had Harry Truman's face and was winging its way back to Independence, Missouri. The phrase came from Mrs. Henry Luce's speech to the convention a couple of nights ago. Billy had heard it on the radio and decided there was no reason it couldn't apply to his success as well as Truman's failure. (Talk about a scheme. Imagine coming up with the idea for *Time* and *Life*. No wonder Henry Luce had landed himself a wife as clever as that.)

After throwing the last paper and turning the bike toward the center of town, he decided he might as well go find Herrick. On his way to the patch of riverbank where he knew Tim would be, he could pass City Hall and see if there were signs of preparation for the stupendous celebration he was hoping for. He sped down John Street past Curwood Castle. Built by Owosso's true favorite son, the late James Oliver Curwood, this stone imitation of a French fortress had always seemed an embarrassing thing to Billy, nothing on the order of the fortresses he'd read about in Howard Pyle's books. Curwood's "folly" (he'd learned the word from Mrs. Porter in sophomore English) had nothing to do with the man's own books, either, these nature novels full of wolves and bears and cayuses (whatever the hell *they* were) that had earned him his money and got made into movies. They were dull books to Billy, but you couldn't deny the success of the scheme. Curwood had turned himself into a brand name, and the proud librarians and Mr. Abner down at the bookstore liked to point out that by the time he died, the year before Billy was born, Curwood had outsold Zane Grey. He'd built the castle next to the house in which he'd toiled away at his first stories, and everybody seemed to think he was a swell guy for not abandoning Owosso after making his bundle. Like every other student at Owosso High, Billy had had to read the man's autobiography—just as, he supposed, all the younger ones would soon have to read Dewey's.

He crossed Main Street and was disappointed to see

nothing in front of City Hall but a bunch of picnic tables. It was still early, he told himself, taking the Columbia down Ball Street until he could cut over to the Shiawassee and—sure enough—spot Herrick, who was lying on his back and looking up toward the sun above the shiny waters, doing absolutely nothing. Billy wondered whether it was encouraging or a little creepy that he didn't have a book beside him. How could he just lie there? Close enough to make out the expression on his face, to see the lips that were slightly puckered in some kind of silent song, Billy cupped his hand to his mouth and came so close to shouting " 'Ey, *Her*-rick!"—his best imitation of Lou Costello calling Abbott—that he could almost hear the words before he said them.

But he didn't say them. Something told him, just this once, to let Tim be, to refrain from disturbing whatever daydream his friend was lost inside. Pretty sure he hadn't been seen, he backed the Columbia off the mud and out of the bushes, taking care not to snap a twig or make a sound, as if he were one of the Shiawassee who long ago had tiptoed here and given the river its name.

THE AFTERNOON WAS SO SLOW THAT ANNE HOPED MR. Abner, once he got back, would tell her to close up and call it a day. She was alone in the bookshop on South Washington, without anything to do since bringing up the five copies of Stanley Walker's 1944 campaign biography that had been lying in the basement for the past four years. *Dewey: An American of This Century* had gone to the printer before D-Day and was terribly out of date, but Mr. Abner hoped he might yet unload three or four of them while the renomination excitement lasted. Anne put the little pile next to Churchill's *Gathering Storm*, beside which, six months from now, if she was still in Owosso, she would be stacking General Eisenhower's memoirs, which Mr. Abner told her were scheduled to appear in time for Christmas shopping.

The whole war had begun to seem as far away as its very first day, that Pearl Harbor Sunday she'd slept late, after the previous night's junior-class dance at Darien High School, back in Connecticut. The Macmurrays would get through the war just fine, her two brothers coming home without a scratch. The biggest change it had made in her own life was bringing her to Michigan in the fall of '43. With her father away for weeks at a time with the OPA in Washington, and her mother indifferent to anything but the vigil she was keeping for her sons, there had been no one especially attentive to her choice of a college. When she suggested going out of state, to Ann Arbor, on no stronger grounds than some pleasant ideas of Michigan from two summer weeks spent with a cousin on Mackinac Island, her mother had said, "That sounds fine, dear," without looking up from the piece of V-mail she was reading.

Here she was, five years later, happily, if modestly, aware that she had become quite a bit harder to ignore. Her personality had come out with her cheekbones; she was a "vivid, literary girl," as one professor had put it in an evaluation she'd read upside down on his desk. She wanted to write a novel, one that had nothing to do with herself. All through the war her imagination had thrived by thinking of real life as what took place elsewhere and got lived by other people. "Elsewhere" had survived the war as an idea, a lure, and the notion that Owosso might be one of its quiet, unexpected precincts had brought her here a year ago: an Ann Arbor roommate had worked for Leo Abner in the summers and knew he could use a college graduate to help him in the shop by recommending things to his women customers. So, as she tried to make her own book come to life, she was spending her afternoons with those women—except that today there had been hardly any customers at all, ladies or gentlemen, which was why she now sat behind the counter reading *The Naked and the Dead,* a book that seemed to need no recommendation at all, that flew out of the shop, sometimes two at a time.

As an aspiring writer, Anne felt obligated to brave her way through it, no matter how rough it was supposed to be, and no matter how suspicious she was of best-sellers. She'd finally plunged in last week, and now, as most of the women customers liked to say, she couldn't put it down. Here, she thought, was what the war had really been, not the high-minded affair served up in the statesmen's memoirs. The other day she'd managed to lose her own copy, which she'd gotten at a 75 percent discount, so she was making do with one from the shelves, which she would take care to replace without dog-earing the pages when six o'clock came around.

It was barely five now, but she hoped the jingling bells on the front door meant that Mr. Abner, back from his errands, was going to tell her to go home.

"Got a date?"

It wasn't Mr. Abner at all. It was Peter Cox, several years older than herself and too attractive for his own good. As he stood in front of her, she looked at the way a thin layer of sweat had pinned his white shirt to his shoulders, and before she could be noticed, she shifted her gaze up to his blond hair and big brown eyes.

"A date for what?"

"History," he said. He was the town's number-one up-and-coming Republican, the newly arrived hot young lawyer at Harold Feller's firm across the street and, she'd heard from Mr. Abner, a candidate for the state legislature.

" 'And Franklin Roosevelt's looks,' " she started singing, " 'give me a thrill.' " She wasn't even a Democrat (though her dad was, a *rara avis* in Darien); she hadn't even been old enough to vote in '44, and wasn't certain if or for whom she'd vote this time, but something inside her insisted that she get under Peter Cox's skin, not give him one more thing in a lifetime of getting everything he wanted.

He put his hand over his heart. "I still have my Navy prayer book with Roosevelt's signature, Miss Macmurray, and I promise I'll treasure it to the day I die. But he's been gone three years, if you haven't noticed, and you surely can't be wild about Harry."

She smiled. "I'm not that wild about politics, Peter. And what's with 'Miss Macmurray'? I know we've only spoken a couple of times, but don't tell me you're putting on your campaign manners already. It's only June."

He sat down, entitled as you please, in Mr. Abner's chair behind the counter. "I'm crushed."

He had that *look*, the one she had noticed a year and a half ago, when he'd been pointed out to her in Ann Arbor; he'd been whizzing through his last year of law school, the one he'd missed when he joined the service. And now here he was in Owosso—with a purpose and a plan. They said he'd picked the town off a wall map at the state GOP's headquarters in Lansing. It showed a senate seat opening up in the Owosso district; an hour later he was on the phone to Harold Feller's office.

Could she really say that *she* had a plan? Her "writing": how many nights a week, back in her room on Oliver Street, did she work at it? Not one in the last two weeks.

"You'll get over it," she said.

"Politics?" asked Peter, knowing perfectly well she meant his being crushed. "I'll never have to. This is the beginning of everything for the Republicans. We've got a great crop all over the state. Over in Grand Rapids, Jerry Ford is running for Congress, and . . ."

"No older than yourself, I'll bet?"

"Five *years* older!"

Anne laughed as she twisted the scarf above her cardigan jacket. "You're keeping track, aren't you?" She wished she hadn't worn it: her neck was her best feature. She knew she was too thin and too tall and that her eyebrows were too thick, but in her neck she had absolute confidence, and here she was covering it up.

"Advanced, aren't we?" Peter asked, pointing to the open copy of *The Naked and the Dead.*

"He's five years *younger* than you are."

"The Army guys I met were the best fellows in the world. Not the bunch of animals he makes them out to be."

"You've read it?"

"Don't have to," said Peter.

What would *he* know? thought Anne. From what she'd heard, he'd spent the war behind some desk in London. "Well, it's very good, and I'd rather read it than Churchill's memoirs."

"Ike's will be coming along pretty soon."

She groaned, but he ignored her and began browsing a shelf. His fingers hesitated at another copy of the Mailer book.

"Go ahead," she urged. "You know you ought to pick it up."

"No, I don't."

He laughed and she began quoting from her own copy. " 'Goldstein thought he was on guard and had fallen asleep. He whispered desperately several times, "I wasn't sleeping. I was only closing my eyes to fool the Japs, I was ready, I swear I was ready." ' "

The bells jingled again. Still not Mr. Abner, but Jack Riley.

"Hi, Anne."

"Hello, Jack. This is Peter Cox."

"Yeah, I know who you are," said Riley, managing a thin smile and extending his hand. "You're running against Harvey Angell. A pleasure."

Anne was sure it wasn't. Jack Riley, who was two inches shorter than Peter, whose hair stood up in brown tonicked sticks and whose eyes were a little too close together—and who for all that was terribly appealing (those intense green eyes never seemed to shut)—was a UAW official in Flint. He was back in Owosso this summer to take care of his sick father, who lived next door to a friend of hers on Williams Street. They had been introduced last Saturday, over a hedge between driveways, as he washed his car. He wasn't through his third sentence explaining the reasons he'd returned to town before the old man was bellowing for him. He'd dropped into the store on Monday, finally asking for the

World Almanac instead of the date with her that she knew he'd come in for. She gave him twenty-five cents off—the book was six months old—but all he managed to say was "Good deal."

Now, back for a second run at it, he turned his attention away from Peter as fast as manners would permit. "Anne, how about a movie tonight? Do you want to see that one with Jane Wyman?"

"Yeah," Peter interrupted. "Ronald Reagan's wife. He's the union man out in Hollywood, isn't he, Jack?"

Riley offered no smile.

"Boys, boys," Anne clucked. "If you're going to fight, it'd better be over me."

"She can't go," Peter told Jack. "I'm taking her out."

"Excuse me?" asked Anne. "I'm nobody's wife, and I don't recall having heard myself say yes or no."

"You must have missed it," said Peter. "Trust me, you said yes. I'm picking you up at seven. You're a cheap date, too. They're serving supper outside City Hall in front of the radio speakers. Only seventy-five cents a plate."

She wanted Jack Riley to sock him. The trouble was she also wanted to accept. She couldn't face one more movie, and she doubted that Peter would ask a second time, whereas she was pretty certain Jack Riley would make a few more polite tries. "How about all three of us going?" she proposed.

"Dewey is a little more than I can stand," said Jack.

"I'll bet the seventy-five cents goes into his campaign coffers, too," Peter mentioned.

"Come on, Jack. Do it for history's sake," said Anne. "Or just to spy for the opposition."

For the first time he smiled, in her direction only. "Okay. I'm used to taking the best bargain I can get. I'll find you both there at seven." He waved good-bye and was out the door to another jangle of bells.

"Now we're stuck with him," said Peter. "I'm backing out."

"Well," said Anne, starting to straighten up the counter, "in that case, 'fug you.' "

"What?" Peter cried.

"Norman Mailer," she explained. "*Very* advanced."

OF COURSE, HE'D HEARD GRIMES, BUT HE WASN'T GOING TO let him know it. Billy's yapping about money and plans and baseball stats was too much to take sometimes, too much antifreeze to the system after hours of his mother's cold silences, which were so loud in their own way that he couldn't think his thoughts. And it was his thoughts he lived in. That's why an hour ago he'd just lain here, not moving a muscle, even though he could feel a bug crawling through his blond hair, could feel it making tracks across his scalp, causing him to wonder if his hair weren't already beginning to thin, the way everyone said Arnie's had just before he left home.

Billy would only have been wanting the two of them to go and watch the Dewey stuff, which Tim had no interest in, and which he couldn't go to anyway, having promised his mother that he'd fix an electric fan for her tonight. He could remember how four years ago she'd let herself get all excited and wouldn't stop telling the story of how Thomas E. Dewey had once taken her out to play tennis and how, once he was President, Roosevelt's war would end and Arnie would be home. She'd made you think that Dewey could raise the dead, that as soon as he was in the White House Dad might even reappear at the dinner table. This time she hadn't mentioned Dewey's name once, and Tim doubted if she could have told the difference, if the two of them came walking down Oliver Street, between Dewey in his homburg hat and Harry Truman in one of those Hawaiian shirts.

If he figured out how to fix the fan, he'd probably take off in Arnie's car for the drive-in outside Corunna. What was playing didn't matter. It wouldn't be *Henry V*, of course. They wouldn't put that on at a drive-in, though Grimes had insisted it was a great make-out movie, on account of no one being able to understand what anyone was saying. As if Billy couldn't really learn something from it if he applied his mind, and as if he'd ever gotten beyond halfway to first base with Margaret Feller.

Tim didn't care if there were no movie at all at the drive-in. It would be enough to sit in the open and look up at the stars, alone but not too alone, the light flickering on the screen and the other people in their other cars, the knowledge of them keeping his mind from going too far down its own road, the way it did when he was too far into the beer. No, secure in the presence of the other cars, he could sit there and try to confound the steady-state theory of the universe, something new that Mr. Sherwood had brought up in science class the week before school ended—scared, fussy Mr. Sherwood, who took such an interest in him and thought he was so deep and would blossom into some kind of minor genius once he went off to Ann Arbor. The steady-state theory was a depressing thing to contemplate, this idea that the whole universe was like an accordion, expanding and contracting, but never doing one thing any more than the other. It made the world seem like a trap, something from which there was no relief, and it seemed to contradict the rules of life here on earth, where for years his own world on Oliver Street had only been shrinking, down to himself and his mother. Mr. Sherwood had lately been full of interest in the big new Palomar telescope, but Tim thought that if the steady-state theory was the big truth it was going to find, they might as well keep the dome closed.

He shifted the book supporting his shoulders and neck; Grimes probably hadn't seen it and by now there were probably a lot of bugs crawling between its pages. It was *Raintree County*, by Ross Lockridge, and he'd nicked it from Abner's the other day, along with a copy of *The Naked and the Dead*, thinking he'd return both when he was through with them. It was only after he got home that he'd realized the Mailer book was the personal property of Miss Macmurray, who had been busy with two customers in the back and never saw him make off with it. In any case, it was *Raintree County* he'd really been after. He was already two hundred pages into it, certain he would find the passage—the key, or at least the clue—that told you why the author, just thirty-three, had decided, right after his book came out, to kill himself.

By NINE-THIRTY IT WAS ALL OVER BUT THE SHOUTING, AND Anne wished that were over, too. Senator Taft had conceded hours ago, and Stassen and Vandenberg (a truer favorite son of Michigan than Dewey, if truth were told) had both given up. Dewey had had his third-ballot victory and was now on his way to the convention arena, all of which the loudspeakers on the steps of City Hall, broadcasting NBC radio's live coverage from Philadelphia, had made deafeningly clear. The crowd of several hundred Owossoans filling the rows of picnic tables at the intersection of Main and Water Streets was in a good, partisan humor, though there were exceptions, like Jack Riley on Anne's right, who had exchanged barely a word with Peter Cox, on her left. They'd long since gone through their seventy-five-cent allotment of beer and ham sandwiches, and Anne was depending on the Fellers— Peter's boss, Harold, and his wife Carol—to keep things civil until the governor could make his acceptance speech.

"You know," said Harold Feller, "I can remember the day in 1924 they laid the cornerstone for that building. I was twenty-three. I still think it's a handsome pile, don't you, Anne?" He pointed to City Hall behind him. Anne smiled and nodded. She liked his blend of pride and self-deprecation. He and his wife had a nice commonsensical ease to them. They were the local gentry, which meant more than it would have in Darien, where everyone was gentry more or less, but there was nothing puffed-up about them. Peter Cox was lucky to have found such a man, even if Harold Feller's law office were no more than a rest stop on his way to the governor's mansion or wherever else Peter was certain the road would lead.

"I call it the Greco-Wolverine style," said Carol Feller, a pretty brunette, a little Myrna Loy–ish, who was laughing at herself for making this joke, which she'd clearly been making for years, about City Hall's combination of classical columns and simple yellow bricks.

"Nothing wrong with little stretches toward grandeur," said her husband. "And speaking of those, Anne, have you ever seen the Dewey birthplace? Look down a block. See the appliance store? The apartment above it is where he actually came into the world. The big place on Oliver came later. By the way, where is Mama Dewey tonight? Does anyone know?"

"At *home,*" grumped Horace Sinclair, who had taken a seat beside Carol Feller, after she'd spotted him puffing through the crowd on his walking stick and insisted he join them. "Where *I* ought to be."

"Oh, stick around, Colonel. We need you for some historical perspective," implored Peter, with a politician's flattery: the "colonel" was a nice touch, Anne thought.

"You mean I'm an old crock," said Horace Sinclair. "And so I am. And I can give you a little perspective on the young Tom Dewey, for what it's worth. Not a particularly pleasant boy. A bit too much confidence and a bit too quick with his fists—don't let that dainty little mustache fool you. A fast-buck operator, too. Used to charge his mother a quarter to mow her lawn."

The Fellers laughed, and said, more or less together: "Billy."

"Who's Billy?" asked Peter.

"Our daughter's ardent suitor," Carol explained. "I'm sure you'll see him before the evening is over, selling souvenirs or peanuts."

"Or campaign buttons for our next President," said Peter, who reached around Anne—managing to brush her back on the way—and clapped Jack Riley on the shoulder. "Cheer up, Jack. You've still got Harry for another six months. And it could have been worse. We could have nominated Taft."

"What makes you so sure I'm for Truman?" asked Riley,

without much of a smile. "How do you know I'm not going to vote for Wallace?"

"Good for you, Jack," said Carol Feller, who meant it, too, in the spirit of fair play and democracy, though she and her husband hardly wished any luck to the expected third-party run by Roosevelt's onetime vice president, who, Anne's father assured her, was little different from Stalin. Jack gave Mrs. Feller a grateful nod, and the party appeared ready to move on from politics, at least the radical kind Jack Riley might actually favor. You couldn't tell: the last two months, ever since somebody had wounded Walter Reuther with a shotgun, the feelings of autoworkers in these parts had been running high.

Anne was happy to change the subject in any case. Politicians bored her. She looked at City Hall and its yellow bricks and thought of the road to the Wizard of Oz. They were all like him, promising they'd change everything, even the weather if you asked them to. As it was, the weather had taken a change toward coolness, and she was now glad she had the cardigan jacket (though she'd gotten rid of the scarf that hid her neck). Whatever additional warmth she might require was being supplied by Peter Cox, whose hand had never made it all the way home from its friendly tap of Jack Riley, and had come to rest across her own shoulders. Once or twice he had also managed to maneuver his leg beneath the broad folds of her walkaway skirt. This was a fast worker, she thought, almost wishing she were padded inside the giant contours of last year's fashions, which she hadn't had the money or inclination to buy, but which offered a woman the protection of a football player's uniform. Being of the lower orders, Jack Riley, who she bet was a better kisser than Peter Cox, had had to behave like a gentleman all evening.

Wasn't that Frank Sherwood, who lived in the same block of apartments she did? He was passing just a few feet away, so she waved him over—and instantly regretted it. He had only been trying to cross the street, and her summons put him into an agony of embarrassment, since he now had to come over and offer the table his feminine handshake and some unprepared mutterings.

"Mr. Sherwood is our resident astronomer," Anne explained to Peter and Jack. "He's out most nights on the roof, looking at the stars."

"I'm just one of the science teachers at the high school," he apologized, his eyes looking toward Carol Feller, who could be counted on for social ease and protection.

"Our daughter Margaret hopes to be in your class next year," she said with a smile. "One of her friends, Tim Herrick, speaks very highly of you."

The sun had long since sunk into the Shiawassee, but Anne could tell that Frank was blushing. Then somebody managed to crank the speakers to an even higher volume, and nothing could be heard except the voice of whoever it was, a thousand miles away in Philadelphia, calling Thomas E. Dewey to the platform.

Frank took this deafening opportunity to wave good-bye to everyone at the table and melt back into the crowd, still carrying a little paper bag that contained, Anne was sure, his dinner. Part of the crowd was up from the benches and on its feet, whooping for Dewey as if he were really about to emerge from behind the big black speakers. Peter Cox was one of those who had risen, the better to cheer and the better to press his hand into Anne's shoulder, to rub it in a way she wished she could resent as much as Jack Riley seemed to.

If the assembled Owossoans were hoping some customized sentence or two might emerge from the square yards of black mesh—a homesick greeting from the local boy who stood upon the mountaintop in Philadelphia—it never came. *"Our task is to fill our victory with such meaning that mankind everywhere, yearning for freedom, will take heart and move forward out of this desperate darkness into the light of freedom's paradise."* Anne was sure Jack Riley had heard a lot hotter speechmaking in the union halls of Flint. Before it was finished, people were back down on the benches, using the bursts of broadcast applause as opportunities to resume their own conversations.

"I'll bet this is the last time we're not in front of a television set for one of these," said Carol Feller. "Margaret is already telling us to get one."

Horace Sinclair made a face—not, as Anne first thought, over the notion of television, which was already broadcasting the convention to those towns that had it, but at the idea of Dewey's victory. "Watch what this does to the town," he said.

"Oh, we'll manage, Horace," said Harold Feller.

"Come on, Colonel," offered Peter. "This is the American century! And Owosso is going to be at the center of things until January twentieth, 1957. *Two* terms, don't you think, Riley? He won't be greedier than that. We'll leave the four-term runs to you Democrats."

"You young men . . . ," said Horace Sinclair.

These three words, obviously a familiar warm-up to lengthy complaints, made Harold Feller laugh. "Horace won't even let Bob Harrelson sell him a *car.*"

Anne was determined, the next time she was alone with him, to give Peter Cox a little lecture on the rudeness of overdoing it, whether it was politics or pawing.

"Oh, look, everybody," said Carol Feller. "Let's have our picture taken for the *Argus.*" A young man with a camera was snapping photos of some of the tables, as if it were a wedding. Peter Cox, knowing that the Fellers were as likely to be chosen for the front page as any couple in Owosso, immediately took charge, gathering everyone into position. As the photographer fiddled with his nighttime flash, Carol Feller effortlessly kept her smile and continued talking, pointing out, with a tilt of her head, yet more groups of people, over here, over there. "That's the Herrick boy I mentioned before, in that car at the edge of the crowd. I worry about him, but not as much as I worry about his mother. I wish she were down here. Something fun like this might do her good."

As the flash went off with an audible burp, it lit the scene in front of Anne's eyes, and she noticed Margaret Feller, Carol's daughter, a couple of tables away with friends her age, looking hungrily at Tim Herrick's blond head in the last second before his car jumped the red light.

There was a second flash, a big one, from a concession booth that had just flung itself up at the foot of City Hall's steps. Dewey was still perorating in Philadelphia, but—what?—he seemed to be here. As several gasps indicated, some people believed he actually was, until they realized, along with everyone else, that they were looking at a giant black-and-white photographic cutout of the governor of New York, around whom Al Jackson, the town's camera and electronics salesman, had draped a friendly arm.

"Billy Grimes will explain it to you!" he told the clutch of people fast assembling.

"That's right!" said Billy, who was holding up a stiff little square of paper, so excited by this job he'd been offered out of the blue a few hours ago that he was barely trying to spot Margaret Feller in the crowd. "I'm Mr. Jackson's new assistant. Starting tomorrow morning, for one dollar, outside the post office, you can have your picture taken with the next President of the United States by the first Polaroid camera in Owosso, Michigan. It'll be in your hands sixty seconds after the shutter clicks!"

The crowd oohed in knowing amazement. They had heard about this camera on the radio, even read about it in the *Argus*.

The whole Feller party had gotten up and now stood at the edge of Al Jackson's display. *"That,"* said Carol, "is Billy." Peter nodded, as Horace Sinclair tapped Jack Riley on the arm. "If you get any buttons from your union boys—I don't care if they're Truman buttons or Wallace buttons—will you send me one?"

"Yes, sir," said Jack, laughing for the first time tonight.

"Good!" boomed Horace Sinclair. "I'd rather have Charlie McCarthy in the White House than see these jackasses turn this town into a tourist trap for the next four years."

"Eight," corrected Peter, with a smile for the old man. "Anne, what do you say? Ready to go home?"

"Yes," she said, "but Jack is taking me." Peter looked at the two of them, trying to hide his disbelief that she could resist him or his brand-new '49 Ford. "I promised him when we first sat down. You didn't hear us. I think you were telling Mrs. Feller why Senator Vandenberg's foreign policy was too much like Truman's for him to have been the candidate. Something like that."

Everyone's eyes turned to Peter.

"Fair enough," he said. "I'll call you." It was a suave recovery, Anne thought, until she and Jack got ten feet on their way and heard Peter calling out, with a politician's terrible heartiness: "Riley!"

They turned around.

"You're fighting two lost causes!"

T W O

June 25

ANNE SQUEEZED THE ATOMIZER ON THE BOTTLE OF SCHIA-
parelli her brother had given her last Christmas. She never
touched it without thinking of the Japanese being blown to
smithereens by the Bomb, and that this particular fragrance
would make better sense on a girl in a Norell jacket brushing
past Walter Winchell at the Stork Club than on one getting
dressed for a day at Abner's Bookshop and an evening with
no plans at all. Still, she thought, this was what she'd chosen
for "the time being," a good name for her unpalpable present, as well as the working title of the novel she was trying to
write (her work-in-stasis, she liked to say when people asked
about it).

As she combed her hair, the curtains blew gently into
the room, revealing maple trees against a sunny sky. In New
York this late in June it would be sweltering, and she would
be sharing a room beside the El with two other girls. Here in
Mrs. Wagner's little two-story block of apartments, curiously
zoned into the green, prosperous world of Oliver Street, all

she had to share was a bathroom, with Frank Sherwood, who was neat as a cat and too meek to complain about her hairpins and lipstick stains, which she could never quite keep off the sink and hand towels. He never made a sound, didn't even play the radio, whereas she was sure he could hear hers, right now, through the wall behind the mirror.

"I feel very pleased to know that Tom Dewey has again been selected to run for President," former mayor Ellis was saying over WOAP. "There is no question that our next President will be a Republican and that our own Tom will be that chief executive." Some enterprising reporter had been out this morning with a tape recorder, getting reactions to the nomination, which were uniformly well-wishing, midwestern proud, even from the head of the Shiawassee County Democratic Party. The only hint of sourness came from a "man on the street" who requested that he not be identified: "I see no reason why he shouldn't be as good as the other candidates. I also see no reason why he shouldn't be better." Anne wondered if this might be old Mr. Sinclair. It sounded like him, and he was surely the early-to-rise type.

She looked out her window, west across Adams and down toward Pine. There was no sign of commotion near Annie Dewey's house. The out-of-town reporters must already have packed up. Straining for a better look, she noticed the Fellers' place, diagonally opposite the candidate's mother, and she decided to take Carol up on her invitation to drop in for coffee some morning soon. Mr. Abner wouldn't mind if she opened up a little late.

It was a big white clapboard with a gay red-shingled roof hanging over dormers and bay windows and a wraparound porch. The front door, bordered by two white columns, faced neither Oliver nor Pine but stood at a forty-five-degree angle to each, fronting onto the corner itself. When Anne appeared, at the kitchen door around the side, Carol seemed no more surprised than if her husband had entered the room still tying his tie. She just said hello and set a cup of coffee on the table. She went to turn down the radio, but the end of an item on WOAP's "Civic Calendar" caught her ear. "The Owosso Armory will be open from seven to eleven o'clock tonight and from eight to five tomorrow. All applicants must be enlisted and qualified by midnight Saturday . . ."

"Applicants for what?" asked Anne.

"The National Guard. They've put a ceiling on Michigan enlistments, and tomorrow is the last day. Mr. Truman is going to sign the draft bill, and if my son Jim were here instead of camping with his Dartmouth buddies somewhere on the upper peninsula, he might have a chance to get into Company I. I'm afraid he's going to arrive home a month from now, dirty and happy as can be, only to find orders taking him to boot camp and Berlin."

Anne noticed that throughout this explanation the corners of Carol's mouth never dropped; she might have been making a humorous complaint against the high cost of living—or HCL, as the newspapers had taken to calling it, as if it were rising too fast for anyone to take the time to say all five syllables.

"No need to rush things with Jim," said Harold Feller. Late for the office, he had just hurried downstairs. "Hello, Anne." He refused an offer of toast from his wife. "I was too young for the First War but had a couple of friends who weren't. And they got over to the Argonne with Company M.

This was just about the smallest city in the country ever to get a Guard unit, and twenty years after we did, we lost more boys than any city its size in the whole United States. That's a fact. And if you don't believe me, you can ask Horace Sinclair."

Mrs. Feller laughed.

"If there's another war," Harold continued, "they'll get Jim one way or the other. There's no need to bring him home by bush telegraph. And no need to be so worried, either." He kissed his wife, and Anne, who was still reminding herself that, against all appearances, this town of sixteen thousand was technically a city, lost any feeling of distaste for what had looked like Carol Feller's unmaternal calm. She guessed that the woman's husband of twenty-five years knew when she was worried and when she wasn't.

"Where's Margaret?" Harold Feller asked his wife.

"Gone off in the Chevy. Ages ago."

He put on his jacket and smiled at Anne. "Any message for Peter?"

"Do get lost, sweetheart," said Carol, snatching her husband's coffee cup and giving him a little shove toward the door. "You're embarrassing Anne." She handed him the Detroit paper and he was on his way.

"*Was* there any message?" asked Carol, who now sat down and gave her guest her full attention.

"No," said Anne.

"Needless to say, we talked all about the two of you before falling asleep last night. Is there anything you want to know about *him*?"

"Harold?"

"No. Peter, of course."

Anne, who could hardly pretend she'd come here for

anything else, warmed to the subject. "Well," she said, "is there a girlfriend?"

"Lots of them," said Carol.

"Oh."

"But no one special. I'm sure that's what he's looking for, and why he's looking at you."

"Does he need a wife? To run for the legislature?"

"No," said Carol, after a moment's pause to think. "Running for Congress requires a wife, I should imagine. The state senate probably lets you get away with being a bachelor."

"I have to say," Anne ventured, "from the way he acted last night, you could never tell he was looking for someone special."

"A little fast with his hands?" asked Carol, who had seen more than enough to require an answer, and pressed forward to a topic on which she *could* use some information. "How was Mr. Riley on your ride home?"

"A perfect gentleman."

"Disappointed?"

"No, not really," said Anne, laughing, and lying.

"I think he's luscious," said Carol Feller. "In a rough sort of way."

"He's taking me to the movies Sunday night."

"What's the picture?"

"The Bishop's Wife," Anne answered, and the two women groaned.

"He's afraid to ask you to something steamy at the Corunna drive-in. In fact, I think he and Peter have both decided to play against type."

"But I don't have a type," Anne protested.

"Oh, Anne, they're just *men*. You can't expect them to be subtle enough to entertain that possibility. But good for Jack Riley, even if he's seeing you as Loretta Young." She made a face. "Let's give Peter an inning, too. I'm having a dinner party a week from tonight, and I'll put him across from you."

"HEY, MISS MACMURRAY! COME ON OVER AND HAVE YOUR picture taken!"

Anne looked down at her thin little Gruen wristwatch. It was already 9:20, and if she was any later, even Leo Abner would likely lose his temper. But how could she disappoint fresh-faced Billy Grimes, who'd spotted her from his new place of business, the sidewalk in front of the post office, a half block down Exchange Street? She hurried across Washington, noticing that Carol's daughter was with him, helping to take customers' money before positioning them against the giant cutout of Dewey.

If Margaret had curls, instead of a ponytail, she would be tossing them, Anne thought: this girl was in a pet, eager to be anywhere but here and doing this. "Hello, Miss Macmurray," she managed to say, as Billy held on to a little boy whose mother was wetting down his cowlick. She was such a pretty girl, with all that strawberry blond hair; why try to hide the freckles under makeup that would start flaking by noon? "He wants me to be here all morning," said Margaret. "I wish I had a job of my own to go to, like you do."

"I wish I *didn't* have one," said Anne.

"Would you just write your book instead?"

In Owosso, it wasn't simply a case of word getting

around. Anne sometimes thought the trees were hung with invisible wire that carried the residents' whispers and thoughts, maybe even their dreams, from one head to another.

"That's what I tell myself."

"Where do you find the time?"

"In the evenings. Sometimes at the library. Tonight, I'm sure, since I've got no other plans."

"Come on, Margaret," Billy pleaded. "Just *one?*" He wanted her to stand next to a farmer who was in town to pick up a package at the post office and ready to splurge a dollar. Like most of Billy's customers, the man seemed more intrigued with the new camera than with the second-time candidate, and here into the bargain was a chance to put his arm around a pretty girl's waist. Margaret, remembering her manners, obliged. She made a thin smile and suppressed a glare at Billy long enough for him to snap the shutter. Then she stormed off to her father's Chevrolet, waving good-bye to Anne and leaving Billy to collect the perplexed farmer's money.

"She's always doing things like that," sighed Billy. "She's not happy unless she gets herself crazy once a week."

"Give me an example. A quick one."

"Oh, like a few summers ago, when she went in with those girls who helped some Jerry prisoners escape. I'm not fooling," he said, noting Anne's look of disbelief. "We had a POW camp outside of town, and some of the German guys were put to work at the canning factory. A few girls on the line got stuck on them and hid them in a basement. Margaret was only thirteen, and had more brains than these girls put together, but when one of them spilled the story to her on line at Kroger's, Margaret put twenty dollars' worth of groceries on Mr. Feller's tab—*food,* for some German soldiers she never even got to meet! She just gave the six bags to the girl who was hiding them."

"What happened to the soldiers?"

"They lived like kings in that basement for a couple of days before they got caught and taken back to the camp. The girls from Roach's got some kind of probation."

"How about Margaret?"

"She didn't even get hollered at. She's Daddy's little girl, you know. Mr. Feller'd let her get away with anything."

So Daddy's little girl had been looking for a grand passion since she was thirteen years old. Tim Herrick's feathery yellow hair, Anne now guessed, belonged in part to those German boys Margaret had never gotten to see.

"I'll tell you one thing," Billy continued. "Those Jerries knew how to work. That's what every farmer around here, not just the cannery boss, will tell you. Wait till this Marshall Plan kicks in and they're back on their feet over there."

Anne smiled. "Billy, I've got to get to work, if I'm going to stay on mine." She wished there were some sign of Margaret's contrite return, so she wouldn't be leaving this poor eager beaver with nothing but his cardboard cutout. "Oh, look," she said. "You've got a customer coming."

"Nah," said Billy, looking down Exchange Street. "It's my boss, Mr. Jackson."

"Hey, Billy!" shouted the fast-walking figure. "Who's your pretty friend?" As he came into closer view, Anne realized that his speed was more nervous than youthful. He must be almost forty. He was *loud,* too, and sweating more than the weather demanded. He pushed up his eyeglasses—black plastic ones instead of the wire contraptions most men in town still curled over their ears—and extended a thin, hairless arm toward her. She let him pump her hand, noticing as he did that his shirtsleeves were actually made short, cut and hemmed that way instead of rolled up.

"You're in a hurry this morning," she said.

"Been in a hurry ever since I got back from France in '45. Worked at Chrysler before the war, but decided to get off the line and into business. Moved my wife Marie and daughter Jennie from Detroit to here and opened the store at 125 West Exchange Street. Haven't seen you there! Come on in and I'll reserve one of these for you. They don't go on sale till fall." He pointed with one short-sleeved arm to the Polaroid camera, while the other reached into his pants pocket for a business card. "Had your picture taken with the next President?"

Anne pleaded appearance. "I'm afraid I'm not as well turned out as Mr. Dewey this morning. Perhaps another time." As she talked, Al Jackson supplied a sort of commentary with his hands, as if he were translating the words of a deaf-mute: a sharply pointed finger that seemed to say "you're absolutely right" about Dewey's grooming; a palms-down seesaw to underline the maybe, maybe not of the last part.

"It's on me, Miss Macmurray. That *is* your name, isn't it? Come on." He commandeered her, as Billy had Margaret, to a place between himself and the candidate, whose photographic mustache and moist, canine eyes were at a level half an inch below her own. She slouched a bit upon noticing she was also taller than Mr. Jackson.

"Hold this," he said, handing her his briefcase. He broke the pose to help Billy with the suddenly balky camera.

"Is there anything in this?" she asked when he got back. "It feels so light."

"That briefcase contains twenty-seven pieces of—smile!—paper, Miss Macmurray." They stepped away from Dewey as Billy began the sixty-second Polaroid countdown. "But they're twenty-seven pages—three sets, one original, two carbons, nine pages apiece—that are going to change everything. Been working on them for weeks. Marie finished typing this morning. They're the future of Owosso, Miss Macmurray. A master plan. Isn't that right, Billy?"

"Thirty-eight, thirty-seven, thirty-six," Billy continued to mutter as he nodded agreement.

"I'm on my way with them to the *Argus*, and City Hall, and then, this afternoon, to WOAP. Which means I could use you, Billy, to mind my store between three and five. Can you do that?"

"Twenty-two, twenty-one, twenty . . ." Vigorous nods.

"Good! And make sure you give Miss Macmurray her discount when she comes in."

He was already halfway toward Washington Street, where she ought to be, and down which she now saw Margaret Feller's Chevrolet tearing at a rate that would provoke scowls from mothers with strollers.

"He almost looks alive, doesn't he?" asked Billy, handing her the still-curly photograph.

Anne pondered Dewey's figure and countenance. "I'm not sure I'd go that far."

"Hurry, baby, *hurry.*"

"Yeah," murmured Jack Riley, trying to, panting, squeezing Louise Rutkowski's bare, thin shoulders even harder, pushing faster. It was Louise who had already finished, a full minute ago, with a neat satisfied shout; he was the one who couldn't quite get there, though he did every Friday at just this time with Louise, here on the beat-up green leather couch in the Flint UAW office he shared with Walt Carroll. Louise dug her nails deeper into his back, and licked his cheek, patiently urgent, and he kept saying yeah, and getting closer, until he'd catch a glimpse of his own socks, which he never had time to remove during one of these meetings, or a pile of REPEAL TAFT-HARTLEY flyers that Walt had neatly stacked. Then he'd lose that ready-to-peak sensation, feel it subside back into his thighs.

He closed his eyes and tried to concentrate, *thinking* about, instead of looking at, Louise, who had flecks of gray in her hair but was amazingly trim for somebody with four grown kids, her taut arms more like a girl's than a forty-five-year-old woman's. She was happy about all this—thrilled, she said—even if she still loved Carl. And why shouldn't she? Everybody loved Carl; even *he* loved Carl, who had sat down with Jack's father during the '37 strike and patted Jack on the shoulder when at sixteen he came with his mother and a thousand other kids and wives to pass food through the windows of the plant. Now Carl was at home, permanently, with a bad back from taking too many chassis down from their hooks on the line; and Jack was here, humping Carl's wife, who was eighteen years older than himself. She'd explained it to him: "I was faithful all through the war, all through those years when the other men were away and, believe me, sweetie, nobody was faithful, not completely, so I'm not going to feel bad about having my fun now, especially not with somebody as gorgeous as you." And that was when she pulled back on his spiky hair and plunged her face into his with a fierceness that usually got him as crazy as she was, but today—

Now, on top of everything else, the phone was ringing.

"Don't, baby, *don't!*"

"I've got to. It's my old man. I told him to—"

"*Don't!*" Louise cried, turning the radio dial sky high, so that WWJ's *South American Way* would drown out the ringing.

"Walt's gonna come in—"

"*No,*" said Louise, quickly changing to "Yes, *yes,*" pretending to be ready again, to be with him now, an idea that got him close to the breaking point, which was what he reached, finally, when the image of Peggy Lee, who was singing "Mañana," came into his mind—that strange blond babe, the little voice like a wisp of smoke escaping a volcano. This was what it took to blow away the picture of Anne Macmurray that had been sneaking into his brain every few seconds. Peggy brought him over the top like there was no tomorrow, no *mañana,* and Louise pretended to go right there with him.

"That's my baby boy," she said, already on her feet and pulling up her stockings. Jack rested his head on the fat green back of the couch, a white towel over his shoulders, like a dazed boxer who'd fought his way to a draw.

"Friday," said Louise, kissing him.

"Yeah."

"You're a good boy, Jack. Call your dad."

Through the frosted-glass panel in the door he saw her slender form retreat toward the daylight, back toward the bus and the market to shop for Carl's supper.

He dialed the phone. "Pop?"

"Where were you?" asked Gene Riley, twenty miles west in Owosso.

"Did you call? I went down the hall to get a Coke. How you feelin'?"

"I'm fine. And listen, speaking of Coke, don't bring any home tonight. Get some beer. I don't give a crap what Dr. Hume says. I'm not going to listen to the fight sipping a Coke."

"Okay," said Jack. "I guess we can make an exception."

"What kind of odds are the fellas giving?"

"On the fight, you mean? I haven't had a chance to hear anything. I don't think there's much betting going on."

"Yeah," said Gene. "They can't get interested if it's just one colored guy against another."

"Pop, I've got to go. I'll bring the beer and some potato chips. Is Mrs. Goldstone gonna bring dinner?"

"That's what you pay her to do, isn't it? Since I can barely do a goddamned thing for myself anymore?"

"All right. You're complaining enough I can tell you're all right. So I'll sign off."

"See you later, Johnny."

Jack sat back for another minute, wiping his face with the towel and thinking about the afternoon ahead: nothing but a meeting on whether the union was happy enough with its new eleven-cent-an-hour increase from GM to join in the planned August celebration of the one-hundred-millionth car to come out of an American plant. He put the towel out of sight and checked his belt to make sure it was fastened, and realized that his twenty minutes with Louise had left him hungry. He'd have to find some lunch somewhere. He'd forgotten his own on the kitchen counter back home; this morning he'd been busy preparing his father's when he looked up at the clock and realized it was time to go. Right now he only had the energy to stare at the splintery wooden floor.

Soon the door had opened and shut, the frosted glass rattling in its square. It was Walt, who looked at him just sitting there and laughed. "You look like you need a mother."

"I need a wife," Jack replied. And not Carl's, either.

ANNE READ THE *ARGUS* FOR A SECOND TIME, THE LAST HALF of her tuna-fish sandwich resting on its post-convention editorial:

> *Their choice for a presidential candidate is almost assured of being the man who will occupy the White House after next January twentieth. The delegates were in effect practically electing a President of the United States.*

The phrasing was as redundant as the election itself appeared to the editors.

But the election's conclusion was the only one they regarded as foregone. Everything else in the *Argus* was a spirited contest: tonight's fight; the evening-gown round of the Miss Owosso competition to be held next week at the Capitol Theatre. In fact, the paper appeared to imagine the town's whole life as a healthy competition, in which the boosterish forces of thrift and industry and get-up-and-go were sure to triumph over all but mortality. Even that foe was conceded to grudgingly: "Mrs. A. Middleton Taken By Death" went the headline of today's obituary, done in the standard formula.

The paper made one feel that Mrs. Middleton and all the dead in Oak Hill Cemetery were victims of a technical knockout, defeated perhaps, but crossing the bar like good sports.

Regardless of the *Argus,* Anne's life in Owosso seemed ever more maddeningly tranquil. In the hours since she'd gotten to the bookstore, she had sold exactly three books: two guides from the *See America* series and one copy of Pearl Buck's new novel. The '44 Dewey biographies remained untouched. The only customer in here now, a tall, thin woman who looked familiar, had walked past them with a curled lip. A Truman supporter? There had to be at least a few in town. Anne reminded herself to draw Jack Riley out on the subject Sunday night.

For the past five minutes the woman had been at the little shelf of home-repair manuals, copying out some fixit instructions that she'd obviously come in here to look up without having to spend $4.50 for the book. Anne's "May I help you?" got a crisp "No, thank you." She refrained from any further prodding and worried about becoming like Leo Abner, too soft for his own good as a businessman. Boredom was making her slipshod. She had the radio on, down low but tuned to *Swingmates,* just to keep herself awake. She turned a page of the *Argus* and *I Love Trouble* caught her eye: the movie she wouldn't be seeing at the Corunna drive-in, where she and Jack Riley wouldn't be necking.

The woman had moved to the knickknacks and notions and picked up a little date book she seemed ready to pay for. With a check, no less, though the book cost only forty cents. Anne ceded her a smile, and then, all at once, taking in the whiteness of her knuckles, and the pink overscrubbed skin of her face, felt flooded with sympathy. Of course, she thought, looking at the tight, precise signature: it was the Herrick boy's mother. She could now even remember when she'd first seen her, a couple of years ago in front of City Hall, on her first visit to the town, with her roommate, the Owosso girl who eventually got her this job. It had been a November day in '45, her junior year. The survivors of Bataan were being displayed and cheered by everyone in town, even a badly burned man in a wheelchair, a victim not of the war but of some horrible childhood accident years before, who'd come to applaud some friend, she guessed, maybe the only boy who had never made a cruel remark or stared at him.

In fact, she could remember Jane Herrick's stare from that fall morning: piercing, intently curious, though Anne had noticed it only when her attention was drawn by the woman's mutterings, a quiet stream of dates and numbers coming out of her like tape from an adding machine, calculations with no apparent meaning to anyone but herself. She had looked at the survivors without hostility or joy, just a sort of demographer's zeal, as if there might be a clue in their faces or bearing as to why they had returned intact and not in a coffin.

They were still coming home, those coffins. Right under the *Argus*'s eight-column headline—GOV. WARREN TO TEAM WITH DEWEY—was the story of "4 More Heroes Coming Back," three from military graves in the Philippines, another from Europe. Every few weeks you'd see the same item about a little color guard being assembled to go down to the Grand Trunk depot and meet the skeleton of some boy who had lain for years beneath an Asian moon or the wings of French nightingales, but still had to be dug up, replanted amidst native flowers and birdcalls before he could be truly dead.

"Thank you," said Anne, putting the check beneath the change tray in her register. (Wait a minute, she thought. Hadn't this woman bought a date book just last month? Was that possible?) Mrs. Herrick said nothing, just put the item into her purse.

Anne watched her go out and turn right. After a minute passed, she went to the door herself and stepped into the sunshine for the first time since arriving this morning. She watched Jane Herrick walk further south on Washington Street, quickly, as if she were a soldier herself, doing double time to the quick beat of some drumming Anne could hear coming from—where? Across the street: the long, slender form of Peter Cox, up on a ladder in his blue striped shirtsleeves, hammering nails into a thick cardboard sign above the entrance to Harold Feller's law office, the sort of sign that was multiplying all over town today. This one went, DEWEY: HONESTY, STRENGTH. She had enough of the first to know she wanted him to turn and wave; enough of the second to keep from calling out to him.

HE SAW HER ALL RIGHT. AS HE STEPPED DOWN TO THE SIDEwalk and looked up to admire his work—absolutely straight, a museum director couldn't have done better—he knew she was there in the corner of his eye. But when he looked across Washington Street, it was toward the south end and—ah, the widow Herrick, poor thing. He'd heard about her from Harold's wife. She must be headed to Oak Hill, to sit alone in the gazebo and think about her boy. If Dewey were smart, he wouldn't harp too much on fear of another war. The last one still had its stone hand on half the hearts in towns like this one. If you were going to talk about the future, you might as well let people believe there'd be one.

What had Riley's war been like? he wondered. Had he spun her some sad heroic tale on the ride home last night?

"Tell me something," said Harris Terry, partner to Harold Feller, when Peter stepped back into the office. "If the economy is so bad, how come you're closing so many mortgages?" He laughed as he asked the question; they were all Dewey men here.

"Personality, Harris." Peter swung his wing-tip shoes up onto his desk. He rolled down his sleeves and flashed his big, white smile. "It'll get you past the Japs, past inflation, even past Mrs. Roosevelt."

"Yeah, personality," said Harold Feller, coming in with a pink phone message for his young associate. "I guess that's why my wife wants you for dinner a week from tonight. Seven-thirty. She told me to tell you."

"I'll be there, boss."

Yeah, personality. Peter had it all right, thought Harold Feller, looking at the blond hair falling into the young man's eyes, and the shirt that had more stripe than white. He liked Peter Cox, and he'd been smart to hire him; but part of him would also like to knock his feet off that desk.

"You men going to listen to the fight at the club?" wondered Harris Terry.

"City or country?" asked Feller, meaning the small club on Ball Street or the golfer's paradise on the northern outskirts of Owosso. Harold was about to say that he and Carol would be going to the country club, when Peter declared:

"City. City Club of Detroit, that is. I'm not going to listen to it on *radio* with you primitives. They've got television in Detroit."

"Carol and I are going to the country club," said Harold Feller, pretending to ignore him. "I suspect she and her friends will play bridge in the dining room, while their primitive husbands gather round the radio at the bar."

"Would you mind taking these along?" Peter handed Feller a bundle of handbills: PETER COX. LEADERSHIP FOR THE 50S.

"Isn't it a bit early in the campaign for this?"

"Ordinarily, yes. But with people so excited about Dewey, I thought I'd give them this advance opportunity to jump on my bandwagon. There'll be a lull in July and August, and then I'll go full tilt in the fall."

"Uh-huh," said Feller, tapping the printed slogan. "The fifties? Wouldn't your term be *ending* in 1950?"

"That's why I'm such a leader, Harold. I keep my eye on the future."

He dialed the telephone number on the slip of pink paper. Mr. Vincent Dent was trying to fill out incorporation papers for his new oil-delivery business, and he couldn't figure out the forms. If he didn't have them filed in Lansing by Wednesday, June 30, he was afraid he'd lose some tax deductions for the fiscal year, and so . . . Peter, who had been handling the matter, listened indulgently—"Yes, Mr. Dent. No, Mr. Dent. Don't trouble yourself about that, Mr. Dent"—while pointing an imaginary gun at his head, a gesture of boredom for Harold Feller and Harris Terry to appreciate. "Mr. Dent, why don't I run over and straighten this out for you? No, no problem at all. I'll be right there. Yes, a cold beer would be very nice."

Feller, who didn't find the gun gesture that funny, said, "I guess this means you'll be gone for the rest of the day?" The grandfather clock hadn't even chimed three-thirty, but Harold didn't feel he could give more than a sarcastic hint. There was no denying that Peter brought in the business.

"I thought I might head down to the river as soon as I set Mr. Dent straight. If that's okay with you, of course. I'd like to do an hour's rowing before setting out for Detroit."

He couldn't just use a canoe, like everyone else who went on the Shiawassee. He had to sit in that little silver scull that looked like a sports car. Feller watched him wave good-bye and start up his brand-new '49 Ford, which already wore a Peter Cox bumper sticker. Pretty flashy, that's for sure: the old bathtubs were slimming down into darts. This model had been unveiled only two weeks ago, and most people who wanted one were on a long waiting list. But not our future state senator. Did he know how that looked? Feller wondered.

Once he pulled out, Peter allowed himself to look across Washington Street and into the bookstore, but there was no sign of Anne, who had probably gone back to her fugging Norman Mailer. He had to drive all of two blocks to reach Vincent Dent's office on Ball Street, where he found the owner thrashing about in adding-machine tape and eraser shavings.

"Boy, am I glad to see you." Dent stood up to get the beer he'd promised, and attempted some small talk with this brainy, rich lawyer fifteen years younger than himself. "So what do you make of this Earl Warren?" he asked, uncapping the bottle of Old Frankenmuth Lager.

"A solid, predictable fellow," said Peter, with the authority of Walter Lippmann. "Not a man to shake things up."

"Will he bring votes to the ticket?"

"Probably some from California. Not that they'll be needed."

Dent nodded, but even a feeling that he was getting the straight skinny couldn't deflect his nervousness about the papers on the table. "Are you sure, Mr. Cox, that this one doesn't have to be in by the thirtieth?" He picked up a pale pink form. "It says on page three . . ."

"Don't worry about page three," said Peter, without looking at page three.

"I'm trying to save as much as possible," said Dent, apologetically, as if his anxiety were a shameful thing compared to Peter's expertise. "We've got my mother living with us now. She's getting on, and—"

"Ah, mothers," said Peter, cocking his head with a sentimental smile. His own mother was in Palm Springs at the moment, probably finishing off the day's first game of bridge. Thank goodness the Cox money flowed in a different direction: Lucy Cox couldn't wait to see her only boy get what he had coming as soon as he could. Back in Grosse Pointe she and his father had long ago moved into respectful silence and respective rooms, and last year she had persuaded the old man—scared him was more like it—into giving Peter sixty thousand dollars now, instead of making him wait for the will. When Peter had displayed a decent hesitation at the news, and suggested he would be perfectly happy to wait until she and Father were dead, she'd assured him, in her smokiest voice: "We died *years* ago, angel." His mother, who had grown up no farther south than Indianapolis, experienced more pleasure from her studied, Tallulah-like pronouncements than any anguish she suffered over the civilized collapse of her marriage; Peter could only play along. "But won't all that money ruin my character, Mother?" "See that it does. I can't stand character. Your father had so much of it."

"Let's look at this other one," said Peter, picking up a yellow form and, Vincent Dent hoped, warming to the task at hand. But as soon as Peter actually looked at it, they were interrupted by a knock on the window. It was Al Jackson.

"Saw you from the street, Mr. Cox. Sorry, Vince, hope you don't mind my barging in." He lifted the department of finance paper out of Peter's hand and replaced it with one of his own nine-page documents. "Yours to keep. The *Argus* has already set it in type. Everyone else'll be seeing it tomorrow."

"Can I get you a beer, Al?"

"Nope, nope, thanks, Vince, no time for that. Now, Mr. Cox, as soon as you finish reading that, you'll see why I'm going to be needing you."

Peter got through less than a paragraph before the grin on his face, watched with curiosity by Vincent Dent, stretched four inches wide. He tapped the table in delight. "Yes, you will, Mr. Jackson! Yes, you will!"

HE OUGHT TO BE OWOSSO'S FAVORITE SON, THOUGHT ANNE, looking up at *Lady With a Parasol*, the Renoir-esque painting that Frederick Frieseke, Owosso High class of 1893, had donated to the town library long after going to make his life in Paris. He'd been dead for nine years now, and gone for nearly fifty, and the few people who remembered him would tell you his crowning glory was a mural he did for the Wanamaker Building in New York City.

Anne studied the painting instead of the three new sentences of *The Time Being* she had managed to write in two hours here on a Friday night and tried to remind herself why she had come *to* a place like this, exactly the sort of town artists fled *from.* Hadn't Frieseke only managed to breathe a smidgen of false new life into an old cliché? Success excepted him from the thousands of painters sitting on the sidewalks of Montmartre and adding one more ill-proportioned Sacré-Coeur to all the ones already in existence. It was, what, 4 A.M., in Paris now, and she'd bet a couple of them were still going at it by citronella candlelight. Wouldn't she be the same if she'd gone to New York to "write"? Weren't the great stories right around her, in the dull American center, parochial lumps of coal waiting to be squeezed into artistic diamonds? HONESTY. STRENGTH. Didn't it take more of both to be *here?*

And yet, how many carats had she pressed today? Those three sentences. The real strength she needed was the kind to keep her eyes open, and the only honesty she'd practiced was in coming here at all: at six o'clock, while closing up for Mr. Abner, she'd remembered telling Margaret Feller how, yes, she would no doubt be working on her book tonight.

As it happened, Margaret was only fifteen feet away, browsing the fiction shelves; dateless, it seemed. Anne supposed Billy was going up and down Oliver Street hawking ice cream and souvenir programs to people sitting home and listening to the fight on the radio.

She waved to the girl, and Margaret strode right over. Obviously, she'd been wanting to, but regarded Anne as too much of a grown-up, or too serious an artist, to be disturbed.

"Hello, Miss Macmurray. Is that your novel?"

"Please call me Anne. Yes, Margaret, that's it."

"How is it coming?"

"Well, I'm struggling with point of view in this scene." She couldn't bear listening to herself. All she was struggling with was an attempt to look at the mostly blank page with a tenth the interest Margaret now displayed toward it. HON-ESTY: she wasn't the least bit honest. This girl was the honest one—you could tell—her sails looking for every bit of breeze, so eager for the horizon she didn't care about falling over the edge.

"Margaret, I'm lying. I've been sitting here bored for over an hour. I'd rather open any book in this library than look at this one, which isn't even a book yet and probably never will be. I can't wait to get out of here. Would you like to have a cup of coffee at that little place on Exchange Street?"

"The Great Lakes? I'd love that! Let me check these out, and I'll meet you outside."

They walked east on Main, away from the site beside the library where a new funeral home would soon be built.

"I suppose everybody's occupied with the fight tonight?" asked Anne.

"Yes," said Margaret, who then thought for a moment. "Well, no, not everybody."

Anne guessed she meant the Herrick boy, but decided against drawing her out. If this forthright girl didn't say more, it meant she didn't want to. At least not right now. So they walked across the Main Street bridge, and Anne con-fined the conversation to the weather and the latest rumor, that a film crew from the *March of Time* would soon be com-ing through town. Beneath the bridge the Shiawassee dipped and bubbled. On their right stood the modest Dewey birthplace, and a few hundred yards left, the tiny castle James Oliver Curwood had built as a writing studio. He had willed it to the town, but the town never seemed to know what to do with it. Lately it had been empty altogether, a fieldstone ghost with three pointed turrets, an oddly continental legacy from someone who had called plain, midwestern Owosso "the nicest place in the world."

A headlight caught the little gold letters on the honor roll outside City Hall. The names of the Owosso war dead, including Pfc. Arnold Herrick's, glinted for a moment like stars. As Margaret and Anne turned north on Water Street, the clock showed it was coming up to nine.

"I hope the Great Lakes will still be open."

"It will be," said Margaret. "They'll want to get some business from the boys signing up for the Guard." She pointed to two lanky young men who had come out of the Armory exchanging goofy mock salutes with each other.

"Your mother told me this morning that she wished your brother were here to sign up. Otherwise the draft—"

"That's Mother all right," said Margaret. "They don't *come* any more sensible. Everything can be *managed*. I mean, the National *Guard*. It's like buying a war on the layaway plan." Anne laughed; she supposed she knew what the girl meant. Better a sudden invasion, with flood and fire, better the chance to be instantly resplendent, than to serve with those who stand and wait one weekend a month.

"I'm sure your mother . . . What's *that?*" asked Anne, drawing Margaret's attention to a big oaktag sign on which a tornado's funnel had been drawn. Beneath the whirling black lines lay the numbers 11 11 11 11 11. "Do you think it's something out of *Revelation?*" Anne recognized the balding young man who stood on the Armory steps holding the sign. He was the minister from the Wesleyan Methodist church on Pine Street. Did Methodists go in for that sort of slam-bang Armageddon?

"It's the tornado story," said Margaret. "You've been here a year and never heard it? A big cyclone came through town on the eleventh of November 1911 at eleven minutes past 11 P.M."

"Like the Armistice?"

"Except for more elevens. Nineteen eleven instead of eighteen, and 11:11 P.M., I swear. After the First War, people decided it had been a sort of prophecy. My father was ten years old when it hit. He was lying in bed in my grandparents' house on Hickory Street. He remembers the window shade being sucked through the window, torn right off its runners, even though the window was only open six inches. It's a miracle their roof didn't come off. People were killed, and buildings blew away all over town. Two churches lost their steeples."

So it was a prophecy that had already been fulfilled. A sign that the Guard unit the town had been so proud of would perish in the Argonne—what Margaret's father had talked about this morning. This young reverend protesting enlistments was reminding people.

"He's brave," said Anne.

Margaret, her instincts activated by the word, looked closely at the shy figure on the steps and seemed to consider him in a new light.

"Really," said Anne, "think of it. That can't be an easy opinion to hold." This reverend was a story, not to mention the tornado itself—every word of it apparently true. There was no need to go to Paris, or even New York. She almost wanted to give Margaret a rain check and go back to the library to work.

They crossed Water Street where it met Exchange. The two new recruits, just ahead of them, were going through the Great Lakes' door. But the moment Margaret and Anne reached the sidewalk, Margaret stopped to look over her shoulder, as if something had told her to. She stared up at the high school, which stood next door to the Armory and used the building for dances and basketball.

Anne turned with her and saw the lit window. Two figures in it had arrested Margaret: Frank Sherwood's intense, bespectacled face was watching someone peer through a telescope.

Tim Herrick was scanning the planets. And Margaret Feller had just seen the sun, moon and stars. Anne looked from Margaret to the window and back, and wanted to tell the girl, as if Margaret really *were* looking at the sun, not to look too directly. But Margaret's face shone with what she saw.

To be that young and to love this hard—

"Oh, Anne, hide!"

Tim Herrick had looked up.

FIVE HUNDRED MILES TO THE EAST, AT YANKEE STADIUM, JERsey Joe Walcott had been knocked out by Joe Louis in the eleventh round. Jack Riley, who at the last minute this afternoon had put some money on the victor, turned on his windshield wipers and continued driving east on Oliver. Passing Anne Macmurray's window, he was depressingly aware of the smell of alcohol—not just the beer on his breath, but the traces of a Sea Breeze left on his neck by a Louis-loving blonde at the Red Fox Tavern twelve miles north of town, where he had ended up going to listen to the fight after his father decided he was too nauseated and cranky to stay up for it. The beer and potato chips Jack had brought back from Flint lay unopened on the kitchen counter. The blonde had been ready, willing and able, but the idea of twice in a single day with two different girls, not that Louise was a girl, seemed scummy, so he'd directed her attention back to Kenny Anderson's orchestra and let her down gently. It was midnight now; Anne Macmurray remained the only thing on his mind, and as the Comstock Apartments receded in his rearview mirror, he wondered if he'd stop smelling of booze by the time he showed up at her doorstep on Sunday night.

Driving northwest, almost straight on toward Jack Riley, though twenty miles away, Peter Cox took his '49 Ford up to 75 and moved his head backward, like a test pilot settling into some satisfying g-stress. Its pleasure was denied him, however, when his silver scull's silver paddle, which he'd forgotten to take out of the back of the car, caught him on the right ear and plunged him back into his bad mood.

Nota bene, as that guy in the English department at Yale used to say: *don't let yourself become a lawyer.* A lifer at it, that is. He had never spent a more boring evening. He'd been surrounded by lawyers in Detroit, all of them squinting and complaining about the picture quality of the television. Which was, admittedly, lousy; but nobody seemed willing to admit the thrill of being able to watch Louis knock Walcott on his behind five hundred miles away. They could only grouse and grumble as if they were actually there in the

Bronx, stuck in the cheap seats. Even five years of closing mortgages and incorporating the Vincent Dents of Owosso would kill him. He had to make every play this year. It was now or never—the same for Miss Anne Macmurray. If there were no encouragement by next week, she could forget him. He took the Ford to 80 and wondered if Harold Feller had passed out his leaflets.

Approaching town, he turned on WOAP, which through the static of distance and rain was giving the news. The Republicans were "packing up from Philadelphia, while meanwhile, here in Owosso, Mr. Al Jackson of Jackson Camera and Electronics has assumed the chairmanship of Citizens for the Future, a committee of businessmen who will be urging the city to adopt a radical development scheme in anticipation of the presidency of favorite son Thomas E. Dewey . . ." Peter raised the volume.

"Mr. Jackson and his associates will be publishing their proposal in tomorrow's *Argus*. It calls for . . ." Margaret Feller, lying on her bed but still fully dressed, turned the dial in search of music, but WGN was just talking and WWJ had already left the air. She shut off the radio and heard voices downstairs. Her parents had come home from the country club, which put an end to all the evening's possibilities but one, the chance to do what she had already done twice this week: wait until they'd gone to bed and then sneak out of the house and down to Park Street to hide behind the hedges and look at Tim Herrick's window. *No; she wouldn't.* It was too terrible either way. If the light was on, she could barely keep from crying out to him, and if it was off she would agonize over his not being there, or agonize that he *was* there, asleep, and breathing softly in the dark without her. Three nights ago had been the worst: the light had been on, but then he had risen, out of nowhere, naked, a god behind the curtain that shimmered like a cirrus cloud. With a movement of his arm, he'd hit the switch and the room had gone dark. But it wasn't the room light he extinguished; it was her. She'd been left to walk home in darkness and torment.

Tonight she had been on the verge of telling Anne Macmurray about him, but had instead told the ridiculous lie that when the two of them looked up at the high school, she had been worried *Billy* might be inside the classroom along with Tim and Mr. Sherwood, and that he would find out she'd really been free this evening, after she'd told him something else. What an embarrassment. But was it possible Anne hadn't even noticed? After all, *she* had been awfully eager to pump *her* about Peter Cox, that stuck-up new lawyer working for her father. Not that there was much to tell, since Margaret had met him only twice. No, he wasn't exactly stuck-up; he was, what was that word she'd underlined in a book the other day? She couldn't think of it, but she knew it fit him perfectly. *Insufferable:* that was it.

She'd had so little to tell Anne about Peter that she was afraid this older woman would lose interest in her, regret asking her to come to the Great Lakes. But then the minister with his tornado sign came in, to smile and joke with the waitress as he had his coffee and pie and hunted for something on the jukebox. It didn't seem possible that anyone could change gears so quickly, go from World War III to Doris Day like that. She'd gone up and introduced herself and said she thought what he'd been doing tonight was interesting, and she'd told him the story of her father and the window shade.

Remembering that now filled her with tenderness for

her dad. There was even a little left over for her mother. Thank goodness they were home, throwing ice into their glasses for a nightcap; now she couldn't walk out the door and down to Park Street. Unless the Great Lakes' coffee kept her awake past the point they came upstairs and turned in.

Seven blocks east, between Hickory and Oak, Horace Sinclair brought down his fist on the yellowing doily atop his dresser. He had just gotten out of his claw-footed tub, and was still dripping from underneath his robe, but he was too agitated to finish drying or pick up his comb. He should never have turned on the radio: ". . . the city to buy up the stretch of riverbank, now mostly private property, running between the Dewey birthplace on West Main and the governor's childhood home on West Oliver. Mr. Jackson envisions a walkway he calls 'Road to Prosperity,' featuring permanent exhibits and structures that will illustrate both Dewey's career and the history of Owosso. At the present time, some of the land, which runs north past Curwood Castle, makes up the backyards of homeowners on John Street. But Mr. Jackson's group . . ." It was a wonder he hadn't slipped on the little octagonal tiles in the bathroom. It was a wonder he wasn't slipping *now,* as he lumbered downstairs to the parlor and squeezed himself between his old chesterfield sofa and the table on which he had set down *Ivanhoe* for the night. He pulled back the drapes' heavy green swag and glowered at Jackson's ranch house across the street. "Son of a bitch!" he shouted, before promptly apologizing to the only other person in the room, an oil painting of the late Mrs. Sinclair. He squeezed back out around the table and sat down, closing his eyes and getting his breath, and making a promise to himself and the portrait. The clock on City Hall, audible even at this distance, chimed twelve—three minutes late by his own reckoning. He pulled himself up from the sofa and slowly climbed the stairs. It had been a long time since he had heard the chimes at midnight, heard them "in the Shakespearean sense," as he was fond of saying about any number of phrases, and a long time since he had charged up any flight of stairs or foreign hill, but he moved with determination now, heading for the buckram box at the back of his dresser, ready to unlock the secret he had kept inside it for fifty-one years.

Meanwhile, back at the ranch, Anne said to herself, kicking off her slippers and turning down the bedspread. *The Time Being* was back in its drawer, but on her mind for one moment more. Could she work the reverend into it? The little she knew about him came from Margaret, who, rather than flirting with the two boys who'd signed up for the Guard, had gone right up to him in the coffee shop, bless her heart, and started asking questions. (*Bless her heart?* She was starting to sound as if she came from here.)

Had she talked too much about Peter? Been too obvious with her questions? What could she really have expected the girl to know? No, she was sure she had let Margaret talk enough herself, about Billy and how sweet, if exasperating, he really was, and her father, and how sweet, if exasperating, *he* really was.

She could hear from the clattering pipes down the hall that Mrs. Wagner was rinsing out her step-ins. On the other side of the wall, the closing of a door, its tongue going into the lock as quietly as the clicking of her brand-new ballpoint pen, told her Frank Sherwood was home. Had he been up on the roof with his own telescope, or with Tim Herrick at the high school all this time? Poor Margaret: that story of how she'd really been searching for Billy up in that window. Did she think she could hide that look, the kind intelligible to everyone in the world? It was the look—

Anne's eyelids sprang up, more open than they'd been all day. It was the same look, she now realized—how had she missed it—that Frank Sherwood had worn while gazing down at the golden head of Tim Herrick. She stared at the floral paper covering the wall between them. Oh, Frank, she thought. *Poor man.*

She reached up to turn off her lamp. The soft pop of its switch was just enough to mask the little noise traveling several blocks from the corner of Goodhue and Saginaw on the rain-soaked breeze. Tim Herrick, taking aim with his late father's Colt .38, had just shot out the streetlight that, before sizzling to its death, stood between his eye and the planet Jupiter.

THREE

"CAREFUL, COLONEL. YOU'LL GET YOUR FEET MUDDY."

Horace Sinclair looked left, down to the Shiawassee River. His eyes were in better shape than his seventy-two-year-old lungs, and they could see, even in the late Saturday-afternoon glare, that the figure getting out of the silver scull belonged to the young lawyer, Cox. He was hauling the absurd little thing onto the bank and approaching to make conversation.

"It'll be paved soon. Easier for walking," said Peter.

"I *like* the earth, Mr. Cox. That's why I've got my feet on it."

Peter smiled as he put on a sweatshirt over his singlet. Horace noted the unmarked smoothness of the arms going into it, and thought of his own, hung with fleshly crepe as if prepared for their own funeral.

"Not in favor of Mr. Jackson's vision, I take it."

"If that's vision, I'll take dark of night," barked Horace. Peter's expression showed his delight in provoking the old man, but Horace took it for something else as well: the camouflage of feeling? How many other young people would have bothered to stop their paddling on a day so fine as this one? He was, of course, a politician, but—

"Well, Colonel, the river has plenty of other pretty stretches that will be left untouched."

"But not this one."

"Is it that castle you don't want diminished by a new setting?" Peter gestured to Curwood's creation across the river and past a couple of empty rowboats that were always tied up in front of it. Horace just snorted.

"Oh, I get it," said Peter. "Did something special happen here, Colonel? I'll bet this was your spot to bring Mrs. Sinclair, back when you were—"

"I beg your pardon!" Horace started to walk away, but a slip of his left foot and Peter's rescuing arm nailed him to the spot.

"Steady, Colonel. Here we go." Peter led the two of them to higher ground, halfway up toward the Armory and high school; Horace accepted his offer of a cigarette.

"You've lived your whole life here?" asked Peter.

"Except for my months in Cuba," said Horace, "and in Florida before that. Training."

Horace now expected a San Juan Hill question, but all Peter asked was: "And you've really never had a car? Like Harold Feller said?"

"I never had the need." He pointed toward a spot a few hundred yards east. "I had my accountant's office, a two-man operation, right back there on Exchange Street, until I retired in '41."

"A good living?"

"It provided much of what Mrs. Sinclair and I wanted. The rest we provided each other."

"Have you got any children, Colonel?"

"We were never so blessed." Horace paused, and looked down the bank. "You're full of questions, Mr. Cox. How about answering them yourself? Shouldn't a fellow your age be starting a family? Every magazine I read says that you're part of a frighteningly fertile generation."

"I haven't got the girl yet."

"I just browsed some books with the one you're hoping to get."

"Am I that obvious?" Peter asked.

"No, I just expect you to have that much sense. She's a delightful young woman. She knows things about this town that some people born here have yet to find out."

"Is that a fact," said Peter.

"You didn't ask me about Teddy Roosevelt, but she did, a couple of months ago, when I was in the shop. Specifically, about the time he came through here in 1901 and gave a talk at the Commons over in West Owosso. A good place for him, too. That's where they used to have the medicine shows."

Peter did not ask what enduring quarrel Horace might have with the old Rough Rider. He settled for observing, "I suppose I can understand why you don't want the place to change."

"Oh, you can?"

"Sure. You know, 'the land of steady habits,' like they call Connecticut."

"Not all habits are steady," Horace pronounced. "Mr. Cox, do you know what I did nearly every workday for forty years—twenty before you were born, and twenty after, while you were at your university in Connecticut? I came to this riverbank and felt a riot of emotion."

Peter paused for a moment before asking, "What did you do with all of it, Colonel?"

"I kept it buried," said Horace, who stubbed out his cigarette and made movements to go.

"Sorry I can't sail you home," said Peter, pointing to the one-seater scull.

"I *always* walk," said Horace. "If you want to do me a favor, fall in love with this river. That's right. With the river. You're already in love with the girl."

THOSE *EYEBROWS*. COULDN'T HE PUT VITALIS ON THEM?

The sight of John L. Lewis's two great facial crops, sticking out like bales of hay that had burst their straps, embarrassed Jack Riley. For once, in the newsreel, Lewis was looking pleased instead of furious, the United Mine Workers having just signed an agreement with the soft-coal operators; but the eyebrows seemed telltale, like some crude secret the labor leader couldn't keep from stealing to the surface, a disgusting version of every man's five-o'clock shadow, which each afternoon reconsigned him to the animal kingdom. Jack checked his own cheeks with his left hand, the one farthest away from her, so she wouldn't think he was about to try something. There was nothing there, of course, couldn't be, since he'd shaved less than two hours ago. He resisted checking the top of his head, to which *he* had applied Vitalis, uselessly: fifteen minutes after he left the house his hair always looked like a field of cowlicks. His mother had never been able to keep down those reddish-brown stalks, no matter how much tonic she slathered on the comb. She'd always given up with a laugh, pushing her face down into the mess to kiss the top of his head. The woman—a walking saint, his father would say—could see the humor in anything. She had actually died laughing.

Tonight, as Jack came down the stairs, the old man, no less cranky than he'd been before the fight two nights ago, had cracked, "Christ, Johnny, you smell like the inside of Reisner's," the barber on Ball Street. The combination of Vitalis and Old Spice maybe was a little sickening, so he'd gone upstairs to towel some of it off. At the moment he could smell only popcorn, which he hoped was all she could smell, too.

At least he wasn't sweating through his shirt. It was almost cold in here, just like the icicles fringing the Capitol Theatre's ads in the *Argus* made a point of promising this time of year. It was still June, but you could tell it was going to be a scorching summer, and since the war people had gotten so eager for air-conditioning that feeling cool was starting to seem as important as keeping warm used to be, back in the early thirties, when the Rileys lived in that beat-to-hell house, two steps above a shack, down by the Ann Arbor Railroad. Now everybody was so sold on being cold in the summer that the Capitol would even book a Christmas picture out of season. *The Bishop's Wife* had been around six months ago, but all its fake snow and jingling bells would make people think the air-conditioning was working even better than it was.

She'd like the movie, wouldn't she? She'd sworn she hadn't seen it, and he was pretty sure he'd gotten away with the lie that he hadn't either. He'd actually watched it with his father and aunt, when she came on a Christmas visit from Chicago. "She's a real *lady,*" Aunt Eileen had said of Loretta Young, meaning not some sex bomb like Lana Turner. The judgment had stuck in his head, and when the picture showed up again he decided it would be his best shot with Anne Macmurray, who, if she were naked, would look just like those goddesses on the plaster medallions framing the stage. Or, goddammit, now framing the sight of some dockworkers on strike in London. Their roaring newsreel heads were five times bigger than life, and if that weren't enough to turn her off union men, Ed Herlihy was informing the audience that His Majesty's Labour government was having to use troops to bring the British people their still pitifully short rations.

This Berlin business was scary, thought Anne. They'd all been concentrating on Dewey three nights ago, when the Russians had finished choking off the city. She'd heard on the radio this morning that every American plane they could find over there would be used to supply the old capital. It wasn't possible, was it? And was *this* possible? Here was Dewey, intoning the same lines she'd heard come out of the radio speakers at City Hall Thursday night. She had seen television only once, through some store windows in New York last Christmas in the middle of a blizzard, a "live" transmission of some puppet show, and having these pictures on the movie screen just three nights after they were shot seemed equally impressive.

Not that the candidate was: *"Our task is to fill our victory with such meaning . . ."* Those same meaningless words again, even less stirring now that she could see the head they came out of. And that *mustache:* did he comb it with Vitalis? It was ridiculously well managed. Didn't his wife ever muss it with a kiss? She supposed it had taken nerve to keep wearing it right through Hitler, but it certainly didn't make her swoon. Still, she'd probably end up voting for him, if only out of local pride and a sense that Truman fell so short of FDR. Dewey did have the voice of a President, she thought, a nice baritone, even if he was just playing scales with this dreary speech. He'd actually trained as a singer, a fact she hadn't known until Friday afternoon, when she picked up that '44 campaign biography—that's how bored she'd been.

"I can't stand him," said Jack Riley, the first spontaneous thing he'd uttered since picking her up on Oliver Street. She looked at his face under the projector's cone of light, and · couldn't get over how alive and appealing it suddenly was. But then she could see him retracting his own expression, as if embarrassed by the outburst. She wanted to say "Don't go away!"—don't go back down into that shell-casing of propriety you keep presenting me with, as if I'm the fragile nurse who's just arrived at the front. *Stay up here and play.* Before he brought her home, she was determined to get one good kiss from that face—the one she'd seen a moment ago, not the tight little profile facing the screen again.

The balcony fell silent. The newsreel, which everyone always talked through, had finished up, and as Samuel Goldwyn's name appeared, the only thing audible was the wrappers on candy bars. Music. And then a snow scene. Loretta Young, unhappy, but *nobly* unhappy, doing some Christmas shopping, longing for some hideous hat with long ribbons that tied under the chin; and Cary Grant behind her on the street. He was an *angel*, "Dudley," if you'd believe it, and more annoying than avenging. He went around this town solving everyone's problems with a wave of his hand. Before it was over he'd be lightening Loretta Young's heart, and nervous, overworked David Niven's, too. So debonair and know-it-all, another Peter Cox, thought Anne, this golden stranger come to town to make everyone thirst for his elixir. It was now the old professor's turn (the same actor, what was his name, who'd played The Man Who Came to Dinner) to be given the beginnings of a little miracle, a preliminary dose of enlightenment. The old man was confessing that the book he'd always claimed to be writing (oh, dear) didn't exist, not a word, and that long ago he'd lost the only girl he ever loved by being afraid to tell her so: "The whole story of my life—frustration. It's a chronic disease, and it's incurable."

She took Jack Riley's hand, just reached over and put it in hers, adding one gentle stroke with her thumb, the kind you'd give to reassure a kitten you wanted to stay on your lap. Maybe he'd suggest they get out of here instead of sticking with this warmed-over *Mrs. Miniver*—for that's what it was, one of those count-your-blessings war pictures they couldn't stop making. Maybe he'd suggest they go to the bar at the Hotel Owosso. She'd listen to his war stories (Italy, she'd heard) if he wanted to tell them. It would be a better start than this.

He gave a scratchy little gulp. "Would you like me to get you anything? A soda?"

Sshh! said Mrs. Hopkins, the twelfth-grade rhetoric teacher.

WITH THE POSSIBLE EXCEPTION OF THE CAPITOL BOWL ON South Washington, there was no interior in town more modern than the coffee shop of the Hotel Owosso. Al Jackson himself was impressed with the chromium counters, fake leather stools and neon tubing, over which Kay Schmidt, the waitress on duty tonight, was running her damp cloth. Things would get busy once the picture let out, but for now there was just one customer: a nice-looking gentleman, Kay thought, not too handsome for his own good, like that young lawyer who had stopped in earlier.

"Want one?" Kay asked the man, seeing him look at the jar near the register.

"What are they?"

Kay spilled a couple of Dewey buttons into his palm.

"Sure," the man said, putting them into his pocket. "I see you're already set for the election in there." He pointed to the hotel's big reception hall, where a small hothouse of red-white-and-blue rosettes had bloomed over the last few days.

"Yeah," said Kay. "They're trying to cash in on a little of the excitement."

"How come no giant picture of the candidate?"

"At the last minute the assistant manager remembered this is actually a hotel," Kay said with a smile. "The only place in town with folks from *out* of town."

"Who might not be for your boy."

"Exactly," said Kay. "The buttons, they figure, won't bother anybody. In fact, I haven't seen more than three people take one. Where are you from?"

"New York. Name's Don Case."

"What brings you to Owosso?"

"Men's shirts. I'll be selling them tomorrow morning, at least I hope so, to Christian's and Storrer's. I work for Hathaway."

"And I used to work for Storrer's," said Kay.

"Did you really?"

"For about six weeks. Until October thirty-first, 1929, the day they opened this place. I remember setting up pumpkins all along the old counter. First thing I ever did here. Mr. Storrer had had the wits scared out of him by the stock market crash and let me and another part-timer go. He had sense."

"Heck of a time to open a hotel."

"It was a good thing they settled for five stories, instead of the twelve they'd been talking about. But there's always been a hotel on this spot." Kay knew by heart the little glass-framed history in the dining room. "The old Ament opened up here in 1844. After that there was the National."

"No kidding," said the salesman. "So a hundred years ago tonight there was a room just where mine is."

"Long as you're on a low floor. Those first hotels weren't very tall."

"Room 214," said the salesman.

"It's kind of like a house that's been moved," said Kay. "Is it the same space or not?"

"We're a couple of philosophers tonight," said the salesman, putting two nickels on the counter and nodding good night. "Take care of yourself."

A few minutes later, back upstairs in room 214, Don Case set out a photograph of his wife and children on the lacquered-pine dresser—set them out just as, not a hundred but fifty-one years before, a young man occupying the same room, or at least the same space in the Ament Hotel, had set out the photograph of a woman. The dresser in those days had been oak; the wallpaper more abundantly floral; the overhead bulb a gas lamp. Setting out the picture was the last thing Jonathan Adams Darrell did that night, before he went over to the wall containing the gas pipe, the one feeding his room light and the lamps on Main Street below, and inserted a delicate awl.

Tonight there were no trees on the sidewalk beneath Don Case's room, but many years ago there had been chestnuts, great leafy ones that Horace Sinclair had climbed as a boy, and from which he'd looked into the window of what was now, as then, room 214. He had not known that when he was twenty-one, at 3 A.M. on a summer's night in 1897, he would have to sneak into that room, the one occupied by the lifeless body of Jonathan Adams Darrell, nor that, in the fifty-one years to follow, he would never again (though no one but the late Mrs. Sinclair ever realized it) set foot in the hotel on Main Street.

"WHY DON'T YOU LET ME WALK *YOU* HOME?" ASKED ANNE.

He'd never felt more like a jerk. The movie had ended and they were back out on Main and there wasn't a thing in the world he could find to say to this girl. His mouth was locked and dry, and on top of his head he could feel the Vitalis stinging a little from fresh sweat. Right now he'd give anything to be over in Flint on the office couch with Louise; with Anne Macmurray the only thing he ought to give was up. He couldn't face sitting across from her in the hotel coffee shop or up at the Red Fox, so he'd said he really needed to get home and take care of his father. Hiding behind his sick old man! And she was making things worse by being nice about it.

"Okay, thanks," he finally replied.

"It's not such a bad night. It's really not *too* hot."

"No, not too."

"Still, all that snow in the movie looked inviting." Nothing. "I guess they used doubles for the skating scene. I can't imagine the actors could really do all those jumps and turns themselves."

"Yeah, I guess."

God, she thought; this was some slow boat to China. As they turned right on Exchange Street, passing between the Argus building and the post office, Anne looked at the other dispersing couples and companionable old ladies, aware that here and there a pair of eyes were pausing to assess this apparent match between the Riley boy and that rather fancy girl from the bookstore. She thought again of the oak trees' invisible telegraph, and wondered what message about her and Jack the other pedestrians could possibly send out on it tonight. The poor man was unable to generate a syllable, let alone the stuff of gossip, as the two of them walked another block, and another, in silence, down to Saginaw, down to Hickory.

He was trying to think about anything but her, to walk as if they were two kids in a double line at school, the silence enforced upon them. He put one foot in front of the other and thought about the WPA water main she didn't know she was walking above; about how his brother Jimmy had helped to build it in '37; and about how that couldn't be anything she'd be interested in. He only hoped she believed his old man was really bad off, that it was just worry which prevented her date from carrying on a conversation.

"Is Dewey the next street?"

"Uh-huh."

"Did they name it after him in '44?"

"No, it was for another Dewey, one of the guys that founded the town. It was Dewey Street even when I was born. One of his ancestors, I guess."

Here was a glint of progress.

"I guess there will be some people who want to rename the whole town for him," she said, hoping this might pull the pin from a grenade.

"I'd move," said Jack, decisively, his eyes coming up from the sidewalk and meeting hers.

"Do you really think Truman has a chance?"

"He ought to. He would if people took a fair look."

"It sounds pretty hopeless to me. Did you hear that the Democrats have asked the Republicans to leave the bunting up in the convention hall in Philadelphia so they can use it themselves a couple of weeks from now? That seems so defeated somehow."

He appeared a bit mystified by the symbolic significance she had in mind, but she could detect a definite warming trend, if only toward the topic. "It wouldn't surprise me if he has a couple of tricks up his sleeve," said Jack, before asking, apologetically, as if he'd forgotten to watch his language, "I guess you're for Dewey, aren't you?"

"I guess I am," she replied. "But I'll tell you what." She put her arm through his. "I'll keep an open mind."

No luck. The new physical arrangement was making him uncomfortable, like a rented tuxedo. If he were relaxed, he'd be dropping his arm over her shoulders. "How long has your mother been gone?"

"Nine years," he answered.

"Any brothers or sisters?"

"Two of each. All of them married and moved away by the time I got back from the Army."

"Where were you, exactly?"

"I finished up at Anzio." He pointed to the scar below his left eye. "January twenty-third, 1944." Seeing her concerned look, he laughed. "It wasn't so bad. I know guys who stayed in it after a lot worse. But my eyesight went out of whack for a year or so, and I came home."

"January twenty-third, 1944," she mused. "I would have been lying on my bed in Ann Arbor reading *Paradise Lost.*"

He'd heard of it, unless he was confusing it with the other one, *Forever Amber.* "Is *Paradise Lost* a book I ought to read?"

"No, not particularly," said Anne, with a sincerity that seemed to surprise them both, and relax them slightly.

They'd reached the Riley home on Williams Street, and Jack, because he was still nervous, or maybe because he regretted wasting most of the last ten minutes in that stupid silence, kept walking her up the driveway, the route he always took into the house, through the garage.

The appealing smell of grease and wood came at her in the dark. She put her hand on an old sled that stood upright against the wall as he went for the light. License plates from the thirties nailed above the rafters; broken gizmos near a watering can that had to have belonged to his mother; a beat-up sofa and a child's bicycle with solid tires: they all flared to life under his hand.

"Johnny? That you?" It was his father, calling from the kitchen.

Jack gave her a helpless look, as if to say "What can I do?" but she put her finger to her lips. Amused, and vaguely excited by the sexual switch—the pretense that Gene Riley might come out any minute with a bulldog to chase away the suitor taking advantage of his boy—the two of them pulled close together, hiding. She brushed his scar with her fingertips and he rushed to cover her other hand, still on the rudder of the sled, with his own.

HE KNEW THE HEELS CLICKING UP THE STAIRS BELONGED TO Anne Macmurray, but with the furtiveness that had become natural to him, Frank Sherwood rushed to brush two tiny flecks of tooth powder off the edge of the basin and rinse them down the sink. He would stay in here until she'd gone to her room. But his strategy backfired. He was so quiet she assumed the bathroom was vacant. She was pulling on the door.

"Oh, I'm sorry," she said.

"That's okay," Frank replied, wiping his mouth and coming out into the hall. "I was through."

"Are you sure?"

"Uh-huh." He smiled and squeezed past her, knowing he had to say something more. "Did you like the movie?"

Anne laughed. "Mrs. Wagner told you where I was?"

"The town crier," said Frank, who picked at an imagined spot on his T-shirt.

"It wasn't very good. Loretta Young. I can't stand those sunken cheeks."

He could ask her about the plot, but he could not ask about the one thing that actually made him curious—Jack Riley, whom with no need of Mrs. Wagner's help he'd seen walking up to the doorbell.

"What did you do tonight, Frank?"

He liked the way she could keep the ball rolling. It made their quick encounters easier than the others he had every day. "I just read a couple of magazines."

"No time with the telescope?" She meant his own, the little one he kept on the roof here.

"I'm only heading up there now. There's so much light in the sky this time of year."

Please don't ask to come up with me. She was awfully intelligent, perfectly nice, but there was nothing he had to say to her.

"Maybe sometime you can show me."

"Sure."

"I saw you at it the other night. Not here; over at the high school."

"Yes," said Frank, quickly. "I was showing one of my students a couple of planets. He's sort of lost, not much to do in the summertime, and he's got an interest in this kind of thing, so I let him . . ."

"That's good," said Anne. "He's lucky. Well, enjoy the stars." She waved good night. "By the way, what'll you be looking for?"

"Jupiter," said Frank, whose hands remained plunged in the pockets of his khaki pants as he started climbing the wooden stairs to the roof.

He was the only one who ever came up here; the oilcloth over his telescope was exactly where he'd draped it the other night. The equipment was in as good shape as it had been when his German aunt Alma, the one who'd kept house for his widowed father and raised Frank in Cincinnati, gave it to him at the end of '41, a present for finishing his master's degree. It spent the beginning of the war packed away—pretty much as he had, over at the naval supply station in Detroit, until they'd let him go in the middle of '43—he was never sure why—and he'd found the job here. He'd always looked forward to showing Aunt Alma the rings of Saturn through the expensive Leitz she'd bought him with her wages from the shoe factory ("The Germans make the best," she'd whispered in the note that arrived in Ann Arbor with the package), but before he left the Navy she and his father were both dead and there was no point in going home to Ohio.

Which was how he'd come here to Owosso, once he found out about the job. Five years later, at thirty-one, he knew that the time spent on his Navy bunk wasn't an interruption of his life but a preparation for the rest of it. Never a date; never a drink; never a slip. He got to live one first glorious season here; but all at once it was over, the whole world gone out of focus. He'd spent the five years since in the same room here, getting up each morning for work, not even taking a trip this summer or last.

He was too nervous to be teaching high-school students. His exotic subject offered some protective aura (the school paper ran stories like MR. SHERWOOD EXPLAINS ATOM BOMB), but he wasn't cut out for a world in which two specks of dandruff, like charged particles, could start a chain reaction of giggles and whispers. He would never be one of the pep-filled class advisors, and he already longed for the days when, after forty, his bachelorhood "confirmed," he would be immune from even the occasional matchmaking joke in the teachers' lounge. His own world, which had flared like a supernova that first spring, had collapsed into itself, a dead star too dense to penetrate. He would be in this town, maybe even the same room, until 1982, when he turned sixty-five.

Between now and then Saturn would travel its whole circle around the sun.

How far would I travel to be where you are? How far is the journey from here to a star? He hummed the tune while removing the lens cap. At the front of the tube he saw his distended reflection, like an intruder on the other side of a peephole: the forehead under the thinning red hair was higher, the chin a bit more pointed. *You're a nice-looking man, Frank.* He remembered and cherished the words, for all the good they would ever again do him.

How he would have liked being here, with this telescope, in the 1890s, the one decade when the downtown streets had been lit with gas. But the earth insisted on burning ever more brightly, as if it had decided that looking for another world took too much effort and it would do its best to be discovered instead. Now the lights of Owosso's business section, installed in '46, were 6600-lumen incandescents. They made early summer nights like this one even harder for the amateur astronomer trying to golf his way from star to star. Frank crouched down, wiping his hands on his T-shirt before angling the scope above some hickory trees on the eastern edge of town. As he swung the tube south, the night sky passed through its lens like a soap bubble through a wand, until all at once a man, large as a housefly, flew into view. It was Gus Farnham, out in his old Curtiss "Jenny," the aircraft sure to be less well lit than Gus, who would bring it down by moonlight in some field far from the airport warden's eye. Frank had heard about the old barnstormer from Mrs. Wagner, but in four years of coming up here he had never aimed the Leitz into a single living room or parked car, and Gus Farnham's plane wasn't enough to make him halt the telescope for more than a second on its arc toward the place he was bringing it, the place he brought it first thing every night he was up here: the patch of sky that, by his reckoning, capped the Oak Hill Cemetery.

"HORACE, YOU'RE OVER HERE," SAID CAROL FELLER, POINT-ing to a chair at one end of her oval table. He would be the extra man, and that was fine with him. It was one of the reasons he liked Mrs. Feller, for knowing better than to sit him beside some widow who would fuss over him or, worse yet, decide by evening's end that she was in line to take the place of the late Mrs. Sinclair.

"Did you hear that Truman may actually decide to run with Mrs. Roosevelt?" asked Dr. Coates, Carol's brother, who had grown up in Owosso but now made a small fortune as a radiologist over in Lansing. He was here tonight with his pert blond wife, Sally, who laughed at the latest rumor about Harry Truman's choice of a vice-presidential candidate. "It sounds like one of those old Eleanor jokes. Remember them?"

"Would that be a progressive thing to do?" asked Harold Feller. "Or would it be hanging on to the past?"

"Hanging on to the wreckage," offered Dr. Coates, whom Carol sat across from Horace.

The past. Of all the advice that Horace Sinclair received from his fellow Owossoans—those self-interested widows; the young matrons aside from Mrs. Feller; the men his own age (usually "cardiac" patients full of frightened optimism about the new regime Dr. Hume had them on)—the piece he most disliked was the injunction against "living so much in the past." It always assumed that the past, while perhaps not a bad place, was too easy a spot for anyone to live in; that abiding there was an "escape" that didn't challenge the mind, which left it as vulnerable as all those septuagenarian hearts. Whereas Horace knew that living in the past demanded much more effort than living in the here and now. As it receded ever further, the past required more and more work for a man to keep up with it, ever greater imaginative stamina to keep chasing it down the tracks. The present asked no more than that he get aboard and take a window seat. Living there showed nothing like a proper regard for life or time; it made them both disposable, like the magazines that had stolen their names. The past was the present treasured and enhanced, an object needing the same care as the late Mrs. Sinclair's silver tea service, the one she had received from her sister in Boston, in 1900, as a wedding present. Horace continued to apply the pink polish to it every Saturday, even though he had never been able to stand the smell through all the decades of his marriage.

Mrs. Sinclair had not actually shared his love of the past, had in fact done her brisk best over the years to keep him "current." His propensity to reside in another time probably came from the other Mrs. Sinclair, his mother, who had frozen her imagination in the fall of 1892, before the following year's depression, which to the Sinclairs had been every bit as Great as the one coming forty years later. It had shut down his father's bicycle shop, and sent Horace himself looking for work at seventeen. By the time he went off to the Spanish War in '98 he was a self-educated man, but destined never to be anything else through all his long years as an accountant on Exchange Street.

"Anne, you're on Horace's right, and Sally, I've got you on his left."

"Everything looks lovely," said Anne. She surveyed the cut-glass dishes and china platters full of roast potatoes and glazed carrots and sliced beef ribboned with gravy. It looked a bit heavy for this early summer night, when all the curtains hung limply against the open windows, but the "lighter seasonal fare" that cookbooks now talked about was more likely to have caught on in New York or San Francisco than here. As it was, she felt hungry, her appetite fired by anxiety over the whereabouts of her half-blind date. Peter Cox had yet to arrive; he'd called to say he was dealing with Vincent Dent's final incorporation panic and would be late. He had missed the two rounds of cocktails, and the chair between Carol Feller and her sister-in-law remained empty.

"Peter said to start, and I'm taking him at his word," said Carol. "Dig in."

Dr. Coates couldn't stay off politics long enough for everyone to serve themselves. After complimenting his sister on the potatoes, he turned to his brother-in-law and said, "The papers are predicting he'll put Taft on the Supreme Court and make Dulles Secretary of State. What do you think, Harold?"

Before the evening's host could reply, the dining room felt its first breeze, the arrival of the missing guest, with a great big smile on his face. "I'm sorry, Mrs. Feller, don't get up." Peter came around to Carol with a bouquet of flowers that he permitted her to sniff, once, before he went off to find and fill a vase in what seemed a single motion. He was Dudley, all right, thought Anne. Everyone watched, without a word, while he set the flowers down on the sideboard as if performing a magic trick. Carol remained seated, just as he'd instructed her, allowing him to circle the table and offer his hand to everyone she now introduced or reacquainted him with. When he reached Anne, and noticed her scolding expression, more sincere than flirtatious, he took her fingers and brought them to his lips in an exaggerated gesture of contrition. As her hand rose toward his tanned face, she thought: He hasn't been with Mr. Dent at all. She would bet he'd been out on the Shiawassee in that little chromium sport canoe. Unexpectedly, she flinched at his kiss. "That tickled," she said, looking him in the eye. "Oh, my goodness, are you growing a mustache?" Her own lips curled in distaste.

Sudden great interest all around, a positive clattering of cutlery, as Carol Feller's guests strained to see for themselves.

"Just a small one, temporary, until Inauguration Day. A pledge taken Tuesday night by every member of the Owosso-Corunna Dewey for President Club. It'll make a great group photo a few weeks from now, don't you think?"

Horace Sinclair snorted, but Peter went brightly on. "I'll bet we get Harold to raise one, too, and Harris Terry down at the office. What about you, Dr. Coates?"

"Not a chance," interrupted Carol. "Especially not for Harold. My father had a great big mustache, practically a walrus. You always felt he was wearing a scarf when he kissed you good night. Don't you remember, Dick?"

"No. He never kissed me good night," said Dr. Coates. "I do remember the back of his right hand."

"Don't listen to Dick," said his sister. "He was the baby of the family and pampered beyond anything recommended in Dr. Spock."

"Mustaches don't seem terribly modern," offered Sally.

"Good," said her husband. "We could use some old-fashioned sense. In fact, I thought Dewey should have called for an Old Deal the other night."

Harold Feller, ever temperate, asked Dr. Coates if, at least so far, he could really find anything to complain about in Harry Truman's response to what had happened in Berlin.

"Hell, yes. He's started something he can't keep up. He'll soon find out he'd have been better off putting that six billion dollars of foreign aid into some more airplanes. And don't get me started about the money in this housing bill."

"It's almost too awful to think about," said Carol, without saying whether she meant Berlin or the idea of Dr. Coates's getting started on slum clearance and homes for veterans. "Did you know," she asked Horace Sinclair, "that Harold and I were in Paris in August of '39? It was supposed to be a second honeymoon; we put the children with their Grandma Coates. Once in France we spent the whole two weeks wondering if there was going to be an invasion."

Harold Feller looked at his wife, figuring she again had Jim's draft status on her mind. He changed the subject with his natural tact. "Speaking of housing," he said, "I see in the *Argus* that the city's finally figured out what to do with the castle." James Oliver Curwood's folly had been leased to the board of education as a place for after-school classes in art and literature. "A good idea, no? The building's been in terrible shape, and the board promises to fix it up once they've moved in. Even Mrs. Curwood out in California is pleased with the deal."

Eyes went toward Horace Sinclair, who was considered

entitled to the final say on any matter connected to Owosso's former times.

"That sounds fine to me. But don't you suppose Mr. Al Jackson will want to chop the whole thing down? Put a plaster-of-Paris White House in its place?"

"Oh," said Carol Feller, "I'm sure Mrs. Curwood would never permit that."

Horace, at this second mention of her name, decided he was lucky the widow Curwood had long since moved away. Otherwise they might try to fix him up with *her.* He knew for a fact that these women had even thought of him as a mate for Annie Dewey, living alone across the street, except for her handyman, Mr. Valentine, these last twenty years. Not that she wasn't a fine woman. Quite undistracted by her son's fame. He'd known her all his life, even when she was Annie Thomas; and more to the point, she knew who *she* was, more a Thomas than a Dewey, from a time in this town when the first name meant more than the second.

Realizing he was lost in thought, and afraid of looking forgetful, he rushed back to the conversational track: "Miss Macmurray, what do you think of all this?"

Knowing Carol wouldn't want the old man excited by controversy, Anne replied, "I'm afraid I've been busy wondering whether Peter wants *his* supporters to adopt any of *his* attributes, like Governor Dewey's mustache."

"Which ones?" asked Peter. "The wonderful smile? The broad shoulders?"

Laughter from nearly everyone, though Sally Coates, who was seeing Peter in action for the first time, merely let her mouth hang open in a pretty little *o*.

"Maybe this," said Anne, touching the dimple in Peter's

chin. No, she hadn't been able to throw him off stride; she had only earned her dessert, by playing her part, the ingenue.

"When do you start your campaign, Mr. Cox?" asked Dr. Coates.

"In earnest? After Labor Day. As I explained to Harold, last week was the right time to trade on a little of the convention excitement. But between now and September I'll lie low and—as I *haven't* yet explained to Harold—take a little time away from the office. Just a couple of weeks," he added, "so I can go up to Mackinac and use the house my parents have there. You ought to come up for a while yourself," he said to Anne.

He'd thrown *her* off stride, and she was furious. Should she say yes? If she did, would she be calling his bluff, or just calling her own, trumping the part of her that tried to pretend he was unattractive?

"I've been there," she settled for saying. "It was my introduction to Michigan, years ago." She would wait for him to follow through, but he didn't get the chance. Horace Sinclair, a little worked up after all, leaned across the table and addressed Peter with some insistence: "You ought to be staying around here. When the city council has to deal with Mr. Jackson's 'plan,' you should make yourself a voice of good sense."

"Oh, I won't be gone long, Colonel." Like the good politician he intended to become, Peter managed to make noncommitment seem like assent.

"Good, because I have a little plan of my own," said Horace, leaning into the table. "I think I can thwart him."

But he was himself thwarted by the arrival of Margaret

Feller and Billy Grimes, who had driven her parents' car halfway to Flint for frozen custard.

"I may send you back there for a couple of gallons on Sunday," said Carol. "Unless you're willing to work the churn for Fourth of July." Margaret groaned at this tradition her mother insisted on keeping; to Margaret's mind it was like picking one day of the year to give up the vacuum for a feather duster.

"Come give your uncle a kiss," said Dr. Coates. Margaret reluctantly obliged. "There we go. I guess any man with a daughter named Margaret can't be all bad."

"At least this one doesn't sing," added Harold Feller.

"Honest to God," said Dr. Coates, displeased with himself for having let up on Truman for ten seconds, "did you hear that at a couple of stops on that cross-country train trip—which we all paid for, by the way—he actually came out on the platform in his *bathrobe?* Dragged the poor girl and her mother out there with him."

Margaret made her way around the table to greet the rest of her parents' guests. Billy was about to follow, when he noticed Mr. Sinclair, who hadn't been around to pay him the other day.

"Grimes," said Horace, nodding.

Too worn out with frustration over Margaret and his own finances to practice Dale Carnegie on the old coot, Billy settled for saying, "Long time no see."

"Can I talk to you?" Margaret whispered to Anne.

"How about a few minutes from now? Just before your mother brings out coffee?"

"I'll be out on the back porch. Signal me? Please?"

Anne finished her second helping while Peter, whether

for his own good or the general one she couldn't tell, turned the conversation from politics to the Detroit Tigers, a subject that, surprisingly enough, brought Sally Coates to life.

"May I help clear?" Anne asked Carol. She followed her into the kitchen, spotting Margaret through the screen door and raising the eyebrows she had plucked this morning. She set down a small stack of plates. "Carol, where can I find the bathroom?"

"Upstairs and to the left."

Upstairs and to the right lay Margaret's room, into which Carol's daughter, following behind, nudged Anne. She closed the door. Anne laughed at the girlish conspiracy and the realization that this seventeen-year-old's room was twice the size of what she herself rented from Mrs. Wagner.

Margaret was concentrating too hard to smile. "How can I get rid of Billy?" she asked.

"Forever?"

"Just for tonight. Before eleven o'clock."

It was 8:45.

"I'm supposed to see Tim Herrick," confessed Margaret, fiddling with the shirttail tied over her bare midriff.

"It's called late-dating, Margaret, and it isn't a crime. Just tell Billy you're sick. But what about your mother and father? How do you get out of the house?"

"Oh, that's no problem. I just sneak out. I've done it lots of times."

What did this girl really want from her? Surely not advice.

As soon as Margaret's eyes met hers again, Anne knew. Her role was to provide the thrilling opportunity for Margaret at last to say the boy's name in that kind of confidential whisper louder than the loudest radio or newsreel or television transmission.

"I don't want to hurt him. Billy, I mean. He and Tim are best friends, you know."

Somehow that didn't seem likely. From Anne's sightings of Tim Herrick, with those cloudy blue eyes and that yellow hair like a prairie fire, he didn't seem the kind of boy who would have a best friend, let alone a harmless little go-getter like Billy Grimes. He seemed more the kind to make somebody desperate—a mother, or a girl like Margaret, or poor Frank Sherwood, probably sitting alone in his room tonight, waiting for the next time the boy would look into that telescope and be blindfolded by the universe, giving Frank the chance to gaze at the back of his head.

"I'm sure you won't hurt Billy. But tell me, Margaret, how did this date get arranged?"

"I ran into Timothy the other night. On the corner by his house."

So now it was "Timothy." What a golden bough of passion this boy had made Oliver Street. "Just like that?" asked Anne.

"Not exactly. I'd gone out. I was taking a walk. I mean—"

"It's all right. I guessed, last Friday night, when you saw him at the high school. But where are you supposed to go with him at eleven o'clock?"

"For a drive. In his brother's old car."

"All right, just try not to upset your parents."

Margaret nodded, as if they would always be the least of her worries. Anne, who could hear someone in the bathroom, said that she herself ought to be getting downstairs.

"How is Peter?" Margaret asked quickly. Having gotten the older woman's approving attention, she was a little giddy now, ready to be on the other end of some girl talk.

"Oh," said Anne, "he's very much himself."

"His favorite thing."

"You don't like him, do you?"

"Not as much as Mr. Riley."

"What do you know about Mr. Riley?"

"Just what I hear from Mother."

"Well, I'm glad to see you two communicate about some things."

"Oh, come on, Anne, aren't you going to tell me any—"

Anne was already on her way back to the party, waving to Margaret as she went down the carpeted staircase, preparing to tell Billy that the girl wasn't feeling well. Should she lay it on thick and say it was the frozen custard that had made her ill?

There wasn't much of a party to return to. Carol was setting down cups and saucers, but Sally Coates had begun washing up in the kitchen, an excuse, it seemed, to put on the radio and listen to the Tigers game. Harold Feller and his brother-in-law had lit their pipes in the living room, and out on the porch Horace Sinclair was reaching into his pocket, better late than never, for some change with which to pay Billy—who took it and ran off down the Fellers' driveway.

"Where is he going?" Anne asked Peter.

"To drive my car back to my place. That way I get to walk around with you when we get out of here. Do you think Margaret will mind that he's gone?"

Anne went back to the table.

"I should have made this evening into one of those 'buffets,' " said Carol, who gave up on reassembling everybody for coffee.

MRS. WAGNER WAS ASLEEP. THE LENS OF FRANK SHERWOOD'S telescope was capped, its black tube under the oilcloth. There wasn't a light on in the Comstock Apartments, but the oak trees' leaves had at last begun to move with a breeze.

"What did you think of the doctor?" Peter asked Anne, as they stood on the steps.

"He *sounds* like somebody who was hit too much as a child. But he's a true believer, at least where your side's concerned."

"I couldn't stand him," said Peter. "Cute wife, though."

"Poor Carol. It was like giving a party on an assembly line."

"Well, that's the future. Everything's going to speed up." His last words were drowned out by the noise of his new '49 Ford, which Billy Grimes was taking on a fifth run down Oliver Street, the sound of George Winslow's orchestra, on WGN, coming out its window.

"What do you mean, 'your side'?" Peter asked all of a sudden. "You said 'your side' about the election. Isn't it yours, too?"

"I'm keeping an open mind."

"Oh, God, he's gotten to you, hasn't he? Riley. That must be why the dinner looked like an 'assembly line' to you."

"All right, Peter. It looked like the floor of the stock exchange. Do you like that better as an image of bustle?"

"A lot better. But when you come up to Mackinac, all your images will be peaceful ones. No cars on the whole island. Only wagons."

"I remember," said Anne. "All right. Which weekend?"

"Which ones do you have free from Riley?"

"Not the next one."

"Okay, two weekends after that."

This was more like poker than dating. Did she even want to go? Didn't she just want to stay here and untie Jack's tongue? At least toward that end her stratagems were sincere, tactics tried out in straightforward good faith: bringing his dad a book on fishing, and the other afternoon a cake—though the price for baking it in Mrs. Wagner's kitchen was having to tell her "everything." Still, all that was better than this neurotic skirmishing. What *was* it about Peter, anyway? He seemed so eager for opposition that he couldn't take victory lying down. As soon as he won an exchange, he insisted on a rematch. Why this should be she wasn't sure, since in other respects he was too much like every older boy she'd known in Darien. They all had more or less the same resumé and future, even if Peter acted oddly delighted about his date with Destiny. The Darien boys treated Destiny more calmly; she was just Success, after all, sort of like the right girl from Rosemary Hall or Miss Porter's. They'd all wind up with her. Peter wanted to step on the gas toward the rendezvous, but Anne hadn't come to Owosso to get into his '49 Ford. She should get serious about her book, but otherwise it *was* all right to be here purposefully without purpose, to wait for something unknown, something different, to overtake her— particularly if that turned out to be Jack. From the moment his garage light had come on and she'd seen those license plates on the wooden walls, she'd really *felt* the difference. In Darien those plates would have been hanging in a self-amused way, pleased with their own jaunty pointlessness. But on the Riley wood they seemed real and proud, without irony, like the height marks parents penciled on a wall, evidence of a family's simple, solid movements with and against gravity.

She would change the subject. "What are you going to do when old Mr. Sinclair approaches you for help?"

"Get out of it. It won't be hard."

"Are you really in favor of this scheme to tear up that whole stretch of the riverbank, right in the middle of the town?"

"A bunch of backyards. That's all it amounts to. Face it, Anne, all of those people with the land, just like everybody else in this town, are going to be famous. Not movie-star famous, but attached to one big piece of somebody else's fame. For the rest of their lives, when they get into a conversation in a club car or a hotel lobby or anyplace out of town and people find out they're from here, people are going to say, 'Oh, that's where President Dewey grew up.' It's not earth-shattering, but it *is* earth-*shaking*, a small tremor, let's say. The earth under this town is moving, just a bit, certainly enough to rearrange a riverbank."

"You keep saying *they*. For the rest of *their* lives."

"Well, *we're* not going to be around here for very long."

"I don't know that."

"You're not going to be here if you're with me."

Ignore it. Don't rise to it. Don't bluff, don't bet, don't fold. And no kiss either. "Promise me one thing, Peter."

"What's that?"

"Don't do anything that will hurt that old man."

Neither of them could see him, but the old man in question, having taken a long detour on his way home, was walking down Shiawassee Street, with great concentration, toward the riverbank.

FOUR

July 8 – 15

Tim Herrick took a gulp of Geyer's lager and said, "Thanks, Gus. What do we owe you?"

His companion behind the Indian Trails bus station, Billy Grimes, knew the exact cost of the bucket Gus Farnham had procured for them from the Top Hat Tap Room. Billy handed over the full eighty-five cents plus a tip. He could settle with Herrick later. There were so *many* things he needed to settle with his supposed best friend.

"You want to join us?" asked Tim, spreading out one section of the July 6 *Argus* on the damp ground near the terminal's brick rear wall. A faint bit of bebop from the night manager's radio came through the window. "Gotta be on the *qui vive*," said Tim, explaining the near-whisper in which he'd extended the invitation. Gus, whose fund of slang had been unmodified by two world wars, just took his dollar and said, "No, thanks. Gonna go see my girl."

"Gus spurns draft," said Tim to Billy, pointing first to the beer bucket and then to a story in the two-day-old paper about how General Eisenhower had resisted the blandishments of Democrats still hoping he might, next week in Philadelphia, save them from Harry Truman.

"Herrick slays himself," said Billy to the still-perplexed Gus, who was hitching up his pants and taking the first steps toward his widowed lady friend in Corunna. "How's *your* gal?" he asked Billy by way of good-bye.

"I haven't seen her much this week."

Herrick didn't say anything. But he knew, which is to say he knew that Billy knew. How could he not? Margaret was no longer home when Billy came around; the Fellers' phone was always busy (lots to discuss with her girlfriends); and this afternoon, during a pickup game at Grand Trunk Athletic Park, there had been that *look* she and Tim shot each other, straight down the first-base line.

"Say hi to your pa," said Gus, waving as he took off.

It was left to Tim to break the silence. "You seen this thing about Civil Aeronautics jobs in Alaska?" he asked, tapping another story in the *Argus*. "$3,306 a year." A sum like that was bound to get a rise out of Billy Grimes.

"It's not as much as it looks. Do you know what it costs to live up there? I bet they don't attract anybody but a bunch of broken-down old guys like Gus."

"Mr. Sherwood told me he picked up Gus's plane in his telescope the other night. He said it was big as a bug."

"He's still giving you telescope lessons?"

"Yeah, we hack around. He's showed me some stuff on Jupiter a couple of times."

"What do you *talk* about with a guy like that? He's a teacher. And what makes you so special that he wants to hang around with you?"

"First of all, I've got a head for what he's talking about. Some of us can calculate more than nickels and dimes, jerkwater." Tim took a long gulp of beer, which he knew Margaret would have been thrilled to see run down his Adam's apple. "And second," he said, pausing to belch, "I think he feels sorry for poor me on account of my poor dead father and poor dead brother."

"I think he's fruity."

"Meaning exactly what?" asked Tim, narrowing his eyes and shifting fast enough to tear two pages of the *Argus* underneath him.

"Meaning nothing exactly." That was the problem with the word; it meant two things at once, and maybe he'd intended it to mean a little of both. "Meaning nuts, I guess. He comes into the camera shop and orders two different kinds of lens wipes, like it makes such a difference, and when another customer asks him what he thinks of the weather, he gets this look on his face like it's some technical question he isn't sure he can answer."

"No."

"No?"

"No, he's not nuts. Nuts is my old lady." Tim knew that, even now, Mrs. Jane Herrick would still be down at Oak Hill Cemetery, revved into a new cycle of grief by the news that yet another body, that of Albert Jack Holmes, d. France, July 2, 1944, had arrived home today in Owosso, at the Ann Arbor train station. The funeral would be Monday at Jennings-Lyons, and Sgt. Holmes' parents, the William Holmeses of Alger Avenue, would be there, as would Jane Herrick, who had never met them or their son.

Calling one's own mother nuts was, as arguments went,

pretty unanswerable, so Billy tried a more oblique attack on Frank Sherwood. "Teachers would be better off having to work summers, instead of doing whatever they do. Reading, I guess."

"What's the last book *you* finished? Dale Carnegie? You ought to read a little more and find a few things out."

"Mr. Quiz Kid."

"I don't mean facts. I mean reasons. Things between the lines. Like the lines of page 464." Tim refilled his wax cup and said no more.

"Okay, I'll bite. Page 464 of what?"

"Raintree County. Go look at the copy down at Abner's. I underlined the place before I slipped it back onto the shelf."

"You returned a book you stole?"

"I didn't want to get Anne into trouble."

Anne. So Margaret's friends were already his friends. Clenching his fist, Billy asked, "So what's the big goddamn secret, anyway? On page 464."

"Why the guy that wrote the book killed himself a few months ago."

"You've lost me." And he had, totally. His best friend had always been a little different, but lately he was scary. Stewed on beer half the time (he'd already drunk the second and was pouring a third), carrying a gun around at night, looking for Jupiter and talking stuff like this. They said craziness ran in families. Maybe nuts wasn't just Mrs. Herrick. Maybe nuts was her son, too. In any case, he'd lost his best friend, and his almost-girlfriend along with him. *To* him. They'd be going off to Jupiter together after fruity Frank Sherwood threw them a bon voyage party. A month ago, when he was telling Margaret about his own determination to escape this town, to make the big money in New York, she'd looked at him and said, "I don't want to escape it. I want to *overcome* Owosso." What had *that* meant? Something else on page 464?

"Whatever happened to Sharon?" Billy asked. Tim was guzzling the third beer like it was malted milk a doctor had prescribed to some skin-and-bones guy getting over TB.

"She's selling pedal pushers at the Ruth Shop." He yawned.

One more small hope—that ladykiller Herrick might still have some interest in the last girl he'd had on his string—now lay dashed at Billy's sneakered feet, among the damp parking-lot weeds and sodden *Argus*. It was Margaret, for keeps; and Billy was angry. "Poor Sharon. Just another slob behind a counter earning a paycheck."

"Christ, are you touchy. I can't help it if my old man believed in a lot of insurance and dropped dead early." It was Alan Herrick's prudence in 1935 that now permitted his widow to spend the day down at Oak Hill, and his surviving son to loaf through the last two summers—behavior Billy looked at disapprovingly.

"I'm gone," Tim said. "You going to want any more of this?"

"No."

"Good." Tim lifted the bucket to his lips and finished off the rest of the Geyer's.

"Where you heading?" asked Billy.

"No place fast." Tim threw the bucket into the bushes. "But in a little while I'll be leaving. Going far, far away." He pointed north, and toward the sky.

Now he was sounding like Jesus, ready to ascend into heaven. Well, thought Billy, even Herrick can't fly.

"*POLITICS FULFILLS MAN'S ESSENTIAL AND PERMANENT FUNCTION as a social being, as a part of God's creation.*"

Al Jackson pointed to the radio in the Hotel Owosso's coffee shop. "Well, she's got that right. I'll give her that, I'll give her that." From Philadelphia, the voice of Frances Perkins, FDR's Secretary of Labor, was complimenting the delegates to the Democratic convention as they sat, in the same wooden chairs the Republicans had occupied three weeks before, probably drenched with sweat.

The radio had been going all night, straight through Senator Barkley's sixty-seven minute keynote speech. Kay Schmidt had paid it no more mind than the kitchen exhaust. She smiled politely at Al before checking the supply of eggs for tomorrow morning and wishing the three men in here would finish, so she could close up.

Things did seem to be reaching a climax. Al Jackson had gotten up from the booth so that the other two, papers spread among their coffee cups, could talk between themselves. At the counter, moving from one stool to another, swiveling, pacing, flipping the cards in the jukebox, pushing up the tops of the creamers and clanking them back down, Al looked like somebody with Saint Vitus' dance. He was a nice enough fellow, but he was making Kay crazy, pawing through the jar of Dewey buttons and spinning the glass sugar dispenser in a series of noisy circles on the formica surface she'd just finished cleaning. "Marie was over at her Gyro-Duce class tonight." It seemed his thought had been prompted by the twirling container. "I think she's just fine myself, but she says she'd like to drop five pounds." Actually, Marie Jackson could drop twenty and never miss them, but Kay figured Al had never stood long enough in one place to get a good look at his wife.

"So, gentlemen?" he called out, striding back to the booth, no longer able to stand the wait.

"Well, Al," said Councilman Morgan. "We're talking a couple of hundred thousand dollars. And that's assuming there are no holdouts among the property owners."

"The city'll make back what it spends before half his first term is over!"

"I hear a couple of the owners are already resisting," said Councilman Royers.

"We've only got to get them into the spirit of the thing!" cried Al. "It's just a piece of their backyards, and they'll be getting a good price."

"They might figure nothing's worth having hundreds of people tramping across what used to be part of their land."

Al looked crestfallen over this possibility, as well as Councilman Morgan's use of "hundreds" instead of "thousands." But he was back with a rebuttal before Kay could reach the booth with one more refill. "The tourists will be hidden by the walls, the big murals behind the exhibits. But time is of the essence. Those walls are going to *take* time— that is, if we get a first-rate painter to paint 'em."

Councilman Royers nodded patiently, doubting somehow that Frederick Frieseke, if he were still kicking around in France, would want to hustle home to Owosso to paint twenty-foot-high likenesses of Lucky Luciano and Lepke and all the other milestones on Dewey's climb to the top. The council had never had to consider such things before. "Al, don't you think the budget you propose for maintaining this whole thing, once it's up, is a little small? The gravel paths alone . . ."

"Volunteers!" Al threw his reassuring grin, like a double-play ball, from Royers to Morgan to Kay. "The chance to be a part of history and take pride in their town! Like the song says, who could ask for anything more?"

"Not you," said Councilman Morgan. "You'll probably sell about five hundred extra rolls of film a week, once all those tourists start coming."

Al looked genuinely hurt.

"I'm just ribbing you," said Morgan.

"With all the town makes from ticket sales and added tax revenues," Al argued, *"everybody* is going to come out ahead. There'll be money to do things we've never been able to think about before. We might even clean up the river!" The Shiawassee, despite James Oliver Curwood's passion for conservation, ran so pollutedly past his castle that ten days ago the state stream control commission in Lansing had declared it unfit for swimming.

"My wife's glad it's off limits this summer," said Royers. "She's always afraid the kids are going to pick up polio."

Al ignored mention of the disease, as if it were one more untidy part of the past that would soon be taken care of. "Phil. Eddie. It's already July twelfth. All I'm asking for is a timetable."

"That we can give you," said Morgan. "A first reading of the proposal before the full council on August third. Second reading and a vote on it round about October seventh."

Thanking Kay for a fresh napkin, Al failed to hide his disappointment. "I don't know that we could have fought the war on a schedule as leisurely as that. You can't make it any faster?"

"Those are the rules," said Royers. "Think of it this way, Al. It'll give you time to whip everybody up, including those yard owners."

"Okay, okay," said Al, reverting to overdrive, wiggling into his pocket for Kay's tip. "But I'm going to go ahead with a few things on my own. That's the only way, if we're going to have this up and running by spring. Jeez, I wish Inauguration Day were still March fourth instead of January twentieth. Did I tell you I talked to somebody over at U of M who thinks he can get us the chair in the law library that Dewey used to sit in every night he was hitting the books? Make a great exhibit!"

At the counter, Kay Schmidt waved good night to Al and the councilmen as the last syllables of Frances Perkins' quavery voice died upon the radio waves between Philadelphia and Owosso. It was when she walked back to the booth and collected the three face-up Franklin D. Roosevelt dimes the men had left for her that she realized whose voice she'd missed coming out of the radio tonight, the only one without a band behind it that had ever made her turn up the sound.

PETER COX STEPPED OFF THE FERRY AND ONTO THE LANDING at Huron Street. The sun shone directly over Fort Mackinac, and the carriage drivers mopped their brows between throws of the dice. There was no particular need for them to look sharp, since at this time of day the disembarking passengers who needed to hire a horse and buggy, the only vehicle permitted on the island, were caught in a seller's market. Peter was not gifted with much patience, and from the time he'd begun coming here as a child he'd always had reservations about the place's antediluvian charms. It was beautiful, but after a week he felt trapped in rehearsal for some school play.

Soon enough a driver whistled for him, and he climbed into the carriage, to be chauffeured at a fast trot over the island's limestone. Watching the cedar trees on the cliffs above, and beneath him the day-tripping Fudgies, pedaling their rented bicycles en route to purchasing the resort's trademark delicacy, he felt restored to his normal measures of proprietariness and peace. He would enjoy himself after all. A round of golf before the afternoon was over, then drinks and dinner at the Grand Hotel with his mother. Her clapboard house fronting the straits was empty for ten months of the year, and each summer she complained anew about having to get a horse-drawn dray full of her possessions on and off the island. That was Mother: she shed vanfuls of mental baggage without a backward glance, but could never travel light on worldly goods.

Mrs. Cox came through the screen door and down the wooden steps. *"How* long are you staying?"

"Two weeks," he said, kissing her cheek.

"Oh," she said, "I thought it was a month." She disguised her relief in a neutral tone that each of them judged a creditable display of warmth. "You'll be in the middle of some company, you know. Your aunt Ada will be here next weekend."

"Then we may be a little crowded. The girl I told you about is coming up then."

"Good. My sister will love the idea of chaperoning."

"Father isn't around, is he?"

"Heavens, no," said Mrs. Cox, looking over her shoulder, as if alarmed by her son's morbid imagination. "We've traded places; he's in Palm Springs. Come inside and get yourself settled."

"What have you been doing?"

"Listening to the radio. I won't be able to stand it when that little rooster takes the podium, so I thought I'd get all my drama in the daytime. They're going to make Senator Barkley run for vice president, the poor thing. He's past seventy, a widower. In fact, they say he's looking for a wife."

"Well, he can squeeze a lot of widowed grandmothers while he's out kissing their daughters' babies. And whoever he chooses can retire with him to the blue grasses of Kentucky next year. Honestly, Mother, do you have any idea what's shaping up? Do you know how many Republicans we're going to pull into the legislature along with yours truly?"

"Peter, if you start telling me all that now, we won't have anything to talk about at dinner. I made a reservation at the hotel for seven. Mr. Woodfill was interested to hear that you were coming back. In fact, he seemed grateful for the warning. You misbehaved there last summer, didn't you?"

"Can't hear you, Mother, can't hear you," said Peter as he carried his suitcase up the narrow wooden stairs. They creaked in the same seasonal spots he had heard them creaking since his parents bought this place in 1925. Even then his old room had seemed too small; now it was positively miniature, more like a diorama than part of an actual house, all its wooden furniture painted a little too brightly. Tonight his ankles would hang over the quilt-covered bed.

Maybe two weeks was too long, however strategic his decision to take them, and however much he already needed to get away from the small-town parade of Vincent Dents, with all their pink mortgage papers and incorporation forms. It would be nice if between now and Anne's arrival that college girl (with whom he *had* misbehaved last year, vigorously, for three days, every moment her parents weren't around) came back. Or another college girl.

He was determined that Anne Macmurray would soon take up permanent residence in his life and mind, but for another ten days she couldn't be present in the former, so he didn't want her cluttering up the latter. Let these two weeks get Riley out of *her* mind. It wouldn't take longer than that.

He had seen her only once since the Fellers' party, by accident, a few days ago. Over breakfast at the Great Lakes the two of them had calmed down a little, making conversation that was more like trench warfare than swordplay. She was strong, this girl, so strong in her *doubts,* about herself and the world and what she was doing in it. This book of hers that she'd owned up to: it was as if she were in Owosso for all these people to use *her,* make her their instrument, their chance to express themselves on her pages. She hadn't put it this way, of course—would have been mortified to— but that was what he understood. She didn't really know what she wanted, and in this she reminded him of no other girl he'd known. If she reminded him of anyone, it was his great-uncle, a congregationalist minister outside Philadelphia who, a few years before Peter was born, resigned from his church in an open letter, saying he shouldn't any longer hold the post when he wasn't "quite completely convinced" of the basis for what he said every Sunday. Not "quite completely convinced." He'd had, Peter was sure, several hundred percent more conviction about what he preached than the rest of the ministers up and down the Main Line, who consubstantiated the mystical proportions of a martini with more zeal than they could muster for the Eucharist. It was a kind of doubt more reverent than faith, and she had it, too.

To be falling in love, after a handful of encounters, with a girl who reminded him of Great-Uncle Waldo! Would he want her if there were no resistance? No. Some of that was always required, if only the semi-resistance of that college girl or the English secretaries on Captain Butcher's staff in Grosvenor Square. Resistance was the grindstone against which he would always sharpen and shine.

Dear Anne,

Just arrived here at my mother's. Enclosed are train and ferry schedules. Whatever you want to do once you're up here is fine—you can stay at the house or the hotel, where we can get you a room even at the last minute. At the house you'd have one quiet enough to write your book in, and far enough removed from mine that you'll hardly know I'm here. In fact, your real trouble will be the attentions of female company. My mother's sister, Ada, an endless talker, will be here too. But don't make that a reason to stay at the Grand. Make it a reason to stay here, so you'll have to beg me to come to your rescue.

Honestly, I'll behave.

Has your "open mind" about the election got room in it for three Democratic parties? It looks as if the plantation owners are going to crash into Wallace's communist friends as they rush through the convention-hall exits.

I should tell you that *I* ran into Jackson, our camera-selling Barnum, at the Great Lakes this morning, just before I set out. He wants me to get up on a stump for his proposal, and I said yes. If the town is going to be a museum, it might as well take on a little bit of Coney Island instead of the fudge-colored amber this place is stuck in. (Even so, you'll love Mackinac, because I'll be here.)

You will be worrying, no doubt, about the old colonel. I won't do anything to send his blood pressure over San Juan Hill. In fact, I'll take care of him the easy way: I'll convert him to Jackson's enterprise.

I'll bring the old man around, and I'll bring you around, too.

Until the 23rd,

Peter

He *would* bring her around. If anyone were the grindstone, it would be he. And yet, when he brought the envelope to his lips, its flap had nothing to brush against. He had shaved off his Dewey mustache the other morning.

"It makes sense this town's biggest industry is death, doesn't it?"

"I know just what you mean," replied Margaret Feller to Tim Herrick. Actually, she did and she didn't. On the one hand, there was no denying where they sat on this summer night: a loading dock at the back of the Owosso Casket Company, which had been making coffins on South Elm Street since Lyman Woodard went into business in 1885. His adjoining furniture factory had suffered mightily in the 1911 cyclone, but had sprung back, and along with the casket operation it still kept the Woodards, the wealthiest family in the city, in their compound of mansions on the western stretch of Oliver Street.

On the other hand, even though Margaret had in the past let the noontime blasts of the Woodard factory whistle camouflage her own ten-second screams of frustration over life in Owosso, she could no longer equate the town with the slow death that comes from being bored. It was only a week ago that Carole Landis had committed suicide in Hollywood—pills—and since that day Margaret had more than once reminded herself, gratefully, that that could so easily have been her. If her first date with Tim hadn't been the success it had, who knows what might have become of her?

But it had been heaven, and the twelve days since had passed in a continual dream: the long, long talks, about everything—their parents, Tim's dead brother, the German soldiers four years ago (imagine telling him that), what the two of them read (he was absolutely right about page 464 of *Raintree County*)—and the long soulful kisses in Arnie's Chevrolet or here behind the casket factory or in back of the Indian Trails terminal. She wished he wouldn't drink so much beer, but he was too much of a gentleman to insist she drink along with him. Half the jerks from school would only be trying to get her drunk.

As far as she was now concerned, this wooden platform was more glamorous than any black-and-white marble floor in those ancient dance movies her parents had years ago dragged her and Jim to when they couldn't find a babysitter. And the Woodard smokestacks were as thrilling as any of those cardboard Manhattan skyscrapers. She hadn't gone so far as telling anyone (certainly not Tim), but she was suddenly, secretly, in love with Owosso, just as she had made peace with her own face, which since Saturday had gone without its morning application of Helena Rubinstein.

"I mean, it's just perfect for my mom," said Tim, after pulling on his beer. "Living in a place that churned out more coffins than any other town in America. Keeping the graveyards well supplied." He raised a toast to a squadron of delivery trucks parked across the asphalt.

"I think your mother is *deep*," said Margaret. "Even if she is sort of sad. I'm sure she understands life a lot more than *my* mother does—just playing bridge and going to all those little charity lunches with her hat and gloves on, never having to actually *see* any of the poor people her friends claim to care about so much. That and matchmaking are nearly all she does."

"How's her Peter Cox project coming?"

"She claims to be neutral between him and Mr. Riley, but of course she isn't, because from her way of looking at it, only Peter is 'appropriate' for Anne. But Peter is up on Mackinac, so things have slowed down for a while."

"How did he get there?" asked Tim, looking at the sky.

"In his '49 Ford—a car that nobody else around here has even gotten delivery of. And then the ferry. Did I tell you Anne is going up the weekend after this one?"

"I want *us* to make a date," said Tim, putting down his bottle and looking right at her with his cool and limpid green eyes. "The Dawn Patrol is coming to the airport two weeks from Sunday. Practically every light-plane flier in the state, hundreds of them, will be touching down. They haven't picked Owosso for this in seven years."

"What do they do once they get here?"

"Finish watching the sun come up, have a huge breakfast, and then take their planes back up for joyrides and sightseeing, even a little racing. They give out a lot of prizes, too. You know, who came the farthest, stuff like that."

"It sounds wonderful," said Margaret, whose head was already swarming with airplanes beautiful as butterflies. If she were still going with Billy, he'd be asking her to the hot-rod races that began their season tonight at the Speedway or—God forbid—next month's cornball county fair.

"You promise?" asked Tim, putting his hands on her shoulders.

"Of course," said Margaret, leaning in for a long, long kiss, during which her mental aircraft looped and dove and swept back up again.

When it was over and her head came to rest on Tim's shoulder, he looked up at the smokestacks, all of them idle but one, which emitted a narrow plume of steam as the night shift sent a thinner stream of glue and shavings toward the Shiawassee than the one pumped in each morning. It seemed to Tim that the whole factory was just a small part, the packaging end, of a much bigger one, life's own, the one producing and growing and curing the corpses themselves, which would be shipped to their final points of delivery, beneath headstones, from Maine to California. Compared to just regular life and death the war itself had been a *small* thing; that's what his mother didn't get. She was like a cop trying to arrest some pathetic bookie without taking any notice of the Mr. Big in charge of the whole operation.

"Have you ever heard of Cass Hough?" he asked.

Margaret, nervous for a second that Cass might be a girl, said she hadn't.

"He's an Englishman some people think broke the

sound barrier back in '42, though they can't prove it. He's going to be the main guest at this year's Dawn Patrol."

Relieved, Margaret asked, "Is there really a big thunderclap when the sound barrier gets broken?" She knew, of course, that there was, but she wanted him to enchant her with explanations while they looked up at the sky.

"It's the place where distance and time slam into each other. There's got to be some little crevice the plane flies right over, some passageway into another dimension."

If Billy were saying all this it would sound like an Action comic, but Tim could tell her he had a map of the place in his pocket and she wouldn't doubt him. And if he kissed her again, *she* would break the sound barrier, fly involuntarily over that threshold they were always hinting at in Girls' Health, the one past which she wouldn't be able to control herself. If only right now he would *say the words,* she could die right here, in perfect happiness; they could put her into the simplest pine coffin in the factory. Tim would cry for a time, but recover when he accepted that she'd been killed by an excess of joy.

"I wish," she said, "that the whole country, not just the Dawn Patrol, had a queen and a king. I'm so sick of Dewey and Truman. This election is so *juvenile,* like picking the head of the student council."

"Who says any of them really rule?" asked Tim, looking off toward the Elm Street gate. "I mean, what makes anybody the President? Just some ancient agreement nobody ever stops to think about. If somebody snuck into the National Archives in the middle of the night and broke open that case they keep the Constitution in, and then ripped it up, would it really exist anymore? Who says all those printed copies have any force? Who says the world everybody agrees on is the same as the world in your head?"

He was so beautiful. He was more beautiful than Robert Daniels, that Ohio boy they were looking for, the one who was in the middle of a killing spree and had his picture in the paper. Except that Tim was good. He and she would be king and queen of their own world, without any subjects.

"Come on," he said, jumping down from the platform. He extended his arms up to her. "I want to show you a *completely* different world."

The car threaded the trees and moonlight, away from the factory and north toward Oliver Street. On the radio that Arnie had installed himself, years after buying the car, Eddy Arnold sang "Anytime," but Margaret wished this would be just *one* time, so perfect, so ultimate, that the Chevrolet would keep driving forever, out of town and through the cornfields and off the edge of the earth.

Behind them, furiously pumping his legs and breathing hard, taking care to remain invisible to the rearview mirror, someone else was hoping their ride would be quick. Otherwise he would lose them, even though he was sure that tonight they would end up where he'd been expecting them to go each of the four nights he'd been following them. The car was soon out of sight, but he kept huffing and puffing toward the place where, sure enough, he found it parked and empty. He slowed down, exhausted, slumping over the handlebars as he slunk away from Tim and Margaret's destination, the rooftop of Frank Sherwood, that son-of-a-bitch Mr. Science, that purveyor of different worlds, the mayor of the goddamned planet Jupiter.

.   .   .

THE CLOCK ON CITY HALL STRUCK MIDNIGHT, AND HORACE Sinclair switched off WGN. Truman had gotten his nomination, but in all the chaos of the convention there was still no telling when he would reach the podium for his acceptance speech. Horace, who now fervently hoped against hope for Truman's victory, sighed with disgust. He tied the belt of his bathrobe around his ample waistline and rocked a bit—one, two, three—until he had the momentum to rise and head for the kitchen.

On the counter he set out a can of frozen orange juice to thaw for morning. You couldn't say he was against every modern convenience. He was even preparing to keep a chart of the daily "pollen count" on the wall calendar from the heating-oil company; a lifelong hay-fever sufferer, he had welcomed the opening of Memorial Hospital's measuring station this week. On days the stuff was really blowing, like today, he sagged something awful. He was too tired to be up at this hour, and yet he knew, as he wiped his hands on a dish towel, that he wouldn't be able to sleep.

His spirits, and no doubt his blood pressure, had been up and down for the past two days. The news of Barkley's selection to run with Truman had given him a boost—"another prosy old man like myself," he'd told Carol Feller yesterday afternoon, right in front of Annie Dewey's house— but tonight he'd been brought low by the announcement of General Pershing's death in Washington. The chill it gave him had nothing to do with age. At eighty-eight, Black Jack had been a good sixteen years older, and when Horace had laid eyes on him fifty years ago near Santiago, it was as boy to man. No, it wasn't old age or the Spanish War that had come to Horace's mind. It was the war after that, specifically the Argonne forest and the service there, under Pershing's command, of Jonathan Adams Darrell's child, that boy who still didn't know what a dark star he'd been born under, thanks to what Horace and Wright George and Boyd Fowler had gone and done that summer night in '97.

Only he and Wright were left, and after this evening of quiet agitation, when his thoughts moved from the Owosso Casket Company to the riverbank to the luckless Truman, whose imminent defeat was the cause of all his misery, Horace realized that he must not wait any longer to send a letter to New York City. He climbed the stairs to his study and rolled up the desktop.

Dear Wright,

Tonight Mr. Kaltenborn was speculating that our two national paragons—I speak, of course, of your governor and His Accidency—will encounter each other face-to-face before the month is out, when both show up to cut the ribbon on your new airport. (Pretty name, Idlewild: too pretty for all the noise and commotion that will bear it.) I suppose your city fathers will have to keep the scissors blunt, lest either one of these two makes a lunge for the other. Of course, young Dewey probably never angers to the point where he's a danger to himself or anyone else. Truman, I gather, is another story, though I have no intention of waiting through the dawn to hear rhetorical evidence of it. I've already witnessed enough of his hapless party at work.

As you can imagine, your hometown is in a lather over the whole thing, lawn signs and mustaches sprouting from the front yards and faces of people who never laid eyes on or particularly liked the disciplined little s.o.b., but there you are, and I suppose it's to be expected. I would be amused if it weren't for another development that distresses me greatly and concerns you, too, I'm afraid. We've got this awful camera salesman—lives right across the street in what he calls a "ranch" house, as if it's some stop on a cattle drive—and he's hell-bent on turning Owosso into Monticello for the Masses, a vacationer's shrine to Our Next President. Chief among his plans is digging up the riverbank along that crucial stretch where you and I and Boyd lost our sense a half century ago.

I cannot bear that this should suddenly haunt us all over again. I feel some terrible judgment roaring down, gathering in the distance like the '11 cyclone. The man's scheme (his name is Jackson) has got to wind through the city council for the next couple of months, and I need to talk to you, Wright. We need to stop him. I don't have the energy to explain it all on paper, but I'm enclosing these cuttings from the *Argus* and asking you to telephone me as soon as you've had a chance to think on this.

"A little little grave, an obscure grave." Even after fifty years we must keep it an undiscovered country.

Urgently,

Horace

AROUND THE BLOCK ON WILLIAMS STREET, WHERE THE houses were smaller and closer together, Anne Macmurray and Jack Riley sat on Jack's front porch, still waiting up to hear Harry Truman. The band in Philadelphia segued from "Hail to the Chief" to "My Old Kentucky Home," in honor of Senator Barkley. Gene Riley's room was upstairs at the back of the house, but Anne and Jack kept the radio so low the crickets almost drowned it out. "Congressman Rayburn," the faraway commentator informed them, "is banging the gavel, trying to quiet the delegates . . ."

Anne realized that the desperate crowd might go on

cheering until 3 A.M. before Jack ran out of things to say. Last month's sudden kiss in the garage had been the first turn of a combination lock, and in the weeks since, during *Call Northside 777* and a dinner in Flint, the tumblers had started dropping. Tonight, politics had acted like nitroglycerine, blowing the safe's door open once and for all. She could hardly shut him up, no matter the subject. Her head was on his shoulder as she looked up at the stars; inside the radio the sweet strains of Stephen Foster mixed with Rayburn's scolding squawk.

"Boy," said Jack, "am I glad you've got your own apartment with its own entrance. I once dated a girl who lived in Mrs. Doucette's rooming house down on Exchange Street, and if I brought her home past eleven, she got the riot act the next morning at breakfast."

"Mrs. Wagner just tortures me with questions."

He adjusted the fan, whose cord ran with the radio's through the living-room window, so that its breeze fell on her more directly. "I never mind the heat," he said. "I guess it's what they call a reaction. Years ago, mornings in the winter in that old house by the train depot, I was the runt of the litter, and my mother would wrap me in her old bathrobe to stop my teeth from chattering. My brothers and sisters would tease the hell out of me."

Anne could picture the mother, smiling and humming, cloaking her darlings in cheerful illusions. How had she managed it with the old man around? A character, her own dad would have said. He'd been friendly enough during dinner, even calling her "doll" a couple of times, but absolute sandpaper on Jack the minute a pot splattered or the phone rang. He was in pain, of course, his stomach bothering him terribly (cancer? Jack hadn't opened up *that* far), but some of it was just ornery assertion, pressed upon Jack in inverse proportion to the old man's growing dependence on him. *And where are you getting these ideas above yourself?* was, she thought, the evening's unspoken question—meant for Jack and prompted by her presence. Gene made her seem like a Buick, or a California vacation, something Jack had his nerve aspiring to, as if he too were developing "champagne tastes on a beer budget."

Her own taste for beer had certainly helped. She was on her third Stroh's, and hadn't touched the pitcher of lemonade that sat catching gnats on the porch railing. Jack had prepared it this afternoon, a last offering, she hoped, to the delicate flower he'd imagined. He seemed relieved that she smoked Luckies and enjoyed plunging her hands into the dishwater; he was so much less nervous with her tonight she was almost disappointed—he hadn't once tugged on those adorable little spikes of hair. The only time he'd shown embarrassment came when he got stalled during a wrangle with the father, something over his own salary (Gene's implication being that it was too high), and like an anxious passenger she'd gotten out to help him push the argument. Her cues and nods rattled him, even as they won her points with the old man—presumably for her loyalty to Jack, and maybe as a display of gumption against himself.

As it was, Jack soon had things rolling again, impressing her if not his father with his command of profit margins and benefit ratios. He was patient and clear in his explanations. She could picture him persuading the fellows in Flint why it was important they get to the meeting this week, or at least give a thought to inflation when the union put in for a smaller increase than they thought it should. He could get a point across, tell a story. (When they went out to walk off dinner, just the two of them, he told her how the water main buried beneath their feet had gotten built.) The one thing he couldn't seem to bring up was Peter, though she wished he would. A vigorously biased assessment might get her to stop thinking about "that one," as she and her best girlfriend in Darien used to call the most impossible boy in their lives at any given moment. She'd been relieved when he went away the other day, and she'd kept the letter that arrived this morning unopened on her dresser.

How different these talks with Jack were from those fusillades of conversation with Peter. Every word she said to Jack was designed to coax and encourage. Add to this desire an urge (so far repressed) to rip off his shirt, and she had a cocktail of longings much stronger than Stroh's beer. She nestled closer to him, pretending it was more breeze from the fan instead of more damp from him that she was after. The two of them were dozing off, still waiting for Truman, as the announcer tried to convey a scene better suited to radio's new competition: the candidates had just been presented with a replica of the Liberty Bell, out of which some doves of peace were taking flight.

While Senator Barkley accepted his nomination, albeit more briefly than he had keynoted the convention, Jack fell fully asleep. His exhalations came in soft little sniffs, like a kitten's, making it impossible for her not to pet him. She shifted so his head was on her shoulder. With her gaze from above, she inventoried the face below the little stalks of hair. Everything was youthful and efficient. There was no decorative dimple, and instead of Peter's high cheekbones, those gaudy epaulets of breeding, Jack's were like retracted artillery. His snub nose was in its small way perfect; the boyish little mouth seemed braced to ward off an aunt's kisses or a brother's fists. His chest rose and fell in time with his breathing, and her eye traveled to an open shirt button inches above his belt, through which she could see a thin line of fine dark hair.

If she weren't careful, she'd reach her hand in. Only recently had this sort of temptation begun to seem a matter of extreme urgency. When she'd first gotten to Ann Arbor, the general dearth of men had made those around seem somehow more superfluous than desirable. Then they'd started flooding home, and she had had her first and only affair, with a dark-eyed boy from Dearborn who'd never been in the service at all. They met in Verse Writing, expressing infatuation with all the spontaneity of the romantic villanelles and octosyllabic couplets they were assigned to write each weekend. When they finally slept together, the boy's thin, perplexed body kept no time with hers; it was as if they'd failed the *terza rima* unit. They gave up after three times, relieved to get on to the brief business of worrying if she were pregnant.

But Jack, after a year when she had barely been able to find a girlfriend, let alone a date, was something else. She just *had* to touch, if not what was beneath it, at least the undone button, but as soon as she did the radio crackled to life: *"I am sorry that the microphones are in the way, but I must leave them the way they are because I have got to be able to see what I am doing—as I am always able to see what I am doing!"*

"Pop?" asked Jack, opening his eyes.

"Truman," said Anne, though she had to admit the

buckshot coming through the Philco—so different from
Dewey's baritone sax and those great bolts of satin cloth un-
rolled by FDR—*was* a bit like Gene Riley.

*"Senator Barkley and I will win this election and make these
Republicans like it—don't you forget that!"*

Anne laughed, but Jack cringed, as if Truman were some
crude friend he'd brought along and he'd only now realized
his mistake. But Anne was laughing in admiration; the school-
yard bluster was preposterous, but you had to hand it to him.
At this point in his fortunes, he ought to be begging, but instead he was dishing it out—to his supporters, no less: *"Never
in the world were the farmers of any republic or any kingdom or any
other country as prosperous as the farmers of the United States; and
if they don't do their duty by the Democratic party, they are the most
ungrateful people in the world!"* Jack sat up and nodded.

Now, unbelievably enough, it was the unions' turn.
Their wages had gone up $99 billion in the past fifteen years,
thanks to Roosevelt and the Democratic party, the "one
friend in politics" they'd ever had. *"And I say to labor what I
have said to the farmers: they are the most ungrateful people in the
world if they pass the Democratic party by this year."*

Giving himself over to it, Jack let out something between a laugh and a war whoop, swinging Anne, as if she
were a girl from Flint and not the maid of Darien, into a
momentary headlock. He planted a kiss on the back of
her neck. A second later he was paying her no mind, just
reaching to turn up the sound and the hell with all the
Dewey-voting neighbors. As Truman went on against "the
convention that met here three weeks ago," and "that
so-called Taft-Hartley Act," and all the rest of the sins of the
do-nothing Eightieth Congress, she and Jack sat smiling like

some long-married couple on a Sunday night, delighted that Jack Benny was hitting his stride.

"I recommended an increase in the minimum wage. What did I get? Nothing! Absolutely nothing!" Social security, civil rights, the Republicans' tax bill: what really came through this litany of mass concerns was a fit of personal pique, a tantrum so strong he had to scold the crowd for even murmuring its astonishment: *"Now, listen!"* How could one not? The two of them hung on each word, straight through to the surprise ending: *"On the twenty-sixth of July, which out in Missouri we call 'Turnip Day,' I am going to call Congress back and ask them to pass laws to halt rising prices, to meet the housing crisis . . . I shall ask them to act upon other vitally needed measures such as aid to education, which they say they are for; a national health program . . ."*

July twenty-sixth. The day she would be coming back from Mackinac.

"Jack, I'd better go. It's past two."

His thoughts had darkened in time with hers. He was frowning as he looked up. "This special session's not a good idea. They'll just say no to him every single day, and he'll look as if he isn't running the country."

"Time for you to go to bed. I don't have to be in till noon, but you'll be lucky if you get five hours. Come on, run me home."

They drove his Ford down Williams to Hickory. Despite the President's barked imperative, it was clear that almost nobody in Owosso but themselves had been listening. Every light was out, including Horace Sinclair's. Jack pointed out the dark gabled house as they turned west on Oliver. "I was sort of hoping the old man would be up. He's about the only person I've run into here who seems to be on the fence."

"Unless you count me," said Anne. "But I think I've fallen off it. I may vote for Truman."

"Are you serious?"

"About the whole election, no; not as much as I ought to be. But about voting for Harry? I think so. Character ought to count for something. He showed it tonight."

"He's a character, all right."

They rode past the Herrick house at the corner of Park. "That's where the boy Margaret's mad for lives."

"They're a sad family," said Jack.

"Did you know the brother? Arnie?"

"We were in school together," was all that Jack replied. Anne took the absence of further comment to be a kind of tribute, the unpresuming silence of a survivor for the lost. The Ford rolled past Christ Church, and Jack changed the subject: "That's where you'll get the best view of Dewey if he comes through between now and Election Day. He'll probably take his mother to Mass, or what do you call it, service."

Anne, a Presbyterian who hadn't been to church since leaving home, glanced at the park surrounding Christ's. "Trust the Episcopalians to need a whole square block."

Jack, who found the Protestants' denominational patchwork a mystery, killed the engine outside the Comstock Apartments. "Mrs. Wagner hasn't been listening to Harry either," said Anne. "Unless she's had him shouting into the dark. Either way, it looks as if I'm safe from questions tomorrow." She leaned into Jack. "Okay. I'll take my kiss here. That way you can get started right for home."

He put his arms around her, the third time all told that he'd done so. But what she suddenly seemed to have in mind was no quick kiss like the one he'd had after the movies or the restaurant in Flint. She was stroking his hair, pulling on his ears, and not doing anything to stop his hands, which seemed released from the invisible cuffs he'd made himself wear all month. It was as if he were with Louise, but without the radio soundtrack, with absolutely no sound at all, not even the crickets. Close as he was to her, he managed to open one eye, the one that had been dark through most of '44. He wanted to *see* her, to realize this wasn't Louise, but his beautiful out-of-state dream. The moonlight caught her face, which continued its passionate business, detonating in him a single moment of memory, his own vision of Fatima: the onscreen sight of Jeanne Eagels, twenty years before, in the dark of the Capitol, with his mother.

When Anne finally spoke, it was as if the screen, back then, had begun talking. "I don't want to go home," she said.

"Me neither," he replied, squeezing her tighter.

"No," she said. "I mean it. Let's turn around." He drew back, puzzled. "That sofa in the garage," she said. He turned the key and pressed the starter, more surprised than if the Christ Church bell had cracked in half, releasing a flight of doves.

F I V E

July 24 – August 1

IT WASN'T TRUE THAT JANE HERRICK NO LONGER READ THE *Argus.* She might have given up home delivery from Billy, but that was because she could not stand the paper's being thrown at her house like a German grenade in the Ardennes. The paper was so important to her as herald of the returning dead that she insisted on a personal connection to any copy of it coming into her home. Before canceling her subscription, she had been troubled by a sense that whatever copy Billy threw was the wrong one, whereas now, by running her thumb up and down the stack of *Argus*es at Kresge's, she could find the one meant for her. The last month's worth of them were stacked in the corner of her bedroom, which no one besides herself had entered in years.

Today's edition, Saturday, July 24, carried news from Ohio of the capture of Robert "Murli" Daniels. Having taken part "in 6 cold-blooded murders in 14 days," he was as unrepentant as he was handsome, but he didn't interest Jane. Tuesday's story of Pershing's burial had been another matter, because it fed one of her mathematical compulsions: calculating forward to the year in which Arnie, were he still alive, would reach the age of the deceased—in this case 2009, the sum of 1921 and 88. That would put him past the millennium, whose arrival she felt sure would lift the seventh of the seals, the atomic bombs over Japan having blasted open the first and second.

There had been no stories of returning soldiers this week, not even in the Flint paper, nothing to clip for the scrapbook, her own Oak Hill, inside the top drawer of her maplewood vanity. She had only glanced at the campaign news, such as yesterday's front-page picture of six men, each wearing a mustache and posed beside a "picture of their idol," Thomas E. Dewey. Lee Janssen, the former Corunna mayor serving as temporary chairman of the Dewey for President Club, had reminded the *Argus*'s reporter that any man wanting to join would have to raise the mustache. Peter Cox, whom she had heard Tim mention in the kitchen (the only place they encountered), was still up on Mackinac and therefore not in the photo, and his absence didn't register with Jane.

She never ventured across the worn hall carpet to her son's room. Each of them allowed the other a separate world within the house, and used the kitchen as a kind of vacuum tube through which to pass essential messages. There was much they might be telling each other, if they weren't leading such busy existences inside their own imaginations. Two weeks ago, for instance, exasperated at the sight of his mother pinning on her small black hat, the one he recognized as her uniform for the more important occasions at Oak Hill, Tim had asked if she was going out to do her part for the "underground economy." He was being what Arnie used to call a "wiseacre." If he were really interested in Owosso's coffin-building connections to death, he might have wondered, as she did, why Howard Jennings and Marvin Lyons, each the son of an undertaker, had both returned safely from the war in order to take over the Jennings-Lyons funeral home from their fathers. This *signified* something, and Jane had almost been ready to discuss it with Tim the other week; but he only wanted to mock her black hat.

Now that Kirk White's house had been moved, Jennings and Lyons' new chapel would be going up next to the library, which would make Jane's consultation of old Owosso High yearbooks, *Argus* back issues and *Polk's City Directory* even more convenient. She lived on anniversaries. They came along like mealtimes in a hospital—regular, necessary and much anticipated occasions. Dark anniversaries as well as happy ones, dates pertaining not only to Arnie but to other dead boys, too: births, graduations, inductions. Her year was as complicated as the Catholics' church calendar, one event after another requiring commemoration, and climaxing just before Christmas—December 17, to be exact, by which time the snows had generally begun and the decorations were up at Christian's department store. This December 17 would be the fourth one since 1944's, which had been the third December 17 you couldn't turn on the radio without hearing Bing Crosby sing "White Christmas"; the last December 17 she had worn her green felt skirt to the Fellers' Christmas party; the December 17 Arnie had been machine-pistoled to death along with eighty-five other American prisoners of war at Malmédy, Belgium.

Last December 17 she had found herself in Gute's Pharmacy, where she heard a customer laugh with the clerk as they used the phrase "Battle of the Bulge" to describe the woman's struggle with her waistline.

Arnie had been buried in a coffin manufactured by the Owosso Casket Company, as had President McKinley, a point of quiet local pride, the week Jane was born in September 1901. Tom Dewey had been a year behind her in school, and they had taken no notice of each other until a fall day in 1918 when she was a new graduate volunteering as a nurse under Mrs. Maud Thompson. She rang the bell at 421 West Oliver, expecting Annie Dewey to open the door and take the gauze flu guards she was distributing, only to be greeted by Tom, who seemed enchanted at the sight of Jane in her own mask. For the duration of the epidemic Mrs. Thompson wanted all the volunteers to be "an advertisement of necessity," but Tom acted as if he were seeing Mata Hari, just Jane's eyes peeking over a veil. And that was why he asked her to play tennis the following day, in a tearing wind. Taking off the mask—it was too ridiculous to play in—restored her face to ordinariness, at least in his eyes; by the end of the third set he had lost interest, and she had acquired a nervous habit, which took her six months to lose, of running the palm of her left hand across her mouth, as if to conceal a flaw. That was what she got for condescending to go out with a senior! Not that it mattered. A year later, she was married to Alan and already expecting Arnie.

She loved that word—*expectant* was even better—because it was how Arnie let her feel, continually, even after he was born. The warmth of his disposition, from the moment his first cries were stilled, was remarked upon by everyone who met him. People were still teasing him for an excess of good nature when he was a beautiful young man of sixteen. He would laugh along with them, even as he blushed right up to his cap of chestnut hair. There was always one day in early spring when the air was so clear and the morning so bright the sun appeared to be more silver than gold: *that* was Arnie's disposition, Jane had decided on one of those days four months after his death.

He'd been one of the first babies born in Memorial Hospital, which opened its doors just days before Jane went into labor. She'd held him up to see the cornerstone laid at City Hall in '24, and a year or so after that he'd begun first grade at the brand-new Emerson School. He'd been first in line for a free ride when the airport opened in 1929, and six years later had his first job running a Skee-Ball booth at the centennial celebrations. When he'd gone into the Navy in '39, just a week after graduating from Owosso High, he'd practically broken her heart. *Why?* she'd asked him again and again. *There isn't any war.* He'd gotten out in '41, three months before Pearl Harbor, and that time, by reversing her argument, telling him there soon *would* be a war, she'd kept him from signing up for a second hitch.

For the next two years it had been just the three of them—herself and Arnie and Tim, who was so much younger he seemed more like Arnie's son than brother. Each day, as if he were the papa, Arnie had gone off to and come home from his job in a teller's cage at State Savings Bank. These had been the best years, these twenty-five months, which she was sure still existed in a part of the universe un-detectable even to that teacher with the telescope, the one who was always giving Tim a look through it. From '41 to '43 she'd kept expecting a girl to come along, but none had, and she'd gotten used to the idea that they would see out the war, the three of them, just as they were. Arnie's prior service, plus his being the sole support of a widowed mother and brother, kept him safe from the draft. There was no way the board could know how much the insurance money amounted to.

But then one night in October of '43 he'd come into the kitchen with tears in his eyes and sat her down and told her he couldn't stay any longer, not with everyone he'd gone to school with off in one place or another from the Solomon Islands to the Kasserine Pass. She had to understand, he said; it wasn't right; she had to know that. And so he shouldered the same bag he'd brought home from the Navy two years before and kissed her good-bye and went out through the back screen door. He left her alone with Tim, who grew into his clothes, moved into his room, and eventually drove his car—becoming, to his mother, an impostor, even while Arnie was still in training down at Fort Benjamin Harrison (another President whose casket had been made in Owosso).

In the weeks after he went into Europe, she followed the progress of the American armored divisions via the little blue pins moved every day from one spot to another on the map of Europe in the Argus's window on Exchange Street. All that fall the pins moved faster and faster, like filings drawing closer to a magnet, until the snow began falling and the radios started playing "White Christmas" and she'd gotten her green felt skirt dry-cleaned specially at Suber's, and then, for one week, the magnet's charge reversed itself and a handful of pins stopped and fell back and dropped from the map.

Now, forty-three months later (just fifty-eight days short of what she had calculated would be Arnie's ten-thousandth day on earth), Jane heard the metal milk box scrape the back porch beneath her window. That girl. She'd forgotten all about her.

"Margaret?" she called out the window. The girl had been waiting so long she'd brought the milk box over to her chair and propped her feet on it. "He *said* two o'clock, but he never keeps his word."

"That's all right, Mrs. Herrick. I don't mind waiting."

"All right, then," said Jane, who shut the window and turned on the electric fan Tim had actually managed to repair last month. For all she knew the girl would wait all night, until Harold and Carol Feller came looking for her.

Yes, Margaret just might. Three weeks into her romance, she had gotten used to Tim's being late, or never arriving at all, and that was all right, because the deep, far-off nature she had fallen in love with was what made him forget, and he always made it up by proposing they do something even more exciting than what they'd planned in the first place. Their being together was like a journey across the mountains; the great peaks were important, not these little molehills of disappointment. And the next great peak would be the Dawn Patrol a week from tomorrow, which Tim could not stop talking about, as if he somehow needed to work her up for the day. She took this as a form of considerateness, his worry that the rally lacked a feminine dimension to interest her. She wanted to tell him that just witnessing *his* pleasure was the greatest thrill she could have designed for herself. In any case, the Dawn Patrol was fixed upon her calendar as irreversibly as Easter or the first day of school.

Footsteps coming up the driveway; 4:10 P.M. on her wristwatch. Was it? No, it was Billy, whose fast gait she ought to have recognized. From the edge of the porch she could see him poised beneath Tim's window, looking up for cigarette smoke, the usual sign of his best friend's presence at home. He then turned toward her and the porch that (she knew, guiltily) had once been the site of a hundred card games and bull sessions between him and his best friend.

She and Billy were each angry the other hadn't turned out to be Tim, but Margaret was bored with waiting, so she invited him up onto the porch. Lonely from her recent absence and Tim's, he accepted.

"We were supposed to, I mean we're going to, drive to Saginaw Bay," she explained.

Billy wanted to say he wished *he* had a dead brother with a car to inherit, but he settled for looking at his own watch, implying as snidely as he could that it was getting a little late for that long a drive, wasn't it? All he had to do was hold the pause, be cruel, but he couldn't. "Do you want to see *Naked City* instead?" he asked. He couldn't even stop himself from adding the slogan—"THE MOST EXCITING STORY OF THE WORLD'S MOST EXCITING CITY!"—just like the old merchandising Billy she'd grown tired of.

"All *three* of us?" she asked.

Well, no, he'd figured on the two of them going alone, but now that she mentioned it, the thought of being with both of them instead of by himself didn't seem so bad.

"That's impossible," said Margaret, pushing the milk box away with her foot.

He looked at her and believed there was only a thin line, one more provocation at most, between remaining

Billy Grimes and becoming Robert "Murli" Daniels. But he wouldn't kill her for the thrill of it; he'd kill both of them, her and Tim, for revenge and peace.

"Margaret?" Mrs. Herrick had come through the screen door. "Oh, hello, Billy," she said, managing a smile. She liked the boy; he had made Arnie laugh.

"Hello, Mrs. Herrick."

"Margaret, I'm afraid you'll wait here all day and most of the night." Couldn't the girl take a hint? No, she supposed she couldn't. Jane had seen her one night, weeks ago, behind the bushes across the street.

"I don't understand," said Margaret, groping for permission to stay where she was. "I really don't know where he could be—"

"I do," said Billy.

"Where?" both women asked, though Margaret inquired with more urgency.

"With Mr. Sherwood, I'll bet."

"You can't look at the stars during the *day*," said Margaret.

"Mr. Sherwood doesn't want to look at the *stars*," Billy shouted, trumping her disgust. "He wants to look at *Tim*."

"What do you mean?" said Margaret.

He was already off the porch and heading for his bicycle, already feeling guilty, maybe even unforgivable, but he said no more. Let them figure it out. He wanted to hurt every one of them, even Mrs. Herrick.

"OH, WASN'T THE TEA DANCE *LOVELY!*"

Ada Gardiner spoke as if, hours later, she'd just realized

the fact all over again. The after-dinner breeze raking the porch of the Grand Hotel reminded her that nothing helps the world like a little effusion.

Anne Macmurray smiled. After thirty hours, and even more of Ada's company than she had expected, she liked the woman, who was as naturally fluffy as her sister, Mrs. Cox, studied to be sharp.

"Charles L. Fischer and his Globe Trotters!" cried Ada, relishing the band's name. "I remember them from twenty years ago, when I first came up here with Lucy and Ray. Peter was just a little boy. I don't think I've heard them in all that time since. Not that I've made a practice of coming every summer, but—"

"They were never around in the thirties," said Mrs. Cox. "But they've reappeared since."

"Mother thinks it's auspicious," explained Peter. "The good times are coming back. The New Deal will be over at last and everything will be all right again. Isn't that right, Mother? What's it you want to see return?"

"Normalcy," said Mrs. Cox, without embarrassment. "Peter likes to mock everyone's sentiments," she told Anne in the instructive tone both mother and son had used to her all day, as if the Coxes were a species apart, unintelligible without constant commentary.

"Especially the sentiments he holds himself," said Anne.

"Exactly," replied Mrs. Cox, pleased she had taught Anne well enough for the girl to make a remark like that. But Anne knew the woman was also pondering the observation. Despite the smoky, gin-voiced cynicism (itself a kind of nostalgia for the twenties), it was clear that sentiments—especially her son's—mattered to her a great deal. The thirties hadn't wounded her with creeping socialism; it was retreating love that had made her suffer.

"Now why exactly would Peter do that?" asked Peter. "Mock his own sentiments."

"A psychologist would call it displacement," said Anne, looking at Mrs. Cox and Ada Gardiner, the three women smiling as if the question had been taken from a radio audience instead of asked by the subject himself. "Indicating a lack of self-confidence."

Ada didn't have much idea what they were talking about, but their teasing Peter made her recall something fond about him. "You know, I remember a *nice* time from the thirties. Wasn't I up here the summer they had that great big costume ball and Peter came dressed as a, I can never get the French word right, a—"

"Pierrot," said Peter. "1934. Celebrating the three-hundredth anniversary of the island's discovery by the French. I'd just turned sixteen."

"And were so handsome!" cried his aunt. "We couldn't get over it. All of a sudden you were a little man."

Not quite, thought Peter, who remembered getting within ten minutes of losing his virginity to a twenty-year-old girl from Pittsburgh.

"A little man wearing tight silk breeches," said his mother. "In love with the line of his own leg. Look sharp, Peter. Here comes Mr. Woodfill."

Promenading down the Grand's 628-foot verandah (not the 880 feet he'd gotten *Ripley's Believe It or Not!* to print), the hotel's owner, a vision of affable formality in his starched collar and fully buttoned double-breasted suit, was greeting his guests.

"They say he's got the chairs in his own parlor bolted into position," Peter whispered to Anne. In the ten days since his arrival, he hadn't seen Mr. Woodfill until now. He'd spent most of his time with some downstate politicians, golfing, riding and discreetly gambling. Or "gaming," as Mr. Woodfill liked to say, mostly when he was denying the existence of such a thing at the Grand.

"Hello, Miss Macmurray!"

Anne and Woodfill had met yesterday, while she was checking into her sixteen-dollar-a-night room and instructing the desk clerk to bill her and not Peter, even if, as the clerk insisted, it had "all been arranged." What she herself had arranged, once she decided she had to go through with this by now very ill-advised visit, was to keep as much distance as possible from Peter. The result had been a lot of time spent in the company of Mrs. Cox and Aunt Ada, including yesterday's late lunch, when she had delighted W. Stewart Woodfill, as she was doing again now, by being dressed up a little more than other members of what he called—through the kind of clenched teeth with which people still said "Japs"—the "younger generation."

"Did you enjoy your dinner?"

"Very much," said Mrs. Cox. "But it's a shame not to see as many regulars as one used to in the dining room."

"Fewer of them each year," said Mr. Woodfill, whose regret was tempered by the booming first-timers' trade.

"Why don't you join my mother and aunt," said Peter, "while I show Anne more of the hotel?"

Declining Peter's chair, but offering Anne a hand as she rose, Mr. Woodfill recommended the Radio Salon as ideal for conversation at this hour.

"I'll tell you what," said Peter. "I think I'm going to run her by the Presidential Apartment. Any chance it's vacant?"

"We've got a party checking into it tomorrow, but I suppose the bell captain might allow you and Miss Macmurray in for a peek."

Anne nodded as Peter led her off. It was clear that Mr. Woodfill could do without any ideas from him.

"The 'Apartment of the President of the U.S.' is a bit of a sore subject," Peter explained. "They did the thing up ten years ago, hoping Roosevelt would stay over during some state Democratic party conference, but the only guy they could get to hang his hat was Jim Farley."

"Of course, all that will change with a Michigan man in the White House, right?"

"You bet, sweetheart."

"So where is it?"

"Who cares?" Peter propelled her into the art deco cocktail lounge, where they sat down amidst a whirl of flanges and chevrons that still seemed giddy over Repeal. "You know," he said, "this is the first time we've been alone since you got here."

"I've been too busy buying fudge with your Aunt Ada and playing golf with your mother."

"Mother. She's pronounced you 'the most extraordinary girl.' Says she can't imagine why I'm interested in you."

Anne said nothing.

"It's a compliment. It means she can't believe I'd make the effort required to keep a girl like *you* interested in *me.*"

"I know," said Anne. "That's what she told me. On the third hole."

He paused for a few seconds. "Okay, I'll go first."

"First?"

"First to tell you why I'm interested. In you. Because you're beautiful, even though you probably think you're only 'good-looking.' Because you're not straining to make an impression like every other woman in here and out on the porch. And because ten years from now, when you've relinquished the handles on the baby carriage, you'll want to grab on to something besides a cocktail shaker and a golf club. You might even go back to your typewriter."

The long-view compliment, she decided, was worth the short-term insult. She kept her gaze steady. "But you *do* want to be holding a cocktail shaker and a hand of bridge. Maybe a gavel, too, but that would only be until five o'clock. Or three."

"So what? You talk as if there's a contradiction. There isn't. I want you to be better than I am."

Her eyes began to water, and just as he was thinking it was because she'd heard the nicest, noblest thing a woman could hear, she blinked and sniffled and looked into her lap and said, "I'm in love with Jack Riley."

"Oh, for Christ's sake!"

She laughed with such relief she had trouble stopping. For three absurd weeks she'd kept her hypocrisy bottled up. The waiter, wondering if she was getting hysterics, finally made his way over to them.

"The lady will have a ginger ale," said Peter.

"The lady will have a Cointreau."

"Are you sure you won't have a beer?" asked Peter. "Straight out of the bottle?"

"The low road doesn't become you, Peter."

"You neither. And you know it, or else you wouldn't have come up here."

Anne looked at the perplexed waiter, and said, "Cointreau, really," before turning back to Peter. "A second ago you didn't want me holding a cocktail shaker. Now I'm not supposed to have a beer. You think you've got me all figured out, that you can write my script, but you can't even get the props straight. By the way, having had dinner with you both, I can tell you that Jack has better table manners." She paused, hoping that he would get madder than she was herself, which wasn't as mad as she should be. "Honestly, Peter, I'm not sure why I did come up here." She stared hard at him, as if he might somehow yield up the answer. "I think I like getting the better of you. It's pretty pointless, but it excites me."

"Well, love *is* exciting."

"No. Well, of course it is, but not this kind of exciting." Love was exciting in the way it was with Jack, something pure and enlarging, a dance in which the partners, instead of thrusting and dipping from one apache move to another, simply held on to each other and moved together.

She took her drink off the waiter's tray, feeling less comfortable in this soft jazzy club chair than on the hard old couch in Jack's garage, where their every move had sent a cloud of dust toward the single light bulb beneath the rafters. Yes, she told herself, Gene Riley's eight-foot porch was a more natural spot for her to be than Mr. Woodfill's 880-foot verandah.

There was one way, of course, to be surer than sure, and that was to make love with Peter. It was unthinkable, but if they could wind themselves down like tops, end the apache dance by collapsing, dumb and spent, on the floor, there would be nothing left between them. The chase would be over and she would be free.

"Peter, please."

"All right. Change of subject. Tell me what I've been missing."

"Back in Owosso? There's a big air show a week from to-morrow, and the city council takes up Mr. Jackson's plan a couple of days after that. The poor old colonel is very upset. Carol Feller swears she can hear him sneezing five blocks away. She's afraid the top of his head will come off."

"We're going to hear from Jackson Monday night at the Dewey Club. Come down and listen."

"Monday? You mean Turnip Day?" Would he smile at that?

No, he wouldn't. "Come with the Fellers. I'd take you myself—Riley or no Riley—but I may not get in the door."

"Why not?"

"Haven't you noticed?" He leaned over and pressed his clean upper lip into hers. She didn't press back.

THE REMAINS OF THE PEACH ICE CREAM WERE STARTING TO melt, but nearly a hundred people had gotten scoops as they waited for the Dewey Club's open meeting to begin at 7:30 P.M. on July 26. Two organizers went out to the hallway of the Matthews Building in search of more folding chairs. "Be glad we didn't make onion sandwiches," said one of them, point-ing to the ice-cream mess while alluding to another youthful culinary favorite of the candidate. The second club member had spent his day licking three-cent stamps and hanging up a giant blow-up photo (courtesy Jackson Camera and Elec-tronics) of the young Tom Dewey as Uncle Sam, posed next to little Miss Columbia by the *Argus*'s photographer on the Fourth of July 1909. Billy Grimes now sat beneath it, handing out Citizens for the Future flyers and avoiding the gaze of Mr. and Mrs. Feller, who were in conversation, down front, with Peter Cox.

"You couldn't get her to come?" Peter asked Carol, sounding less sure of himself than usual.

"I'm afraid not. But I had more luck with the older woman you asked me to soft-soap." She handed him a small stack of letters. "She's underlined a few bits, which are the only ones you're allowed to use. And if you don't think she means it, just ask Reverend Davis or any of her bridge circle what it feels like to have Annie Dewey bite your head off."

"Forewarned," said Peter.

"She's even taken my head off," said Harold Feller.

"And you're a fine, mild fellow, Harold."

"That's right, Peter. Up to a point I am."

Peter knew what was coming, and to escape the question about why he hadn't bothered coming in to the office today, he pretended to return a wave from Vincent Dent in the third row.

Peter took one of the chairs on the rostrum just as the club secretary test-tapped the microphone and began the meeting: "You know," he said, waiting for the last of the audience to take their seats, "back in 1940, our first Dewey for President Club had no need for a microphone. I think all of us who were in it could probably have fit into one booth down at the Great Lakes."

Christ, thought Peter. The guy had actually written this stuff on index cards.

"But we did have a club back in '40, because some of us already knew that the best man to be President of the United States was a thirty-eight-year-old district attorney whose only mistake was ever leaving Michigan for New York."

Peter grinned wide and tilted his head back. No one would realize his laughter was pantomime, not even the high-school girls down in front, friends of Margaret Feller's who, Carol said, were here because Peter was so "dreamy."

"In 1944 this club sent out a hundred and fifty thousand Dewey for President buttons. I can see a few of you are wearing those tonight, and probably appreciating our foresight in leaving the year off them."

Focusing on a clock at the back of the room, Peter tuned out the voice of this amiable stiff. The guy couldn't really be excited about Dewey, could he? Pretending was one thing, but actually buying the whole cardboard package? The elevator shoes; never having missed a day of school; playing the gentleman farmer in upstate New York; having his press secretary announce his candidacy, like it was an afternoon appointment. What they said was probably true: You had to know him really well to dislike him. None of this kept Dewey from being absolutely preferable to that strutting little Missouri jackass, but there *was* something insidious, an irritating grain of truth, in that rhyme—Keep America Human with Truman. Humanity itself might be overrated, but what if you suspected that the bulk of your life's acquaintance—all those punctually plastered guests at your parents' cocktail hours, with their indisputable skill in running the world—fell into that inhuman counterspecies to which Dewey was accused of belonging?

Come on, buddy, come on. He already knew what he himself was going to say, and all he wanted to do was say it and get out of here and get his paddle into the river while there was a last half hour of sunlight. He wouldn't take more than a jab at foreign policy—not with everyone in such an all-for-one-and-one-for-all mood over Berlin, and with *Iron*

Curtain playing down the street. He'd keep it simple, the way the alcoholics did, and end with the little hometown touch of these letters Carol had gotten him.

". . . and further down the ticket, the man it is now my pleasure to present: an outstanding Michigander, an Ivy League scholar, a distinguished veteran, a skilled attorney with Feller, Terry and Nast, and the next senator from the Twenty-third District of this state—Peter Cox!"

He winked at Margaret's friends and got up from his chair. "Good evening, ladies and gentlemen. My name is Peter Cox" (you couldn't say it too many times) "and I'm happy to be one candidate who moved *to* Owosso." (General applause; wait two suspenseful beats after it subsides; solemnly lower voice.) "Tomorrow morning President Truman will ask the Congress for a tax on profits and the authority to control prices. It's fitting, I think, that he should make these requests during a 'special session' whose convening demonstrates that he has no more respect for the Constitution than he does for the laws of economics and the rights of the American small businessman." (Smattering of applause; probably would be more if there'd been an awestruck mention of "the American worker" in the same sentence. It had gotten so you couldn't give even a Republican speech unless it came out like sounding like "The House I Live In.") "The President, a failed businessman himself, isn't happy unless every druggist and grocer and haberdasher is feeling the pinch." (No need to mention that Truman went bust with Harding in the White House.)

"The Eightieth Congress, whose record is one of exceptional accomplishment, is about to do the country its greatest service yet by defeating every single proposal that comes its way from 1600 Pennsylvania Avenue in the next few weeks." (If Dewey were bolder, he'd get out and lead that Congress, send it his own program and start acting like the President six months before his own inauguration.) "And I daresay the Eightieth Congress will give the President reason to regret the tantrum that's brought it back into session. The House Un-American Activities Committee, under the leadership of J. Parnell Thomas and sparked by the energy of young Republicans like Congressman Nixon of California, is going to use the opportunity to hold some extra hearings, and a few Washington friends of mine say they're likely to produce a couple of interesting surprises." (Impressed glances between members of the audience realizing they would have a state senator with his own connections in the nation's capital. All right, that little hint was enough about Communism and, by implication, foreign affairs. It was time to balance the cosmopolitan outsider with the humble, happy-to-be-here local boy. Pull letters from pocket. Take a long pause.)

"You know, if my mother doesn't get a letter from me each week, I hear about it but good." (Carol Feller whispered "Oh, brother" to Harold. Margaret's friends were further enchanted.) "I suspect Tom Dewey has it just the same." (Laughter from all who these days were pretending to know Annie Dewey better than they did.) "I draw that conclusion not just because the governor is the kind of man he is, but also because Mrs. Dewey has allowed me to share with you a couple of lines that her son has found the time to send home to her here in Owosso. Now, the governor is more of a gentleman than I am" (fat chance of anyone believing that, with the two-hundred-dollar summer suit he had on) "and, as you know, his public comments on Mr. Truman's shang-haiing of the Congress have been more restrained than mine. But lest you think his silence has been dictated by po-litical prudence or secret worry, let me tell you what he tells his mother: 'The special session is a nuisance, but no more . . .' " (Big, big applause. Thanks, once more, to their next state senator, they were getting some inside dope un-known to even those press boys who'd left a month ago and wouldn't be back until November.) "The candidate, who as you know has two sons of his own, also writes his mother that there's 'no rush' about planning 'accommodations at the White House for the family, if I am elected.' " (Big laugh at the emphasized "if.") "Governor Dewey would be too modest to note it himself" (yeah, right), "but there are polls now showing him ahead even in the state of Florida" (a small gasp from the history teacher), "which means that the solid South is looking about as solid as Mr. Truman's haberdash-ery in 1921." (Applause.)

"I'd like the people in the back rows near the window to turn around and look across the street to the Colvin Home Appliance Shop. I'm sure you all recognize the apartment above it as being not only the current residence of Charlie Bernard (he'd found "Bernard, Charles S." in the street di-rectory), but the first home, the birthplace, of the thirty-fourth President of the United States." (Biggest applause of the evening.) "We all know when and where the Dewey story reaches its climax—on January twentieth in a White House that will be renovated in more ways than one. But that little building across the street is where the Dewey story began, right here in Owosso; and it's along the banks of our own Shiawassee River" (he was beginning to make himself sick) "that it took its first steps, toward Annie Dewey's big, friendly house on Oliver Street.

"That little stretch of land now belongs to history, and to the country as a whole. It's our job in Owosso to manage it with the largest and most faithful sense of purpose we can muster. As you know, a week from now our city council will be holding its first discussion of this matter, so I'm going to acknowledge your patience and graciousness in listening to me and" (it was 7:53; he'd be on the water by 8:10) "turn this meeting over to the next speaker, our neighbor Al Jackson, who has asked for and been given the Dewey for President Club's permission to speak on behalf of Citizens for the Future. Al, won't you come up here?" (Polite, mixed-feelings applause for Jackson, who was running up the middle aisle.) "Thank you, ladies and gentlemen, and good night!" (Bigger, much bigger, applause. He was going to take 65 percent of this town.)

Another wink for Margaret's friends. By the time Jackson unveiled his god-awful six-by-four-foot "artist's conception" of the new riverbank, no one would realize Peter Cox was gone. He made his way up the side aisle, handing Annie Dewey's letters to Carol ("Going home to write Mom?" she asked) and clapping the Grimes kid on the shoulder. The boy looked haggard.

"Where's all that get-up-and-go, Billy?"

"It got up and went."

"Girl trouble?"

"Yeah."

"Join the club."

.   .   .

IN THE EARLY LIGHT OF AUGUST 1, A LEFTOVER PIECE OF RIB-
bon fluttered on the ground at Idlewild Airport. Yesterday's
joint dedication by the President and Governor Dewey had
proceeded peaceably. In fact, Dewey had been astonished to
hear Truman, as if caught up in the spirit of modernity, whisper into his ear: "You'll want to do something about the
plumbing after you move in." Was the little rooster less confident than he pretended? Or was it his idea of mockery, a
little psychological warfare from somebody with nothing
to lose?

Five hundred miles away, at the Owosso Community Airport, the smells of dew and gasoline mixed on the air with
those of frying steak and eggs, as the first hundred or so
planes flying in for the Dawn Patrol completed their landings. Before the morning was out, a hundred more were expected, along with another thousand spectators to join the
thousand already there. In one of the improvised outdoor
hangars, Gus Farnham polished the fuselage of his Curtiss
"Jenny." Next to him the AM radio inside a decommissioned
Brewster Fighter pulled in Chicago's WGN. Jane Powell sang
about its being a most unusual day, before giving up the
air to an announcer who had the latest from England on
seventeen-year-old Bob Mathias's progress in the Olympic
decathlon.

Walking between the rows of planes, Tim Herrick and
Margaret Feller looked like a young couple browsing Bob
Harrelson's Chevrolet showroom, but Margaret was so giddy
that the field and sky seemed to her like a cartoon: the perfect shapes of the colorful planes swooping down and blowing raspberries of motor noise, the whole effect sort of sweet
and silly, like a gaggle of puffing little-engines-that-could.

She half expected the wingtips to be wearing white Mickey Mouse gloves that would wipe beads of sweat from chubby faces behind the propellers.

The applicant must be 16 years of age or over. The applicant shall have logged at least 35 hours of solo flight time . . . Included in the foregoing are at least 5 hours of cross-country flying, of which at least 3 hours shall have been solo, providing for at least one flight over a course of not less than 50 miles with at least two full-stop landings at different points on such a course. In addition, the appli-cant shall satisfactorily accomplish a written examination covering prevailing weather conditions in the United States . . . A lot of the boys—whose mothers, if they'd grown up in town, could tell them the cautionary tale of how James Oliver Curwood's son had died in a flying accident right here in 1930—got to the table with information on private-pilot ratings and scooped up the leaflets. To Margaret's surprise, Tim put back the one she handed to him, saying, "Nah. I don't really want a license."

From behind a table selling V-8, Nestle's Quik, and or-ange drink, Billy Grimes, whom Al Jackson had given the weekend off, watched Tim and Margaret as if they were a movie whose sound had died. He would never be able to re-pair it, never again get close enough to hear either one. Billy stared at the two of them, as if the intensity of his gaze might resolder the wire that had once made them the two main posts in his life's circuit. There wasn't the faintest sizzle of re-newed connection.

Twenty yards away, Anne Macmurray was avoiding gazes, not pressing them. "It didn't take him long," she said to Carol Feller, who had also seen the new blonde sitting on the trunk of Peter's Ford.

"Second thoughts?" asked Carol.

"No."

"Well, he's not having them either."

Anne wished that Jack would hurry and get back here with the coffee.

"Second thoughts about you, that is. I don't think you've heard the last of him."

"And the blonde?"

"She's not really a thought," said Carol. "More like a daydream. You darling man!" she exclaimed, taking two of the four cardboard cups Jack had in his well-scrubbed hands. "Now all I've got to do is find Harold. He drifted over to the Navy pilots' booth while you were gone, Jack." It was peculiar having a husband who'd been too young for the First War and too old for the Second. The accident of time had left Harold with funds of curiosity and deference he would never be able to spend. "What is it you two are signed up to do?" Carol asked as she started off.

"Jack is going to spot one of the runways."

He would be the most perfect of mates, she decided. She told herself their children would fall off the roof and land like laughing angels in his arms. As they drank their coffee and strolled by a row of Beechcraft, Jack kept one arm around her shoulders and pointed with his coffee cup, resuming an earlier explanation of the difference between an aileron and a stabilizer, something he remembered from four months helping to retool the Ford line in '42, before the draft took him. "The stabilizer is fixed but the aileron lets you roll." She glanced toward Peter Cox, but he and the blonde had already quit the scene.

"Hi, Frank." Jack set down his coffee cup on the high-school science department's table and shook hands with

Frank Sherwood, who was out here this morning to talk about the dead-reckoning method of celestial navigation to anyone who cared to listen, even if the technique was unlikely to be useful to fliers of small planes so far from an ocean.

Frank nodded to Anne. "I thought you might be here. I heard you getting up this morning."

"I'm never as quiet as Frank," Anne explained to Jack. "He's a much more considerate neighbor than I am."

"Oh, I didn't mean—" said Frank.

"It's true!" cried Anne. "He's Mrs. Wagner's favorite." She picked up one of his star charts and admired it. Without taking time to think, she said, "I saw your prize astronomy pupil looking at some planes with Margaret Feller." Anne thanked her lucky stars that, in the course of spinning some comic tales of what went on under Mrs. Wagner's roof, she hadn't told Jack what she'd figured out about poor Frank.

Frank straightened the pile of charts. "This celestial navigation is actually pretty earthbound stuff."

"How so?" asked Jack.

"Well, with real astronomy the earth hardly counts. But when you navigate by the stars you've got to see things in relation to where you are." As he spoke this explanation to Jack Riley's open, intelligent face, Frank decided Anne Macmurray was a lucky girl. So many faces this morning had seemed twitchy and peculiar, as if they weren't used to getting up so early. Margaret Feller had given him the oddest, most pained look, and the Grimes kid had gotten positively tongue-tied when he went up to him for a soda.

Jack pointed to the Owosso High banner. "Are they paying you for this, Frank?"

"Nope. This is just a break from that big summer vacation they're always telling us makes up for everything else."

"Are you going to get home before summer's over?" asked Anne, who felt guilty to be thinking how much easier it would be to have Jack spend the night, and slip out undetected the following morning, if Frank weren't on the other side of the wall.

"No, I'll be staying around. I don't really have anybody back in Ohio anymore." He looked up at the wind sock, which was half-filled but pointing as best it could in the direction of Oak Hill. This was home now; he knew that.

"Welcome!" shouted the retired Air Force major in charge of the Dawn Patrol. He urged people to make for seats behind the ropes so that the competitive drills could get under way. The throng tossed their paper cups and began a dutiful shuffle, while the major read off a list of 1948's big aviation events, from the first jet carrier landing to the first nonstop Paris–New York commercial flight ("just sixteen hours") to the death of Orville Wright. But the eyes of the migrating crowd were already on the first two planes, a couple of Hughes racers with open cockpits, their goggled, helmeted pilots facing into the wind and waiting for the sound of the starting gun to pull back on their sticks and take off. A moment after they were up, to everyone's cheers, the silver planes took 270-degree turns in opposite directions, each describing an arc that suggested a hot-air balloon. Before they were out of sight, another pair were aloft, executing loops that Margaret couldn't stop pointing to. Her gesture was more than exuberance in the presence of beauty; it was oddly functional, because unless prompted Tim didn't seem inclined to look at the stunts.

As Anne, without knowing what to call them, admired chandelles performed by the latest two pilots, Carol Feller sidled up and said, "I promised Harold I'd be like the League of Women Voters and stay strictly neutral. But the one you've got here is awfully nice."

Anne watched Jack watching the precision spins from the place where he'd volunteered to stand along the ropes, like a policeman at a parade. One little girl was actually holding on to his leg. "He is, isn't he?" she replied to Carol.

Frank Sherwood regarded the geometry of two skywriters who, as they swept through barrel rolls and an Immelmann turn, appeared to be connecting dots in the sky, skeining the sun-camouflaged stars into a pattern, a face or design that would soon emerge and stun them all into silence.

Billy observed Mr. Sherwood as he made what Billy took to be the impressively detached observations of the pure scientist. Billy wished he could take back the thought he had planted in Mrs. Herrick's addled head, but he knew that that was no more possible than this antique Bristol Boxkite's being able to erase its white plumes of skywriting.

Five minutes later it was the ground, not the sky, that the planes were whitening. A long green strip held the targets for a precision bomb drop, the climax of the morning's competitions. Bag after bag of flour fell, exploding without a whistle or thud, puff after white puff dappling the grass and exciting the crowd's applause. Harold Feller, still caught between the wars, watched in silence, his emotions too encrypted for even himself to read. His daughter looked at Tim Herrick in another kind of bafflement, trying to descry the thoughts inside him, to understand what was keeping his attention from all these events he had talked about for weeks, why his eyes kept darting toward the parked planes and not the ones competing overhead. Carol Feller studied her daughter and wondered why she seemed febrile with devotion over her new love, like an ecstatic nun, rather than just purring with ordinary happiness. Jack Riley watched the fiftieth sack of flour explode upon the soldierless ground and knew exactly what he was remembering and why he wouldn't think any more about it. He would occupy his mind with the sensation of having his thumb chewed by the little girl to whom he'd offered it.

When all the planes were down and their pilots all applauded, the major turned things over to Cass Hough, the English daredevil, who pulled a card from an envelope and announced that none other than Doris Singer, their own Miss Owosso, who had just the other week made the state finals but lost the prize of being Miss Michigan, had been chosen Miss Dawn Patrol.

"Come on," said Tim. "Help me."

He needed Margaret to go back with him to the car, in whose trunk he had another trunk, a big one, half the size of an old steamer. Would she help him carry it to Gus's plane? "It's a surprise," said Tim. "I'm going to cover it up with a blanket. He won't even notice till after he's put the plane back in his barn."

"What's in it?" asked Margaret, as she walked backwards with it, covering the three hundred yards between Arnie's Chevrolet and Gus's plane. Gus himself was sure to be at the just-opened beer stand.

"Cans of soup, evaporated milk, stuff like that. Gus is a lot poorer than people think. He can use all of it, and it's easier for him to just find it than have to say thank you."

Gus's plane might look smaller than Harold Feller's Oldsmobile, but there was a surprising amount of room behind the old leather passenger's seat. The trunk hid easily under a blanket that had been lying in a clutter of tools and beer bottles.

"That's great," said Tim. "Why don't you get a place for us on the rides line? I'll be there in another minute. I just want to leave him a note. A couple of these things need instructions."

He was, she decided, too embarrassed to have her see him complete this act of charity, and she wanted to be as considerate of his feelings as he was of Gus's. So she gave him a kiss and ran off to join her girlfriends, who were still dismissing the charms of Doris Singer, as they waited for the first plane, ahead of the long line of ticket holders, to rev up and take off. The skies had been silent for nearly a half hour, and the crowd was beginning to miss the noisy motorized duets. Soon enough, though, an uncertain hum filled the air. Margaret's friends stood on their toes to see the first of the twenty-five-cents-a-ride planes take off. But as the erratic buzz grew more raucous, there was still no plane visible ahead. All at once it became clear that the sound was above and behind them. They turned and looked up to see, sticking out of a low-flying cockpit, not a helmet and goggles, but a head of golden hair, streaming in the wind as the plane went, accidentally, into a quarter roll, before the pilot righted it and waved good-bye to his girlfriend below, pulling up on the stick and disappearing into a sun so bright it seemed more silver than gold.

By nightfall the desk of police chief Ted Rice had on it a report of August's first serious theft, that of a Curtiss JN-4D, as well as one for the month's first missing person, Timothy Herrick, seventeen, late of 105 Park Street.

S I X

August 3

"MR. CHAMBERS, WILL YOU RAISE YOUR VOICE A LITTLE, PLEASE?
When and where were you born?"

"I was born April 1, 1901, in Philadelphia."

"How long have you been associated with Time *magazine?"*

"Nine years."

"Prior to that time, what was your occupation?"

"I was a member of the Communist Party . . ."

The interrogation of Whittaker Chambers by Robert
Stripling, chief investigator for the House Un-American
Activities Committee, had gotten under way in Washington
on the morning of August 3, and that evening Horace Sinclair read portions of it in the Detroit paper. The late Mrs.
Sinclair had developed in him a taste for genteel mystery
novels, ones in which truth emerged at the point of a question instead of a gun. Exactly what had transpired years ago
between Chambers and a diplomat named Alger Hiss looked
as if it might play out like one of the books Horace came
home with each week from the Owosso Public Library, the la-

beled skull on their spines promising a good night's sleep after a bit of mental exercise.

He hoped the story would soon crowd others off the front page. He could not stand the annual round of Hiroshima anniversary features, which would reach a peak this weekend, emphasizing rebirth and a lack of hard feelings. Horace had no stomach for the bipartisan certainty that dropping the bomb had been necessary, even kind, in light of the casualties a land assault would have led to. Of course, no invasion of Japan would have been the cakewalk his own cavalry unit performed in Cuba half a century ago, but who could say what the bomb's long-term effects would be? The smoke from it was a whirlwind begging to be reaped. The first time Horace had seen the photographs he'd noticed not a mushroom, but a sort of truncated crucifix, as if this new cross to which man was nailing himself refused to support his head; he would have to hang it in shame. This week the pictures were back, the cloud and the rubble and the craters, the heaps of lives buried and dug out and, the papers would have you believe, resurrected. And all he could think of was one small crater, hastily dug and frantically filled, fifty-one summers ago. The black buckram box stood on his dining-room table, and there had still been no letter from Wright George. If he failed to respond, Horace would have to take matters into his own hands, soon, and in the dead of night.

How he envied the Herrick boy—free and far away, if he was still alive. After three days, people were beginning to doubt anyone would ever find him. It was like looking for a needle that had blown out of one haystack into who-knew-which other. Each day the *Argus* ran the same unsmiling picture, a much-enlarged head from a group photo of the high-school baseball team. The paper had by now familiarized readers with the fact that 1948 had seen great progress in the proliferation of VHF omnidirectional radar stations, which sent out beams toward every point on the compass instead of the mere four that older systems had. Of course, in order to use the new radar, planes had to have updated receivers, and—well, there was no radio of any kind in Gus Farnham's biplane. The paper printed the background material on radar to fill column inches of a big local story that had very little else to offer the typesetter. All anyone had were theories, which mostly involved the plane's having come down over water, since on Sunday there had been no crashes reported anywhere on the southern peninsula. There were those who guessed Tim had flown over Pointe Aux Barques and fallen into Lake Huron, and those who said westward, over Big Sable Point and into Lake Michigan. A few speculators, no more informed than anybody else, thought he might have made it all the way to Wisconsin. But if so, where was he? No one seemed to think he'd gone southeast or into Lake Erie—if he had, surely somebody out of all the millions of people in Detroit and Toledo would have noticed him. Though he acknowledged having taken him up a couple of times, Gus Farnham claimed to have given the boy no flying lessons: "I guess he picked it up by watching," Gus told both the *Argus* and Chief Rice. Tim Herrick had never asked to take the controls, let alone mentioned any scheme to skip town.

The *Argus* reporter ended today's article by noting that Margaret Feller, 17, of 430 West Oliver Street, was still "distraught" after questioning by police, and that William

Grimes, also 17, of 352 Pine, a longtime *Argus* carrier with an excellent record, was mailing flyers with Tim Herrick's picture on them to dozens of towns throughout the state that his friend was known to have visited, mentioned, or just driven through in his brother's old Chevrolet. Mrs. Herrick had been "in seclusion" since Monday, when she had returned, in her own car, from a Marine's reburial in Battle Creek and learned of her son's disappearance.

Horace's clock chimed six-thirty. If he got ready now, he could comfortably walk to City Hall and arrive in time for the first public reading of Jackson's scheme before the city council. He rose from his chesterfield sofa and went into the kitchen to refresh himself by sticking his head into the icebox and keeping it there, eyes closed and vapor swirling, for a good fifteen seconds. He brought his suspenders back up over his shoulders and gathered the papers he had been working with at the dining-room table, his own handsome prose descriptions of two of the town's oldest structures: the Woodard Paymaster Building, a tiny wooden cabin from which Campbell Gregory, fifty years before, had each week handed Owosso men the wages they'd earned making chairs and coffins; and Elias Comstock's cabin, 112 years old this May, the first regular dwelling place in town, so much improved and added on to by Judge Comstock and subsequent owners that it eventually seemed like a piece of furniture, or a secret, inside a bigger house. These endangered buildings were the real history of the town, what the council ought to be spending its money on instead of throwing up this cornball Casbah along the river. That's the argument he would get up and make tonight. To coddle his voice he had smoked neither pipe nor cigarettes all afternoon, and before he put these papers inside the old soft briefcase he used to take to the office on Exchange Street, he would swallow a teaspoonful of honey.

He was ready. He pushed his glasses up on his nose and turned off the light above the dining-room table. The fringe on its shade shook a little, as Horace stole one more glance at the buckram box, hoping against hope that when he returned tonight he might be able to put it away forever.

"GO, MR. ABNER. REALLY," ANNE INSISTED. "YOU WON'T GET a seat unless you do."

Leo Abner still appeared reluctant. When he'd decided to keep the shop open till seven-thirty on summer Tuesdays, he'd told Anne she wouldn't have to stay.

"Go," she said, giving him a little push. "I've got to wait for Jack, in any case."

"All right, you talked me into it."

Anne laughed. "You want it to go through, don't you?"

At this mention of Al Jackson's plan, whose presentation at City Hall was Leo Abner's destination, the bookstore owner's expression crumpled back toward guilt. "I shouldn't, should I? Maybe I'm being selfish. Maybe I've just decided it would be good for business—all the postcards and Dewey books we'd sell to the visitors." He couldn't bring himself to use the uncourtly "tourists."

"But you know, Anne"—he'd finally dropped "Miss Macmurray," now that Jack Riley ("your beau") offered her sufficient protection against familiarity—"part of me just *likes* the idea."

This confession no longer surprised her. Since coming

back from Mackinac she'd heard a half dozen town elders, hierarchical club women and their privacy-loving husbands, express an embarrassed enthusiasm for the Dewey Walk, which was what everyone had taken to calling it. ("Road to Prosperity" had been dropped, probably for its faint echoes of Hoover.) Al Jackson might still be something of a brash outsider, but all the color and chatter he'd made people imagine along the riverbank stirred in them memories of the long carnival summer of '36, when the town had celebrated its centennial and floated for weeks upon the puffings of calliopes.

"There's no reason you shouldn't like the idea, Mr. Abner."

He put his hat back on. "The two of you will come along later?"

"Both of us. Now *go.*"

It was 7:20, and before Jack arrived she could perform one small chore, wrapping up a copy of *Kingsblood Royal,* the most recent Sinclair Lewis, for Mrs. Henry Hamel on Lee Street. It would replace the copy of *Raintree County* the police had taken from her yesterday. Since Sunday morning Margaret, between bouts of crying and silence, had mentioned the novel a number of times, whenever Chief Rice and his deputies inquired about what the *Argus* now called Timothy Herrick's "state of mind." She'd admitted that late in June Tim had stolen (and then replaced) a copy of the book from Abner's, and had occasionally mentioned the relevance of page 464 to the author's recent suicide. So yesterday a policeman had come into the shop looking for the book, which Anne's card file showed as having been sold to Mrs. Hamel on July 9. A visit to Lee Street revealed that page 464 had been underlined and starred by someone besides Mrs. Hamel, who reacted with more sheepishness than surprise: she had never made it past page 50. She let the officer take the book with him, and Leo Abner instructed Anne to send her something else, with the shop's apologies for having sold defaced merchandise.

Anne now looked at page 464 on the store's only other copy of *Raintree County* and considered the lines Tim had marked in the volume whose summer odyssey had ended on Chief Rice's desk:

> *The figure on the floor sighed and said mournfully,*
> *—Whip me, honey. I deserve it.*
> *Johnny picked up the whip and tossed it into a corner of* *the room.*
> *—Get up, you crazy little thing, he said.*
> *—Go on and lash me, she said with savage intensity. You're* *too good to me, Johnny, and I don't deserve it. I wish you'd beat me* *good and hard.*
> *Johnny leaned over and pulled her to her feet. She was crying* *and kissing him at the same time.*

Anne had been surprised to find such a passage lurking in this big, bloated Carl Sandburg production. (The book *had* been seized by the Philadelphia vice squad back in March, but vice squads were always seizing something.) A little bit of Krafft-Ebing back in Ann Arbor had taught her there were men excited by such things (Kinsey, she now realized, must also have something on it), but Margaret insisted that Tim had spoken of these lines only as the clue to why a few months ago Ross Lockridge had killed himself, just when he'd realized his big best-selling dreams. Anne had brought the novel home last night and skimmed enough of it to gather that the problem with Susanna (the girl who wanted whipping) was the guilty secret of her Negro blood. Lockridge had had his own torments, according to the magazines, including *The New Yorker*'s sophisticated pan of his book, a review that managed to call him "Lockwood" throughout.

Suicide was all the police had to hear about to start working that as Tim Herrick's motivation, a line of thought infuriating to poor Margaret, who maintained that Tim had no guilty secrets and was only interested in what happened to Lockridge as an example of the world's cruelty. Besides, if Tim wanted to kill himself, why would he bother to do it from a plane? Why not just jump off the water tower? Or take a page from Lockridge and run the engine of Arnie's Chevrolet with the garage door closed? And where *was* this plane they were thinking he'd deliberately crashed?

Anne was pretty sure Margaret had it right. Whatever had propelled Tim Herrick into the air, she was sure it wasn't *Raintree County,* a book so messy she might have to rethink her own thoughts about small-town literary inspiration. No, this novel (like poor Margaret, alas) was only one fever in that boy's brain. Did Margaret know more about the other ones than she was letting on? She had, after all, helped him load the plane. Everyone from Carol Feller to Chief Rice was hoping Margaret might break down and tell Anne what she was withholding from everybody else. Meanwhile, Anne had her own theory.

The bells jingled. The shop door opened and the shade behind it went down, pulled by Jack Riley, who took the Kinsey report out of Anne's hands. He kissed her and said, "Let's not go."

"I *want* to," she insisted. "I feel like Mr. Abner. It's pretty silly, but sort of exciting all the same."

"I'll tell you what's exciting," said Jack. "We'll go home and cook dinner and put Pop to bed and then go out to the garage." It was their mad love nest now. "You've even decorated it!" she'd cried Saturday night, after discovering he'd replaced an oil can that dripped onto the couch's bolster with a small vase full of violets. Gene Riley, who could now barely negotiate the stairs inside, let alone leave the house, would never notice them. The things she brought to Williams Street herself, a book from the shop or a bottle of Chianti or a can opener to replace the one that seemed broken, were reverently set down by Jack in the living room or kitchen, rooms that, as they shared them, seemed to excite him as much as the garage. He never pressed her to go outside, not because he still felt the need to play the well-mannered working stiff, and not because he wasn't a regular crazy boy once they got there; just because nothing seemed to make him happier—the kind of happy that depends on a certain disbelief—than to sit on the sofa, the doily-covered one inside, dozing off with his head on her shoulder, sniffing like a kitten. Upstairs, pills would have put Gene into a deep sleep. (It *was* cancer, she now knew, and only a matter of time.)

"We can heat up what Mrs. Goldstone made last night and turn on the radio and listen to *The Night Watchman*. What do you say? You don't want to hear a bunch of local politicians going at each other all night."

"Haven't you fed your dad already?"

"He wasn't hungry. I'm practically force-feeding him now."

"I know."

"Look, you want to go. That's okay. *I'll* skip it. I'll walk you over to City Hall and see what's going on in Rice's office, see if that CAA guy from Lansing has left any more search ideas." For the past two nights Jack had been part of the effort to find Tim Herrick, crisscrossing cornfields twenty miles away for as long as the light held out.

"No, don't. There won't be anything more you can do tonight. Let's split the difference. Come to *part* of the meeting with me. We'll leave early and go home and see if your dad has any more of an appetite."

"Deal." The word "home," she realized, was making him smile. It was as if she'd put "our" before it. She looked at her watch and put away the scissors and string. Mrs. Hamel's parcel could wait until tomorrow. Without even peeking at the graphs, Jack replaced Kinsey in the empty space on the shelf.

"Jack, I think I know where Tim is. I'll bet you he's safe and sound with Margaret's brother, on the upper peninsula, where Jim and his friends have been camping all summer. I think Tim somehow made it there after Margaret, without meaning to, put the idea into his head. That's what she realizes now, and that's why she's so upset. I tried this idea out on Carol last night and—"

He shook his head as he held the door for her. "Margaret may have been thinking that, but she was wrong. Jim Feller called home today for the first time in three weeks. He and his buddies are in Montana. They've been on the road with all their camping gear since July eighteenth, thumbing rides from trucks. Carol called me in Flint while you were out on your lunch hour. She didn't want to leave a long, complicated message with Mr. Abner."

Anne looked at him, surprised.

"I didn't want to call and upset you for the whole afternoon." He stroked her pretty head.

"Now these are just samples," said Al Jackson, holding up two tempera-painted panels. Laughter, and then applause, for the first.

"We all remember Otto, of course."

Of course, Al did not remember Otto Sprague, the Washington Street druggist who at the time of the cyclone had served as mayor, and fifteen years after that as postmaster. Otto had died before Al came to Owosso. But, as Peter Cox could see, nobody seemed to care that Al was lying. They were too occupied with enjoying Otto's likeness. The painting showed him looking out from behind some old apothecary jars, as the pre-mustachioed Tom Dewey swept the shop floor. In his youth, Dewey had worked more jobs than Billy Grimes, and Al, or the retired teacher he'd hired to paint the scale-model panels, had decided this one was the most picturesque.

The other piece of oaktag Al was holding would come to life much further down the Dewey Walk. It depicted the candidate just four years ago in Oklahoma City, on the night he'd finally taken off the gloves against FDR (a baleful background figure done in somber hues). The speech, as no one but Peter seemed to recall, had been a disaster; the newspapers criticized Dewey for an unseemly attack upon the commander-in-chief who'd brought them to the edge of victory.

In fact, the stumble was still echoing in Dewey's reluctance to speak ill of the current incumbent: he'd yet to say a word against the special session. But painted twenty feet high, even Oklahoma City would seem a triumph.

"I'm surprised you came," Anne whispered to Carol Feller, who had saved her and Jack a pair of seats.

"If we'd stayed home, Margaret would think we were waiting to catch her getting a phone call from him."

"How bad would that be?" asked Harold Feller, as he had obviously asked at least once before that evening. "We'd at least know the boy was alive." The strain was showing on his face.

Peter looked away from the four of them, preferring that they watch him instead and take note of the little clutch of people who during any burst of laughter or applause were asking him questions about the HUAC hearings and Mr. Chambers. Did his Washington friends know what might happen next? He tried to give the impression that he wasn't at liberty to say, even though this past week he hadn't talked on the telephone to anyone but a secretary from Lansing— his principal diversion since he'd dropped Vincent Dent's incorporation forms, a month late, on her desk at the state department of finance. He now realized he hadn't even, despite a promise to himself and Anne, called up Horace Sinclair, who was in the fourth row looking loaded for bear.

Al Jackson had jumped the gun by holding up the paintings. First they had to read the resolution, Councilman Royers reminded him. It was actually a whole set of resolves, eighteen in all, involving everything from competitive bidding to funds for insurance and crossing guards to the installation of traffic meters on Water, Exchange and Main streets.

The audience clapped at the end of the list, less for its sub-
stance than for Royers' heroic recitation. Councilman Morgan, reminding them that he was doing this only so the
proposal could stay on the floor for discussion, seconded the
resolution. *Now*, his nod indicated, Al could begin his pitch.

And pitch he did, without notes or interruption, explaining how the visitor would march up the west side of the
riverbank past such simple sights as the law-library chair
(Dewey's transfer from Ann Arbor to Columbia would go un-
depicted) as well as the more sensational ones, among them
a towering, glowering Waxey Gordon, the bootlegger being
led off to a papier-mâché prison (five days before Repeal) by
the young prosecutor. Directly across the water would be a
one-to-twenty replica of the Albany, New York, governor's
mansion, in front of which, after having covered the DA
years and crossed the as-yet-to-be-built footbridge, the visitor
could buy a glass of Frankenmuth or Geyer's lager. The
bridge itself would be strung with authentic banners from
each Dewey campaign.

Al anticipated every objection he could think of,
vacuuming them up like dustballs. "The whole exhibit will
be small enough so's everybody coming to see it can leave
the same day they get here. It's not as if we're going to need
a whole lot of new hotel space. The Hotel Owosso will do
nicely."

"You mean they'll make out nicely," said Myron Warren,
a shoe repairer in the second row, who laughed at his
own joke.

"And for those of you worrying about traffic, you've got
to remember that M-21 isn't going to stay a two-lane road
forever. Before long it's going to be the chief highway crossing the lower peninsula."

A murmur from the front row.

"People are going to be bothering Mrs. Dewey in any case," said Al, directly addressing the murmurer. "Now let me say something about the added business and revenue we can expect . . ."

Peter watched their Rotarian eyes glisten over all the geegaws and lunches and gas they'd be selling. Only a few of them remained unmoved. What direct gain, after all, would accrue to Dr. Starns, the optometrist, or Bill Gordon, the roofer over on Chipman? No day-tripper was going to need new glasses or shingles to complete his visit to this funhouse. Peter could see the left-out stealing peeved looks at the ones who stood to cash in: the proprietors of White's Bakery and Knapp's Super Service and the Top Hat Tap Room (who hoped that no one came around asking if Gus Farnham ever shared the beer he bought there with any minors).

Another group seemed hopefully uncertain: might a few of the tourists be so taken with Owosso that they'd stay to buy houses from Thane Neal's realty office? Would any of them, in a burst of patriotic decorum, stop in to Reisner's barbershop before hitting the Walk? The key to Jackson's success, Peter decided, lay with those who had no hope of re-alizing any added business but were smiling anyway, like Mike Hodges, an upholsterer on East Main who was either impressed by Al Jackson's budgetary statistics or just tickled by the prospect of visitors walking past those looming dioramas.

"Do you think they could get Roosevelt's cigarette to puff out smoke?" one old lady asked her husband. "Like Times Square?"

"That's a wonderful idea!" he responded.

A retired stenography teacher stood up and waited for

quiet before declaring: "I think James Oliver Curwood would be *appalled* by this defacement of the river. The castle he built upon it was something beautiful, made out of nature's own stones. He would hate these papier-mâché monstrosities being constructed from partisanship and greed."

Councilman Royers calmed the waters. "Nobody can speak for the dead, ma'am."

Peter was surprised—almost as surprised as Anne—to see Jack Riley's hand go up.

"Is it democratic to do this before the election?" he asked. "Is a town supposed to bet its money on one candidate over another, even if the candidate is a favorite son?"

A smattering of applause; a vigorous, grateful nod from Horace Sinclair. The crowd, hushed by the contention, listened to Al: "Everybody knows those Republican delegates in Philadelphia were picking a President. Everybody knows how this election is going to turn out. We've got a responsibility to get started. The sooner we do, the sooner we'll turn a profit. A profit that, under President Dewey, won't all go to taxes." *Hear, hear,* from a few businessmen.

"Does anyone here remember Amos Gould?" Horace Sinclair, without being recognized, was on his feet, the boom in his voice overriding its scratchy touch of hay fever. "Well, even I'm too young to remember him." The old man, winning Peter's admiration, waited for his laugh before going on. "But I know who he was. He was the first mayor of this city and he built the old house at 100 West Oliver in 1843. It's been chopped up for apartments now and—no disrespect to anyone living there—the history of the place is being plastered over and subdivided out of all recognition. There are a dozen buildings like it in Owosso, ones that don't have any plaques on them, even though they represent the *real* history of the town that produced Thomas E. Dewey. If you want to get a sense of his life, you should learn to recognize them instead of staring goggle-eyed at this carnival Mr. Jackson is proposing to throw up along the river." As if he were Robert Stripling reaching a dramatic moment with Whittaker Chambers, he turned around and faced Al. "Mr. Jackson, may I be so bold as to inquire if anyone has asked Governor Dewey about this big idea of yours?"

"He's in the middle of a presidential campaign, Mr. Sinclair."

"Do you mean the future of Owosso itself isn't important enough to bother him with?" Horace wheeled around and faced the crowd. "How many of you know where to find the Paymaster Building, or the Comstock cabin? Or even know what they are? Here, let me show you." He took to the aisle and began passing out his stenciled descriptions of the two fragile piles, along with a suggested appropriation for fixing them up. It was a dramatic enough maneuver, thought Peter, but it quickly lost steam: Horace hadn't brought nearly enough copies, and the councilmen weren't going to wait for him to finish his distribution before resuming the meeting.

Passing among the bakers and gas-station owners and just ordinary excited citizens, Horace felt ridiculous and frail, like that cabin that had been built over without a second thought. What had made him think this counter-proposal would move them more than Jackson's gaudy little Lido? What made him think he could believe in it himself? It was only a cover-up, and he was disgusted by his own arguments. (As if he cared what Thomas E. Dewey thought of anything, Owosso included!) He ran out of handbills halfway up the aisle and kept moving toward the door. He departed just as he heard Jackson, looking ahead to the groundbreaking, say something about "driving piles into the riverbank."

Damn it, thought Peter. He had hoped he might fulfill his promise to Anne by catching the old man even tonight, flattering him about his point of view before talking him out of it. Well, Anne and Riley would have to comfort him instead. They also were making for the exit.

After another half hour, the discussion was hardly exhausted, but Councilman Morgan called for a show of hands by his colleagues. By five to two, and to substantial cheers, the plan was carried forward to a second meeting and a final vote in October.

The crowd, uninterested in sewage treatment and new fire helmets, tonight's other items of business, were already on their feet. Peter could hear one librarian ask another if she didn't think their friend Trudy would be perfect playing Cokey Flo Brown, the Dewey witness who'd put away Lucky Luciano, on those Saturdays when real people in costumes, the way they'd started doing it in Williamsburg, Virginia, would take their parts in front of the murals.

"Ladies and gentlemen! Ladies and gentlemen!" cried Councilman Royers, who finally got those departing to turn around. "May I remind you that over the next few days, extensive on-foot searches for Tim Herrick and Gus Farnham's plane will be conducted in Clinton and Livingston counties? Please see the bulletin board outside Chief Rice's office for details, and please give of your time as generously as possible."

. . .

HORACE FLICKED THE UAW'S TRUMAN BUTTON ONTO THE
late Mrs. Sinclair's lemon-slice dish before dissolving, exhausted, onto the sofa. If Gene Riley's son hadn't given him
a ride from City Hall, he would never have made it home.
What a fiasco the evening had been! What a feeble attempt
to avoid what was coming! He had hoped to arrive home
tonight and, after fifty-one years, throw away the contents of
the buckram box. Instead, if he'd had any left, he would be
flinging his silly historical handbills into the wicker wastebasket by his reading chair.

He looked at the box on the dining-room table. It
seemed to be clicking in the moonlight, waiting to spring
to life, the way dead bacteria, scientists claimed, could
wiggle back into existence if they were freed from the amber that had held them for millions of years. Whenever
he was in Christ Episcopal, he thought about how the contents of the cornerstone, buried in 1859, were similarly
seething with suppressed vitality, awaiting the church's
centennial and their planned release. Christ's was where
they had all met back in the eighties, in the boys' choir led
by the rector's daughter: himself and Wright George and
Boyd Fowler and Jon, poor Jon, who even then had lived
from one enthusiasm to another, swept along on his own
good nature, every loving or unkind word striking him
five times harder than it would anyone else. "God should
have brought him into the world as a dog," Wright had
said when it was all over, and the others took the remark
for what it was, a compliment, and elaborated upon it, until
they decided on the particular breed of retriever whose

guilelessness and feelings shone brightest on its eyes. That was Jon.

He switched on the dining-room lamp. Its fringed shade shook, raking the table with shadows. He opened the box, not to destroy its contents, but to surrender to them, to let them hurt him all over again. The letter had never had an envelope, just an engraving of the Ament Hotel in an oval-shaped cloud, at the top of the stationery:

Dear Horace,

Forgive me this, but I am wandering alone in a blizzard, looking for the one single light that could be in any of a hundred directions on the compass. I am too tired to go on. Please take care of my mother.

J.A.D.

The fold was still in the paper, with the last three words Jon ever wrote, "To Horace Sinclair," on the back. Jon had hoped the clerk would find it in the middle of the night, when he walked the second-floor corridor and heard a faint hiss and smelled something sweet and saw no light at the threshhold. And that's just what had happened. Once inside, the clerk pinched off the gas, but it was too late. The blue skin and strangely red lips sent him, in a panic, to the Sinclair house five blocks north on Ball Street. There, still in a shed, stood a half dozen bicycles from his father's failed shop, so Horace gave one to the young man and the two of them rode as fast as they could back to the hotel. Up in room 214, the clerk swore the face was bluer now, an even bolder contrast to the sepia tones of Alice Banks, the girl from Lennon whose photograph had been set out on the dresser.

Only eight months had passed since the Saturday afternoon Alice came into Owosso and bought fabric from Jonathan Adams Darrell, the boutonniered new clerk on the second floor of D. M. Christian's. Before long she was coming in each Saturday, to meet him at the counter of Otto Sprague's first drugstore or to hold hands at the Salisbury Opera House before Jon drove her back to Lennon in his carriage, both of them dreading the sight of George F. Behan's grain elevator, which signaled their arrival at Thomas Banks's small house, which he'd built as close to the elevator as one safely could, the elevator being where he worked and, despite another man's owning it, the pride of his life. By early June Alice, as feckless as Jon, was expecting a child, and Thomas Banks decided it would be more effective to banish his daughter than her detested suitor. For the two weeks before Jon cut into the gas pipe, Alice had been someplace so tightly guarded that no letter from her could reach him. Jon's haggard pleadings had fallen on the equally deaf ears of Thomas Banks and his wife.

"Bring me the register," Horace whispered to the clerk, who ran and got it so that Horace might rip out its last used page, the one he was now pulling out of the buckram box. "Jonathan Adams Darrell" was written beneath the name of a salesman from Chicago, who had slept through the night's furtive commotion three rooms down the hall.

"Can you remember the rest of these names?"

"Yes," said the clerk.

"Then copy them onto the next empty page downstairs. Do you remember his name?" asked Horace, pointing, without looking, at Jon's still body.

"No," said the clerk, who was smart enough to guess this

was the right answer, and calm enough now to scent opportunity, to give off a deliberate hint of unreliability, what Horace would have to satisfy three days later with fifty dollars withdrawn from the Owosso Savings Bank. The receipt for that transaction, also in the buckram box, was stamped "100 W. Oliver Street," the address of the Amos Gould house, out of which the bank had operated in those days, a fact he neglected to put into the handbills he'd passed out tonight. By the end of the summer of '97 the clerk was gone from Owosso, managing some Harvey House out west.

Two of the ninety-five telephones then in Owosso were owned by the Ament Hotel and Wright George's parents. At 3:15 A.M. Horace got the operator to ring the Georges' number, trusting that Wright would be the one to pick up. "Meet me in front of your house in ten minutes, and have your father's wagon ready." By 3:30 they had roused Boyd Fowler, and by four they had stolen a mahogany coffin from Boyd's place of business, the Owosso Casket Company. Before the sun came up they had buried Jon in the soft riverbank behind the shuttered mill. No lights gave them away: there was then no Armory, no high school, no purposeless castle just across the water.

Along with Jon's note, the page of the register, the bank receipt and the photo of Alice, there was a copy of the pact Horace had talked them into signing. They had put the original into Jon's stolen coffin, a paper averring that they had buried Jon so as not to give Thomas Banks the satisfaction, nor Alice Banks the agony, of knowing what had happened. Horace would write Mr. Banks that a despairing, desperate Jon, determined never to return to Michigan or communicate with Alice again, had shipped out with the Navy; so it was safe to bring her home and be happy with the misery Mr. Banks had caused them all. As for Jon's mother, she required no material assistance, and Horace convinced himself he had spared her with the same lie, which she was able to believe, since she had never liked Alice Banks and let Jon know it: it made sense that he was bitter enough never to write home from San Diego or Manila Bay or any of the other ports of call where from time to time she imagined him over the next and last ten years of her life.

Horace took another look at the buckram box and wondered if *he* had any possibility of another ten years. Could he live through the unearthing of all this? Survive the *Argus* story that was sure to reach Jon's son, a fifty-year-old man who, as Horace knew from years of secretly keeping track, still lived in Detroit? Useless speculation; as useless as continuing to wonder if Wright George would answer his letter. The only question worth asking was whether or not Horace Sinclair could still wield a shovel.

MARGARET LAY AWAKE, LOOKING THROUGH HER OPEN WINdow. She was still sure—at least for moments at a time—that he would come to her, or get her a message, explain what his voyage had been about, and what it had to do with her. The thought that it had *nothing* to do with her, that he had betrayed their weeks together, was still unthinkable, though, also for moments at a time, she had been tempted to consider this. To stop herself, she would concentrate on her enemies, chief among them Billy, whose every effort at helping, like those ridiculous flyers, seemed an I-told-you-so. Then there was the parade of Tim's old girlfriends, like Sharon

Daly, eager to get themselves into the *Argus* and on WOAP, coming forward to list all the places *they* had gone with Tim in Arnie's Chevrolet, as if Tim might have flown his plane back to one of them as some lovesick gesture.

In the darkest part of her heart, she suspected her parents—as she suspected they suspected her—of having had something to do with what happened Sunday morning.

But what had happened *since* then? Where had he landed the plane, and what had he been doing? She *did* believe he was alive, but she remained incapable of picturing him outside the cockpit with his feet on the ground, breaking into the provisions she had helped him load. Did this mean the thread connecting them was too thin to transmit an image?

HE SUSPECTED BOTH OF THEM; THEY WERE IN IT TOGETHER. That's what Billy thought as he walked east on Oliver away from Margaret Feller's window. Herrick was making a place for her, establishing a beachhead, where she would soon join him, having "overcome" Owosso at last. It was as if his own life were some game of ten little Indians; Billy Grimes, who had more practical ideas for getting out of this town than any of them, would be the one forced to stay behind. He could have made a lot extra helping Mr. Jackson at the city council meeting tonight. Would Herrick ever realize he cared enough about his friend to give that up and work on his latest flyers? He'd dropped them off at Chief Rice's office (the town would pay the postage), and now he was just walking, watching the lightning bugs go on and off, like substitutes for the forsythia petals of spring. At least, by luck, he was on the north sidewalk; across Oliver, he could make out Jane Herrick coming in the opposite direction, and he didn't want to have to talk to her. What was she doing out at midnight? It was creepy even to think about, so he'd think about his fifty-to-one shot, his best fantasy for the way this whole thing might turn out, with Tim returning unharmed, and Margaret so furious at his having hotfooted it off without her that she never spoke to him again. He, Billy, would have both of them back to himself.

But all this was too improbable to keep his mind off old lady Herrick. Was she wishing Tim were dead? Shot down by some insane Nazi exile living on the northern peninsula? Which would make him another casualty to bury and remember? Or had she, like some crazy Quaker, you couldn't tell with her, *told* him to run off—to avoid August 30, when every Shiawassee County male born between 1923 and 1930, which included Herrick and yours truly, was supposed to register for the draft? "24 YOUTHS VOLUNTEER FOR ARMED SERVICES—LARGEST PEACETIME CONTINGENT": that's what the *Argus* had just bragged about. But anybody who did the numbers could tell you that was pretty small compared to the *involuntary* contingent they'd soon be assembling.

JANE APPROACHED THE COMSTOCK APARTMENTS, HER MATHematical compulsions operating as she pushed the bell for number 331. Subtract that many days from August 3 and you were back at September 7, the birthday of Charles Beck, a Corunna boy who'd lost a foot on Okinawa, which wasn't the same thing as being dead, but which still meant something. She brushed off a couple of small leaves that had attached themselves to her green felt skirt, which wasn't right for the season and hadn't been pressed in more than three years, but which she'd still put on for this visit.

Frank Sherwood opened the door, unnerved, as she'd hoped he would be.

"Mrs. Herrick. Please come upstairs." He'd thought it might be Anne, that she'd forgotten her key.

Jane looked around the room.

"Can I offer you a cup of tea?" asked Frank. "It takes a few minutes to get the water going on this hotplate, but I can do it." He turned it on without waiting for an answer, taking down a second cup and a package of Tetley's, which he'd drunk since '43 and knew was her brand because he'd seen *him* buying it, back then, in Kroger's.

"*Principles of Celestial Navigation.*" Jane picked up the book as she read out the title.

"It's from the school library," explained Frank. "I got it out because it was the only thing my chairman and I could think of for me to do on Sunday. I had this little booth at the air show—"

He realized she wasn't looking at him. She was regarding the electric ring under the saucepan, watching it turn redder and redder, as if the hotplate were really Saturn, and had dropped in tonight on its long circuit around the sun.

"I'm sure that Tim is okay, Mrs. Herrick. You know, that plane was in surprisingly good shape. That's what the airport warden said: 'Say what you want about Gus, he really took care of the plane. He was out there working it every Saturday, working on everything from the—' "

"Mr. Sherwood," said Jane, moving her gaze from the hotplate's ring to Frank's eyes, gathering in her lungs and throat the same voice she had shouted into the Ardennes forest on a December night in '44, in a dream. Tonight she was right here in Owosso, awake, but the words that came out of her were the same ones she'd cried in her sleep three and a half years ago: *"What have you done with my son?"*

SEVEN

August 9 – 23

DEWEY'S CAMPAIGN PLANS QUICKENING;
SILENT OVER SPECIAL SESSION

Peter picked up Anne's *Argus* from the counter near the register.

"He may be 'silent' over the session," she said, "but the session is over, period." It was Monday, August 9, two days after Congress had adjourned. Along with price controls, the House had even rejected, as too liberal, a housing bill backed by the arch-conservative Senator Taft. Truman could now gleefully complain about the do-nothing Eightieth Congress for the twelve weeks until Election Day.

"That's some forthright candidate you've got, Peter."

"Who do you think will break his silence first?" he asked. "Dewey or the Herrick kid?"

A terrible joke (after nearly ten days the search for Tim had been quietly called off), but she was pleased to find herself laughing. It meant she had at last relaxed with Peter

Cox. She was now officially Jack's girl, recognized as such by all, including Peter. Their skirmishes were over; he had surrendered the other night, gracefully she thought, when she and Jack ran into him in front of the Capitol Theatre. He'd actually shaken Jack's right hand, while Jack's left one stayed around her waist. It wasn't exactly signing papers on the deck of the *Missouri,* but she detected a touch of formality in it. With all that behind them, Peter could now cross the street and drop into the shop at lunchtime like some friendly trade delegation on a routine mission.

Peter wished she hadn't laughed at his joke. He already knew she had a streak of black humor, but he would have preferred still being enough of a threat to require scolding. Instead, as she unpacked a box of novels from Lippincott, she motioned him into the chair behind the counter. "Put your feet up," she said. "I hear from Carol it's what you do at the office."

"Okay." He swung them onto Leo Abner's blotter.

"How about *your* campaign plans? Are they 'quickening'?"

"I'm not making much noise yet, but I'm not lying quite so low as the top of the ticket. I'll be at a meeting of the Shiawassee County Young Republicans later in the week, where the Wayne University *Collegian*'s star reporter will tell everybody about the wonderfully modern Dewey machine he saw operating in Philadelphia." He dropped his head to his chest and made snoring noises.

"Is this boy from Owosso? Maybe they can paint him into the convention panel of the Dewey Walk."

"God, you're really for that thing."

"I am. I am genuinely for it and for Harry Truman."

"It's so cornball," said Peter.

"The Walk or Harry?"

"Both."

"Neither. Harry's going to go down fighting, and all those things on the Walk will say more to people than Dewey himself ever will. You remember our conversation after Carol's dinner party? When you said the Walk was more important than those backyards, on account of history and fame or something like that? You were trying to talk me into it. Well, I am talked into it, but not for your reasons, and certainly not to lure the tourists. I like it because it's peculiar; it'll be one of a kind, not something from a chain store. They say the future will be places like that ready-made town they're going to put on a potato farm outside New York— each house like every other. But how many towns had a coffin factory, or a woman who crippled herself working on the slanted floor of her husband's merry-go-round? If Owosso is the place that produced Dewey, at least it's the *only* place that produced him. So let's put up the Walk."

"What does Jack think?"

This was the first time Peter had spoken his name as a simple fact, something requiring no particular tone of voice, only the recognition facts routinely got.

"He just wants them to wait. He still thinks it's indecent to do anything before the election." She called out to a customer at the back of the store. "It's $1.95, Mrs. Smart. Sorry about the missing cover, but that's eighty cents off."

"How's his father?" asked Peter.

Anne walked back to the counter to give him his answer, cancer being one fact that demanded not just recognition but a shameful hush. "He's slipping. Jack thinks they'll put him in a hospital within another week. Either here or in Lansing."

"I hope he doesn't have to get poked by Dr. Coates. *That* must be some bedside manner."

Dr. Coates? Oh, Carol's brother, the rabid radiologist. "I'm afraid poor old Gene is way past the X-ray stage."

Cancer could shut even Peter up; she had to jump over the silence. "Well," she sighed, tapping the paper, "Dr. Coates won't have to worry about money being squandered on little apartments for veterans. Honestly, Peter, when they won't even pass *Taft*'s housing bill! It's like saying Mr. Bumble's been too generous with the porridge."

She spoke, he thought, like somebody who would be turning into a Democrat even if she weren't dating one; she talked as if she wanted to have a *discussion,* that so-much-less-sexy version of an argument.

"If you don't want houses that all look alike," he replied, "why do you want the government to build skyscraper slums?"

"People have got to live *someplace.* And why do you say they'll be slums?"

"You're right. They won't be. Because Congress isn't going to build them."

She paused to ring up Mrs. Smart's copy of *The Ides of March.* And because she wasn't going to give him the sort of argument he wanted, she shifted the subject.

"I'm getting excited about the election, which I never would have expected. I think my dad was the only Democrat in Darien, and I could never understand why he bothered tacking signs to the trees each fall, and driving old ladies to the polls when he knew they were going to vote for Landon. But I'm beginning to feel it."

Was it, Peter wondered, her romance with the town—
the one she was willing herself into for the sake of her
book—or the one she was having with Riley? The first, he decided. Evenings spent pouring Jack his beer and listening to
why everyone needed more wages to make fewer widgets
might have made her "Truly for Truman," but it was this
novel of hers that was leaving room for the Dewey Walk.

"Well, I'm bored with the whole thing. That's the way it
is with foregone conclusions. Even the war was boring after
New Year's '45."

Which he'd spent smashed on champagne in Grosvenor
Square, she bet. While Jack was thanking God his eye had
twitched back to life.

"How's your girl from Lansing? The one with the tax
department."

"She's retiring."

"More like the pink slip, I'd say. From you." It was the
closest she'd come to flirting, and it was over before she got
back to the box of books from Lippincott.

He'd had enough. He swung his legs off the counter
and started for the door.

"Oh, Peter! I forgot. Your mother is going to think I'm
as rude as can be. I only this morning got around to writing
her a thank-you letter for everything on Mackinac. I haven't
even mailed it yet. If you talk to her—"

"I'll tell her you've been busy." The bells jingled and he
waved good-bye from the sidewalk.

Crossing Washington Street, he felt inside his pocket for
a letter that assured the pointlessness of Anne's, one he'd
found waiting at home last night, its absurd postmark—
RENO—falling over the three-cent Statue of Liberty. After
thirty-four years of marriage his mother was in the Biggest

Little City in the World, living at a dude ranch to establish residency for a divorce.

Once back at his desk, his feet squarely under it, he read Lucy Cox's handwriting for the third time:

August 5, 1948

Dear Peter,

This isn't *too* much of a shock, is it? There's a slot machine in the stable, and another in the powder room, and everyone is terribly nice. It's a big hen party with half the girls already "looking." Except for all the liquor, it reminds me of the semester I had at Smith forty years ago, before your grandfather brought me home—the greatest sorrow of my life, as I'm sure I've told you.

I've already begun to receive invitations: dinner next Saturday night at the archbishop of Reno's. Yes, Reno has an archbishop, but a very liberal one, I hear, so I probably won't find Senator McCarran at his table. You'll have to make that conquest yourself, whenever you manage to graduate to Washington.

The requirement here is six weeks, and they say one should figure on another two before getting everything straightened out, but I'll be back in time for your election. Try to call me some morning at the number on the stationery. And put your mind at ease. Your father has agreed to it, and nothing has changed from your standpoint. I'm talking about the money, of course.

With love from your
Mother

Of course she was talking about the money, and about everything except why she had suddenly gone and done this, now, fifteen years after he had seen what bound her and his father just disappear, like an animal that had run off. Back then he had asked, again and again, to no answer but a smile: *What's the matter?* From that time on the house had felt muffled, except during the cocktail hour, when with their friends his parents roared into false gaiety, each of their voices echoing like a room robbed of its furniture.

He wouldn't hear men and women that loud again until the war, when the soldiers and secretaries throwing themselves at one another talked at a volume two notches higher than necessary. But their noise, he remembered noticing, lacked that echo. Something packed it, something from within, maybe an awareness of the person back home they were betraying and somehow loving the more for doing it.

He could remember envying all that temporary passion, and wishing *he* had someone at home to betray, but by the time he'd gone over to London he'd long since learned to imitate his parents' indifference to love. He'd started practicing his own version of invincibility the summer he'd been the Pierrot up on Mackinac, the summer after things had gone wrong at home. As he'd told Harris Terry weeks ago, it was *personality* that closed the deals, that got you past the Japs or Mrs. Roosevelt or you name it.

Could he name *them?* There had been so many girls he no longer could.

His mother's letter had so much of her silvery nonchalance that it had taken him three hours after reading it—as he lay in bed on Park Street, letting the phone ring in the dark (the tax-department secretary)—to realize the obvious, if still unexplained, matter behind it. Something had *happened,* something to make her feel there was now a reason for her and Father to be officially apart instead of officially together, as they had been for so long, like two parallel-parked Lincolns. But what was it?

This afternoon he was no closer to guessing. He stuck it out at the office for longer than usual, interrupting himself only to look out the window and across the street at Abner's. Any sight of her was blocked by the glare, which made the bookshop's window a blue rectangle, into which the occasional customer would be painted just before entering the shop. At 4:45 Jack Riley arrived and disappeared inside. Were they down to a thirty-five-hour week in Flint? Or had he come home early to take care of his old man? Either way, he was in there, while Peter sat across the street, so deep in the picture's background it didn't even count.

His only route forward seemed to be the Dewey Walk, that "peculiar" one-of-a-kind boulevard she'd decided she liked. It was the service road he had to stay on.

Unless, he all at once realized, Dewey himself could be used to bring Peter Cox and Anne Macmurray together.

"Harris! I'm leaving for the day. If Harold comes looking for me, tell him—"

"That you're on the river? Or that you had to nip over to the tax department in Lansing? Poor Vince Dent's affairs must be *extraordinarily* complicated."

"No, Harris, you can tell him I've gone up to Oliver Street to see the mother of our next President."

BERTRAM HAD JUST BEEN WOUNDED IN A DUEL, FATALLY IT seemed, but Horace Sinclair, who had finally finished *Ivanhoe* and now had *Guy Mannering* open on his lap, was paying more attention to WGN, the *Chicago Tribune* station with a ten-state range, named for the World's Greatest Newspaper. The announcer was listing the long—and, to Horace, quite pointless—itineraries of the presidential candidates. The public ought to demand that Dewey and Truman get on the same stage and argue things out like shrunken devolutions of Lincoln and Douglas. Instead, the two of them would spend the next three months flying and locomoting all across the country, avoiding each other like a lover and a cuckold.

In other news, the announcer declared, the House of Representatives (for all its parsimony these past weeks) had agreed to spend $65 million to build the United Nations a headquarters in New York. Horace frowned, not because he disapproved of the U.N. (it was a comfortable old idea, like the failed League of Nations), but because the item renewed the rage he'd felt over a billboard he'd seen this morning. COMING SOON TO THIS SITE, it said, big as life, stuck in the riverbank and visible from the Main Street bridge he'd been walking over on his way to the library. OWOSSO'S HERITAGE WALKWAY. CELEBRATING ITS NATIVE SON, THOMAS E. DEWEY, 34TH PRESIDENT OF THE UNITED STATES. It couldn't be more than twenty feet from Jon's bones, there on the slope between the Armory and the river.

He'd turned right around and come home, where he spent the afternoon with *Guy Mannering*, from his own shelves, when he wasn't making calls to City Hall. None of the council were around, but he finally reached Ed Royers at home, only to receive a nursemaid's soothings. "Now, Horace, don't get yourself in a lather. Al put it up himself. We didn't give him a dime, or any seal of approval. Yes, strictly speaking, it's premature, but what harm's it doing?"

He'd hung up with a loud slam, a bad habit the late Mrs. Sinclair had cured him of long ago, but which had come back, like excessive smoking and eating peas with a knife, in his years as a widower. That lonely status was "no excuse for such behavior" (the words she would have used if she were still here), but it was a better one than all the luxurious reasons Wright George had finally sent explaining his inability to come to Owosso anytime soon. His wife was sick; they'd promised visits to their children in other parts of the country; he'd turned his ankle, really rather badly, on the golf course. Without a wife or children or the breath to play golf, Horace had sat seething the last few nights, knowing Wright was doing his best to forget what Horace had told him. He was hoping that fate or luck would prevent the discovery.

Discovery was only half of it, thought Horace. The *desecration* bothered him as much as the thought of Jackson's contractors driving their steam shovels into the earth and finding the other box inside the no doubt long-rotted mahogany one. The airtight silver case, the one in which he and Wright and Boyd had each put a self-identifying token, was sure to be there amidst the broken-hearted bones.

Each evening since Wright's letter, Horace had sat here in his chair, getting perhaps a dozen pages deeper into *Guy Mannering*, until the wave of exhaustion met and overwhelmed the wave of dread riding his overworked arteries. Then, if he hadn't fallen asleep in the chair, he would hoist himself up for the slow climb upstairs to the late Mrs. Sinclair's side of the bed, where he would drift into a messy assortment of dreams.

He was dozing in the chair even now, but a footfall on the wooden porch came and roused him. Either Grimes arriving to collect, or Mrs. Goldstone (recently recommended by Carol Feller) to drop off the two roast chickens he would live off for the next week.

"Come in!" Horace shouted, glad he had his wallet in his pocket and could avoid the effort of rising.

"Colonel."

"What are you doing here?" It was the young lawyer, Cox, the one he'd once had some hopes for against Jackson.

For a moment, as the ceiling fan blew his blond hair up and down in the dark room, Peter appeared at a loss, unprepared for the energy of the man's hostility. "Get yourself a drink," Horace growled, pointing to the tray of liquors a foot away from the silver tea service. "And turn off that radio." The bottles, stoppered with cut glass, looked warm and syrupy. Peter poured himself what he guessed was sherry, trying as he did to keep smiling at Horace, whose massive head with its still-full share of slicked-back hair looked, in the room's shadows, like the bronze promontory of a war memorial.

"I'm disappointed in you," said Horace.

"How come?" asked Peter, taking the seat he hadn't been offered.

"I heard about what you said at the Dewey Club."

"Ah," said Peter. "Introducing Mr. Jackson's plan."

He was squinting at the old man, wishing he would turn on a light. Instead, from his chair Horace pulled the curtains' drawstring and closed them a final six inches against the detested sight of the camera salesman's ranch house.

"What's so terrible about it, Colonel?"

"You've already heard me on that subject. You were at the council meeting."

"Where you proposed restoring some of our older buildings."

The "our" only further inflamed Horace. It was perhaps three months since this young man had arrived in Owosso, after selecting it with a politician's dowsing rod.

"Why can't we do both, Colonel? Organize some private funding for the Paymaster Building and, you know, the other one, I forget its name, if the council won't appropriate anything. I'd be glad to contribute something myself."

"Stop soft-soaping me. I'm only one vote, Mr. Cox. I left the Army before Thomas E. Dewey was born, carrying, despite my erstwhile nickname, the rank of lieutenant."

"Is there something personal in this passion, Mr. Sinclair?" That was the sort of motive Peter could understand, the sort that had brought him here.

"Not one bit!" Horace shouted, with a different, more urgent, agitation. "That riverbank is what carries the life of this town. Poking holes in it is like firing gunshots into a person! I'm just one old man, but I—"

"Tell me about Annie Dewey," said Peter, as quietly as he could and still be heard.

The change of subject baffled Horace into meekness. Had he missed a question? He was about to start doing his memory exercise, the one he murmured to himself as proof against senility—*Taylor, Fillmore, Pierce, Buchanan*—when he heard Peter Cox say, just as quietly as before: "Please, tell me about her."

"She's as fine a woman as you'll find in the state of Michigan."

"But crusty, too, I've heard."

"Nothing wrong with crustiness."

"No, indeed."

"Mr. Cox, just what is it that you want? You make me nervous."

"I don't mean to, Colonel."

"Then what is it?"

"I need to talk to Mrs. Dewey, and I'm having trouble getting to her."

"Really."

"Mr. Valentine, her houseman, just answered the door, and when he called my name up to her, she said sorry, she wasn't able to see me. Now or at any other time, apparently."

Probably decided the one sharpie she'd raised was enough, thought Horace. Or maybe she figured she'd already done this young man enough of a favor; he had heard about that little stunt with the letters at the club meeting. Or maybe she was just getting cautious. There would be plenty of stories about her in the next twelve weeks. Somebody was bound to revive the old rumor that she had once belonged to the Committee of One Million, which she hadn't. But if she had? Did that make her the only person to discover there will always be some disreputable people advocating your own reputable opinion? Most of the voters on this street had been isolationist until Pearl Harbor.

"What do you want from her?"

"I want her to bring her son to Owosso between now and Election Day."

"Why can't he decide to come on his own?"

"Would you? If you were he? I mean, why waste the time? This isn't exactly a toss-up town. In any case, the Dewey Club hasn't had any nibbles from the national organization."

"I'm sure the governor just wants to avoid making some

controversial remark—like how good it feels to be back in his hometown."

Peter leaned forward and nodded, as if Horace had just gotten the point. "I'm sure, if he were here, he'd avoid *all* controversy. In fact, if some reporter from the campaign train were to ask him what he thought of this immense tribute the town was undertaking to build, I think prudence would pretty much obligate him to say he was touched, but that if it were up to him he'd like to see the money go to, let's say, orphanages and war heroes." He paused. "A remark like that could put a damper on the whole project."

Horace, who by now *had* gotten the point, and was wondering what was in it for Peter Cox, reopened the curtains several inches and fixed him with a hard look.

Peter knew he couldn't go to the Fellers for help with this: it seemed the loan of the letters had apparently used up any line of credit he had through them with Mrs. Dewey, and Carol, if not Harold, was sure to smoke out an ulterior motive. He forced himself not to glance at Al Jackson's suddenly visible house; he returned Horace's stare without blinking. "I want him here, Colonel. I want everybody pitching in to get ready for him. I want a lot of fuss."

Horace ran his finger over *Guy Mannering*'s spine. He looked away from Peter as if he might be considering it; and to give him a moment, Peter looked around the room, from the heavy sconces to the full-sized radio cabinet to the silver tea service.

"Colonel, did you and Mrs. Sinclair ever think of getting a divorce?"

The question, out of the blue and in a different tone from the one he'd been hearing, offended Horace not at all.

It prompted no alarm or antisenility exercises. It was as if Peter Cox, for whatever reason, had finally asked him something worth answering.

"No, Mr. Cox, we didn't."

"I wonder if people who get divorced ever *really* separate themselves from each other. I wonder if that's possible."

Horace put *Guy Mannering* on the table and closed his eyes. "Son, one can't undo *anything.*"

Peter rose and made ready to go. Instead of shaking Horace's hand, he gently closed the curtains for him. "Call Mrs. Dewey, Colonel."

FRANK SHERWOOD LOOKED THROUGH THE OPEN WINDOW and wondered how he might land. He wasn't thinking seriously about jumping, but defenestration was back in the news. This time, unlike the one before with the Czech foreign minister, there seemed no question that the victim, Mrs. Oksana Kosenkina, had descended of her own free will from the third floor of the Soviet consulate in New York. The fifty-two-year-old teacher, a visitor from the U.S.S.R., had failed to show up for the boat home on July 31. The consular authorities were now claiming to have rescued her from White Russian exiles, but Mrs. Kosenkina, from her hospital bed, insisted that the Soviets had taken her prisoner inside their building on Sixty-first Street.

Here in the Comstock Apartments Frank felt similarly stateless. He was cut off from the small patch of memory he'd counted as home, deemed an enemy by his last living connection to it, Jane Herrick, with whom he'd never spoken a word until a week ago Tuesday night.

Tim had to be dead. Frank pictured him lying inside his crumpled plane, as yet undetected by the party of hikers or hunters who would eventually find him, a skeleton in a broken fuselage, his things still in the footlocker the paper had mentioned every day until they tired of the story. In the locker Frank imagined a clean white shirt, like the one they always found with the Japanese soldiers being pulled out of hiding in the jungle, the shirt they kept for the day they'd be flying over Washington, the shirt Tim might have packed to wear when he got to wherever he thought he was going.

The police had shown up three days after the Dawn Patrol. Had she sent them? It was awful either way. One of Chief Rice's deputies asked what he knew of Tim's "habits" while examining Frank's bookcase and night table and, finally, the contents of his top desk drawer. He missed two nearly identical pictures marked "September '43," both of them showing two young men a little drunk outside the Red Fox tavern, their arms draped over each other, looking to the slightly drunk third party with the camera like just what they were, a schoolteacher and a bank teller loosening up after work.

The patrolman had asked to go up to the roof and have a look through this telescope he'd heard about, and Frank had obliged, wishing that the daylight hiding Jupiter might somehow hide him as well.

"Are you staying around this summer, Mr. Sherwood?"

"Of course," he'd answered.

There was nowhere else to go, so he would stay, hearing in his head, over and over, that unexpected conversation he'd had with her, as if it were an *Encyclopedia Britannica* film he had to show four different classes in a single day. He would keep thinking of what he should have said instead of "I just gave him some astronomy lessons." He should have said, "I've visited his brother's grave as often as you, sometimes even when you were there, though you didn't know it. As soon as I saw you coming, or until I'd see you leave, I'd sit in the gazebo or lurk behind the Bell mausoleum."

But he hadn't said this. And Jane Herrick had just stared at him, as if he were the German officer who would reappear in her dreams forever, always available for questioning, always without an answer.

Had Frank felt able to question her, he would have asked if she had received a letter written later than the last he'd gotten, the one dated November 30, 1944. He would have asked: When his effects came home before his bones, did you find a key chain with the sun and the moon embossed on a silver disk? By any chance did you put it into the coffin at Oak Hill? There were nights without number that he had wanted to claw the earth and dig down for it, dig for the bones themselves, while she and Tim, a boy he could never figure, and could never dare to talk to about his brother, were sleeping over on Park Street.

He looked at the telephone. *Owosso 6410.* He knew that was still their number, because he checked it every year in *Polk's City Directory.* He had never rung it, but he had a stronger desire than ever to do so now, to dial his neighbor, the only other living soul in the land of dead Herricks.

CHIEF RICE'S DEPUTY HAD TWICE BEEN TO SEE JANE.

On his first visit, he asked if he might have a look at Tim's room. She said yes, but did not accompany him upstairs; she had almost never gone into the room between '44 and the day Tim disappeared, and she had no desire to now. After his search, the deputy remarked to her upon the room's unusual tidiness for a boy Tim's age. The fastidiousness extended to the fifth of whiskey tucked exactly into the first-baseman's mitt in a bureau drawer, though the officer confined his observation of that detail to his notepad. To Mrs. Herrick he talked of the neat stacks of magazines and schoolbooks, the folded clothes and sorted coins, before asking if she had straightened things up since last seeing Tim. She answered no, and continued listening to the policeman's description of the room as if it were a postcard from abroad.

His second visit, sparked by the *Raintree County* speculations, yielded no hidden notes or *X*-marked maps, no letters from Margaret Feller or anybody up on the northern peninsula. Mrs. Herrick did manage to identify the copy of Michie & Harlow's *Practical Astronomy* that he brought down. Despite its being uninscribed, she remembered it as a present from Frank Sherwood. This merited some underlining in the deputy's notebook. After showing himself out, he went back to City Hall astonished at the woman's overall lack of knowledge about her son, a fact that made her mention of Frank Sherwood conspicuous.

After the officer's two visits, and her own to Frank Sherwood's, Jane had concluded that Tim was dead. Her "three men," as she had called them in the gay middle days of her marriage, were all gone now. By today, Friday the thirteenth, even the girl from the *Argus* had stopped calling.

August 13. On this day in history (not the anniversaries cited by the paper, but the ones she mentally assembled),

Arnold Herrick had received a diphtheria vaccination (1931), and Byron O'Clair of Laingsburg had been killed in the Solomon Islands (1943).

Tim was deader than Arnie. Her older son had bones and a monument, which her fealty had animated with something like life. She had no theories about where Tim had gone or how he had died, nothing that took her beyond that single impulsive trip to the Comstock Apartments, prompted by the sight of the astronomy handbook and, after she'd identified it, the deputy's mention of Frank Sherwood's booth at the air show.

Whenever she saw him on the street, Frank seemed to *look* at her, the way people once in a while accused her of looking at them. She knew he was mixed up in this, somehow. Her train of thought went nowhere with the feeling, but lately the papers announced no military funeral that would take her mind off it. She was angry at Tim for being dead, for appropriating her grief the way he had taken everything else belonging to Arnie.

Her despair no longer nourished; it consumed. She could not sleep and was forgetting the simplest things, like her key chain with the sun and moon, which she'd left dangling from the front-door lock all night after coming back from Frank Sherwood's apartment.

FOR THE FIFTH NIGHT IN A ROW, ANNE AND JACK SAT IN THE second-floor waiting room at Memorial Hospital, holding hands.

He was beginning to get her. He'd known better than to suggest *The Emperor Waltz* at the Capitol this weekend. Forget

the music and frills: she would have no more interest in seeing Bing Crosby than he would. *The Bishop's Wife* had become
a standing joke between them, a story he imagined her
telling friends a year from now—*their* friends, when they
were out from under this business with Pop and had time to
make them. What he really liked to picture was her telling
the story to their daughter, twenty years from now, though
he feared pressing his luck, even in his imagination.

When he'd suggested the livestock parade at the Shiawassee County Fair, he knew she could be counted on to say
yes, even after he admitted, like a New Yorker who's never
seen the Statue of Liberty, that he'd never been to it. Nights
now, when they were home from the hospital after eating
someplace down on Main or Exchange, she'd go back to the
house with him and work for an hour on her book, which
she claimed to be making progress on at last—"thanks to
you," she'd said. He'd sit across from her, reading the Detroit papers (he'd never been able to stand the *Argus,* even
before it got drunk on Dewey) or a book she'd brought
home from Abner's. Now that Pop was in the hospital, she
stayed over most nights, upstairs, though once they'd gone
out to the garage for old time's sake, both of them laughing
over the idea, and so excited they'd practically tripped on
the back steps.

She liked doing it, not just for itself, the way it was with
Louise, but because it took her someplace else. She liked
him to talk at the beginning, not the filthy stuff that years
ago that girl from Kroger's had loved to hear, but hummings
and murmurs, which at first had made him feel like an engine, but then, when his murmurs changed, automatically, to
little whispered words, like "good" and "fine," he felt like a

kid, which was what she seemed to like best, judging from the sharpness with which she'd start taking in breath. It was then she'd tell him she felt crazy about him, at which point he'd stop murmuring and act his age. He'd rip out her last hairpin and squeeze it until it nearly broke the skin on his palm. He'd lick the rouge from her cheek and leave the spot redder than it had been before.

He'd broken things off with Louise, two weeks ago, the first Friday morning he could get up the nerve. She'd ripped up a few dozen of Walt's Taft-Hartley flyers and flung them in his face and called him a son of a bitch before she calmed down and, in her own words, took it like a man. She'd come by a couple of times since, asking questions about Anne and, with no sarcasm, offering advice: "Take a trip someplace, if only for a day. Be someplace where the only thing you know is each other. That's the way to get to know her."

The other night Louise had come by the hospital with Carl; she'd stayed here in the waiting room with Anne while the two men went in to see his father. He'd practically been jumping out of his skin the whole time, but he needn't have worried. Carl had focused completely on Gene, talking about the '37 strike as if Gene were really taking it in instead of looking up confused and angry.

Coming back out he'd heard Anne and Louise talking about him and what a good son he was and how Gene was too ornery to die. With one signal, communicated to him by a movement of her head as she and Carl were starting back for Flint, Louise gave Anne her seal of approval. Later at the house he considered telling Anne about her, about why it had been and how it was over, but he'd stopped short, because it wasn't something you told your girl—not even this one, who made no secret about having a small past of her own, and who would, in the middle of dinner, start guessing about the Fellers' sex life. "Jesus, Anne," he'd say with his mouth full of corn, and she would brighten up, enjoying this the same way she seemed to like the idea, when he was murmuring in bed, that she was the one leading the dance.

Gene had been asleep when they arrived a half hour ago, and there was little chance he would awaken before visiting hours ended, but the two of them, their nightly schedule established, lingered amidst the green linoleum and translucent glass cubes that divided the waiting room from the nurses' station. Anne read *Collier's,* barely realizing her right hand was in Jack's as she turned the magazine's pages with her left.

His rough, rumpled beauty brought forth something extra from her own smoother kind; she felt like the plain white egg she'd seen resting on mica chips in the window of a New York jeweler a couple of years ago. The egg's bland perfection was suddenly the more dazzling for its surroundings. And yet, as she and Jack walked together on Washington or Main, receiving the appreciative looks she liked and he didn't notice, she was aware of being the tougher customer, the one who, just the other day, when they were in Storrer's getting Gene a pair of pajamas for the hospital, wouldn't let the salesman get away with a nasty remark about Harry Truman. Jack knew all the party-supplied statistics and arguments, but when she tried to put forth a few of them second-hand, he turned red and started nudging her toward the socks counter, as if this weren't the time or place. "Anne, I've known that man since I was six." As often as not, she felt herself protecting him, from one kind of awkwardness or another—despite the physical command she enjoyed being under more every day, and despite his still-occasional attempts to shield her from things that were supposed to upset her, be they the doctor's details about pancreatic cancer or the state park service's best estimates of how long a seventeen-year-old boy might have survived in the woods.

They were waiting for Gene to die, of course. It was almost like a birth. If she weren't holding Jack's hand, she could picture him pacing this waiting room like an expectant father. It had been less than two months since *The Bishop's Wife*, but she had taken to imagining a future for them. A few years in Ann Arbor, with Jack going to school on the GI Bill?

Suddenly, not one siren, but two. Fifteen minutes ago they'd heard the hospital's red Cadillac ambulance pull out of the parking lot, and now it was returning, behind a police ambulance sounding the treble note in a frantic harmony. The head nurse went squeaking across the linoleum on her crepe soles, standing on tiptoe to get a better look through the window. Whatever it was, the commotion soon dissipated into the emergency room a floor below, while Jack and Anne resumed their pointless watching of the clock.

Within ten minutes, two groups began forming on the second floor, adults and young people, both of them distressed and smoking earnestly. Between the two and belonging to neither sat a short, thin fellow in a tan jacket who had his hand near his face, as if trying to conceal the fact that he'd just done some crying. It took Anne a moment to realize who he was.

"Billy?" She pointed him out to Jack before she got up and crossed the room. "What's going on?"

For a second he looked as if he wanted to hide behind the translucent glass. But once Billy started up, his narrative

ran with the same don't-let-them-interrupt-you drive as his
sales pitches.

"Bill Stone lost control of his Ford V-8 out at the Speedway. Actually, it isn't his, it belongs to some guy from Howell,
and it's a complete wreck now. Stone souped it up and drove
it in the first race. He busted through a pole, lost control of
the thing completely and sort of flew up into the grandstand.
He flipped over three times, must have gone a hundred feet
before he came to a stop. People got clipped and creamed
the whole way along, and one man wound up pinned
under it."

Anne winced, and let Jack, who'd come over to listen,
too, put his arm around her waist. Billy went on—"The
guy that got pinned has gone to the hospital in St. Johns
with a few of the others, but they brought at least six people
here—" until Jack interrupted him with a question.

"Why are *you* here?"

Billy looked at him, surprised that the current central
fact of his own life could elude anyone.

"It's Margaret. Her left ankle's broken and both her legs
are cut. You see, everybody was looking at the front-runners.
Stone's Ford was dead last. No one was paying any attention
to it. Nobody saw him coming." He paused for a second, trying to skip over the moments when Margaret and the
others were injured. "Stone walked away from it. He just
opened the door and got out. A few minutes after it happened some people were saying he'd been thrown clear, but
it didn't happen like that. He hung on. It was like watching
one of the bull riders at that rodeo down in New Buffalo
last spring. I saw him behind the wheel just before the
second flip."

"They should close that place down," said Anne. "There were those two drivers who got killed last month—"

"Tonight's card was a benefit for them! One guy's widow was there. She was talking to Bill Stone after he got out of his car. Miss Macmurray, they didn't even shut the place down *tonight*. They're running the rest of the card right now. Leo Kosecki's Chevrolet is in the feature race."

Jack asked Billy where Margaret's parents were.

"On their way home from Lansing. Somebody called them."

"Is Margaret calm?" Anne asked.

"I don't know," said Billy, with a look of wonderment at how she could be unaware of another central fact—namely, that he hadn't been with her. "She was at the race with a couple of her girlfriends. It must have been the first time she's gone out since the Dawn Patrol. I was sitting miles above her. I only saw her being put onto the stretcher. She was crying. I followed the ambulance on my bicycle."

What a miserable summer, Anne thought. "Have you had anything to eat?"

"I had some stuff at the Speedway. I'm not really hungry."

Anne was sure he wanted to cry, and that he wouldn't let himself do it in front of Jack Riley. She looked at Jack, not just to convey this reading of the situation with her eyes, but to see if she *could* convey it, like a test of the emergency broadcast system, or the sort of shortwave communication a man and woman didn't necessarily develop until they'd been together for years.

Jack took the hint. "I'll go downstairs and wait for the Fellers."

Once he'd left, Billy stood next to Anne, fingering the glass cubes and looking down at his high-top sneakers. "I didn't even want to go tonight, but one of my sisters told me she'd heard Margaret would be there with a couple of friends. I'd never been able to get her to go with me; I must've asked her a dozen times last summer. I knew I still wouldn't get a chance to talk to her tonight, and I didn't plan on bothering her, really—" He looked up at Anne, imploring her to believe him on this small point. "I just wanted to see her."

"You wanted to see her happy," said Anne. "Out doing normal things again."

Billy nodded, and asked, by the way, what she and Mr. Riley were here for tonight.

"Jack's father," said Anne, pointing to room 208. "He's very sick."

"Are you two going to get married?"

Refreshed by the question's childish good sense, Anne brushed one of the freckled cheeks onto which Billy had still not permitted tears to fall. "Let's go find Margaret," she said. "Before her parents get here."

"Will the doctors let us in?" He'd already started walking.

"We'll get in."

A floor below, away from some crying women in sleeveless dresses, and some men who didn't realize they were stroking their young sons' crew-cut hair, the eight injured spectators who had been brought to Owosso Memorial were being attended to by as many doctors and nurses as could be called in for an extra shift. "When you think about it," went the relieved refrain, "it was a miracle." And Anne supposed it had been. No one else had gotten hurt as badly as that man taken to St. Johns, and someone was saying even he might pull through. She threaded her way through the emergency room and down the first-floor corridor, noticing a boy and girl in matching arm slings, as if they'd gotten themselves up for a costume party; one doctor was explaining to an unconvinced father that his daughter's broken collarbone was not the end of the world.

Through the half-open door of an examination room, Anne and Billy spotted Margaret sitting up. Her left leg, swollen but clean, was propped up on a chair back.

It was such a ladylike injury, Margaret thought. Instead of X-rays, she might be waiting for someone to fling his cape over a mud puddle. She could also see in the mirror that she looked about thirteen: along with color, the panic and pain had drained years from her face. But she was calm, clear-eyed, as if she'd finally woken from a dream and admitted, once and for all, that no magical boy or message was going to fly through her window and say that all was well. If a hot rod could bowl twenty people over like a pair of strikes, what kind of fiery crater must a plane falling from the sky have made? How thin *was* the rope attaching us to this world? What could she cling to? She shook off a chill and slid her hand down the waxy paper on the examining table.

"Margaret, I'm so sorry."

She looked up at the sound of Anne's voice, and upon seeing Billy she burst into tears.

"I'm sorry, too." She was looking at him as she said the words.

Speechless, he turned to Anne for some sort of permission, before taking the few steps left to reach Margaret and put his arm, very gently, around her shoulders, his shaking thumb coming to rest upon her miraculously unbroken collarbone.

"If you're okay by next week, do you want to go to the Capitol? The picture's going to have Marlene Dietrich." In sudden alarm, not knowing what transformations the month had effected, he added a question: "Is she still your favorite? If you're in a wheelchair, I can push."

Margaret, through her tears, kissed his hand and said that she would love that.

EIGHT

August 24 – September 28

LABOR DAY BEGAN ITS APPROACH WITH PEOPLE HOPING THAT a thunderstorm might sweep away the dog days gripping Owosso and much of the country. Twenty Michiganders had died from the heat, and locally several events preyed on already tired nerves. There were no further mishaps at the Speedway, but up near the country club a child's birthday party ended with one little girl's being run over and killed. Over in Vernon a diagnosis confirmed the rumor that two kids had come down with polio.

The campaign needed a cloudburst, too. President Truman was supposed to arrive in Detroit for a holiday rally in Cadillac Square. His speech, some said, would finally provoke Dewey to step outside and mix things up, but fresh evidence of the challenger's imperturbability continued to make news. On August 24, when the temperature reached ninety-eight degrees, Dewey brought his two sons to Yankee Stadium and went on from there to his office in the Roosevelt Hotel for some "personal business." Just watching him made one feel cooler; even Norman Thomas was forecasting his victory.

The peacetime draft arrived on the thirtieth, and Billy Grimes, who would turn eighteen before the year was out, reported to the Owosso Armory with Margaret's brother, Jim, to register. Though her son had only just gotten back from his travels and would be returning to Dartmouth in another two weeks, Carol Feller banished her anxieties about Berlin to make the boys a big breakfast amidst the usual morning bustle. Peter Cox was at her table, too, conferring with Harold about someone's lawsuit against the Speedway.

Billy watched the smooth young attorney without envy. After all, here *he* was, back in his girl's kitchen, while Peter had lost any chance of success with Anne Macmurray. According to Margaret, who had regained enough interest in life to look out her window, there were nights when Anne never made it all the way home from Jack Riley's house down on Williams. Billy was encouraged to hear her report this behavior with excited approval: Margaret's admiration for Miss Macmurray was so thorough, she might be inclined to imitate her in this sphere of activity.

Outside the Armory the Methodist minister once again stood with his 11-11-11-11-11 tornado. Inside, approaching the registration table, Billy noted the name HERRICK, TIMOTHY L., just a few below his own on the ledger. What would they mark in the box at the end of the day? AWOL? That would actually be sort of swell. It would seem as if Tim had *today* made one of those defiant gestures that used to let him feel alive. But Billy knew the only reason they hadn't drawn a line through Tim's name was its being too soon to declare him "legally" what everyone knew he was, which was dead.

Seeing their names together, the way they had traveled alphabetically since the two of them started grade school, made it seem, for a last moment, impossible that they wouldn't be sharing whatever lay ahead, even fighting their way toward Berlin. They had, in a way, shared even Margaret. She had returned to Billy as if waking up from a dream, and been more affectionate these last two weeks than in all the years he'd known her. Yet he could never rid himself of the feeling that she remained, in some way, Tim's girl, in a world beyond this one, where Tim was dead and wouldn't relinquish her.

If Tim and Margaret had gone all the way—something he could not bring himself to ask or imagine—then she *was* still Tim's girl, at least until the two of them, he and Margaret, finally made love to each other. Which made the need for that to happen even greater than the biological imperative conceded by *The Boy Scout Handbook*.

In the meantime, Margaret would be the one to share Berlin with him. On Friday night, as the holiday weekend began, the two of them watched Marlene Dietrich and John Lund romance their way through the rubble of the German capital. As it happened, Margaret did not require a wheelchair; she had already gone from crutches to a cane. With her ankle still in a cast, she had to take Billy's arm when they got out of her father's Chevrolet on Main Street. She leaned on him more heavily than she needed to, and once they took their seats he stroked her hair as if she had accomplished something heroic by her journey from the curb. She spent almost the whole movie with her head on his shoulder, and to his astonished delight her whispered commentary showed a preference for Jean Arthur, as the no-nonsense Congresswoman Frost, there in occupied Germany to investigate looseness and corruption, over Dietrich, the black-marketeering *femme fatale* who sang at the cabaret. Billy had always loved that scratchy little voice Jean Arthur had; it came up like ice-cream soda through a straw, a little sting in its sweetness. And in this movie she was even a Republican.

Margaret had seen some sort of light. Two months ago she had been mooning over that mass murderer, but tonight, on the way down Washington Street in the car, when she'd mentioned Robert Mitchum's arrest for dope she'd crinkled her nose in disgust. Billy wasn't going to say he told her so, because when she'd been wrapped up in her dream of Tim he couldn't tell her anything. He preferred to think that she'd been brought to her senses by suffering. Both of them had; they were now wise beyond their years. All last night and this morning, seven hundred of their fellow students had lined up outside Owosso High, trying to make sure they'd be assigned one of the second-floor lockers for the coming school year. By the time the sun came up, a window had been broken and the principal called the cops—all because everyone said you didn't rate if you had to lock on the first floor. He and Margaret not only didn't bother to camp out with everybody else, they just shook their heads when one of Margaret's friends told them about the melee. And, no, they weren't interested in taking a couple of the Wallace buttons some of the kids had gotten hold of—as if wearing one would be such a big shock to their parents. The two of them were grown up now. They'd be ready to blow this town in a year. Maybe, before they did, they'd even skip the prom.

. . .

S TANDING AT THE SIDE OF THE RAIL CAR, AROUND THE COR-
ner from its rear platform, Jack couldn't see Harry Truman,
but he was close enough to hear him without the microphone: "I understand in your state college out here the veterans are sleeping three deep in a gymnasium, and that
there was a time when your Republican city council here in
Lansing could have helped remedy that situation. They decided not to do it!" Jack had driven to Lansing two hours ago
and was waiting to board the train and ride with the President from here to Detroit to Hamtramck to Pontiac and finally Flint, where he would get off and find Anne. She'd
promised to be standing by the fourth post of the railing
around the grass in the park, where Truman would speak
after a short drive from the station.

He and Walt had gotten the call last Friday from
Reuther's own office: one of them could be part of the UAW
delegation on the train. It didn't seem fair—given everything Walt had been doing against Taft-Hartley, while he'd
been distracted by his father and Anne—but Walt insisted
they toss a nickel. Jack picked the buffalo side, which landed
face up, so here he was with, believe it or not, his heart
pounding, thinking about how eight hours from now he
might be telling his girl he'd exchanged a couple of words
with the President of the United States.

Truman himself seemed unjustifiably calm. He urged
everyone to register and make sure they made it to the polls
on November 2—reminding them, as had become his habit,
that they deserved whatever they got if they didn't. But having said that, he declared, "I shall be perfectly satisfied with

the result. I know what that result will be," as if he knew something they didn't. A minute later the train was off on its two-and-a-half-hour run to Detroit. For most of it Jack had to stand, jammed in with an army of small-town mayors, AF of L officials, newspaper reporters and an actual Medal of Honor winner who'd come aboard at Grand Rapids. It was a hot, chaotic ride, the way the press boys said it would be for the whole two months after September 17, when the "whistlestop" campaign would pull out of Washington in earnest. Toledo was the last town on today's schedule, and a guy from the *Blade* predicted "Harry'll be coming onto that platform like a cuckoo out of a clock" until Election Day.

According to one reporter used to making counts, there were 300,000 people in Cadillac Square by 1:30. He said his Republican publisher would see that the figure got edited down to 150,000, but you could trust him: he'd specialized in this kind of thing from war-bond rallies to V-J Day, and there were 300,000 people out there. Even when the minor politicians warming up the crowd couldn't get it to cheer, the hum of people's voices gave the square the sound of another world. It reminded Jack of the '37 strike, when he'd stood behind the ropes with his mother and noticed this look of anticipation on all the women and even the kids. Today's crowd was in a lighter mood, of course, but there was still this look of waiting to be fed, if only a message or a war cry instead of the actual food they'd been worrying about eleven years ago.

He stepped off the train clutching the pass that would let him back on, and worked his way around the end, where at 1:40 he caught his first glimpse of Truman. The President emerged from the car, through the blue curtains, and started talking just as soon as his spectacles caught the sunlight. "As you know, I speak plainly sometimes. In fact, I speak bluntly sometimes. I am going to speak plainly and bluntly today." No, he wasn't the rooster they liked to compare him to, and he wasn't the cuckoo in a clock; but he did, Jack thought, seem half machine. It was as if some engine down in his stomach kept feeding him the words, firing them out of his mouth like rivets. Anybody in this crowd who'd spent his life hooked up to a line, picking up and bolting and setting down whatever the belt drove past, until he felt he was part of the mechanism, so connected to it he had trouble dreaming about anything else, had to feel connected to Harry right now, if only in the "subconscious," to use that word Anne liked.

This was the second time Jack had ever seen Reuther, who looked more like a politician, or even a college professor, than Truman. He just stood there listening, quietly holding his hat, probably still wearing bandages under the suit. Jack wondered about the size of the hole the shotgun had put into him, but he wondered for only a moment; you might be able to take your eyes off Harry, but you couldn't take your ears off him. "You all remember how a Democratic administration turned the greatest depression in history into the most prosperous era the country has ever seen!"

While Jack pounded his palms together with everyone else, a cold trickle of doubt leaked into his belief in all that. Hadn't a lot of people the Rileys knew been worse off in '37, after a whole term of FDR, than they'd been at the beginning of '33? Even Pop might admit that. Maybe it *was* only the war that turned things around. No, he thought, still clapping, pulverizing the heresy between his hands: today he was proud and excited to be union, and anyway, as people never remembered to ask themselves, how much worse might '37 have been after another four years of Hoover?

"Remember that the reactionary of today is a shrewd man. He is in many ways much shrewder than the reactionaries of the twenties. He is a man with a calculating machine where his heart ought to be!" They would lose the election, but they might at least carry Michigan. Seeing all the crowds along the tracks, you wondered how they could lose it. What kind of place *was* Owosso, anyway? How could it be part of a state full of towns like Hamtramck, where the train arrived for a quick stop at 2:45, just long enough for Truman to tell the crowd: "I understand that you are 97 percent Democratic. Now I wonder what's the matter with that other 3 percent? See what you can do about that in November!" It was practically the same in Pontiac, where the President told his supporters that voting the Republicans in for no other reason than that they'd been out for sixteen years would be like going back to making buggies because four decades had passed since they started turning out automobiles. Keeping up his attack on Capitol Hill, he laid claim to "the greatest veto record in the history of Congress except for Grover Cleveland," a fact Jack reminded himself to pass on to Horace Sinclair, the only person he could think of likely to be impressed by it.

It was 7:00 before the train pulled into Flint station and Jack Riley met the President of the United States. He'd been assigned to a bus three vehicles behind Truman's car, but before the motorcade started off a state party official matched his lapel tag to his name on a list and brought him to a line of twenty local people standing by the limousine's open door. Truman was shaking everyone's hand with the regularity of a loom.

"Son," he said, giving one quick pump to Jack's arm. Jack had several times rehearsed what would be his own four words should this occasion arise, but before the sounds of "Good luck, Mr. President" could reach his lips, Truman was two men further down the line, snapping off a salute to the World War I vet who headed up the local VFW chapter.

Thirty thousand people packed the park, but Anne was exactly where she said she'd be, in her long skirt and sleeveless white blouse. Her hair was loose, the way he'd been hoping to see it as he pictured this moment all morning and afternoon. She looked as natural to the spot as she ever could have to Darien.

"Anne!"

She heard him on the first shout, and though she couldn't see him, she waved the TRUMAN-BARKLEY pennant she'd bought an hour ago from a grittier, city version of Billy Grimes.

"Stay where you are!" he cried. "I'll come to you!" He excused his way through the twelve-deep crowd standing between them, his apologies lost in the shouts of approval that had already commenced for Truman, who was rattling through reminders of labor's contribution to the war. It was when the President attacked the next piece of reactionary "poppycock" that Jack reached Anne, and kissed her, and felt richer than any of the Republicans profiting from the "rich man's tax bill," felt in fact that he had robbed them of one fabulous prize that should have been their own.

"I shook his hand," he said, and they kissed again. Anne heard the President of the United States talk about choosing hope over fear, as she kissed Jack's neck and twirled two of those little stalks of hair that were sticking up in the summer heat. The roaring and rhetoric made her want to go out and post the minimum wage in factories, attend discussions of the Four Freedoms with dark-skinned delegates to the U.N. It was only further proof that what had happened between her and Jack was the real thing.

"The speech was a little different in every town," he said.

"Did you get a picture?"

"A CIO guy I knew was taking some at the train station. I think I'm in one of them; I can call him up."

"You're sunburned."

"I know. I was only off the train for an hour at a time, but I can feel it."

"I've been here since three-thirty. The car is miles away."

"How was Pop?"

"I went up to his room when I went over to get the car." Gene Riley was out of the hospital, doped up and in his own bed, at least for a while. A nurse came in the daytime, but Jack felt bad about all Anne was doing to help, each evening and early every morning.

"Was he awake?"

"On and off. I put the radio on in his room. The rally was just getting started in Detroit. I told him you were there."

"Did he get it?"

"Even better. He thought *he* was there, too."

PETER HAD COVERED THE TWO MONTHS' RENT ON HIS CAM-paign office in the Matthews Building with a check his mother sent from Reno. He was paying his one devoted staffer, Mrs. Bruce, whose husband had just retired from Johnson Controls, out of his own pocket. Given her ardor for his prospects and the Republican cause, he probably could have gotten her as a volunteer. When she wasn't rolling envelopes through the old Underwood he'd borrowed from the basement of Feller, Terry & Nast, she was either gazing at his four-color campaign poster or staring out at the Dewey birthplace.

A month from now he would need extra help to tack up signs and pass out leaflets. Billy Grimes would be perfect, but for the foreseeable future Al Jackson had full use of his after-school services. There was another reason, too, why Billy couldn't join the Cox campaign. Apparently, Margaret Feller didn't share her friends' estimation of the candidate's dreaminess. Or so Carol Feller had tactfully hinted, while explaining how Billy wasn't doing anything these days that might risk expulsion from his paradise regained.

"Oh, you're just exactly right," said Mrs. Bruce, as she banged on the Underwood. She was taking down Peter's reply to the President's Detroit speech, which he had to get to the *Argus* before four o'clock. He should have done this days ago, but he'd been hoping to play off a reply from on high, and the Dewey camp's rejoinder to Truman had been less than thundering. It had even been less than personal. On Tuesday night, Harold Stassen, the governor's opponent in the primaries, acted as his surrogate in Detroit, giving a nationwide radio address from the Masonic Temple there. Dewey listened in "with great interest" from his Pawling, New York farm, but otherwise—said a spokesman—had no comment. Peter had heard the speech here in the office with Mrs. Bruce, the two of them sorting voter lists as she nodded in time to each burst of applause from Detroit.

"Okay, let's see now. 'And keeping reporters from the *Argus* and WOAP off the campaign train, despite earlier assurances that they could ride along with everyone else, only added' . . . how about . . . 'undemocratic insult to the economic injury Mr. Truman has already done the state.' That ought to do it."

"Oh, yes," said Mrs. Bruce, who hit the keys with an aggression she hoped would be worthy of the point. "But do you really want to begin that sentence with a conjunction?"

"I'll leave that up to you, Mrs. Bruce. I've got to get going."

"Are you going to be in the picture?" The *March of Time* was back in Owosso, filming a short that would be shown in theatres after Dewey's election, and a rumor of the shooting schedule had made its way through town. The cameramen should be setting up in front of Annie Dewey's about now, and Mrs. Bruce couldn't imagine Peter Cox having any other destination.

Too vain to tell her no one had requested to film him, he settled for asking, as generously as he could manage, "Are you sure you don't want to come along?"

"Oh, I couldn't," said Mrs. Bruce, inserting a fresh sheet of stationery into the Underwood. "I've got to make this perfect by four o'clock." She couldn't tell him that her own best chance of getting into the film lay in staying here and waving from the window when the crew reached the Dewey birthplace an hour from now. Surely one of the cameramen would, what was that word, "pan" across the street to catch her standing between the two posters that filled the second-story window, one of Governor Dewey and the other of Mr. Cox—she didn't know who was handsomer. Mr. Bruce had laughed when she confessed her hope of playing some small female role along the Dewey Walk next spring; it would be even worse to look overeager about the newsreel and have Mr. Cox think her ridiculous.

"Thank you, Mrs. Bruce. My conjunctions are equally grateful, I'm sure."

The clock on top of City Hall said five minutes to three. Turning north up Water Street, Peter figured he had enough time to get there: he couldn't imagine the *March of Time* letting its cameras roll before the grammar schools at each end of Oliver Street disgorged a horde of cycling kiddies to swell the huzzahing throng.

The throng's housewives, being kept back by Chief Rice himself, already stood three deep at the curb, trampling cables as they watched the sound man hiding a boom mike behind the porch's latticework for when Annie Dewey emerged to wave and speak whatever piece she'd prepared.

Was there no female dogsbody to whom Peter could flash a smile and introduce himself, giving her the photogenic idea of having Mrs. D. pose with this other bright hope of Owosso, a taller, better-looking surrogate for her unavoidably absent son? The newsreel's postelection premiere meant the picture wouldn't do him any good, but a word or two with Mrs. Dewey, unmediated by that Cerberus Mr. Valentine, still might. Alas, there was no girl around to put him in the picture. He was as far outside the frame as he'd imagined himself while looking at the bookshop window.

"Dewey! Dewey! Dewey!" the housewives chanted, before their cycling progeny took up the cry. Do we *what*, he wanted to ask. Do we barge across the lawn and just shake her hand? It wasn't possible. As soon as she emerged, the director, if you could call a newsreel shooter that, sat her down on the porch's striped glider. She was with a woman about the governor's age. (Miss Liberty of 1909 from the *Argus*'s pages? All grown up?) Whatever the First-Mother-to-be was saying remained inaudible to the sidewalk audience; the microphone was designed to record, not project. But Peter could see how relaxed she was in her print dress. The steel specs and tightly waved hair belied the way she let the seat glide a little, back and forth, as she answered the man's questions.

And then, after less than two minutes, she was gone, the way poor Bess Truman was going to be all fall, snatched back inside after being dragged out onto the caboose's platform to offer her dour wave. The microphone came down from behind the latticework, and the kids positioned their bicycles to chase the big lettered truck as soon as it took off for the next shot. The housewives began to disperse, and with a feeling of futility Peter took from his pockets some LEADERSHIP FOR THE FIFTIES flyers. If he accomplished nothing else this afternoon, he would get rid of them.

"Are these about the Dewey Walk?" asked a plump redhead trying to keep a baby bottle inside junior's mouth.

"Actually, they're—"

"Oh," she said, disappointed. "Maybe you should try my friend over there." She shifted the baby to her other shoulder and started for home.

"Here," said Peter to the friend. "Take 'em all. If you know anybody you think may be interested, I'd appreciate your passing them along."

He couldn't get away from here fast enough, but his first steps east brought only more annoyance. There in front of the Comstock Apartments sat Riley's fat green Ford, a battered dowager compared to the sweet little debutante Peter had left parked behind the Matthews Building. Three o'clock and the guy was already at her apartment, home from Flint for the day. Peter knew all about the sick father, but what good did this hovering do? If you asked him, it was morbid. She ought to—

"Turn around and say hello. Only don't hit me with your nose."

"Where did you come from? And what's wrong with my nose?"

"It's growing." Anne read from his campaign flyer: " . . . 'will implement state programs to complement President Dewey's national ones on behalf of housing for veterans.' You've made that poor gal who handed me this an accomplice to libel."

"Do you want to hear Dewey's record in New York on housing?"

"No."

"Good. Tell me where you're coming from instead."

"Having tea with Mrs. George Dewey."

"Son of a bitch. Sorry. How did you get in there?"

"Carol brought me. A call for tea-drinking lady extras went out yesterday."

He studied her expression. It was taking its pleasure not from the dousing of spotlight it had had, but from the small uniqueness of the event. She looked as if she'd managed to speak with the man who once ran that carousel not too far from the coffin factory.

"What's she like?" he asked.

"A hell of a character, to quote my dad. Have you noticed how many of the older people in this town *are*? Her, the poor colonel you've neglected, Jack's dad. Do you think we've lost something, I mean all the ones in our genera—"

"What did she say?"

"Well, pardon me for thinking big. She asked me what was selling well, so I told her. Then she asked if I'd read the latest James Gould Cozzens, and I said no, and she fixed me with a look."

"What sort of look?"

"The sort that said, 'You call yourself a bookseller?' "

They reached Riley's car. "We can drop you home," Anne offered. "Jack's waiting inside. Just let me go and rescue him from Mrs. Wagner. I'm supposed to cook an early dinner and then put in a couple of extra hours at the shop, while he's at the hospital." Gene had been brought back there yesterday.

Riley reemerged with her almost instantly. Was he that eager to be sprung from the landlady, or did Anne already have him trained? Maybe he had her trained, too. His shirt was better pressed than Peter's own, and he certainly hadn't gotten it done at Suber's.

"Hi, Peter."

"How are you." It was a two-door, and it made more sense for him to ride the five blocks up front, but he got into the back seat as if he knew that was his place.

"Jack was on the President's train Monday. Tell him about it, honey."

Monitoring the rearview mirror, Peter watched Jack smile at her. "It was a nice little piece of history. A very little one, I guess."

"I would have enjoyed reading more about it," said Peter. "People back here didn't see much beyond what the

AP had. The Democrats blocked the *Argus* and WOAP guys from getting on at Grand Rapids."

"I don't know anything about that," said Jack, honking his horn at a straggling cyclist. Anne helped the kid out with a they-went-thataway gesture, before saying, "Yes, Peter. I heard that. And do you know what I think?"

"Tell me," he said, leaning forward between the two of them.

"I say big deal. Dewey has practically every newspaper in the country endorsing him, and don't tell me *they're* going to cover this campaign fairly. Why shouldn't a little unfairness on the other side even things out? And don't go giving me any lectures about what we fought the war for."

"Are your UAW boys staying in line, Jack? Wallace gave it to them pretty hard the other day."

"Would it make you happy if they voted for him?"

"It wouldn't make *me* happy," said Anne, turning back toward Peter. "Even *you've* got to admit Truman isn't afraid to displease his friends when he's got to. Who was ready to draft the railroad strikers last year?"

"Oh, he understands intimidation all right. Jack, how many UAW workers had to pay the three-dollar fine for not showing up in Detroit on Monday?"

"Nobody had to pay three cents," said Jack, making a sharp right onto Park Street.

"It seems to me," Anne added, "the only one who's in-timidated is Dewey. Hiding behind Stassen!" As soon as the car stopped, she got out and pushed the front seat forward. "You're home, Peter."

"Hardly," he answered. "But thanks for the lift. You, too, Jack."

The tires didn't quite screech, but the happy couple were on their way toward Williams Street before he could add a good-bye wave.

He hadn't been walking here in the first place, and as soon as they turned the corner, Peter doubled back up Park and across Oliver toward his original destination, the gabled house between Hickory and Oak. Though September was proving almost as hot as August, there was no sign of life or iced tea on the open porch. He went up the front walk, glancing at each curtained window, thinking how stifling it had to be in there. The heavy green drapes of the parlor were parted a couple of inches at most, just far enough for him to get a look inside. He called through them: "Colonel, this will never do."

Horace roused himself from what he still called his afternoon "doze," though that was now just one of three or four long naps.

"Are you still hounding me?"

Peter let himself in and switched on a light, sure that the pointless expense of electricity would agitate the old man less than opening the curtains onto the outside world. "Why the terrible mood?"

Horace picked up the paper Billy Grimes had delivered yesterday afternoon. POLLING OUTFIT SUSPENDS WORK ON PRESIDENTIAL RACE, ran the offending headline. Elmo Roper had announced he would not keep asking people a question whose answer they had already made clear.

"Don't worry, Colonel. I can still get you plenty of information. Dewey takes his own polls."

"That's supposed to make me feel better!"

"At some point, Colonel, you're going to tell me if all

this upset is really about just papier-mâché and paint. I have a feeling it isn't."

This overture only further inflamed Horace. "I am too old for psychiatry, and you are too young to try and pretend you're my friend. As if friends did one any good!"

"Who's let you down?"

"In particular, my friend Wright George, who grew up a few streets from here before he went east. I've invited him for a visit, but he's full of excuses." Horace declined to elaborate. He merely turned and pointed to a letter, apparently as offensive as the *Argus*, on the dining-room table. It lay by the uncleared remains of some roast chicken on a plate. Peter looked at the old man in profile, noting the new grayness and sag to his jowls. He had declined noticeably since their last visit.

"I imagine you've been posing for the cameras," Horace said.

"Doing my damnedest to. But I can't get at *her*. It's like getting an audience with Queen Mary."

"Queen Mary—another woman made of more outstanding stuff than her son."

"Those two don't even speak."

"Whereas Annie Dewey and the young governor *do*. Don't think I don't know what you're trying to bring up again. Well, it so happens I walked Mrs. Dewey home from church on Sunday."

"Did you now?" said Peter, pouring himself some of the syrupy cordial. He took a seat behind the dining-room table, at a distance comfortable to the old man's farsighted eyes. "And what came up in conversation?"

"The 'Dewey Walk,'" said Horace, puckering the words as insipidly as he could.

"What did she say?"

"Whatever it was, she said it between herself and me."

"Colonel, a few years ago when I was on the staff of good old Captain Harry Butcher, I was probably the best man in London at keeping secr—"

"She says it's the most damned fool idea she's ever heard of!" Horace seemed to look at the remark he'd unloosed, as if it stood suspended in the air for him to measure whatever hope it held.

"That should make you happy," said Peter.

"It does not," replied Horace. "Because she clearly won't say a public word about it. Between now and the election she's not going to do a thing to discourage anybody, anywhere, who's pushing her son. By the time she's ready to speak up, the thing will be half built."

"You must have talked about something else as well."

"Yes, we did, Mr. Cox. About your fondest desire. That little campaign visit you think will pump up your majority. Now does that make *you* happy? I suggested it to her as a 'wonderful' idea." More puckering, on the order of "Dewey Walk."

"Her reply?"

" 'Tom's his own law.' " He could see Peter's response coming and waved it off. "You would have been proud of me, Mr. Cox. I argued, 'Surely *you've* got special influence with him.' "

"Well, she must. Mustn't she?"

"I don't have the slightest idea. Now, look, Mr. Cox, I *mentioned* it. Are you going to keep harassing me? Like another bad memory?"

No, he'd finished his pitch, and even that wasn't what had really brought him here. It was the letter from Reno, and his *own* bad memories of a father who, as the years went by, could barely speak to him, let alone yell. Peter liked this old man's bark, and wanted to know about the bite: the one the colonel had given life, and the one life was still taking out of his hide. But most of all he wanted to know what real, remembered passion kept pumping out all that uxorious tribute. What sort of union could stay unriven by all except death?

"Tell me about *her*, Colonel." Peter was pointing to the portrait of the late Mrs. Sinclair.

ONE DAY BEFORE THE END OF SUMMER, WHAT SEEMED THE first decent breeze of the season came through the trees of Saint Paul's Roman Catholic cemetery at the end of South Chipman. Two graves stood open, one of them fully dug and ready to receive a coffin, the other just barely begun, temporarily abandoned by the workmen in deference to the feelings of those gathered for a funeral at the first.

Anne Macmurray looked over toward the unready plot. Stuck in the dried-out ground at its border was a pitchfork. She nudged Jack. He looked at it and smiled, recalling their argument last night, as the wake wound down and the Rileys mixed reminiscences with Pat-and-Mike jokes. The conversation had turned to politics, with Jack saying he didn't think Truman should have accused Dewey of "sticking a pitchfork in the farmer's back." The President had gotten carried away at the National Plowing Contest in Dexter, Iowa. But a Riley cousin who grew corn in Fountain County, Indiana, begged to differ with Johnny. If he'd been around there in the thirties, he wouldn't mince words either. Jack, in the darker of his two suits, what he called his negotiating outfit, said it did Truman no good to sound like the worst hotheads in the CIO. When Anne took the cousin's side and started teasing him, the rest of the Rileys had felt confirmed in their feeling that this girl was all right.

Throughout the quick prayers that preceded the lowering of Gene's body, the pitchfork stood at macabre attention. Anne kept to a polite place in the second row, behind the brothers and sisters who had come back to town, even though her favorite among them, Lorraine, had for two days already been calling her "Annie" and treating her like one of the family. "Thanks for all you did for my dad," she'd said, handing her a little pin for a present, as matter-of-factly as if she'd brought a side dish over for supper. Anne wondered what Jack had written or said to her over the telephone, but the Rileys were so transparent she could see her reviews posted on their faces.

As the priest went through the last words of the Apostles' Creed, Jack felt Anne squeeze his hand from behind. He was feeling oddly happy. The last time he'd been on these grounds had been the morning they'd buried his mother. Today he could barely remember that. He felt as if Gene had finally gotten a hard-earned vacation from his pain, and that everyone here was full of fine, honest feeling—glossing over Gene's faults, to be sure, but more natural and even festive than people were on those union picnics he never could stand. Mixed into the line of family and old friends (this was the first time he'd ever seen Louise in a hat) were a half dozen people who'd turned out for Anne, which made him wonder, pleasurably, what she'd been telling them about him these last three months. The

Fellers had come, along with Margaret and Billy Grimes, like in-laws from another state, a prosperous branch of the family you only saw at funerals and weddings. It was decent of Frank Sherwood to skip a couple of classes and show up; and if Peter Cox had decided to do him a favor by staying away, he was grateful for that, too.

"I'm sorry for you," said Jane Herrick with much-practiced dignity. He barely knew her by sight, and wondered what had brought her out. The First War had ended before Gene even finished training for it. Horace Sinclair, still wearing the Truman button Jack had given him, shuffled slowly through the line, his elbow cradled by Mrs. Goldstone, who had driven him here. *"You'll* be needing dinners for a little while," she said to Jack, her eyes bright with kindness and what he could still recognize as Depression fear: she'd started cooking for other people when the Owosso Sugar Company closed in '34. "I can bring you things for a week or so. How about that?"

"Thanks," he said in the same automatic way he'd been saying it for three days, waiting for this strangely enjoyable party to come to an end, so he could at last, and for the first time ever, be alone with Anne.

Walt Carroll and two other guys from the office were bringing up the rear. Walt told him to take his time coming back, but Jack insisted he'd be in on Wednesday. He still felt bad about having won the toss for the Labor Day train.

People had begun to walk toward their cars. The body, by prior agreement, would be lowered outside everybody's presence. Anne came forward and threaded her arm through Jack's, pointing to a couple he at first didn't recognize. From the back they appeared to be making hesitant conversation, maybe one of them offering the other a lift; as they set off together, he realized that the two thin figures were Frank Sherwood and Jane Herrick.

"Now what is that about?" Anne whispered.

He looked at her and didn't answer. He was seeing only her *interest* in it, the way she was adding it up, figuring it out, not for gossip's sake, but to understand some piece of the world she hadn't understood before. And while she watched Frank and Mrs. Herrick, she didn't worry about anyone watching her. He'd never met a girl who cared less about being looked at—or not looked at. Or who could take a compliment with less fuss.

"Will you marry me?" he asked. "I know this isn't the place, I know it's ridiculous, but—"

She looked away for a second, back toward all the rows of headstones, newly carved or weatherbeaten: the men and women mated for life and now eternity; the babies of another time, dead the year they were born; long-lived maiden aunts buried with their parents, the dates so strangely aligned it took a visitor a few seconds to sort out the blood ties; the boys who'd gone down into the ground, for a second time, as Jane Herrick listened to "Taps"; the dozens of men who, right in this town, had built the caskets they lay in.

"There's nothing wrong with this place, Jack. Yes, I'll marry you."

HE FELT AS IF HE'D DRIVEN OVER FROM NEW HAVEN ON A date, and the desk clerk at this dude ranch outside Reno were a dormitory matron at Vassar. He hadn't been allowed what she called "up," though all the rooms were spread out in two big one-story buildings, like giant versions of Al Jackson's house.

His mother had come into the lounge looking wonderful, a new jangle of turquoise on her wrist, her hair freshly silvered by the sun. They each had a martini resting on the wagon-wheel table, and she was leafing through three issues of the *Argus* that Mrs. Bruce had airmailed him.

"Oh, there's your name, dear." She'd found the small item about a debate he'd been in before a government club at the Corunna high school. "Right next to this article about the Dewey boardwalk, or whatever it is. COUNCIL TO VOTE OCT. 7. You mentioned that to me up on Mackinac. You're for it, if I recall."

"Yes."

"It must be good politics."

"Yeah," said Peter, impatiently.

Lucy Cox continued reading aloud, delighted by the project's comical controversies, like the question of whether space should be left on the east bank, south of, say, the high school, so that depictions of the Dewey administration's achievements could be added to representations of the candidate's rise. She finished an inch of her drink before putting the paper down.

"Peter," she finally said. "Exactly why are you here? I could scarcely believe it when I got your call from town."

"Well, Mother, I could scarcely believe it when I got your letter from 'town.' That Reno postmark was something of a shock."

"My letter was perfectly straightforward."

"Exactly, Mother. As if this were all routine. *Why?*"

"Why not?"

"No, Mother. That may have been the question for the last fifteen years. The question now is *why*."

"Peter, this litigious style doesn't suit us."

"It's appropriate. I don't want to play word games. I'm sick of playing them with girls, let alone my own mother."

"A special girl?"

"Answer my question."

She lifted her purse from its place between two spokes of the wagon wheel, and extracted a snapshot. "I found this a couple of months ago. Not long before I last saw you."

"Father," he said. "From about—"

"Nineteen-thirty-three. September."

"So?"

"Look at the expression."

"Happiness."

"*Perfect* happiness. It was taken a few weeks after he met her."

"Met whom?"

"The *girlfriend*. Oh, please, Peter."

He spun the wagon wheel about forty degrees. "I suppose I've always guessed that." He paused before raising his voice. "So you're here because fifteen years later you're angry all over again."

"No, I'm here because fifteen years later I've stopped being angry. When I saw that picture I stopped being angry *for the first time*. All I could see and remember was his perfect happiness, which I destroyed. Believe me, when I got through with the two of them, there was nothing left. Of course, I didn't figure on there being nothing left of me, either."

"That's not true, Mother."

"Of course it is. Now stop interrupting me. I'm giving you your money's worth. When I saw that picture, I was enthralled. I wanted that happiness restored."

"Father's long since forgiven you, I'm sure."

"Why should he? I haven't forgiven him. Peter, I'm not talking about *his* happiness. I'm talking about *mine.* I want to be happy. I've spent fifteen years being victorious. A headless, winged victory. It is September twenty-eighth, 1948, Peter. I am fifty-nine years old, and I want to be happy."

The possibility that his mother might cry, or that her eyes might at least, however briefly, glisten, seemed to him as shocking as the idea of the Winged Victory itself flying down the steps of the Louvre.

In her more familiar, theatrical voice, Lucy Cox came to his rescue. "Do you know who's enchanting?"

"Who?" asked Peter. Yes, he wanted to talk about Anne. How impressive Mother had found her on Mackinac. What an unusual beauty she had. How he must have her at all costs—even some gesture as bold as Mrs. Cox's own Reno venture.

"Senator Barkley."

"Christ, Mother, if you tell me *you're* for Truman—"

"Don't be ridiculous. I'm going to need a sound economy in which to shelter my alimony. But I *like* the man. He keeps up this cheerful front when all the while he's desperately lonely. You can see it in every photograph. He'd rather have a new wife than this ridiculous job he's running for."

Peter said nothing.

"I'm looking for a husband, Peter. Someone about fifteen years younger than Senator Barkley."

Peter gave the wagon wheel another spin. His mother

reached over and stopped it. "I'm looking for someone who, maybe for one minute, maybe for only as long as it took to click the shutter, will make me feel the way your father felt in that picture."

He rode back to Reno, trying to stay angry. Mother was like a hypnotist who had emerged from her own spell; she was leaving the theatre, not terribly concerned that her audience—himself, his father—was still "under." He wanted to find a card game, or just a slot machine, to keep from pondering what she'd said. He drove down Virginia Street toward his motel, the neon reminding him of Mrs. Sinclair's silver tea service, so well polished it had managed, the other week, to reflect the single sliver of light allowed through the colonel's curtains. His mother sounded as if she were looking for ecstasy, as if she might suddenly decamp to California like Aldous Huxley; Mrs. Sinclair, to hear the colonel tell it, had never shown anything but serenity. The old man had shimmered like the tea set when extolling her. Did he want the town to stay as it had always been so that he could continue picturing her there? Was it as simple as that?

At the desk in the lobby he put down change for the paper. Too bad he would be going home before October 7. Richard Nixon would be out here that day to give a speech on "Cold War Treason." Peter Cox would be watching the Owosso City Council vote on the Dewey Walk.

"Can you get me some ice?"

"Of course. You've got a message. A Mrs. Bruce called from Michigan. She asked that you call her back and not worry about the hour or the time difference."

Had the office flooded? Had the colonel thrashed Al

Jackson with that fifty-year-old walking stick he'd brought home from the Cuban jungle?

Back in his room Peter waited for the operator to make a connection.

"Hello?"

"It's me, Mrs. Bruce. Can you hear me all right?"

"Oh, yes, Mr. Cox!"

"What's the trouble?"

"*Trouble?* Anything *but* trouble, Mr. Cox. He's *coming!*"

Peter hesitated as her words ran through the wires.

"Did you hear me, Mr. Cox? Governor Dewey is coming to Owosso!"

NINE

October 4 – 2 2

ON OCTOBER 4, THE DAY PETER COX ARRIVED HOME FROM
Nevada, Dewey's men in New York had still not picked an
exact date for the governor's visit. At the Great Lakes and
the Hotel Owosso's coffee shop, some argued that *after* the
election was better, since greeting a President-elect would be
even more momentous than greeting a presidential candidate. To which others rejoined: In that case, you might as
well wait until next spring, when he can come back as the actual President. They wanted the visit *now,* just as they didn't
like having to wait until after November 2 to see themselves
in the *March of Time.*

This second group got its wish on Thursday, October 7,
the day of the city council meeting, when the candidate's
men finally made up their minds and the *Argus* could announce: MONSTER RECEPTION TO BE TENDERED DEWEY HERE;
EXPECTED OCTOBER 23. The council meeting, at which a few
sparks had still been expected to fly, wound up being poorly
attended, while over at the Elks temple, where the Dewey for

President Club was reorganizing itself as a reception committee, you couldn't find a seat. The sudden change in by-laws
was a bit confusing: the club itself continued in existence,
even though the new committee, in an all-for-one spirit of
civic pride and hospitality, had taken on a Democrat. Bruce
Wilson, the young biology teacher at Owosso High, satisfied
a couple of objections by explaining what Luther Burbank
had done with hybrids, and after that the group felt free to
move on to the latest flurries of incoming news. Each hour
seemed to bring the name of another state politician who
promised to join the governor during his only Michigan appearance of the whole campaign. A stack of decisions had to
be taken, from the very basic (should the parade end at
City Hall or Willman Field?) to the more subtle (how should
the city and its merchants split the cost of decorating the
downtown?).

At 9:15, Al Jackson came running in, out of breath with
a sheaf of oaktag under his arm, to announce that the council had just approved the Dewey Walk by a vote of six to one.
The single dissenter was Chester Burnham, who they all
knew was an old friend of Horace Sinclair's.

Someone asked if Horace had even shown up tonight.

"Didn't see him," said Al. "But that's all in the past. We
built the future tonight! That's what's important!"

A couple of people who never would warm up to Al, at
least not all the way, turned their attention back to the
club/committee's mimeographed agenda. They'd been
doing just fine without Al, and now that he'd gotten his
way about the Walk—which for all its permanence seemed
less important than the parade two Saturdays from now—
couldn't he leave them alone?

He couldn't. Within ten minutes he was revved up by the can-do wartime speed of the proceedings— racing from one colloquy to another, interrupting the organizers, answering questions he hadn't been asked. The vice president of the club, who either was or was not the co-chairman of the reception committee, felt ready to tell him to pipe down, when the question arose of what the parade floats would actually depict and whether they could be built in two weeks.

"Whole universe took only six days!" shouted Al, who before anyone could stop him was at the lectern roiling his oaktag sheets. Their liquid noise was far less audible than he: "We've already started! All we need to do is build a version of what we'll be putting along the river. Look! 'The Family Fireplace,' 'College Days,' 'Gotham Courtroom' . . ."

Even Al's detractors took his point.

"I thought so!" said Al, who before anyone actually said anything was standing the panels up along the bottom of the stage. "Talk about an unveiling! It'll be like new-model day in Detroit. Now all you've got to do is pick who gets to play who. Good luck to everybody—so long as they know getting picked for the parade doesn't give them any leg up when we pick people for next year by the river. That'll be done later, fair and square."

At the back of the temple, Peter Cox toyed with the idea of playing Tom Dewey's father in his newspaper office. Standing atop a great moving crepe-paper version of what was once the Owosso Times Building would have its advantages. Showing himself off with a touch of gray powder at the temples; their next state senator playing father to the latest father of the country. Of course, it might look like too literal a jump on Dewey's bandwagon, too obvious a grab at his

starched little coattails. Maybe it would be better just to secure a dignified place on the speakers' platform wherever
they decided to wind up the parade.

He'd have a day or two to decide. There was something
more important to attend to now.

"What was that phone number they mentioned, Mrs.
Bruce?"

From her position below his right shoulder, she looked
up from her notepad. "The volunteer line?"

"Yes. Could you write it down?"

"Owosso 2188," she said, tearing off a sheet of steno-
graphic paper.

"Thanks," he said, heading out toward his car. Which
would be the best place to leave it? In her mailbox on Oliver
or under the door of Abner's?

ON MONDAY AFTERNOON FRANK SHERWOOD ROUNDED THE
stairwell between the first and second floors of Owosso High.
As always when he found the landing here deserted, he felt
relief. Most days, before the 8:15 bell and between class peri-
ods, it was filled with the athletic kings of the hill and their
girlfriends, the "hearties," as an Anglophilic colleague in the
history department liked to call them. They never actually
said anything when he walked by, but whenever he passed,
he was waiting for it, imagining he'd heard some noise or
seen some gesture that showed they could guess what their
parents could not. (He particularly dreaded one pedagogi-
cal invention taking hold in some parts of the country: the
junior high school. From everything he'd heard, dividing
the educational trek into three stages instead of two meant
the kids arrived at high school one year later and even more

sophisticated, having just spent puberty cut off from the smallest ones.)

But today was easy. He sat down to mark tests at his desk in front of an empty classroom and listened to the half-strength blowings of the band practicing outside for the Dewey parade. Most of the boys, along with most of the men teachers, were off pheasant hunting on this first day of the season: a peculiar little privilege that had survived the generations and was not without benefit for those who stayed behind. Frank had gotten to cancel two decimated classes.

They weren't bad kids—he smiled to think of the boy who'd come back last year with a live turkey vulture for bird-loving Bruce Wilson in Biology—but it would be easier to live without them. Once or twice he'd thought of going along on the hunt; Arnie had shot pheasants, and the chance to stumble down paths that he once walked was almost inducement enough. But every year he declined, content to wonder what had happened to the gun, trying to picture it in a corner of the garage on Park Street. It seemed doubtful that Tim had inherited it. Last year on this day, when Frank went off to an afternoon movie at the Capitol, he'd spotted the boy in the third row, asleep and, he was pretty sure, drunk.

He'd thought of going to the movies today, but then he noticed that his first canceled class would only run into lunchtime—still too early for the first show. So he'd decided to go down to Oak Hill instead. He just sat in the gazebo for a half hour. Since suffering through those visits from Jane Herrick and Ted Rice's deputy, he'd been afraid to go near the grave itself, lest somebody spot him there and decide it was suspicious. He hadn't even gone to his old inconspicuous spot behind the Bell mausoleum. The last thing he wanted to do was watch her at the headstone: it was a lovely morning and there was every reason to think she might be down there.

She scared him more than the police. A few weeks ago, at Gene Riley's funeral, she'd come up to him and started making odd conversation about how Saint Paul's was nice enough in its way, but as cemeteries went it really couldn't compare to Oak Hill. She'd even asked him for a ride home, which he'd been too flummoxed not to offer, even though he feared a barrage of new questions, ones that had occurred to her in the weeks since his denials that night back in his apartment. But they'd ridden all the way along Chipman and Oliver in a crazy, screaming silence.

The quiet here in room 211, as four distant clarinets dominated two distant trumpets on "The Sidewalks of New York," made him as peaceful as he ever was in this building. Marking the third incorrect rendition in a row of the formula for hydrochloric acid, he tried to tell himself that he would be more interested a month from now, when the curriculum put them through a unit of astronomy.

A knock.

"Come in," he said, disappointed that the five minutes he still had coming to him, thanks to the pheasants, would now be spoiled.

The wooden door opened, and he saw her standing before him, pieces of wet green grass stuck to the darker green of the same skirt she'd had on when she rang his bell in August. With fast, pointless instinct, he shut his grade book. Was there a policeman behind her?

"Do you mind if I sit down?" she asked, with a kind of desperate clarity, as if she were speaking the one line she had in an Owosso Community Players production and was afraid she wouldn't get it out.

"They've all gone pheasant hunting," he said, with the same overenunciation, as if he had misheard a cue and delivered *his* line out of sequence.

She sat down in the front row, placing her folded newspaper on the paddle desk. She fidgeted a bit and tried smiling. "They never did have enough of these for southpaws." She waited a moment before going on. "My son Arnie used to hunt pheasants. Tim was never much interested."

"Did—" To his absolute horror, he realized he had started to ask what ever happened to Arnie's gun. He caught himself, and beneath the desktop dug the point of his red pencil into his thumb. "I don't think we're going to get much of anything done this fall. Every club in the school is involved in one way or another with the rally for Dewey, and as soon as that's over everyone will be getting ready for the homecoming game." The night before, down on the river, as they screamed and petted their way through a pep rally, he would have to supervise the bonfire, a quasi-scientific duty that fell to him every year.

"That snake," she said. "I never like it. It reminds me of maneuvers. Or some terrible medical probe." She was talking about the giant conga line of seniors that roared through the downtown. Her images for it, disgorged by her obsession, touched him unexpectedly. Surprised at himself, but without checking the movement, he came out from behind the desk and stood less than two feet from her. He looked down at the newspaper item she had circled with a wax pencil: eighteen Shiawassee County boys were reporting to Flint for pre-induction physicals.

"I can hear those seniors all the way to my corner of Park Street," she said. "You like quiet, too, I suppose."

Was this a trap? He offered nothing.

"I saw you at Oak Hill this morning," she said. "Sitting in the gazebo. It's a wonderful place to go for peace and quiet, isn't it?"

It was a trap, he was sure, and he had to figure out what wild supposition might be coming next.

"Have you lost someone who's there?" she asked.

"All my family are buried in Cincinnati." He said it with self-imposed calm, in such a low monotone that no one in a theatre could have heard him. She nodded, respectfully. His having dead of his own, wherever they were, was clearly important to her, like a demonstration of good manners.

"Thank you for dropping me home the other week," she said, looking up.

He had to reply. "I'm glad you said hello to me at Mr. Riley's funeral." No, he wasn't; no more glad than that she'd come here. What did she want, and why wouldn't she come out and say it and then leave him alone forever?

"There was something I wanted to tell you then," she said.

Inside his jacket pocket, he pressed on the red pencil with what he calculated as the maximum force it could stand without snapping in two. He waited. But whatever it was she had to say, she couldn't make herself do it. Some compulsive numbers came out instead.

"I suppose you saw the *Argus* for September 29th. Two weeks ago Wednesday? 358,967 dead. The official count. Not made or released until thirty-seven months after the second surrender. And 150,000, still just a round number, already home or to be returned."

As if pushed by a giant ball of ticker tape, Frank began to retreat behind his desk.

"Mr. Sherwood, I'm sorry," said Jane, in a tone suddenly lucid with pleading. "I don't know where Tim is, and you don't either. I never paid the least bit of attention to him. I'm glad that you gave him some."

He paused in front of the blackboard. He kept his back to her and waited for her to finish.

"Someone put a foolish suggestion into my head. I don't think I ever believed it. I think I tore after you because I was angry with myself. I wanted to make the attention you gave him into something bad, so I wouldn't have to feel guilty about not giving it to him myself. I know this doesn't make sense—"

He heard her voice trailing off, retreating into the confusion of the other world, the one in which she spent most of each day. He wanted to wheel around and catch her, keep her *here*, but he couldn't make himself do it, couldn't take his eyes off the blackboard, this same panel of it he'd stared at one afternoon four years ago, when, five minutes after seeing the words OWOSSO MAN IN ARDENNES MASSACRE in the Teachers' Lounge copy of the *Argus,* he'd come in here, as they talked and laughed and passed notes behind his back, to pick up a piece of chalk and, in a trance, write down the second law of thermodynamics.

"I should go," she murmured.

"No, please, don't," he said, turning around. "May I give you a ride home?"

"No. Thank you," she said, extracting a ring of keys from her purse. "I have my car today."

He saw the sun and moon dangling from the chain. His mouth dropped open. He was staring straight into a total eclipse.

"I know why you were angry at me," he said. "It's because we're the same. It's not just liking quiet and the cemetery. We're alone in this town, and this is a hard place to *be* alone. It makes you angry to be yourself. A week from this Saturday night, through all the roar of the parade, I'll stand in the middle of the crowd on the sidewalk and still be alone."

"Please don't go to the parade," she said. "Come to my house for dinner instead."

THEY'D REMOVED SIX BUICKS FROM THE ROSS SHOWROOM TO make space for the reception committee's operation. At eight o'clock on Monday night, the eighteenth, the big selling floor and the sidewalk at Main and John were as busy as any stretch of downtown on a Saturday afternoon. All day long Mrs. Bruce had been running back and forth from Peter's headquarters to the library to her own card table here. She'd just come from the reference section with what she hoped was accurate information about which implements at the Putnam farm (site of some youthful Dewey work experience) might have been automated. There was no point building a fake tractor if a hundred people along Main Street were going to hoot at an anachronism, and not even the county Farm Bureau, which was sponsoring the float, had seemed completely sure.

Rushing back in, she bumped into two club officers returning from Detroit with complaints that they'd been high-hatted by some campaign official with bigger things on his mind than one town's parade. "What do you expect?" said one to the other. "They play *bridge* on the campaign train."

At the back of the showroom there was a poker game in progress, which local merchants would drift in and out of for a few hands after depositing the latest load of paint or lumber or crepe paper, whose rolls were now piled up like newsprint wheels at the *Argus* plant. Nearby bolts of cloth bunting looked silky and regal compared to all the flimsy crinkle, but none of this red-white-and-blue swag would be hung from any outdoor lamppost until Thursday at the earliest, not with the forecast looking as uncertain as it did.

Peter Cox, who'd just sat down at the card table, was intrigued to hear about the Victory Special's bridge game; he would be cleaning up if he were aboard. He'd given up on the idea of playing Dewey senior and settled into his role as liaison man to the offices of Governor Sigler and Senator Vandenberg, both of whom would be on hand this weekend. And nobody was going to high-hat *him* when Dewey's New York representative arrived in town tomorrow.

"Honey, you need a cup of coffee." He could detect the hearty voice of Kay Schmidt, here with a donation of food from the hotel, imploring Anne Macmurray to give herself a break from the busiest table of all, where she and Carol Feller and a couple of other ladies were trying to find 150 beds for various dignitaries and reporters who'd be staying over Saturday night.

"Mrs. Schmidt," she replied. "I need a *drink*." It was exactly the sort of remark she knew how to get away with—one notch below Nice Girl, but nowhere near to pushing it. The people who heard it would go home saying she had "pizazz" and wasn't the least bit stuck-up. It was curious, thought Peter: she *knew* what she was doing, was calibrating it exactly for effect, even though she had no need to. She would have made the remark anyway, said it *naturally*. The calculation was redundant, and as soon as she employed it she'd be on to herself, would feel a trace of guilt, which was, he thought, as he watched her flip through a card file, one of the reasons, somewhere near the middle of the list, that he was in love with her.

"Rosebud!" he cried, having at last, after twenty minutes without going over to her, found the moment. They were bringing in the bobsled, Dewey's own, promised by his mother and now delivered by Mr. Valentine. It would ride atop float number two, the idyllic childhood winter scene, if they ever got all this paraphernalia down to the site where the floats themselves were being built.

Orson Welles had obviously made it to Darien. She was looking up amidst the oohs and aahs (it was a kid's *sled*, for Christ's sake) and giving him a smile.

"Where are we taking this stuff?" shouted a newcomer.

"The old sugar company," answered a man struggling with a plywood witness stand.

Mrs. Goldstone, who was dropping off two casseroles (at a considerable discount) and picking up two empty pans, became momentarily lost in angry memories; she was not entirely comfortable with the idea that these happy crepe-paper confections would be rising from the unweeded grounds of the factory whose closing, fourteen years ago, had ruined her husband's pride.

"Thanks for the phone number, but I was way ahead of you," said Anne, once he finally walked over to her.

"I figured you would be."

"I would have been there that first night, but we were with Billy Grimes' father, straightening out Gene's insurance. Not that there was much to straighten out."

"Certainly not as much as Billy Grimes will be carrying twenty years from now."

"Right. The kind that makes you a profit. Term. Or the other kind. I knew all this the night it was explained to me."

"So what is Billy playing? A newsboy? Bobsledder? Farmer?"

"You jest," said Carol Feller, on her way to give Mrs. Goldstone a hand. "Do you know how much money there is to be made Saturday night? He'll be hawking souvenirs and running errands for every reporter on Main Street. Probably selling them Truman buttons, too."

"And where will *you* be Saturday night?" Anne asked Peter.

"The reviewing stand, of course."

"Then stand next to me. I'm a sort of lady-in-waiting for Mother Dewey. Carol is, too. It's kind of a sequel to the *March of Time.*"

"*The Road to Buffalo.* That's where he's heading after church on Sunday. Inside information, of course." He paused. "So what does Riley think of all this?"

"He's a model of tolerance."

"I wouldn't be."

"No, you wouldn't be."

And you wouldn't want me to be. "What's your job between now and then?"

"After tonight I'm on the floats. If the speed they're going at is any indication, don't ask me how they're going to get the Walk up by next spring."

"If things are that much behind schedule," said Peter, "I'll have to lend a hand myself." He hoped that Riley's toleration wasn't so broad he'd be out there next to them, hammering with his overmuscled arm.

"My God, Peter, you could have calluses by the week-end!"

"What time does the late shift start?"

"Seven o'clock for the next four nights. Sign up on the clipboard near the front door. They'll have floodlights set up, and the band will be having its practice out there, to keep people in the mood."

"Oh, boy," he said. "Lots of Sousa."

"Maybe they'll make a mistake and throw in 'Happy Days Are Here Again.' "

"Why stop there? How about 'Brother, Can You Spare a Dime'?"

"Do you know how much I'm going to hate you by the end of the week?"

No, you're not. "Yes, Mrs. Bruce?" She was tugging at his sleeve.

"I'm sorry to interrupt, Mr. Cox, but you've *got* to talk to Mrs. Waters. She's putting *six* names down for some of the cars. Those people are going to be *crushed* before the parade reaches Willman Field."

"Excuse me," said Peter, in a sonorous Raymond Massey voice. "Executive decisions."

"Of course," said Anne.

He followed Mrs. Bruce to the trouble, humming "You and the Night and the Music" as he went.

JACK AND ANNE WERE FINISHING THEIR COFFEE IN THE DIN-ing room above Christian's department store.

"Is it this parade?" she asked. She could understand his being tired—he'd been working long hours in Flint, trying to make up for the past three months—but she didn't know what was making him blue.

"No," he answered. "I'm glad you're doing it."

"Is it the arrest then?"

"A little bit, I suppose." The excitement over Dewey was bad enough—it made his own Labor Day contact with Truman less special, to himself and maybe to her. But the arrest, over in Pontiac, after so many months, of a *union* man in the shooting of Walter Reuther: it was hard not be be brought low by that. The guy was even an officer in a Ford local—it wasn't impossible Jack had met him. To top it off, it looked as if he'd also robbed a CIO co-op store. Just a hoodlum, in other words.

"Did anything go on in the shop today?"

"Not much. Leo put in his order for Eisenhower's memoirs."

"I wonder if we might have won with him," Jack said, more to the coffee cup than her.

"I don't know, Jack." She looked at her watch and couldn't think of a cheerful thing to say.

"Lorraine called me this morning. We finished up everything about Dad. They all want me to have the house."

She knew that Gene had left no will, but that was it? Just some informal chat among the brothers and sisters? No pieces of paper with percentages and dates?

"None of them is nearby anymore, and she went on about how I'd taken care of Dad and all that."

"The Rileys are a lot more civilized than the Macmurray brothers would be, I'll tell you that."

"Do you want me to sell it? If I do, I'll give Lorraine and the rest of them some of the money, but we could keep a lot of it, and get a GI mortgage on some place elsewhere. Flint's not much, but there are some nice spots just outside it. Or we could stay and fix the house up any way you like."

She could picture herself walking home on days like this, down Oliver Street, past Mrs. Wagner, who would have turned into an anecdote; waving to Carol Feller, whom she would eventually be like, their both having lived in the neighborhood for years and years. She would go through the garage, and look at the sofa and the license plates, which would still be there, before walking through the back door and up to her study, though she'd call it something else, that funny little room at the back of the house, right next to the one Gene had done some of his dying in. She'd paint it light blue.

"Oh, turn that up," said Jack. "You've got to hear this." The waitress refilled their cups and raised the volume of the Flint station.

"Jack, I've heard it. It's a rehash. The story is a week old."

". . . in Beaucoup, Illinois, where Governor Dewey's Victory Special nearly backed into a supportive crowd because of a mistake by the trainman. 'That's the first lunatic I've had for an engineer,' said the distressed candidate, who added that the man 'should be shot at sunrise.' But as no one had been hurt, Dewey offered the man a pre-presidential reprieve before heading on to Oklahoma City."

"Like he's Louis the Fourteenth," said Jack. "Can you believe that? 'Shot at sunrise'? And the announcer was laughing, could you hear him, like it was a funny story."

"Down, boy," she said, massaging the place between his neck and shoulders in a way that interested the waitress more than anything the radio had said.

"Can I turn it down now?" the girl asked. "My boss doesn't like—"

"At least he doesn't have you shot at sunrise, does he?"

"I wouldn't be here if he did." She winked at him and took away their plates.

"You've dated her," said Anne. "Oh, God, I knew it."

"Once. Ages ago. What's that got to do with Dewey?"

"Nothing. That's why I brought it up. Listen, why don't you concentrate on Harry's crowds? They say they're enormous." At single stops in places like San Antonio, two hundred thousand people had been turning out to see Truman step through the blue velvet curtains and start firing at the Republicans.

"They also say they're just coming out to see a President," said Jack.

"Well," said Anne, wiping her mouth. "Maybe they're right. I guess I'm coming out to see the next one. And you are, too."

"Do I have to?" he asked, with a hint of lower lip.

"P—. Oh, God, I almost said *pwease*. I'm on the verge of talking baby talk in a public place. Either you've got to get less adorable or you've got to take me out of here. I'm late as it is."

"Okay, let's go." He put down a five-dollar bill and they headed out.

"If you agree to come Saturday night, we can go out to the Corunna drive-in as soon as it's finished. The midnight show. Something bloody. Bleached blondes, John Garfield, that kind of stuff."

"Not *The Bishop's Wife*."

"Liar!" she shouted, slapping him on the arm. "I forgot

to tell you! Your aunt Eileen, at the funeral, told me you'd already *seen* that movie before you took me. She was asking about our first date, and I mentioned it, and she looked all confused and said, 'I'm sure that's what Gene and Johnny took me to at Christmastime.' "

"That's before I knew you were an—"

"Adventuress. Come on, we've got to hustle."

They got into the car.

"So what about the house?" he asked.

"Let's keep it."

"You don't want something new? No ranch like the Jacksons'?"

"No. I'd like the old colonel to feel free to drop by."

He reached over and touched her knee. "We can make that little room at the back into a kid's room."

Of course. She'd been seeing bookshelves, but this was a truer projection of the future, just a little further distant than the one she'd projected herself. She remembered the sight of him at the air show, her vision of children falling safely into his arms. She squeezed his hand but said nothing, and he yawned: "I'll take a nap. Then pick you up at eleven."

"No, go to sleep. I'll get a ride. Really. I'll call and wake you if I don't. I promise."

"Okay." He pulled the Chevy in through the rusted gates of the Owosso Sugar Company and tried to smile. "I can't believe you're helping out that overprivileged little s.o.b."

She kissed him on the cheek. "He's not *that* bad."

"Are you kidding? 'Shot at sunrise'?"

"Oh, you mean Dewey. No, he's awful." She pointed to

a huge wall of crepe paper. "Look! They've got the birth-place up!"

"TUFT, STAPLE, FLUFF. TUFT, STAPLE, FLUFF. OH, FORGET IT. You're hopeless." Anne took the botched crepe-paper flower from Peter and put it on the pile she was making, six a minute, for one of the floats. "Just cut off foot-long strips. Did you ever hold a skein of yarn for your mother?"

"Mother doesn't knit."

They were sitting cross-legged beside one of the scenes that would be hoisted onto flatbed trucks Saturday after-noon. The floats committee, headed by Gordon Graham, had hired a Detroit company to do the heavier construction, and a host of volunteers were putting floral pelts onto any-thing already hammered together. Anne twisted another four buds into bloom before Mrs. Bruce, her hands full of lists, came up to Peter.

"The ones in this column will turn down Oakwood, and these will go down Dewey. Both will wind up at the field." Peter glanced at the rosters of cars and dignitaries, imagin-ing these two divergent strands of the parade taking a couple of wrong turns and crashing back into each other like clus-ters of Keystone Kops.

"Very good, Mrs. Bruce. I'm sure you'll keep them in line." The poor thing; his compliments, like cups of coffee, were getting her through the week. When she'd gone, he turned back to Anne and asked, "Is that all you're going to do?"

"You mean make flowers? Probably. We need a few Indi-ans along with the chiefs."

"As one of the chiefs, I'm pleased to tell you that I per-
sonally vetoed the 'platform' idea." The more intense parti-
sans of the Dewey Club had wanted a giant rendering of the
GOP platform, or at least its highlights, spelled out in crepe-
paper rosettes and waiting for the candidate when he arrived
at the reviewing stand.

"That was big of you," said Anne. "Although there was
no danger the actual platform would have collapsed from
any substantial extra weight. It's not like, well, this, for example." She cleared her throat like a singer on prize day and
started reciting the more ambitious pledges of the Democratic party. " 'Repeal Taft-Hartley. Increase minimum wage to
seventy-five cents an hour. Increase social security payments
50 percent. Control prices—"

"Save it for Saturday night. There'll be three ambu-
lances and two First Aid stations along the route. You can
blow hot air at me when there's somebody around to dis-
pense oxygen."

"There'll be no *time* to propagandize. After all, the program starts at 10:05. Not 10:06. Not 10:04. 10:05."

"Nothing wrong with a little military precision."

"Baloney. It's not military; it's what all those efficiency
experts working for him learned in business school. 'The
governor will speak from 10:30 to 10:45.' I hope he doesn't
start on Communism or inflation at 10:44."

"It wouldn't matter. We can deal with the big things
quickly. It's not like 'the moon, the stars, and all the planets'
have fallen on us." He mimicked Truman's description of
what taking over from FDR had felt like.

"Why don't you imitate Dewey? They say he can strut sitting down."

Before she knew it, and without letting go of the crepe paper, Peter was doing a dozen mazurka kicks, the polished shoes on his long curled-up legs kicking at her pile of paper flowers.

"Where on earth did you learn to do that?"

"At a party in London," he answered, resuming a seated position and cutting off another foot of crepe paper. He nodded modestly to Mrs. Bruce, who had taken awestruck notice of the ten-second performance.

"And speaking of foreign parts," Anne said, "where exactly have you been? I mean for a whole chunk of the past month. Carol guessed Palm Springs. Golfing with your father. Do you know Harold's going to fire you at this rate?"

"No, he's not. He's going to keep me around for two more years until I win the House seat here and head for Washington. And I wasn't in Palm Springs. I was in Reno."

"Divorcing some successor to the secretary from Lansing? Boy, that didn't last long."

"No, I was with my mother. Seeing her through her divorce from my father."

She stopped tufting to look at him. "You're not joking." Picking up the stapler, she added, "I'm truly surprised."

"So was I. It all had to do with a picture in a drawer."

"Explain."

"I can't."

He really couldn't. The look on his face told her he couldn't stand to.

He saw that she was reading him. "It's not a big deal. It's surprising they lasted as long as they did. It was practically an arranged marriage; their fathers were two minor midwestern maharajahs who exchanged them thirty years ago."

She didn't know what to say. "Well, I guess even India is independent now."

"And will be the worse off for it. They're not a nation; they're the *idea* of a nation. And don't go giving me that Eleanor look."

"What Eleanor look?"

"You know. The sorrowful bucktoothed pout."

"I don't have buck teeth."

"I've noticed."

"On Saturday, when you're near the oxygen, I'll recite the Four Freedoms along with Harry's platform."

All right, enough of this. "I hear you're getting married. Pretty sudden, isn't it?"

"Not really," she said, keeping her eyes on the staple gun. "I would think you'd approve. You certainly can't say it's 'arranged.' "

"Sure it is."

"What?" She looked at him.

"He's a wonderful fellow, I'm sure, but—"

"Stop right there."

"But he's an idea. At least to you he is. He's like this place, where you've come to write your book. You went in search of something you didn't know. You think embracing the unfamiliar is the test of imagination. You probably think it's the test of love."

"Look who's talking! Everyone knows how *you* came here. You picked Owosso off a map at the state party head-quarters!"

"It's different. I come here, but then I leave. I go *on* adventuring. In fact, I'm the only person within a hundred yards of you who's likely to fall on his face in the next ten years."

"Peter, I'm going to vote for you on November second. And you're going to wish me congratulations. Now."

"Have I ever told you remind me of my great-uncle Waldo?"

AS SHE RUFFLED CREPE PAPER INTO SNOW FOR THE BOBSLED scene, Margaret kept up a more or less steady stream of conversation with her girlfriends. There was something soothing about the repetitive motions, "like making baskets in the state asylum," she joked. Two floats away she could see Mary Ann Morton, the oldest of the girls who'd hid the German prisoner, the ringleader, really. She was helping to letter the University of Michigan sign on the college-days scene, while both of her children toddled from one construction to another. Her husband worked at Woodard's, and Margaret supposed he was home tonight, falling asleep in front of the radio.

She felt peaceful enough here, but Owosso—even this frilly, toy version of it—was no longer magical, not the way it had been behind the casket factory in July. Truth be told, there were *lots* of places just like Kansas, or home. Her life was fine. School went effortlessly; next marking period she could expect an A from even Mrs. Hopkins. On Friday nights she went out in a group, and on Saturdays she and Billy went to the movies, necking incrementally, though she kept the week-to-week differential barely perceptible. She certainly didn't *dis*like it, but she had no trouble keeping herself in line. The other night she had even complimented her mother, who was now thirty yards away helping the Jaycees set up a First Aid van. Thanks to Mrs. Harold Feller the reception committee had already found all 150 beds needed for Saturday night's stayovers. You couldn't say she wasn't resourceful.

Margaret waved to Anne Macmurray. How much less exotic she seemed these days, compared to the end of June. She, too, was now a part of home. There was a rumor she'd gotten engaged to Jack Riley.

Where was Billy? He ought to be back from the Buick showroom, where he'd gone to get approval for two last consignments of Flint-made Dewey pennants. He'd be paying three of their classmates to help sell them Saturday night; he'd already contracted out his Polaroid-camera job to a sophomore.

At last Margaret noticed him making his way through the whole busy open-air workshop, coming toward her, actually slapping a couple of backs and giving little pep talks as he went, like a factory foreman or Mr. Jackson.

"Boy, *everybody's* here!" he cried. "How come you're not over with the band?"

"He let us go if we had our parts down. It's not like I haven't been playing flute since I was ten."

"Half the teachers are here tonight, even the ones who live outside town." He looked around. "Have you seen Mr. Sherwood?"

She wished he wouldn't bring this up. It showed a guilty conscience, which Margaret supposed wasn't a bad thing for anyone to have, but the subject stirred memories of everything that had happened in August. "I doubt he's here. I would have seen him talking to Anne."

For a second Billy looked sad. "Well, you can't expect everyone to show." If only Frank Sherwood would get back into the swing of things, or get into it for the first time, Billy could make up for what he'd done. According to Dale Carnegie, three-quarters of the people you met were starving for sympathy. If Billy could just spend a half hour with Mr. Sherwood, asking him a lot of questions about *himself*, then accounts might be settled.

"Your father was looking for you," said Margaret.

Billy glanced around. "He's still trying to force a couple of college applications on me. It's like he's serving a subpoena."

"Tell him you'll go if he gets you a car." They didn't even have her father's tonight. They'd be getting a ride back with her mother, but only as far as downtown, where a group from Christ Episcopal would be meeting in a corner of the Ross showroom to make plans for Dewey's appearance at the ten o'clock service Sunday morning. It would be another mob scene, only twelve hours after the one before.

"Are you about ready?" It was Carol Feller calling to the two of them.

"I think so," answered Margaret, who noticed that Anne Macmurray had joined her mother. Both of them were approaching the bobsled.

"Good," said Carol. "That way Anne can come with us. She won't have to call poor Jack and wake him up. Billy, did your father find you?"

"Nope," he said, and the three females laughed. Margaret thought that within another month he would give in and apply. It would make sense, of course, though it would put an end to the only unconventional part of Billy that existed.

As the car drove along Main Street, he asked Anne if she had been in a sorority at Ann Arbor. So far fraternities were the only aspect of the college idea to which he'd warmed up: they struck him as a good place to make connections, like the golf course, where you could do what the books called "client development." He caddied a couple of times a month to learn the social rules of the game.

"Just the literary society," said Anne. "You wouldn't believe how unfashionable. About half of us have unwashed hair in the yearbook picture."

From the back seat Margaret noticed that Anne's own hair, freshly washed and glossy, was cut shorter, more like everyone else's, than at the beginning of the summer.

Near the spot where the road crossed the river, Carol pointed northward toward Curwood Castle. "Have they started the renovations?"

"I don't think so," said Anne. "Leo Abner said the school board's fallen behind on its part of the agreement, maybe with all the commotion about the Walk and the parade."

"Well, someone's started on it," said Carol. There was a single light shining inside one of the faux-Norman turrets.

ON THURSDAY NIGHT THE ROSS BUICK SHOWROOM REVERberated with applause for Lawrence Banner, head of the decorations committee. Everyone agreed that downtown was looking wonderful; with no rain in sight the bunting would still be fluffy on Saturday. The Dewey Club's president clarified some elements of the program—Mayor Crawford *would* speak, but Senator Vandenberg would introduce Dewey, who would review the parade at Willman, not downtown. "Does everybody have that straight? Good. Then I'll tell you the best news of the week. The latest polling figures give Governor Dewey a full eight-point lead nationwide." Routine applause preceded a detailed rundown of the thirty-car chain that would follow Dewey to the field.

Anne looked at Peter and he looked back, with what she decided was the appropriate expression of apology. It was safe to go over to him, before everyone pulled out for the evening's work at the sugar factory. In fact, it was only prudent that they speak, to keep that little conversation last night from being a big thing.

"Here," he said, handing her a pamphlet for his opponent in the state-senate race. "You're entitled to change your mind. You'll see that Harvey P. Angell speaks your language." The back page had highlights from the Democratic platform.

"Hmm," she said. "It is a hard choice, isn't it?"

"Or you could think of it this way. Voting for me will increase my margin and propel me out of town faster. If I only squeak through, they may not nominate me for Congress until '52."

She handed him back the pamphlet and took one of his own from the handkerchief pocket of his suit.

"Who are these people on the back of 'Peter Cox: Leadership for the Fifties,' by Peter Cox? The ones you're standing with."

"My substitute famiy. A fifth-grade teacher and two kindergarteners from a school in Corunna. People who don't bother reading the caption will think they're the wife and kiddies."

She slipped it into her purse. "Have you got any brothers and sisters, Peter? I don't think you've ever told me."

"No."

"A mixed blessing."

"How so?"

"Well, the Macmurray boys have their moments, but most of the time they leave a lot to be desired. God, it's so different with Jack's family." She wanted to tell him the story of the house, about Jack's casual inheritance of it, but decided not to.

"So," said Peter, indicating the bustle in the showroom with his outstretched arm. "Are you going to put all of this into your book?"

"If my book weren't stopped dead already, it would stop in 1911. At least that's the plan."

"Let's see," he said, "1911. What was going on? Teddy Roosevelt starting to get disillusioned with Taft. Thinking he ought to have run for a third term after all. What else? Maybe—"

"There was a tornado here, Peter. It wrecked a whole patch of the town. You'd better bone up on your local history before you debate Harvey P. Angell again. Someone may catch you."

FOUR HOURS LATER PETER WATCHED THE FIRST REAL WINDS of fall push the clouds over Horace Sinclair's gabled house. It was after eleven, not a light was on, and the whole place had a Charles Addams feel, heightened by some harpsichord music from—where *was* it coming from? The wind spun the notes around him so trickily that, just inside Horace's hedged property, he couldn't tell. It had to be another house, but which? One all the way around the corner on Hickory?

In fact, the music *was* coming from Horace's house, or

more precisely, the garage that had never housed a car. A keener look from Peter revealed its door was open just a crack; music—and light—were leaking through. He approached, taking care not to be heard over the spangles of sound, which he now realized were more heavenly than creepy.

The old man, his back toward Peter, was lifting shovels from their holders in a rack, taking them up, one by one, and holding them over his head. He would then mime the movements of digging. Before Peter could decide whether Horace was testing their utility or practicing an eccentric form of calisthenics, his attention was diverted to the source of the melody, something between a music box and a Victrola. A brass plate with holes in it revolved on a turntable; the thing seemed to work on the same principle as a player piano. The machine moved quickly; its enchanting metallic waltz would be over in a minute.

"What's it called?"

The old man wheeled around. "Damn near scared me to death!" His face blazed with guilt.

"You act as if it's not your own garage."

"It certainly isn't *yours!*" Horace thundered.

"Come on, Colonel, what is that?"

"That's my Reginaphone," said Horace, putting down a shovel and recovering his breath. He invited Peter to come closer, to look at the patent number, from 1893. "It belonged to Mrs. Sinclair when she was a young woman."

"Why isn't it in the house?"

"She put it out here years ago. She preferred the radio."

Peter sat down on the workbench. "Heard anything more from, what's your friend's name?"

"Wright George. He is not coming." Horace spoke the last three syllables with disdainful emphasis, then regarded the lone pitchfork hanging with the shovels. He was one man, trying to figure out how to do the work of two. He turned back to Peter and asked, "Why aren't you getting ready for this carnival?"

"I've already been down there tonight. It's late, you know, Colonel."

"I know."

At the far end of the workbench Peter noticed a buckram box, which the last time he was here had been on the dining-room table.

"I'll be surprised," said Horace, "if any self-respecting railroad man agrees to bring the precious candidate to town Saturday night. Not after that incident wherever it was in Illinois, the town with that silly French name. DeTrop? Toot sweet?"

"Beaucoup," corrected Peter. "As in *merci beaucoup.*"

"Mercy is in short supply. It's never *beaucoup.*" Horace paused before barking: "Why do you never announce your purpose in coming here?"

Peter smiled. "I've come to talk about Sunday morning."

"You mean the ten o'clock service."

"That's right. I always keep my part of a bargain. I know a reporter from the *Sun-Times* who'll be there. I've arranged to have him ask Dewey a question about the Walk—in such a way he'll almost have to discourage it."

"I've given up on the Dewey Walk," said Horace. "Given up on any chance it won't be built."

"Come on, Colonel. You've earned this last try. You went and talked to Mrs. Dewey, after all. And it seems to have worked. The governor *is* coming."

"Your Chicago friend can do whatever he likes. I'm proceeding as if Mr. Jackson's Walk is going up." He forced himself not to look at the shovels.

"Proceeding?" asked Peter.

"Resigning myself."

"Colonel, why do people put things out in garages?" Peter touched a pair of crates beneath the Reginaphone. "I mean, if you want to get rid of things, why not throw them clear away?"

"You can't get rid of the past, Mr. Cox. The past is not a matter of time. It's a place. Somewhere just out of reach."

"You sound like H. G. Wells."

"No, I don't, because I know no machine will take you to it. It's right here, rearranged, hiding like the face drawn into a tree in one of those children's puzzles. People who appreciate the past work harder to see it. They know it's there. They can sometimes see the beard, or the eyes, or the nose. But never the whole thing." He looked at the box. "The world is divided into two kinds of people, Mr. Cox. Those who, when they pass a house, wonder who lives there, and those who, when they pass it, wonder who *used* to live there. I belong to the second group, but no matter which anyone belongs to, he still runs out of time. I've run out of time."

"So have I," said Peter.

Horace snorted.

"Really, Colonel, I have. There are only two days left in my campaign, and I'm further behind than when I started."

"What are you talking about? I'm not senile." *Cleveland, Harrison, Cleveland, McKinley.* "Election Day is November second, and you're *exactly* the sort of man we'll be electing from now on."

"Not that campaign, Colonel. Another one."

"Ah," said Horace, getting a general idea and sounding almost apologetic. For a moment, ten years dropped off him. "Who is she?" he asked, thinking it had to be somebody new.

"Anne Macmurray."

All at once Horace could feel himself angrier than ever before at Peter Cox. He struggled to measure his tones. "She is a lovely girl. Very special. And it's past time you gave up on her. She is going to marry Riley's boy. I heard all about it from Mrs. Goldstone. Mr. Cox, *he* is good enough for her."

"Colonel, why don't you go in and get us a drink? A real one, not the cordials. When you come out, you can tell me how you courted Mrs. Sinclair."

"If you're interested in that, you might as well come inside."

"No," said Peter. "I like it out here. I might play the Reginaphone."

"All right, suit yourself. I'll bring out some whiskey and some ice."

Horace went inside, leaving Peter alone with the Reginaphone, which he cranked, and the buckram box, which he opened.

JACK HAD NEVER BEEN TO THE CITY CLUB, BUT LATE FRIDAY night, when he arrived to pick Anne up from the sugar-factory grounds, Carol Feller insisted he join a group that would be there celebrating the readiness of everything for Dewey's arrival.

They drove up Main, where the 6600-lumen incandescents brought to life the bunting and the candidate's black-and-white face, endlessly repeated, pole after pole. The

Hotel Owosso was full, music from a swing band sailing through its open doors.

Upstairs at the City Club, along with Peter Cox, Harris Terry and Councilman Royers, Harold Feller waited for his wife. He was in an expansive mood—life was much better than it had been in August—and delighted to see Carol arrive with a group, even if the club had grown short of chairs and waiters. "I'll do the honors," he said, taking the newcomers' drink orders as soon as he found them something to sit on.

When he made it back with the tray, Harris Terry was taking the last sip of his second highball and asking where the young people were. "Not that you three aren't young," he said to Anne and Jack and Peter, "but I meant Margaret and her swain."

"Billy," said Harold Feller, "is probably selling the last roll of crepe paper at three times the price." He felt so right with the world he could even accept the idea of Billy Grimes as a son-in-law, should Margaret somehow make it through four years in Ann Arbor as contented with her lot as she now appeared to be.

"There is no further need for crepe paper," Carol informed her husband and Harris Terry and Ed Royers. "Everything is completely finished. Ready for Freddie."

"How's it looking?" asked Terry.

"Like a dream," said Anne. "It's such a wholesome sight; it's only the *extent* of it that seems opulent, as if Marie Antoinette were in charge of the prom."

"Let 'em eat crepe," said Peter.

"Well, this will fuel Al's megalomania," mused Ed Royers, laughing.

"Has anybody figured out what they're going to do with the traffic?" asked Jack. It was the most neutral, sportsman-like question he could think of.

"They'll start blocking off the streets at three tomorrow afternoon," answered Royers.

"Imagine what January twentieth in Washington is going to be like," said Terry. "The *Argus* says they've already got Truman's farewell parties planned. A lot of the Cabinet are renegotiating their leases so they won't be stuck paying rent."

"Harry may have a few cards left to play," said Anne. Everyone knew about her postconvention enthusiasm for the President (what Peter called the New Zeal), and they indulged it like someone's unaccountable fondness for a mangy dog. Even Jack could still be surprised by the ardor of it.

"You mean cards like the Vinson mission?" asked Peter.

"Now, Peter," cautioned Harold, "that's been canceled."

"But for it to have been *thought* of!" The President's idea of sending the Chief Justice on a trip to Moscow to negotiate with Stalin—a scheme vetoed by General Marshall—had dealt Truman an embarrassment he could scarcely afford.

"Yeah," said Peter, entering his relentless mode, "that's really giving the Russians hell."

"Too bad he isn't as tough as Dewey," said Jack. "He could invite Stalin over here and have him shot at sunrise."

"Oh," said Peter, "the engineer. Jeez, Jack, he's just trying to regulate the railroads. You're all for the regulation of every interstate thing under the sun, aren't you?"

"Enough," said Anne. "That particular train has pulled out. 'With a little jerk,' as someone wrote."

"I think we ought to make the incident a booth along the Dewey Walk," said Peter. "Give our Democratic visitors a chance to work themselves up."

"Or maybe," said Jack, "you could make it into a game for the Republicans. Shoot the engineer and win a kewpie doll."

"I like the way you think!" said Peter, raising his glass. "Tell me, Annie, what are you going to play out there next spring? And have you thought about growing gracefully into the older character parts as the years go by? Maybe even Mama Dewey herself along about 1990? You'll be, what, sixty-five?"

"Anne, you and I both need a snack," said Carol. "We skipped dinner, if you remember." The two women headed off to see if the kitchen was open. Before they were out of earshot Anne heard Jack suggesting that the next time Peter looked at a map for a legislative seat, he think about picking Rat's Ass, Alabama. She missed the reply, but Carol caught it. "Peter says he can't run there, because Rat's Ass is part of the Democratic plantation. You know, the solid South. Don't worry, Anne, they'll cool down. By the way, has Peter been drinking?"

"Not enough. Nothing takes the edge off him."

"Well, Harold will keep him in line." They joined a group in search of sandwiches.

"Why won't he *quit?*" asked Anne.

"Because he hasn't won."

"But he's *lost*. And is that all he wants? To win?"

"No," said Carol. "He may be a politician, but he wants *you*." The two women looked back toward the circle of chairs they'd just left. The noise was growing.

"I have to confess I hate seeing some of the changes occurring here," said Carol, diverting Anne's gaze to other parts of the room. "Everything is already getting spruced up and unrecognizable. A year from now all the ashtrays and glasses will probably look like souvenirs from Princess Elizabeth's wedding, except they'll have pictures of Tom and Frances Dewey on them."

"Maybe they will for a while," said Anne. "But not by 1990. I mean, surely everybody will be over it by then."

"Don't bet on it. Have you ever been to Marion, Ohio? You'd think Caesar were buried there instead of Harding."

Anne seemed to drift away from the conversation. It was as if she were off in another place, hearing and answering Carol by radio, half her mind working along some track that ran parallel to the words. *1990.* Between now and then the country would plow itself up ten times. These elections weren't a matter of democracy; they were a self-induced reinvention, history's protest that, even with the occasional war, it would bore itself to death without a new era every four years. How could the country get ten lives while she, living here, would get only one?

"Wouldn't I somehow be *older* than sixty-five in 1990? It feels as if I should."

"It feels to me as if I've every right not to be *dead* by then, but I will be."

While Carol took possession of two sandwiches, Anne saw a picture of the next fifty years passing, one in which the town remained the same and everything around it—this abstract, galactic swirl—spun and crackled and continually reconfigured itself, a terrible, inviting vortex. She would be asking Jack to shield her sight from the lightning while, the whole time, she peered through the cracks between his fingers.

"Chicken salad all right?" asked Carol. "They're out of everything else."

"Yes," said Anne, trying to turn off her mind's eye. The two women started back toward the circle of chairs holding their husband and fiancé. The younger men's voices, which had subsided for a minute, were regaining volume. Shouts of "Taft-Hartley" and "Pendergast machine" and "ignoramus" were pitched and batted back, while Harold Feller and Harris Terry tried, like umpires, to be heard.

"We know what this is really about!" Jack shouted.

Judging from everyone's sudden silence, including Harold's and Harris Terry's, Anne realized that everyone *did* know what it was really about, a situation so mortifying she had to shut her eyes. Behind their lids she once more saw Owosso, forever denied a second tornado, as the still point in the swirling universe, and she understood that only one thing, something inevitable, and imminent, and necessary, could halt the swirling. To her immense relief it was exactly what happened next, when Jack, without getting up from his chair, leaned over and knocked Peter's block off.

T E N

October 23

THE SEVEN BRASS BANDS AND THE FLOODLIGHTS AND HOW-
ever many thousand people were shouting on the sidewalks
seemed ready to crack the nighttime sky, to puncture it like
an eggshell. They were living in a Dewey world now. There
weren't even real movies anymore: the Capitol's marquee
proclaimed THE DEWEY STORY! *MARCH OF TIME* STARTS TO-
MORROW! CONTINUOUS SHOWINGS! It had been decided
somewhere that the nine-minute newsreel, starring Himself,
would be released to Owosso early; the rest of the country
would get it after victory footage from election night was
added.

Residents had been urged to eat dinner at home and
save space for visitors in the big chow lines set up at the high
school, the Lutheran church and who knew where else. Jack
had made himself two hamburgers after Anne left for Jackson, Michigan, at four o'clock with the reception committee.
She'd boarded the Victory Special there about three hours
ago, arriving with it in Owosso on the dot, at 9:10. Fifteen

minutes earlier, the parade had stepped off with a roar toward Willman Field, where the candidate would be waiting. As soon as the last float passed by, Jack would get down there, to the place he and Anne had arranged for her to spot him, a reversal of what they'd done in Flint.

Down at Willman, when they brought Dewey out, Jack planned to turn his back on him, at least for a second. He wouldn't give him the bird or make a thumbs-down; just this quiet, rude gesture. No one would notice, and he'd do it only to please himself. As it was, his status as a gentleman seemed unshakeable. Last night, while Peter's shiner sprang to life as neat as Dewey's mustache, he'd expected to be thrown out of the City Club like some common brawler. But an immediate consensus formed that Peter had been the instigator, provoking Jack "beyond endurance," as Mr. Terry put it. Councilman Royers had even clapped him on the back. In a daze, as if he'd taken the punch instead of thrown it, he could hear Harold Feller saying, "Peter, eject yourself." Which is what Peter did, while Royers scared up a last round of drinks and joked about "Jersey Jack" and, like the Fellers and Mr. Terry, refused to hear any apology out of him.

The only one who seemed unhappy was himself. He was glad to have slugged the guy, but it was John L. Lewis's eyebrows all over again. In front of Anne he'd done something "common," as his eighth-grade English teacher liked to put it; or, to use a phrase Anne sometimes applied to Truman bashers who got on her nerves in the newspaper, he'd "reverted to type." But nobody else saw it that way. By the time they left the club, the incident was growing into a nice little legend. Back on Williams Street Anne couldn't stop talking, telling him what a pain in the neck Peter had made himself all week. She'd rattled on as if she were afraid to subside. It was the first time she'd stayed over since the Saturday before, and there had been no little-boy warm-up to the lovemaking; she'd wanted things right away and then again in the morning, before she jumped out of bed and walked all around the house, up and down the stairs, fast, slicing the air with her arms the way Louise always did with that bony nervous energy. She talked about the color each room could be, how they could knock a hole in the wall between the kitchen and dining room, and how up in the attic, with a little remodeling, there'd be space for another bedroom, a place for "Junior's little brother." She kept it up, laughing all the time, though not the way his mother would have; more like someone after a little too much gas at the dentist's. He put it down to her being both exhausted and all jazzed up now that the big day was finally here.

He wished he could share the excitement. As it was, he felt crankier than his father had been at the end. Irked by the noise, he was just standing here, not cracking a smile, annoyed by the debate going on behind him about whether the crowd was ten thousand or fifteen thousand. Whatever it was, the Republican editors would jack it up; he knew that much from his day in Detroit. He'd actually clipped today's *Argus* editorial to give to Walt Carroll, who lived in Flint and couldn't imagine what Jack had had to put up with ever since moving back to Owosso last spring. "He is approaching the climax of his public career," the Campbell brothers' paper had said of its candidate. "On November 2 the people of this nation make him their chief executive." Not even *will* make him. But the real crap came, as Anne had pointed out, two paragraphs later: "He had to make his own place in life through ability and the sheer force of sticking to the job at hand. There are many American people who forget the opportunities for self-expression and advancement in this nation. They are too prone to call it quits when the going gets rough and let the government or someone else carry them along. Tom Dewey never did that . . ."

Dewey's life had been a parade from the beginning! As the bobsled rode past and the crowd cheered for the boys on top of float number 2, including Phil Welch, Dewey's fourteen-year-old second cousin, Jack tried concentrating his gaze on the undercarriage of the flatbed truck, to see if he could guess its make from that alone. But he couldn't stop remembering the way the wind raced through that shotgun house down by the depot while he and Lorraine shivered with flu. And now here came heroic young Dewey milking cows on the Putnam farm and then selling magazines outside the Owosso Times Building, where he probably made more money than the full-grown Gene Riley did before the union came in and made his job worth having.

ACROSS THE STREET BILLY HAD KEPT AN EYE OUT FOR MARgaret, who responded to his two-handed wave with a smile and a wink, never missing a note as the sixty-eight-piece Owosso High School band, marching between floats one and two, blared out "The Victors." He revered her composure; a Grenadier guard outside Buckingham Palace couldn't do better. And now that they'd had their prearranged greeting, he could get back to supervising his sales force. He was six kids' boss tonight. The old Columbia was turning out to be a godsend, the only conceivable means of shuttling between here and Willman, but come Monday morning he should at last have enough money for a decent used car. No, nothing as flashy as Peter Cox's new Ford, but also no antique like Arnie Herrick's Chevrolet, which he guessed was slowly dying of suffocation in Mrs. Herrick's garage. He'd be paying cash, too, before his father got any ideas about how the wads he'd accumulated up in his room and at the State Savings Bank might better go toward next year's tuition bills.

He knew he was getting sucked toward MSC or Central Michigan, and it only made sense if he was going to hold on to Margaret. It was a matter of keeping one's machinery up to date, resisting depreciation, which is what his Owosso High diploma was bound to suffer in her eyes if he didn't make some big score over the next four years. He didn't have the grades for Ann Arbor, where she'd certainly get in and go, but even a Central Michigan degree might keep him looking solvent to her.

Jesus, though: if there were this many people on Main Street every Saturday night, he could be rich before 1950 rolled around.

WITHOUT A FLUTE AT HER LIPS, MARGARET WOULD HAVE failed to notice how damp it was tonight. The noise and light were deceptive; the ease with which she was keeping her whistle wet told the real story of how much moisture the air held. Her girlfriends had brought some spiked cider to the parade's assembly point, and when everything was over they were going to ride out of town and finish it off. She'd go home by herself, since Billy would be selling his stuff until one in the morning and she didn't want to have to fight to keep her eyes open at church tomorrow. Everyone said there'd be a better view of Governor Dewey from the back pew of Christ Episcopal than the front row of the stadium.

She wondered if they'd have fireworks after he spoke tonight. That might get her more in the mood—not that she *wasn't* in it, but she kept thinking that somehow November 2 itself would have to be more exciting than tonight, which for all its size and sound struck her as missing something, maybe a salute with a cannon, or just one plane overhead, skywriting a message.

"RILEY! RILEY!" OVER THE DIN, FROM ACROSS THE STREET, Jack made out the voice of Carl Rutkowski. Carl's ruined arm had to rely on Louise to do its waving, but his voice was every bit as strong as when Jack had heard it singing "Which Side Are You On?" in '37. Not one to mind her manners or the rules, Louise had now darted into the street, between float number eight and the Durand High School band, which was coming right at her. She made it across and started tugging him to join her and Carl.

"You're gonna get us trampled," Jack protested.

"Okay, we'll wait till after the next float. Where's Anne?"

"Down at the field. With the reception committee. And probably wearing a Truman button."

"From what I hear," said Louise, "she could get away with it. Tell me why I should like this girl so much," she added, giving Jack's rear a squeeze.

"Jeez, Louise."

"To coin a phrase. For Christ's sake, Jack, there's a half dozen tubas between us and Carl, and he can hardly see past the curb as it is. What did you do about dinner? We had ours at the Elks' temple, and dessert at the Lutheran church. They overstocked both places, and they should've known better. People don't want to sit down and eat before something like this. They only want what they can wolf down on the sidewalk or in the stands."

"I hope Dewey's operation gets stuck with the bills."

"I hope somebody has the sense to get the stuff to the Salvation Army before it rots. If you're as miserable as you look, why don't you stop watching this and drive a truckload of leftovers to Flint?"

"Why are *you* watching this?" He pointed to her own Truman button.

"Because I love a party. And I can get away with the button just like Anne can, though for a different reason."

"What's the difference?"

"She can get away with it because she's charming. I can get away with it because if anybody gives me a hard time I'll bite their damned head off."

Even Louise couldn't make herself heard over the wave of sound now engulfing their block of Main. Float number nine, the last one, had just surprised the crowd by turning on its own set of lights. Jack looked up and recognized what it was: the White House, two huge frosty white tiers of crepe paper with a dozen lit, trimmed windows blinking on and off.

"Christ," said Louise, laughing. "They should have stuck Dewey on top of it. He really *would* look like he was on a wedding cake."

·   ·   ·

"LET ME HELP YOU WASH UP."

"Oh, no," said Jane Herrick. "I'm just going to run water into the pots, so things won't stick. Please, go sit in the front parlor. I'll be in with coffee in a moment."

Frank was sure she wanted the water's noise, not its function. Five minutes ago, at nine-twenty, the sound of drums, along with some fainter buzz that must have been the crowd, had begun reaching the house, making her nervous, as if the two of them were the only people at home on Park Street. Quite possibly they were, and the sense of that had made the room a desert island, filled it too full of imminent revelation. She needed, he knew, to take refuge in the music of the faucet, lest the drumbeats crack the evening's fragile formality, which so far had sheltered the two of them like the glazed bowl holding the stewed carrots.

There had not been one word about Tim, let alone Arnie, unless you counted a single reference to "my babies," one thrilling bump along a road of early-biographical recitation. She'd established a certain superiority over the parade by telling him a story about flu masks and her own personal meeting with Thomas E. Dewey; the tale of their tennis game followed. Both epidemic and sport were described colorlessly, except for some brief statistical flourishes—body counts and set scores. She had a picture of Dewey, from the 1919 *Spic*, the high school yearbook Frank had fortunately never had to "advise." Showing it had led to discussion of the piece in today's *Argus*—"page twelve, columns two and three," she'd said—in which a college roommate of the candidate's took exception to his stuffy image. Jane assured Frank the roommate was wrong.

The house was beyond stuffy, so he secretly raised the

parlor window another inch. Since hot air rose, the upstairs was bound to be even worse, but ever since he'd stepped through the front door it was the upstairs that had suggested itself as a place of heavenly breezes and spilling treasures, the place with a room behind whose door Arnie had slept.

Frank had not been in this house until tonight. Arnie's never having asked him over was proof of the intensity between them, something forbidden, dangerous, too likely to give itself away in the home Arnie shared with his mother and kid brother. Throughout Mrs. Herrick's dinner conversation, Frank had fought the impulse to get up from the table and maraud through these domestic precincts, to suck up the sight of every knicknack and carpet runner he'd had to picture in his mind for five—or, to put it as she might, five and one-fifth—years. Excusing himself before they sat down to the table, he'd gone as far as the downstairs bathroom. Once inside he'd been afraid to open the medicine chest, but he'd run his hands over the tiles and mirrors before noticing, amidst a clutter of Q-tips and sachets on a little open shelf, a pin from that college on Gute's Hill, where Arnie had taken those night classes while working at the State Savings Bank. Could he steal it? Would she notice? He'd settled for making a mental note to touch, before he left the house, the moon-and-sun key chain, which he'd already seen lying on a table in the foyer.

Now, in the front parlor, the sound of the eastward-moving parade grew louder, closer. He watched her bring in the tray, and asked if he could help, but she set it down and poured the coffee herself. Her jaw clenched against the possibility of spillage and the irritating drums. Before she stirred the cups, a spurt of numerical facts gleaned from the *Argus* and pertaining to frankfurters, wind instruments and the number of cars on the Victory Special emerged from her. He knew why she was so interested in this parade she clearly resented: because Arnie, if he weren't dead, would be in the thick of it, the way he had thrown himself into the centennial when he was a boy, and before that been one of the first babies out of Memorial Hospital, facts Frank had heard Arnie impart, laughing at his own rube-ish pride, one night in the Chevrolet.

"Will you still vote for Governor Dewey?" Frank finally thought to ask. It was the most personal question he had raised all evening, but right now he felt he could get away with it. A sudden intimacy seemed to demand it: he loved her for hating the parade, and for making him hate it, too.

"Oh, no," she replied. "I don't vote."

He was disappointed. He'd wanted to tell her he planned to cast his own ballot for Truman, but her remark was at some other level, the wide-eyed one she'd been jumping on and off all night, a place where he could no more join her than he could reach the bedroom upstairs.

"History is not in our hands," she elaborated. "It will unfold just as it's planning to, whether we send Tom to the White House or keep Mr. Truman there."

He nodded, and she stepped back down, her eyes resuming the look of the here and now.

"And what keeps *you* here, Mr. Sherwood? In Owosso, I mean."

"I don't know, Mrs. Herrick." The lie was so big it demanded a varnish of truth. "I don't really have a home anymore." But that was a lie, too; his home was the one he shared with her, in secret alternation, down at Oak Hill.

"There's no one special? Here or anywhere else?"

"No, there's no one special." Could she mean a woman? Had her suspicions receded so far as to leave him beached in full normality?

"Was there ever?" She was almost girlish now, teasing him.

"Once," he said, with the full measure of daring he'd permit himself tonight. "Someone who's not here any more."

"Why don't you get away?" she asked, her eyes undilated, fully focused on him; the two of them, for all her misapprehension, stood on the same level.

"I'm not really looking," he said. It was a true statement, but he hated the social laugh with which he accompanied it.

"I don't necessarily mean some*one,*" she said, still present, still fully lucid. "Just some*thing,* maybe." She sighed. "You know, towns like these . . ." She stopped herself, as if, without experience of anything else, she had no right to criticize.

"My neighbor, Anne Macmurray, tells me she came *here* to find something."

Jane shook her head, unimpressed by whatever this girl in the bookshop thought she was doing.

"How old are you, Frank?"

"Thirty-one."

She instantly did the arithmetic. "When I was thirty-one, I was absolutely happy." She meant, he understood, that all her men were still alive, and that he should be happy, too, at least for a while longer. He saw her struggling to stay where she was, to avoid falling down the statistical well of her obsession. She was trying to remain with him, on the plane of sympathy. She fought the widening of her eyes like a patient trying to blink away an optometrist's drops.

"Do you have any money?" she asked.

"Seven hundred dollars. In the State Savings Bank," he added, determined not to dare anything further.

"My son used to work there."

"Oh?" Each foray into truth demanded its own shameful camouflage. He could remember the day he'd opened the account, August 18, 1943, and the four times he'd come back during the next two weeks, depositing amounts that were comically, suspiciously small. He had kept going in, just before closing time, until it finally happened: Mr. Herrick, as his teller's pin read, suggested they go out and get themselves a glass of beer.

"My son used to say, if he had a lot of money, he'd go to New York."

"He did?" There was no lie in the question. Frank's surprise was genuine. He'd never heard Arnie indicate anything but cheerful acceptance of his role in life, a widowed mother's comfort and a kid brother's father. Responsibility was his sunlight; he sought it like a photosynthesizing plant. "Another day, another dollar" was fine by his sunny disposition, which asked for nothing outside this one-horse town but the chance to shoot pheasants a couple of times a year and go to the movies on Saturday night. Unless the chance to sustain some *new* happiness, a deeper, dangerous one, had secretly begun unsettling him?

"When did he say that?" Frank asked.

"A few weeks before he left. He was sitting in the chair you're in now. The radio was on, playing 'This Can't Be Love' one night after dinner, and I asked him why he looked so"—she paused to find the word—"enchanted, that's how he looked, and it wasn't because of the song itself. It was more that it was coming 'live,' in the very moment, from New York. For some reason that fact struck him, as if he were realizing it for the first time. Some friend of his had just explained radio waves to him, and this common thing was suddenly magical. 'Life would be easy there,' he said, as if he were standing, right then, on a corner in the middle of Manhattan."

Surely it was the need for responsibility that had made him join up when he didn't have to. That's what Frank told himself most nights; there was nothing that could have changed things. But on other nights, when he had a need to feel guilty, and ecstatic, he let himself wonder: *Did he go because of me? Because staying here was too dangerous for us both?* That Arnie had gone into the Army to get away from him was the surest proof of love he could have given, more passionate and generous than refusing to invite him home.

Life would be easy there. Was it possible that for one moment, before too much responsibility killed him, the way too much light will kill a plant, he had struggled to lean his nature away from it? Had he been looking for a way out, one the two of them could share?

"I think some part of him is there even now." As Jane said this, her eyes were widening, becoming just wild enough for him to fear she would now drown him with figures about the actual locations of the glorious dead. But it didn't happen. All at once she was back here and calm.

"Can you hear it?" she asked. "It's stopped."

It was almost ten o'clock. The parade had reached the field and could no longer be heard here at the corner of

Oliver and Park. Her mind could rest. The silence of the grave could settle over her once more. "Thank you," she said, leaning over to touch Frank's knee. "Thank you for being with me."

THE SEVEN THOUSAND PEOPLE IN THE STANDS WERE *FREEZING.* Why hadn't he thought of a blanket concession? Billy Grimes paused on the edge of Willman Field to admire the Dewey operation. There was the special podium, flown into town in advance of the candidate; the four rows of press tables topped with sharp pencils and special telephones, like restaurant tables in the movies. And there was the huge canopy, folded up but standing by, in case the skies opened and the 250 people who would be on the still less than half-occupied platform needed cover.

Peter Cox sat on a folding chair far from the podium, holding the side of his face that didn't hurt. All day he'd kept ice on his injured eye and cheek. "Insulted," that dainty coroner's word, was actually a better term than "injured" for what had happened to his head. He'd lain alone in the dark last night, not picking up the phone (he was sure it was Mother, still in Reno), and thinking about how Riley, after that cornball sucker punch, had managed to emerge the crowd's favorite. All he had done was raise a few important points, national and local, before Studs Lonigan started in with the fists.

For one instant, before his vision cleared, he'd thought he had actually come out the winner, that Riley would be thrown out of the City Club, and the Feller party, including Anne, would do what good Americans now did with anyone they'd just seen bombed to kingdom come: shower them with the spoils of war. In his case, that would have been Anne, but it hadn't turned out that way. Out of the corner of his good eye, as Harold handed him his hat, he'd noticed her standing there, safely draped with Riley's arm, the one that had belted him.

At three o'clock this afternoon, he'd checked his face in the mirror and decided it was not yet sufficiently presentable to travel all the way out to Jackson with the reception committee. And he did not mean unpresentable to *her*. The contest was finished and she was welcome to Riley. He'd gone off to the kitchen to make another ice pack and climbed into bed with it, getting up only an hour ago. His head still hurt, but the darkness was doing wonders for his looks.

What he felt was more like a hangover than anything else, and when the stands and platform started popping with the light of flashbulbs, hundreds of them, he ached the way one did when a window shade snapped up the morning after a four-highball night. He could swear that the tips of his perfectly shaped ears hurt. What had caused this outburst of light, anyway? Clearly it was related to the sound now drilling the deepest interior of his skull. Turning a bit to the left, no pleasant task, he realized that the radio drums had given way to real ones. The crowd had risen to its feet—did *he* have to?—and was whooping it up for the National Guard. (The same company that had gotten creamed in the First War? He'd read a little local history the other day, after she shook him up with that tornado story.) They were cutting smart military turns, clearing a path.

Yes, there it was at last, a sleek green convertible, like a new dollar bill, carrying Thomas E. Dewey into the stadium ahead of the parade. Real roars now, at exactly 10:00. Peter looked down at the candidate, who was standing as tall as his rumored elevator shoes would allow, accepting (the word had never been more accurate) the cheers of the crowd. The cars of the reception committee motored in his wake, Al Jackson running beside them like a welterweight doing road-work; he wouldn't be cooped up in a car when the nine-float prototype of his personal World's Fair was rolling in. He bounded up the platform, before the candidate, as if he were about to drive in the golden spike. Renewed roars as the VIPs—Anne, too—filed up and stood before their fold-ing chairs. Special ululations for Mother Dewey. Anne was with the Fellers in the front row, giving a big wave, much big-ger than the shy one being dispensed by Annie Dewey's daughter-in-law, otherwise known as the candidate's wife. She was waving to Riley, of course, signaling him. Peter fol-lowed Anne's eyes and arm to the general vicinity they were trying to reach, and sure enough, he spotted him, in an old hunting jacket, right behind the baseline and a row of cops.

As near as Peter could figure out, the Dewey Club presi-dent was now introducing the introducers' introducers. He wished he'd paid a little more attention to Mrs. Bruce all week; he'd have a better idea of how much he had to en-dure, how many speech-lengths of watching her short dark curls and her clean white collar, just three seats left of Mama Dewey, and only two more than that from her son. He was better off far away from her. He wouldn't be craning his neck to see if she'd acknowledge him; he wouldn't be trying to catch her licking her lips, his favorite nervous gesture of hers, second only to the way she ran her left hand along her neck, which he could tell she was vain about.

"You can write this down," shouted Senator Vandenberg a moment later, his two hundred pounds as unbuttoned as Dewey's slimness seemed corseted. "When election night is over—and it's going to be over early—Governor Dewey will have four hundred electoral votes and the soon-to-be-former President a mere one hundred thirty-one!" The crowd ate it up, and "Van" flashed a big Dutch grin. The night wind ruffled the curtain of hair combed over his shining dome, and he went on to tell them how, come January 20, "the hates and hubbub of splinter government will move out! So will the Reds and red herrings! So will the bureaucratic despotism of the last sixteen years!" None of the swells on the platform, least of all Vandenberg, had been for Dewey before June, but if the gallant old boy was feeling any regret that, with a little more pushing, this could all have been his, he gave no sign of it. He was as happy as Barkley in a bevy of widows. And where was Mrs. V.? Peter wondered, imagining a helpmeet as vitalizing as the late Mrs. Sinclair.

As the band kept the applause going, Peter felt a touch on his shoulder.

"I can't find much to clap for, but I'm still pleased to see you."

God, they'd invited everyone. It was Harvey P. Angell, his Democratic opponent.

"Well, Harvey, on most days Vandenberg sounds more like Truman than Dewey."

"I know!" said Angell, who Peter could tell was about to make some sincere remark about what everyone now called "bipartisanship" and how, when it came to foreign policy, politics stopped at the water's edge. He wished he would just shake hands and go. For one thing, turning in his chair to look Harvey in the face made his own face hurt too much, and for another, this accountant from Durand was so damned nice that his presence made Peter feel guilty about the thirty-point margin he expected to bury him with.

"Gosh," said Angell, noticing Peter's eye. "What happened to you?"

"I was attacked by one of your supporters, Harvey."

Angell looked stunned, as if he might have a goon squad he didn't know about.

"Relax, Harvey. I've just got girl trouble."

"Oh," said Angell. "You know, Peter, the other week, at that debate in Corunna, my wife noticed you were single. When this election's over, win or lose, we'd love to have you over to dinner. My wife's cousin is a great girl, a couple of years younger than you and pretty as can be. Her name's Mary and she works for the FSA."

This guy was killing him. "Okay, Harvey," he replied in a whisper, grateful for a hush that signaled the beginning of the next speech. "We'll talk."

Mayor Kenneth Crawford confined himself pretty much to expressions of delight and logistical warning. The official reception for invited guests would take place on the platform immediately following the governor's speech; the band would continue playing throughout it, and the mayor hoped the citizenry would depart the stadium in an orderly but prompt fashion, so that the parade cars and buses might have a clear route back to the Hotel Owosso and the candidate could get home to his mother's house on Oliver Street without any undue delay.

Peter noticed Harold Feller getting cues from Carol and standing up to communicate something to somebody out in

the crowd. Harold was tapping his watch and making a beck-
oning gesture, still incomplete when Vandenberg's colleague, Senator Homer Ferguson, started speechifying. Mrs.
Bruce, two places down, turned in her seat to run the fourth
check she'd performed so far on Peter's eye.

It was simple, Peter realized, as Ferguson gave way to
Governor Sigler; he'd get Mrs. Bruce to kill Riley, just take
her in his arms one night next week after turning out the
lights in the Matthews Building. *Mrs. Bruce, there's something I
need you to do . . .*

"AND STRUCK TERROR INTO THE HEART OF
EVERY THUG IN THE GREAT, BELEAGUERED CITY OF
NEW YORK—"

That was it. His eye was throbbing and Sigler's shouts
made his ear want to fold over on itself. He was getting out
of here. He could listen to Dewey's speech on his car radio
and get a picture of himself shaking the anointed's hand at
Christ Episcopal tomorrow morning.

"Excuse me, please. Excuse me." He did it with the ele-
gant stealth he'd once used to such good effect at parties in
Grosvenor Square, at the perfectly judged moment for an
assignation to get under way. "Pardon me, thank you, pardon me . . ." Barely missed, he reached the four wooden
stairs and nodded to the cop who was giving a safe conduct
to somebody coming up.

Riley? Harold Feller was waving him up past Peter and
around the last row on the platform, where Anne took
charge and brought him, practically in a crouch, toward the
little patch of ground behind the podium, where Dewey was
holding a discreet levee as the speeches continued.

After a whisper from Carol, Annie Dewey lit up in plea-

sure, as if she'd been waiting for ages to meet this beau belonging to Miss Macmurray, who had clearly been wonderful
company as they rode the victorious rails from Jackson. And
then, sure enough—this was more unbelievable than Harvey
P. Angell—it was time for Jack Riley, this goddamn Taft
Hartley-repealing pugilist, to politely offer his hand to the
real next President of the United States, not the lame duck
he'd met on Labor Day—and for Thomas E. Dewey, still
eager to please mama, to give a warm clap on the back to this
obviously splendid fellow.

"WE DON'T SMEAR OUR OPPONENT. WE DON'T ABUSE HIM. WE
don't call him the ugly names we hear poured out in recent
years by zealots."

Dewey's words slid through the ten sets of phone circuits strung along South Washington and out of Peter's car
radio as he drove his '49 Ford north up the deserted street.
Streamers, handbills and tufts of cotton candy blew about in
the night, getting caught in his wipers as they brushed the
windshield's freezing damp.

"In Owosso, nobody has succeeded in setting labor
against management or making people think in terms of
classes. 'Class warfare' and 'social distinctions' are terms that
have no meaning here. Nobody has succeeded in setting the
farmer against the storekeeper, the factory man or the laboring man. Everybody works for a living, we're all useful, we all
depend on each other and we know it."

The beautiful, plummy voice seemed to be coming from
the huge pictures in every window. A corner of the DEWEY:
HONESTY, STRENGTH sign above the door to Feller, Terry &

Nast was flapping in the chill breeze, but across the street Leo Abner had taken care to keep all decoration inside his bookshop. A warm electric light fell upon red-white-and-blue cloth swaddling a 1944 campaign poster of the governor.

Just before 10:36 Peter looked at his watch, crossed Main Street and drove on toward Exchange. Here, too, all was deserted, as if some piper of the night had led the whole town, children and grown-ups, away from their hearths and into a forest. Peter parked the car on Water Street, across from the Armory and high school, and walked through the space between the buildings, as quietly as he could, until the ground began sloping downward toward the Shiawassee. There he paused. Only two lights were visible: one across the river in a room at the top of the castle, the other a lantern beside a boat tied up at the bank on this side.

The old man was digging, as Peter knew he would be. The other night, once he'd opened the buckram box and scanned the papers inside, all of it—the shovels and the colonel's depth of feeling against the Dewey Walk and his disappointment in Wright George—had made sense. And what better time would there be for him to go down and dig than late on the night when every person in town was sure to be two miles away?

Even so, the old man was running out of time. It was 10:40 now, just five minutes before Dewey would make his precision finish and the population of Owosso, on foot and in cars, would start coming back north. Peter could hear the colonel's grunts, his plaintive exhalations after piling each shovelful of wet earth upon the others. He was up to his chest in the hole he'd dug, wondering if he'd remembered the right spot. Peter debated whether to stop him, to lift him out of the pit before his heart gave out, but as the old man's cries grew louder, more and more alive with pain, Peter decided to let him play out this last act of his secret drama.

Another shovelful, and another cry; another and another, until Peter could feel his feet beginning to intervene with a will of their own. But they stopped dead when Horace let out a long, high wail. He thumped the shovel, two, three times on what it had struck, and began a new, more frantic series of scoops, less vertical than horizontal. Each one made a scraping sound, as another few square inches of coffin came visible. Before two more minutes passed, Horace threw the shovel against the pile of soil he'd removed and began trying to lift one end of the box with his bare hands. Nothing budged, but he kept trying, until he sobbed with frustration. He paused to look at his pocket watch and fell backwards onto the still half-buried coffin. He cried out against his own foolishness.

All at once a splash, and then a ripple in the water, and then a wake, human-sized, traveling across the narrow river from the castle side. Taking advantage of the sound, which had caught Horace's attention and brought his head warily above the earth's surface, Peter crept lower down the bank to a clump of bushes, waiting for what would come up near the rowboat.

It was a boy, clad only in a pair of summer shorts, his wet hair shining in the moonlight. He was racing up the bank to the open grave, pulling the old man out of it.

The colonel, no doubt thinking he was in a dream or past his death, protested not at all as the boy picked up the shovel and finished digging out enough dirt to free the casket. "Come on," he said to the old man, dragging the box by

its handles to the water's edge. With a small assist from the
exhausted colonel, he loaded it into the rowboat. Then he
helped the old man get in and took hold of the oars. He gestured with his head for Horace to unfasten the rope.

"I know you," said the frightened Horace Sinclair.

The boy just nodded, and at 10:48 Peter watched the
old man and Tim Herrick set off with the body of Jonathan
Adams Darrell on a half-minute sail to Curwood Castle.

BY THE TIME HE CRAWLED OUT OF THE ROWBOAT, HORACE
was so dazed with exhaustion and disbelief he barely realized
he was being led, along with Jon's bones, inside the sixteen-
inch stone walls of old man Curwood's folly. Horace had already been middle-aged when the writer built the place in
1922; after getting over his initial fear that something to
match it would soon go up on the other side of the river, he
had continued to dislike the pile for its simple incongruity,
though he would admit, before too many years went by, that
it had grown on him. In fact, this summer another old-timer
had reminded Horace of that change of heart, suggesting he
might eventually make peace with the Dewey Walk, too.

The boy dragged the muddy coffin and the lantern into
the middle of the castle's big room. The peaked rafters and
flickering light reminded Horace of the church in which
Jon's coffin might have had its funeral years before, if he and
Wright and Boyd hadn't lost their heads, though the ecclesi-
astical look of the place actually had to do with Curwood's
worship of himself. There were flags all around the room,
for every nation that had sent a guest to the castle; to entertain them the best-selling author would project the tame
movies made from his wild printed yarns.

Horace was thoroughly confused. He knew he was with the Herrick boy, the one who'd been missing, but he could not keep straight how the boy had gotten home and how long he'd been in the castle. It was easier for Horace to convey the story of "this guy," as the boy referred to Jon, or at least his bones. After so many years of rehearsing it to himself, the tale came out as automatically as the Our Father on a Sunday morning.

"So you dug him up before the guys digging the Dewey Walk could find him?"

Horace nodded and asked the only question he would all night. "What can I do with him now?"

His own plan had been to sail the coffin a third of a mile up the river, to hide it away from the Walk site and rebury it another night. But it was too late for that: through the stone walls and the cracked window he and the boy could hear the honking horns and singing voices of the crowd returning from Willman Field.

"I know a place outside town where we could bring it."

Horace could sense that the boy was used to being no longer himself; his febrile enthusiasm showed that he judged Horace a daft kindred spirit. "But we've got to wait until the coast is clear. I'll telephone you, someday soon, probably in the middle of the night. But for now I've got to lie low. I'll put him up in the turret, and I'll clean the carpet down here so nobody who comes in gets suspicious. Some men from the school board have come by twice, in the afternoons. They talk about their plan to fix up the castle, but they never go upstairs. I listen to them from the top of the winding stairs. Can you walk home all right?" He seemed amazed by Horace's lack of a car, which was, to say the least, going to complicate the reburial possibilities.

Horace, so tired that for one terrible moment he was unsure he wasn't talking to Jon himself, said yes. And Tim (for that was his name, not Arnie, as Horace kept thinking) promised he would keep Mr. Sinclair's secret if Mr. Sinclair would keep his.

Pursued by the voices and horns, Horace made his way to the bridge on Shiawassee Street, trying to avoid the eyes of his neighbors. He detoured all the way to King before turning east. Once home, he collapsed upon his sofa, and realized that he had left his shovel and lantern with the boy. Would Tim keep them well hidden from the school board? And remember to bring them when they reburied Jon? Would he really remember his pledge and come?

ELEVEN

October 24 – November 2

ON SUNDAY MORNING, THE GOVERNOR WALKED DOWN THE
aisle of Christ Episcopal right on time and then took a
seat in his mother's pew, about three-quarters of the way
down the right side. The church fairly shone with elbow
grease and excitement, but no mention of the candidate's
presence was ever made from the pulpit. The service was
like a game of exegesis. One listened to the eighty-fourth
Psalm and tried to figure out its applicability to the occasion. The hymn, "Lead Us, Heavenly Father, O'er the
World's Tempestuous Sea," was a giveaway, but Reverend
Davis's sermon conveyed only the most covert blessing
on Dewey's polite crusade to retake Jerusalem from the
New-Dealing infidels: "In this solemn hour when the fate
of the world is in the balance, 'Let us take care to maintain
a conscience that is void of offense toward God and man.'"
A truly attentive listener might have found some holes in
the tropes: "It is mandatory that we say what we mean, and
mean what we say," declared the minister, not considering

that it was Truman who excelled at the first and Dewey the second.

Peter had been attending church regularly since Labor Day, but this morning he was so preoccupied by other matters that when the organist began playing the recessional, "My Country 'Tis of Thee," he thought for a moment he was back in Grosvenor Square drinking the health of George VI. What he'd witnessed down on the riverbank twelve hours before kept his mind off the immediate scene. Was the Herrick kid still holed up in the castle with the bones of Jonathan Adams Darrell? Did his crazy mother have any idea he was there, or even alive? Peter searched the pews behind Dewey for Horace Sinclair but saw no sign of him. Presumably he was at home sleeping off his night's labor; after the service, he was not on the church steps to hear Peter's *Sun-Times* friend, as promised, ask the governor if he felt entirely comfortable with the money Owosso would soon be spending on its monument to his political success. The candidate replied, serenely: "I regard it as a delightful tribute to democracy and the wonderful town that produced me. I'm quite unworthy of it, but the people of Owosso have the good sense to decide such things for themselves." And now, if you would excuse him, he was ready to escort Mrs. Dewey and their sons to the portion of the weekend they'd been looking forward to most: a turkey dinner at his mother's house. "Good morning, gentlemen!" The departing worshipers applauded and set off after him down to 421 West Oliver, where some stayed all afternoon, gawking through Annie Dewey's lace curtains.

Well, thought Peter, walking home in the opposite direction, that was that. He'd kept his promise to the colonel, but the green light had gone to Al Jackson. Would it matter now? With the exhumation of the body, would the old man care any longer? Not if he'd managed to get the bones out of the castle and reburied away from anyone's notice.

Peter asked and re-asked himself the obvious questions. How long had young Herrick been inside Curwood's folly? How had he gotten back to Owosso, and where was the plane? Had anyone helped him get home, and was anybody—Margaret Feller, let's say—helping him to stay? Somehow Peter didn't think so: he'd seen her coming into church with her father and mother. They'd even exchanged a few words, and he'd found her a perfect lady, dulled by her sorrow but a good deal warmer to him than usual. She was riding her parents' new wave of sympathy for poor, chastened Peter.

His friend from the *Sun-Times* left town five minutes after the service, promising to mail Peter the picture he'd gotten of him and Dewey and Rev. Davis. For an instant Peter thought of telling the reporter how, inside that little castle he'd probably noticed, there was a far better story than this orgy of hometown adulation. But he checked himself. If it got out that he was messed up in the Tim Herrick mystery, if only by providing its solution, who knew what suspicions might be raised? Harvey P. Angell might wind up getting elected over his own protests that he was sure Peter Cox hadn't done anything wrong.

Should he tell Anne the story, give it to her for her novel? No, she'd only remind him he was the accessory to a crime, which he probably was, before telling Riley to break down the castle walls with his bare, heroic hands. But there was more than the practical angle. Peter wanted to let the kid play out whatever he was doing, the same way he'd decided not to halt the colonel's strenuous digging. In a way he envied both of them; each seemed closer to accomplishing something than he himself had gotten with his campaign to wrest Anne from Riley.

There was something foolishly consoling in this new secret he had, and on Sunday night he drove across the Main Street bridge, looking to see if the kid had nerve enough to keep the light on. When he slowed down to peer, he could make out just a flicker: Horace Sinclair's lantern, he would bet, a dimmer substitute for an electric bulb. One good rain had washed away any signs of Horace's digging; the dirt, if not the coffin, must have been replaced by the kid.

FIVE DAYS AFTER THE PARADE, JUST FIVE NIGHTS BEFORE THE election, Peter saw Anne again. Sitting dateless in the Capitol Theatre, watching an early-evening showing of *The Dewey Story*, he was startled by the sight of her, for a few quick seconds, in Mama Dewey's parlor, before she and Owosso disappeared from the film, making room for a review of the candidate's march toward the White House, that sequence of events soon to be made even more dully familiar by the Dewey Walk.

The Fellers were being especially friendly. Harold let his absences from the office go unremarked upon, and Carol had him over to dinner, where they talked of Other Things. They were treating him with the kindness one shows a loser, which was what he would continue feeling like Tuesday night, even after Harvey Angell rang up from Durand.

He wouldn't be surprised if Dewey wound up feeling the same. The campaign had hit a nasty end, Truman outdoing himself for sheer buffoonishness by comparing the Republican candidate to Hitler. Dewey's wife had kept her husband from fighting back—or so Peter had heard from an insider friend in New York. Politically, the wife was the wiser of the two, but Peter had to wonder if five days from now, on top of the Roosevelt Hotel and striding the free world, Dewey would be feeling every bit a President and not entirely a man.

THE MORNING AFTER THE PARADE HORACE AWAKENED TOO late to go to Christ Episcopal, but he had long since given up that any answer Dewey gave Cox's friend from the *Sun-Times* would make a difference; he wondered only if his own absence from the service would be remarked upon. This small worry joined the new guilty spectres in his brain. What would happen if the boy was discovered with the body? What sort of monster would Horace Sinclair be thought for having, in addition to his youthful crime, failed to tell Mrs. Herrick her son was still alive and well? Each day for the next week he thought of going to her house and confessing all, and each day his new awful secret held him back as firmly as the old. On Friday afternoon, the twenty-ninth, he saw her walking down Oliver Street with the science teacher, Sherwood, and came within a second of calling out the window; but the moment passed and he never said a word, just calculated how, once he got what he wanted from the boy, he would be able to inform her with an anonymous note, and hope that Tim didn't pay him back betrayal for betrayal.

Oh, why had he never learned to drive a car? This stupid piece of imagined fealty to the past would now prevent him from keeping his pact with it. He had not dared go back to the castle, not even in the hours before dawn, though down along the river night was hardly night now, not with the floodlight Jackson had started shining upon the billboard announcing the Dewey Walk. For the past week Horace had confined his time outdoors to brief morning walks, awaiting discovery at every turn. "The thief doth fear each bush an officer," he whispered, dreading the look of everyone he knew, most of all Peter Cox. The cessation of those unexpected, knowing visits of his now seemed more ominous than the visits themselves. Whatever happened, whenever it did, Horace felt sure it would be even worse than the consequences of leaving the body where it had been.

LATE ON SATURDAY AFTERNOON, THE THIRTIETH, FRANK went into Abner's, knowing that Anne Macmurray was off for the day and couldn't bother him with all her fond, well-meaning questions, worse in their way than Mrs. Wagner's. He scanned the shelves for something he could bring to Jane's, passing up Lloyd C. Douglas and *Doctor Faustus* and anything about the war in favor of some man named Robinson's history of the British post office, a paradise of numbers and linkages that Leo Abner, probably unable to resist some sales rep with the tale of a new baby at home, had agreed to stock.

A few hours later he arrived for dinner and gave the book to Jane, just before blurting out his confession: "I can't go back to school next week. I won't. I was staring at my grade book all morning, and at two o'clock this afternoon I threw it away."

"Quit," she said, without a pause. "Get your money when the bank opens Monday morning and leave without delay." The emergency enlivened her, made her seem just a normal person in the heat of an important moment. Clasping his arms, she literally pushed on him, moving his body two inches to the right, as if helping him dodge a bullet. "Just go. Don't even give them notice."

Frank laughed, letting himself enjoy the impossibility.

"I'll drop you off at the Grand Trunk depot. You can take the train from Durand to Chicago and then leave on the Broadway Limited for New York. It pulls out at 4:30."

How did she know these things? Had she studied the regular commercial timetables while memorizing troop trains and doing the ratio of those who boarded to those who survived?

"I'll give you the Durand-to-Chicago fare," she said. "A going-away present."

From the moment a week ago when she'd leaned over to touch and thank him, it had become Jane Herrick's mission in life to rectify a miscount of the dead that had consigned Frank Sherwood's spirit six feet under. Her duty, as she somehow saw it, was to repatriate him among the living, to get him back *to* some corner of a vital foreign field. Mixed in with the more fantastic ingredients of her motive was a simple, sensible desire to convince Frank that Owosso was no place for him. Somewhere else, like New York, he could find what he should be looking for—something unspoken but presumably other than a girl, of which Owosso afforded many.

He tried changing the subject. "Do you want to go up on the roof later?" He meant the roof of his place, where they'd gone this week after dinners at the Hotel Owosso and a nice restaurant in Lansing. He was teaching her the rudiments of astronomy, whose distances and brightness factors were a natural for her statistical mind; she took his own awareness of them as further evidence of his displacement, his being worlds away from where he belonged. He'd been showing her Jupiter, not stopping the telescope along its arc above Oak Hill.

Jane didn't answer. She led him to the table and made him sit down. "Arnie never liked corn," she said, pointing to the plates, as if baffled by the vegetable's reappearance. Frank thrilled to hear this fact, because it was one he remembered. As the week passed, he'd had the feeling she saw him as a living substitute whose own attractiveness, like that of nylon stockings, established itself unexpectedly.

"Picture yourself in the Pullman," she urged.

"I've never been in a sleeper."

"That means for a while you'll sit up, with your tie still fastened. You'll be a little too nervous to loosen it. It's nine o'clock and you're two hundred miles out of Chicago, still twelve hours away from New York. You're fingering the quarter you have left over from the fifty-cent haircut you had right on the train. You used the third quarter to tip the barber, who never once nicked you as the train sped along the rails."

All the cosmic arrangements he was used to calculating had never really allowed him to project himself anywhere; the dry dates and numbers she gathered in grief were, he now understood, kindling for an imagination that let her go backwards and forwards to live and relive life, as it might be, as it had been, with more detail than most people noticed while it happened in real time, right before them.

"Will you get into bed or go to the club car? Maybe try and find the library they say exists on that train?"

He pushed some corn away with his fork. There was a wild, sickening intimacy to what she was doing. It was as if she'd loosened a button on his shirt, or was saying the words he could remember from long ago—*you know you want to*—as she drew him into a game that, yes, he did want to play. *You're a nice-looking man, Frank.*

"What's above you?" she asked. "On the rack."

"Two suitcases," he said. "And the telescope. In the aluminum packing tube."

She nodded encouragement. "When you wake up in the Pullman it'll be Tuesday morning."

"Just when they're really beginning to miss me at school. The first day they'll figure I felt too sick to call in, but on the second, even with the voting lines in the gym to distract them, they'll know something's really wrong. An investigation will 'ensue,' as the *Argus* would put it, and that will lead to the discovery that on Monday morning Mr. Sherwood withdrew every last cent—$706.48—from his account at the State Savings Bank."

She smiled at him. *Now you're getting it.*

On Sunday night, through the wall, he heard Anne and Jack Riley laughing over Jack Benny. He packed the two suitcases and left whatever wouldn't fit. He went up to the roof to dismantle the telescope, humming "This Can't Be Love" as he cleaned it off with the chamois cloth. Monday morning, as soon as he was through waiting on the longer of two lines at the bank, the one that led to Arnie's old window, he called Jane to tell her what he had done and to ask if she would actually give him the ride to Durand. He almost asked her to come for him in the old Chevrolet, which he was sure still sat in her garage, but he didn't want to risk revelation for the sake of a talisman. As it was, when they got to the depot, he handed her an envelope with the instruction not to open it until she heard from him again. She nodded, uncompelled to ask whether that would be in ten days or ten years or some exponential measure of astronomers' time. She just took the envelope and said good-bye.

MRS. BRUCE WAS ALREADY CLOSING THE BOOKS. HAVING JUST paid Billy Grimes' two friends twelve dollars to adorn a hundred telephone poles with new likenesses of Peter Cox, and having already bought champagne for tomorrow night's victory party, the campaign had made its final expenditures. All of tomorrow's drivers were strictly volunteers, and when a half hour ago they became overbooked, Mr. Cox, like an angel, had offered to ride the last old lady on the list. What a thrill she would have when he showed up to take her from Mason Street to the high school.

Everything was running smooth as silk, though Mrs. Bruce could have done without this co-ed on the telephone across the room. Her job was setting up election-night interviews with out-of-state reporters here to cover the hometown angle. Mr. Cox might make jokes about his "duty" to represent the wave of young Republican officeholders who would be coming in with Dewey, but Mrs. Bruce knew it was precisely because he thought of such things that he was going places. There was no reason she couldn't be making these calls herself, but he'd told her the account books and drivers were too important to have her diverted from them. She couldn't help letting her imagination get ahead of itself, picturing what she might be doing on this very night four or six years from now, when Peter Cox ran for the U.S. Senate or the governor's mansion.

In the office's other room, the candidate sat with his feet up on the desk, looking at the wall clock. It was getting on toward 8 P.M., and he had run out of things to do. He'd talked to the Kiwanis Club in Perry, shaken hands in front of Christian's and checked his mother into the Hotel Owosso. He'd told her there was plenty of room with him on Park Street, but she'd insisted. It wasn't that she expected some sock-strewn bachelor's lair; she wanted to be part of the out-of-town crowd in order to meet that younger version of Senator Barkley. Late tomorrow night she'd join the locals celebrating here in the Matthews Building and over at the City Club.

WHAT DEWEY WILL DO, announced the cover of *Changing Times,* the top magazine on the stack by Peter's feet. He'd spent part of the day listlessly reading them, instead of plotting what moves he should make as soon as the returns showed him elected. He'd remembered to set up the out-of-town papers and radio guys, but there was another score of local follow-up actions he should be getting ready to perform, phone calls and thank-you notes and the rest of it, to put a little early-as-possible oomph into his springboard for '50 or '52; and he couldn't interest himself to the point of even making a list. He'd do his interviews, take Harvey Angell's painfully gracious phone call—and then what?

The ice that was falling off his mother seemed to be repacking itself around him. Take that co-ed in the outer office: he'd made sure to hire the best-looking of the three that had responded to the notice on the door, but since this morning he'd offered her barely more than a hello. Even a few weeks ago he'd have been all over the young lady, probably inviting her to their own private election-night party. As it was, he couldn't bring himself to go near her; this luscious sweater girl seemed coated with the thumbsucking repellent his mother used to make the maid apply to him.

He tried to interest himself in the Chicago papers. The *Tribune*'s editorial was ordering Republican readers to the polls, warning against overconfidence. The editors so despised Dewey, this white-glove candidate incapable of flinging red meat, that, like Rev. Davis, they couldn't bring themselves to speak his name. Still, he was all that would deliver them from Roosevelt's ghost.

A knock on the door. Oh, *not* Mrs. Bruce telling him one more thing the sweater girl had done wrong or the name of another biddy needing a chauffeur to the voting booth. "Come in," he sighed.

"For luck," said Anne, taking a small package from the oversized pocket of her coat.

"You shouldn't have," said Peter.

"I shouldn't have," she replied, while he unwrapped a copy of Dewey's 1944 campaign biography.

"These still aren't moving," she said. "Leo let me have it at cost."

"Inscribed, to boot."

"Inscribed."

"'To Peter, on the eve of his first election victory. With a reminder that he now has until 1964 to reach the White House without being older than Thomas E. Dewey. Fondly, Anne.'"

"You don't know what to say," she said.

"I don't know what to say. Want one of these in exchange?" He handed her a copy of Sunday's church program. "I didn't see you there."

"No, I never made it. After Saturday night I figured there was a limit to how much Dewey I could foist on Jack."

"Ah, yes. We all know he has his Dewey limits."

"Do-we ever. Have you got any plans for your, what do they call it? Pre-incumbency? The time between now and January."

"Not many. Making up to Harold some of the time I've cheated him out of. Maybe looking for a little apartment in Lansing. I won't want to make the drive every day. And you?"

"Oh, the usual."

"Have you set the date?"

"More or less. March sixth, or maybe the thirteenth."

"I've got one, too."

"A date?"

"A date. With Harvey P. Angell's wife's cousin. A fix-up."

She gave him a weak smile. "I'd better get going. I've got to stop off at the Abners'. Leo's wife is sick, and—yes, Peter—I want to get home in time for Truman's speech."

"Say good night, Harry."

"Good night, Harry."

As she buttoned her coat, he leaned across the space between them and kissed her, if only on the cheek, for the first time since Mackinac in July. "Good-bye, Gracie."

OUTSIDE THE MATTHEWS BUILDING, BY THE LIGHT OF A streetlamp, she opened the church program, determined not to regret the perfectly sensible gesture she had just performed. The three of them were going to be living in the same town, after all. She'd heard about Dewey's name never being mentioned by the minister, a classy, very American touch, she thought, but they'd certainly made up for it in this handout, which went on about "a native son who by his ability and integrity has won the admiration of the American people." The Reverend Davis referred contentedly to how the pollsters' "prophecy" of Dewey's election awaited fulfillment, though, as she slipped the program back into her coat pocket, his last line—"We earnestly pray that God will guide, protect and bless him in any vocation to which he may be called"—seemed to the writer in her just a little off-kilter, as if the diction of modesty had gotten tinged with the tones of religious mystery.

She would never make it back to Jack by the time she'd promised. Before she went to the Abners' on Washington Street, she had to stop at her apartment, where—oh, let it not be true—Mrs. Wagner seemed to be lying in wait. But no, the blue coat coming toward her was not Mrs. Wagner's. The cut and fabric were too fashionable, and the kerchief was protecting hair that had just come from the beauty parlor.

"There you are!" called a deep, confident voice, as if Anne were late for an appointment. The voice belonged, she could now see, to Lucy Cox, whose skin was two shades darker than it had been on Mackinac back in July.

"For goodness' sake," said Anne. "Hello." (Had she ever sent that thank-you note?) "You must be in town for Peter's big day." She *could not* tell her she had just been up to see him. She would get the wrong idea completely.

"Yes," said Mrs. Cox. "I'm at the hotel. Look, I got a new

Dewey button in the coffee shop. I'd left my old one on my light jacket, which I was wearing up until a week ago."

What did one say? That one was "sorry"? She settled for "Yes, I heard that you'd been out West."

"That's right. He took it rather hard, unfortunately."

Anne fumbled. "I'm afraid I don't know Mr. Cox, but I'm sure he'll feel better as time goes—"

"Not Mr. Cox. Peter. Peter took it hard."

"Oh."

"I arrived in town this morning, and was coming to invite you to a lunch party I'm giving at the hotel on Wednesday, to celebrate. I had your address on that lovely note of yours that got forwarded. It's pretty short notice, I know, so I thought I'd walk over and ask you in person."

"Mrs. Cox, I'm sorry, but I won't be able to—"

"That's all right, dear. He says he won't be able to make it either."

"He?"

"The guest of honor. Peter."

"Why is that?"

"I honestly don't know. And that's the *real* reason I came by. I thought you might. All I did was mention this little lunch, while he was checking me into the hotel, and he said, no, not possible, he expected to have some business to take care of on Wednesday. What business? I asked. And all I got was this look. So I thought you might know. What business?"

"I don't know, Mrs. Cox. Perhaps he's just trying not to tempt the gods. You know, by agreeing to a victory lunch in advance."

"My dear, has Peter ever struck you as lacking in confidence?"

"Well, no."

"There's something on his mind, and I can't figure out what it is. I haven't been paying him much attention these last ten or fifteen years."

JACK SAT ON THE COUCH, LISTENING TO TRUMAN AND WAIT-ing for Anne to come home. Years from now, he thought, whenever the two of them happened to hear that voice, in an old newsreel or on some radio program, they'd recall it the way other couples did "our song." Listening to it now made him want to get a record of it.

He was keeping her dinner warm in the oven, though he didn't expect her to stay the night. He was still registered to vote in Flint, and would have to be up at five-thirty to help Walt dispatch the fleet of union drivers ferrying widows and crippled veterans to and from the polls. It was going to be a long day's work for a short evening of disappointment, but he'd promised Anne he'd start back for Owosso as soon as voting stopped at 8 P.M.

He had never voted at home. In '44 he'd filled out his ballot in Europe, and four years before that had been under twenty-one, though he could remember Gene going around the block that time to vote for Roosevelt, complaining about the idea of a third term but saying the worst thing about Willkie was he came from some town in Indiana "a little too goddamned like this one."

Next time he and Anne would both be standing in line at the big Emerson elementary school. The business of the house had been settled: they would keep this one and start fixing it up between now and the wedding. Before they got around to anything that could be called remodeling, they'd be busy with simple repairs, all the stuff Gene had had to let slide.

Tomorrow night they'd be saying good-bye to Truman from the City Club, where Anne would be with the Fellers. They had told him to make sure he came by as soon as he returned from Flint, which was fine with him: it would be more practice for Christmas in Connecticut. Anne had already bought their train tickets, and he was less nervous about the whole thing than he might have been. He'd decided their engagement was hardly the most surprising thing you could think of. Asked to name that, he'd have to say it was John L. Lewis (that secret symbol of all his own shortcomings) practically endorsing Dewey! A temper tantrum left over from last year's dispute with Truman, and pretty idiotic, but it did show you that anything could happen.

He wouldn't say it to Walt, but Jack knew that good times were ahead, whoever got in. Along with all its new power, the whole country was bound to get richer. This small house, which had once brought deliverance to the Rileys, would now be only what the real-estate agents called a "starter" for him and Anne. It would do them for Junior and maybe Junior's little brother, but when the third one came along they'd trade up to something bigger.

"I know," said Anne, a second after Jack heard the door. "I'm late. Leo's wife is sick, and when I brought them over some things from the drugstore, the three of us got to talking." She looked at the clock: it was twenty to ten.

"You haven't missed much," said Jack, turning off the oven and taking out her plate.

"I will miss *him,*" she said, pointing to the radio. *"Tonight*

*I am at my home here in Independence—Independence, Missouri—
with Mrs. Truman and Margaret. We are here to vote tomorrow as
citizens of this Republic. I hope that all of you who are entitled to
vote will exercise that great privilege."* For a moment the two of
them listened in silence, as if she were thinking what he had
a minute ago, and they were an old man and wife hearing
"Alice Blue Gown."

"The high school's going to be mobbed," Anne said.
Maybe she'd walk there to vote with Frank Sherwood, if Mrs.
Wagner didn't nab her first.

"Walt wants all his voters up early. He's told the drivers
to pick them up before lunch. He figures as the day draws
on, even before any returns come in, they're going to see
less and less point to it." He set down her plate and she
kissed him.

*"I believe that the Democratic party is the party of the people. I
believe that through the Democratic party all classes of our citizens
will receive fairer treatment and more security."*

"At least," said Jack, "he admits that classes exist. Remember Dewey talking at Willman? He said there was no
such thing."

Anne said nothing. Jack and Truman were right, but it
was Dewey's illusion she now needed to believe, the feeling
that these differences mattered not at all, that even if they
had once complicated life, they had long since been
bridged.

*"As you mark your ballots tomorrow, I want every housewife to
ask herself: Will this protect my home and my children for the future?
I want every husband to ask himself: Is this best for my wife and
family?"*

Jack looked across the table at the future Mrs. Riley, who

was looking at the radio as if actually trying to answer Truman's questions.

"Do you want ketchup?" he asked her.

"I'm sorry," she said, seeing his look of disappointment at her still-full plate. "I guess I'm not that hungry." She took a couple of bites before saying, "Can we go to bed?" knowing that they couldn't, not just yet, not until she helped him put up the storm window in Gene's old room, where the sill was rotting from all the rain getting in. She knew that Jack had to be up at five-thirty, and that even if she stayed, she'd have to sneak out extra early, since Mrs. Wagner was bound to tap on her door while making an early run to the polls. She knew he wouldn't be able to do what she most needed him to tonight, which was make love to her.

"Go to the polls tomorrow, and vote your convictions, your hopes, and your faith—"

The President spoke, she thought, as if those three things were always the same. She held her empty fork and envied him, before saying, with she hoped no trace of a quaver in her voice: "Jack, honey, let's find that storm window."

BY THE TIME HARRY TRUMAN ROSE AT 5 A.M. ON ELECTION day, Thomas E. Dewey had already beaten him, 11 to 1, in Hart's Location, New Hampshire, though the big story was that Hart's Location had defeated Dixville Notch in the race to have a first-in-the-nation count go out over wire services and radio. Most of the country, including Owosso, had awakened to fairly mild fall weather. The Shiawassee County clerk, Sherman Welch, husband of Dewey's first cousin and father of fourteen-year-old Phil on the bobsled float, had arranged for 20 percent more ballots to be printed than ever before. Owosso did its voting by machine, but Dewey's presence at the head of the ticket was expected to swell the turnout in the outlying towns as well. Welch's office was urging people to show up at the polls as early as possible.

This warning was quite unnecessary to Horace Sinclair, who was in line at 7:00 A.M., as he had been every first-Tuesday-after-the-first-Monday-in-November since picking McKinley over Bryan. At the Emerson School only three people stood ahead of him, one of them being Peter Cox, who hoped to flash his smile to the line of voters when he came out of the booth.

Upon emerging, he had time for just a brief exchange with Horace.

"I tried, Colonel. You saw what he said to my *Sun-Times* buddy."

"Well," said Horace, looking straight ahead, "we don't always get what we hope for."

"I know," said Peter. "I didn't either."

Figuring he meant the Macmurray girl, Horace replied, "I'm sorry about that," though he wasn't. "You'll have your other victory later today."

"Sixty-five percent, Colonel. See if I'm not right. And remember, there's nothing wrong with splitting your ticket."

Horace no more required Peter's advice than he had Sherman Welch's. He was in and out of the booth in the space of ten seconds, voting for Truman and nobody else. He hurried home as fast as his ever more wobbly legs would carry him. Once there, he bolted the door and did not raise the blinds. He opened up *The Lady of the Lake,* hoping she would put him to sleep before lunchtime. She succeeded, keeping him there into the early evening, except for two quick interruptions: the thump of the *Argus* (thrown through the passenger window of Billy Grimes' new 1941 Ford) and Mrs. Goldstone's delivery of half a turkey with three tiny American flags flying from toothpicks.

Horace ate two slices off it and waited until eight o'clock before turning on the radio. He would not listen to WOAP tonight, for the same reason he had left the *Argus* outside his locked door: to avoid a lot of mush about the hometown prodigy. He would go with the ABC station from Flint, even though it was promising Dr. Gallup and Walter Winchell, neither of whom he could stand. Gallup, of course, was merely the messenger bearing bad news, though he'd been bearing it, to Horace's discomfort, for months now. But Winchell, whose rat-a-tat-tat reminded him of Truman's, was a teller of other people's secrets, the most infernal, automated busybody the world had ever seen. Horace could imagine him declaiming to Mr. and Mrs. North America and all the ships at sea the story of Jonathan Adams Darrell, whose bones, unbeknownst to everyone, were lying inside a little castle in Owosso, Michigan. Before Winchell was through, the tale would probably involve drugged starlets and Nazi spies, instead of just the original, sad fifty-year-old facts and the pathetic postscript of a weary old man and missing local boy.

It was too late to undo things. It was too late for everything. The polls had just closed, according to the Flint announcer, who told his listeners that the day's good weather assured a big farm vote across the whole region and, as a result of that if nothing else, the election of Thomas E. Dewey.

·   ·   ·

"FIFTY, RIGHT?" ASKED BILLY GRIMES.

"Fifty," he was assured by the Campbell brothers' sales manager. The *Argus* was planning to put out an Extra shortly after midnight, and Billy was reserving a full bale of what were sure to be highly saleable collectors' items. He was also carrying the best camera and night lens he could borrow from Mr. Jackson's shop. Photographers from *Time* and *Life* and the newsreels had already fanned out through town to shoot the local-color celebrations, but if they spent as much time drinking as his father said these journalists did, they might be grateful for the chance to buy some extra pictures from a kid who really knew the neighborhood.

It was past ten now, and the crowd outside the Argus was stretching down Park toward Christian's and the Capitol. A special late showing of *The Big Sleep* was in progress there, but Billy had just heard from one of the *Time* stringers that hardly anybody was in the audience. By a week from tomorrow, when *So Evil My Love* started playing, things would be back to normal and the place packed with the usual Wednesday first-night crowd.

But what was he thinking? Things were never going to be the same here. Along with the tourists coming to see the Walk, these reporters would be back any time Dewey did something big in the next eight years, the way they used to descend on Hyde Park and Warm Springs to see if the President's own neighbors liked what he was up to.

Billy went through the lobby and looked at the tote board set up with a chalk-rimmed box for each county in Michigan and state in the country. Truman was ahead in both counts, but as the loudspeakers kept assuring the crowd on the street, that was only to be expected: the big cities, where the bulk of the President's voters lived, always reported first. Billy knew that in an hour or two Harry's percentages would take a sickening plunge, the way, whenever you got to the point in a movie where the stock market crashed, ticker tape slipped like sand through the broker's hands. The only thing missing would be those fast, squeaky violin notes changing into groans from a bass fiddle.

"Miss Macmurray! Mr. and Mrs. Feller!" He waved to them on the other side of Exchange, figuring they had detoured by the Argus on their way to the City Club. He knew from Margaret that Anne was having dinner with them, and that afterwards they were going to celebrate the results downtown. Jack Riley, who was being treated these days like he was practically a member, planned to join them when he got back from Flint.

Margaret might make it there herself, if rehearsals at school for *Dear Ruth* finished up early enough. When she'd told him this, he'd reacted with an anxious look, as if she might expect him to show up, too. But then she'd remembered the killing he'd told her he could make off the pictures and the Extra, and she'd responded with a tired smile, as if they were already married and he was calling to say he'd be working late at the office.

THE CITY CLUB WAS JAMMED WITH MEMBERS AND THEIR guests, three times as many as the night before the parade. Extra waiters had been hired for the occasion, but there was no hope of finding a seat in the main dining room. Harold and Anne and Carol squeezed onto a spot of the dance floor as close to the bar as they could get. The radio was tuned to WGN, but the voices of the crowd kept drowning it out.

"Jack!" cried Carol Feller. She'd spotted him over by the entrance to the Long Room, looking bewildered but somehow pleased. "Over here!" she shouted, glad that at least this part of her arrangements had worked out. A moment ago she'd been disappointed to learn from Mrs. Osmond's daughter that Margaret had decided to head straight home after the rehearsal. "Was she feeling all right?" Carol had asked. "Oh, she's fine, Mrs. Feller. She said she was just a little tired." There were times these days when Carol wished her daughter were again feeling angry or even sullen—just not quite so in need of a multivitamin. But there was no time to think about that now, and she felt lifted by Jack Riley's cheerful approach. He gave her, after Anne, a big kiss.

"How was the day?" his fiancée asked.

"Not bad for just going through the motions." He laughed and raised his voice over the radio, which was now being turned up.

"Half the cars were overloaded," he explained. "We had four ladies instead of three in some of the back seats, and they joked all the way to the polling place about who was the fattest. Mostly I'm happy for Walt. Walt's the guy I work with," he explained to the Fellers. "He did a great job turning them out, and they'll notice that in Detroit. It shows we can get well enough organized for something like this that, another time, when we've actually got a shot, we'll make the most of it." His last few words were louder than necessary, because the room was quieting down. Ed Royers was standing on the bar, waving his arms up and down in an effort to hush everybody. The crowd understood why as soon as it heard the announcer, two hundred miles away in the Chicago Tribune tower on Michigan Avenue: " . . . and yes, I've just been handed the first edition of the world's greatest newspaper for November third, 1948, and the headline, ladies and gentlemen, is a brief three words that say it all: DEWEY DEFEATS TRUMAN."

The rest of what he said died in the roar. The extra barmen, like a Busby Berkeley chorus line, succeeded in a simultaneous popping of three champagne corks. The crowd chanted Dewey's name, and Harold and Carol kissed each other hard, both of them surprised to be so moved that this had actually happened in the town where they had lived all their lives. Anne planted her lips on Jack's right cheek and brushed the left one tenderly with her hand. He returned her glistening it's-not-so-bad smile with a kind of amused relief, before turning to shake Harold's hand. A New Year's feeling had come over the hall. It seemed like two minutes past midnight, not twenty minutes after ten, and almost peculiar that the little band had struck up "Peg O' My Heart" instead of "Auld Lang Syne."

"I just thought of something," said Carol. "Where is Al Jackson?"

"In Detroit," said the man behind her. "He wanted to watch on the television. I heard he was going to offer himself to the cameras down there. He's set up some fireworks behind his billboard, and he's left instructions with someone here to shoot them off at the moment it's 'absolutely official.'"

"Poor Al," said Carol, miming his herky-jerky gestures, "how will he describe the Walk without his paintings and props?"

"What makes you think he didn't bring them?" said Harold. "Harris!" he called out. "Make your way here."

Harris Terry struggled to reach his partner's little group, bringing with him a different mood altogether.

"What's the matter?" asked Harold.

"I'm not sure," replied Harris, who valued his reputation for caution. "And I don't want to be the wet blanket at this party, but I was just looking over some teletype at the Argus and there's some peculiar stuff going on. An awful lot of House and Senate seats in the East seem to be going back to the Democrats, and so far Sigler's not doing well at all."

"Really?" asked Harold, whose interest in the governor's fortunes, after the Dewey news, was less than burning.

"As I say, I don't want to make too much out of it, but come January, Dewey may be having a tougher time with Congress than anyone expected."

"I'm beginning to enjoy this," said Jack. He gave Anne's shoulder a squeeze and wondered why she didn't seem in higher spirits herself. Her adopted town was now famous, and it looked as if her new party had still done better in the voting booth than anyone expected. Shouldn't she be at least half as pleased as she'd been Labor Day afternoon? An image of her in that white sleeveless blouse, waving the pennant to catch his eye, came to him now, a memory of perfection. "Is anything wrong, honey?"

"I guess I'm just a little worried about Frank Sherwood," she answered. "No one's seen him since yesterday morning." Though this was news to Jack, it had been Topic B at the Fellers' dinner table.

"Anne, stop worrying," said Harold, who didn't relish another missing-person drama, not after what Tim Herrick's disappearance had put them through this summer. "He's a grown man. When he's over whatever is eating him, he'll come to his senses and get back to school."

"What do you say," suggested Harris Terry, "we all walk over to the Matthews Building and drop in on Peter? The figures show *him* elected for sure, and I'll bet even Jersey Jack here can find it in his heart to shake his hand."

"Gentleman Jack would be an absolute sport about it, Mr. Terry, but I'm going to spare him that," said Anne. "He's already been enough of a sport tonight. I think we're going to check with my landlady to see if Frank's come back or left a message. And then we'll cry over the farm vote in front of Jack's radio."

"I'll walk her safely home after that," said Jack. Carol Feller smiled at his obvious concern that Harris Terry, whose son had been born five months after he and Jeannie got married thirty years ago, might be getting the wrong, which was to say the right, idea. But Harris still seemed preoccupied by the teletype he'd seen at the Argus. He'd not made the slightest movement toward the bar and was really fidgeting to get out of here and over to Peter's headquarters.

The Fellers joined him on the two-block walk to the Matthews Building. Before turning west, Carol looked the other way down Exchange and saw that the crowd outside the newspaper office, instead of burgeoning, was actually smaller and less noisy than the one they'd passed on their way to the club. Whatever the people down there were listening to, it wasn't WGN. The bar that the three of them now passed on their way to Main and Water was certainly full, but as far as she could tell from looking through its window, the patrons weren't celebrating, just concentrating on their drinks. City Hall, across from Peter's office, looked deserted; she'd expected to see Mayor Crawford out on the steps with a dozen flashbulbs going off in his face.

But euphoria was still in business on the second floor of the Matthews Building. The radio there was tuned not to WOAP or any of the network stations, but to a dance band in Flint. A little crowd milled about in front of a blackboard sliced by a giant chalked check mark, whose front tip touched the x in Cox. At just after eleven o'clock nearly all the returns in the state senate race had been counted, and Peter stood elected by a vote of 8,508 to 6,213.

"So where's the victor?" asked Carol.

"Gone for the moment," crowed Mrs. Bruce, who had already collected her kiss of gratitude. "He stepped out a few minutes ago, after getting a call from New York." Mrs. Bruce was still not sure whether the call had been from a reporter or someone with the Dewey campaign, but she did know it hadn't required any arranging by that co-ed, who was sitting across the room and having, by Mrs. Bruce's count, her third glass of champagne. "Here," she said to the Fellers, handing them an open bottle. "Drink up!" Carol thanked her, and went with Harold and Harris Terry to a card table beneath a blow-up photo of Peter and Dewey from the *Chicago Sun-Times*. "Let's stay awhile," she said. There was more room in here than at the City Club, and the atmosphere was a lot better than the weirdly subdued one on the streets outside.

The only candidate in the room was Harvey P. Angell, who an hour ago had come over from Corunna to offer Peter Cox his congratulations. He had stayed on to talk with the state-senator-elect's mother, who had brought along a gentleman from the *Dallas Morning News* who was staying a floor above her in the Hotel Owosso. The three of them had gone through their own bottle of champagne and moved, at Mrs. Cox's insistence, from talking about Peter to about how nice the winter weather in Dallas could be.

A little before midnight Harris Terry hung up the phone he'd been on and, more grim-faced than before, rejoined the Fellers. "Iowa's gone for Truman," he said in a whisper.

"Oh, come *on!*" said Harold, who was in his cups by now and determined to hold Harris to his pledge not to be a wet blanket. "I don't believe you."

"Add up those numbers," said Harris, pointing to the blackboard, whose figures showed what seemed to him the one certain Republican victory of the night.

Harold put on his eyeglasses and affected great concentration. "A landslide," he said. "Sort of. For our overly handsome, generally exasperating and, with any luck, soon-to-be-departing young associate."

"Not the *result,* Harold. The *total,* for the two candidates together. What does it tell you?"

"Nothing," said Harold.

"I think what Harris is trying to say," said Carol, "is that Sherman Welch may be stuck with a lot of unused paper ballots."

"If Republican voters in Shiawassee County aren't coming out the way they were supposed to," said Harris, "how do you think it is in parts of the country that *don't* call Tom Dewey their favorite son?"

Harold gave his partner a good-natured poke in the ribs and went up to the radio, which for the last hour had been switched back and forth, through friendly shouts of disapproval, between the dance-band station and one with the returns. "Do you mind?" he asked the couple next to it.

"Be my guest," the husband said.

Harold slurred the dial over to NBC and Mr. Kaltenborn, who after a moment said that Mr. Truman might, even at this late hour, be a million ahead in the popular count, but when the rest of the farm vote and the West came in, the President would be beaten for sure.

"See?" said Harold, coming back to his wife and Harris for a refill.

OUT ON MAIN STREET, BILLY GRIMES PEDALED WEST ON HIS Columbia bicycle. Anticipating the sort of snarled traffic there'd been a couple of weeks ago, he'd left his Ford parked in his father's garage. He was on his way with the camera to the Dewey birthplace, hoping to get some good exterior shots. It was 12:20 A.M., and the canvas of his empty *Argus* delivery-boy's bag clucked in the night breeze. At 11:55 the Campbells' managing editor had announced that there would be no Extra proclaiming Dewey's victory. The results were still too close to call, and Owosso readers would have to wait for tomorrow's regular edition. So Billy had told the sales manager to save him fifty copies of that one, which would still have considerable value, if not quite what it would have with the word EXTRA emblazoned across the front. For now, he'd just get on with the picture taking, though he couldn't say much for this particular spot. Beneath Charlie Bernard's second-floor apartment, the bunting left over from October 23 hung limp and unlit, and outside the modest brick building where Thomas E. Dewey came into the world on March 24, 1902, not a soul was standing.

•   •   •

HE'D FOUND A BROOM AND DUSTPAN IN THE BASEMENT AND swept the carpet and stairs so completely the school-board people never realized a coffin containing Mr. Sinclair's old friend had spent a night in the main room of James Oliver Curwood's castle.

Since then the box of bones had been up in the turret, where he'd dragged it. The Owosso Casket Company's small brass plate, all cleaned up, glinted in the light from the lamp over which Tim had draped a sweater. (The kerosene was long since gone from the old man's lantern.) The coffin makers had good reason to put their names so proudly on their work: the box had held up beautifully over fifty years. There were one or two patches of rot, but the whole thing was still intact and sealed shut. Only the lining must have disintegrated; as he'd dragged and pushed it up the winding stairs Tim could hear the skeleton rattling against the sides.

He had not been tempted to raise the lid, but he had never felt spooked, either. So this was suicide. How unfinal it appeared to be. Jonathan Adams Darrell seemed, in a way, still *here.* Tim could remember how the old man, while telling the poor guy's story, had every so often looked over to the box, as if he expected the person in it to nod or correct him. Somewhere six feet under Bloomington, Indiana, Tim figured, Ross Lockridge was still here, too, not as completely gone from the world as he'd hoped to be.

He wished he had *Raintree County* with him now. In the two and a half weeks he'd been in the castle, he'd had to make do with the Curwood novels on the shelves near the fireplace downstairs. Once through *Green Timber* and *The Courage of Captain Plum,* he'd given up, preferring to imagine his own stories from the movie posters lining the walls up to the turret. He'd even been tempted to write something himself, maybe the tale of his adventures since August, on the big black L. C. Smith typewriter near the staircase. But there was no paper in the drawer beneath it, and no telling whether the sound of the keys would carry to the houses over on John Street.

Mixed in with the movie posters was a framed front-page Extra from the *Argus*. JAMES OLIVER CURWOOD'S ILLNESS FATAL, said the headline for August 14, 1927. He'd been sick with a streptococcic infection for just ten days, and the suddenness of his departure made the paper talk about him as if he were missing instead of dead. Maybe no one was ever more than halfway into eternity; maybe everyone was ready to spring back to something like life, on the order of Jonathan Adams Darrell, or that replanted ghost regiment his mother was still saluting.

A clanging noise made him jump. He turned to the casket, as if to ask the bones: Did you hear that? Someone was definitely downstairs. He reached under the sweater to click off the light as quietly as possible, but a second after he did, he could tell that the big chandelier a floor below had flared to life. And now the staircase light had come on. Somebody was coming up.

"Some fortress," said a sarcastic voice. It was Peter Cox, the lawyer Margaret couldn't stand, the one who worked for her father. "All I had to do was pry off a rusty grate over one of the basement windows."

"I got in the same way," said Tim, with an eagerness that made no sense, except that this was the first conversation he'd had with anyone since the night he brought the old man in.

"Introduce me to your friend," said Peter, pointing to the casket.

"His name's Jon."

"Right. And he disappeared, sort of like you, a long time ago." Peter sat down at the typing table. "You look almost as skinny as he must be, Tim. Did the old colonel tell you that his friend killed himself?"

"*I* never tried to kill myself," said Tim.

"Then just what did you try to do?"

"I tried to come *alive!*" His voice was full of indignation and just a hint of teenage self-pity. Above all, it was bursting with the desire to tell somebody besides befuddled old Mr. Sinclair his story. "I had to get away from that house I was living in. It was more a coffin than the one *he's* in! And my dead brother was more alive than me." The words trailed off in a sudden, unexpected exhaustion.

"Where did you go?"

"A big field outside Kerby. I knew about this abandoned shed where I could hide the plane."

Peter laughed. "Ten miles?" The kid hadn't traveled outside the district he'd just won.

"A little less," said Tim, more proud than defensive.

"And you needed a plane for that?"

"Yes," he said. "If I took a plane, people would assume I went farther away. It would be easier for me to hide."

"The purloined letter."

"Huh?"

"Who helped you?"

"Nobody."

"Nobody? What have you been living off?"

"A locker full of stuff I had in the plane. Plus stuff I'd put in the shed beforehand."

"What about here?"

"Some boxes of stuff I brought in two weeks ago. I hitch-hiked with them in the middle of the night. Some guy thought I was a rich kid coming home." His voice dropped from pride to worry. "I'm starting to run out."

"Does Gus Farnham know where you are?"

"No."

"Margaret Feller?"

"No! Have you seen her? What's been happening to her?"

"She's had a broken ankle on top of her broken heart, and now she's dating your best friend."

"Does anyone besides you know I'm here?"

"No."

"How did you find out?"

"I've been keeping my eye on the old man. Tell me why you came back."

"For her. For Margaret."

Peter said nothing.

"I think I love her," said Tim, rushing to fill the void. He was still so famished for company he feared Peter might leave if he stopped talking. "I'm in over my head," he said, now on the verge of tears. "I'm afraid to come out. I'm afraid that my mother will have a heart attack, that they'll arrest me for stealing Gus's plane, or for sending the police on a wild-goose chase. I'm afraid Margaret won't have anything to do with me, that she won't forgive me." He struggled to get hold of himself. "I only wanted to disappear. I thought I could resurface somewhere else, creep out of that mausoleum I'd been living in since 1944. I thought I could figure every-thing out in that shed. But I stayed drunk for the whole first week, and then the three whiskey bottles were gone. I haven't had a drink since. After a couple more weeks I started going stir-crazy. I'd only come out at night to hitch-hike someplace and then come back. I finally decided to come here. I thought I could look out on everybody without their seeing me and I'd finally figure out what to do. Instead I've been in here with this dead body. On top of everything I made this crazy promise to the old man that I haven't been able to keep. In the middle of the night, just after he left, I managed to fill up the hole on the other side of the river. But I need a car to do the rest, and I haven't been able to steal one."

Peter could see the boy trying to put the particular complication of Horace Sinclair and Jonathan Adams Darrell out of his mind as he walked across the turret to one of the tiny windows on the opposite side. "See?" he said, pointing across the river toward the high school. "Sometimes at lunch the kids come down on the riverbank. Once or twice I've seen her with her girlfriends." He turned back around from the window. "Did you ever have anybody in love with you when you didn't deserve it?"

Peter, who had not gotten up, didn't answer. He was thinking about the Margaret Feller he'd last seen at her parents' dinner table: a polite young lady, half dead behind the eyes.

"I've got to talk to her, Mr. Cox. Away from here. Out of town. But I'm afraid if I try to get in touch with her the cops or her parents will find me first."

Why, Peter wondered, as he'd been wondering for two weeks, should he resurrect this boy for Margaret Feller? The kid would be back on the bottle inside of a week, after he'd ravished the girl like a hungry parolee. He was as bad a risk as you could find in this town.

But at least he was a risk. "All right, buddy boy, listen up. At eight o'clock tomorrow morning you're going to be at Ruby's Cafe, at the highway junction in Perry. You know where that is? Good, because that's where you're going to be waiting for her."

"How am I going to get there?"

He felt like Winchell bringing in Lepke. "I'm going to take you."

"Now?"

"No, sometime after 3 A.M. That's when I'll be coming back here for you. And before we head over to Perry, we're going to bring Mr. Darrell home."

"You mean bury him? Where?"

"Right where he was. As fast as two of us can dig, by the lowest flame my Ronson will hold."

"We can't," said Tim. "I promised Mr. Sinclair. He dug him out of there so the Dewey Walk won't get built on top of him."

"Kid," said Peter, looking at his watch. It was just twenty-five minutes since he'd talked to his old Yale friend in the candidate's suite at the Roosevelt Hotel. "Trust me. There isn't going to be any Dewey Walk."

T W E L V E

N o v e m b e r 3

WHEN JANE HERRICK'S TELEPHONE RANG THREE HOURS later, the sound did not wake her up. She was already awake, because she had not yet been to bed. She was hardly the only person in Owosso up at 3 A.M., but she was probably the only one rereading the *Argus*'s October 28 edition, specifically its article on the end of the pheasant-hunting season. "Although final returns are not yet in, it was estimated that more than 500,000 legal birds were shot this year, about a 10 percent better take than last year." Factoring in the article's further piece of information that "less than 300,000 hunters stalked the woods compared to some 350,000 nimrods in 1947," Jane began doing the math that would tell her, to the second decimal point, how many more birds would have died this year had Arnie's gun been in his living hands instead of a corner of her garage.

"Hello?" she said matter-of-factly.

"Hello!" responded a voice she recognized, despite its being a bit more thick and distant, on the edge of slurring, than what she was used to. "I came all this way and I'm still just two hundred feet away from Mrs. Dewey! Except they're *vertical* feet." Frank Sherwood, through his laughter, was trying to convey his location—a telephone booth off the main bar in the Roosevelt Hotel in New York City, where, as everyone in Owosso, even Jane, knew, Annie Dewey now occupied a room of the governor's fifteenth-floor suite.

Jane said nothing, and Frank's words rolled on. "They say she's gone to sleep. Things are pretty glum. We got over here around midnight and the ballroom was jammed, but the crowd's down to a couple of hundred now, and nobody's saying much. The bar's still full, and I guess some of them haven't given up. We think there's even a secret service guy waiting around, just in case. The only guy drinking coffee."

"Who are you with, Frank?"

"Some fellow I met at the theatre. I had standing room at a show called *Born Yesterday,*" he explained, looking, for confirmation, at the Lyceum Theatre playbill he still clutched in the hand also holding his drink. "I was going to try and see *Mister Roberts,* Henry Fonda's in it, but I figured who needed three more hours of the Navy? So I walked over to this show I'd never heard of and saw the last act standing up."

"And that's where you met this friend?"

"Right!" said Frank. He was surprised at how sharp Jane seemed tonight. "He was standing right next to me, and we got to talking and decided to come over to the Roosevelt, where all the action was supposed to be. Except it's getting deader by the minute." He laughed again.

"You're not staying there, are you?"

"No, I've got a room just a block from Penn Station. I

checked into it as soon as I got off the train. I've got it for the rest of the week."

"Tell me about today. What else have you been doing since you got there?"

"I went to the planetarium. Pretty silly, huh? But it was the first thing I thought of. That was in the morning. Afterwards I walked up and down Fifth Avenue and clear across Fifty-seventh Street in both directions. I haven't been to Macy's, but I went into Lord & Taylor. You could fit Christian's into the shoe department!" He'd already used that last line, a couple of hours ago on this guy from the theatre, but he liked the polished way it came out now, the little extra ring rehearsal had given it. All day long he'd been overhearing people talk that way.

"What's the weather like?"

"Kind of nice. No rain, even though they predicted it. Just a lot of clouds. There aren't any stars out, just the ones at the planetarium. I already know my telescope's going to be useless here with all the light on the ground. But do you know what you *can* see?"

"What, Frank?"

"A giant beacon sweeping the south sky. I noticed it before I knew what it was. It's coming from Times Square, from the newspaper tower. It means Truman's ahead. If the arc shifts north, it means Dewey's in front. When either of them has it won, it'll lock into position, north or south." For a sentimental split-second, a piece of him regretted that he wouldn't be able to explain this scientific marvel tomorrow morning during third period. "What's happening in Owosso?" he asked.

"Nothing's happening in Owosso," Jane replied.

Frank imagined she hadn't been out of her house all day, not to vote or go to the cemetery or anything else. He also thought he might be sobering up. The distance between them was lengthening fast; Jane's remoteness was making itself felt the way it always did after a while, even face-to-face. It was up to him to keep the conversation going, to say what he needed to before the sound between them died and the operator came on asking him to put in the rest of the change he'd gotten from the group at the bar. And he couldn't keep his new friend waiting forever. By now there were so few people around he could hear the radio playing in the lobby. Just music; the station was taking a break from the returns. He couldn't make out the song, but he wondered if it might somehow be "This Can't Be Love." He was too drunk to concentrate on the remote possibility, so for a moment he just closed his eyes and let himself feel something he'd never felt before, the sensation that he was the happiest person in the room.

He swallowed the rest of his drink. "Jane, do you remember the envelope I gave you Monday afternoon?"

"Yes, I've got it right here."

"Open it."

Someone else would have asked, "Are you sure?" or "Right now?" but this was Jane he was talking to, and the next thing he heard was her slitting the flap. He waited, and saw in his mind's eye exactly what she was seeing: the photograph that matched the one in his wallet, two young men in shirtsleeves, their arms draped over each other outside the Red Fox tavern.

·   ·   ·

AT 9 A.M. HARRY TRUMAN WAS TWO MILLION VOTES AHEAD, with Illinois sitting on his side of the electoral college. Crossing the street to the Fellers', Anne looked back at 421 West Oliver and wondered if Annie Dewey wouldn't be less pained waiting out the end behind her own lace curtains than in New York City. There wasn't a single person on the sidewalk, and Anne doubted there would have been even if the owner were home. Any remaining chance the house had of ever being declared a national monument now depended on Ohio.

"Do you remember my brother in Lansing?" asked Carol, handing her a cup of coffee. "He just called. He's ready to lead an invasion force against Illinois." Anne smiled absently.

"Where's Jack?" asked Carol. "He ought to be over here toilet-papering our trees, or something like that."

"He drove off to Flint a nervous wreck. He still thinks it's too good to be true. And Harold?"

"Upstairs sleeping off Peter's victory champagne. He has no idea of the rude awakening he's in for. There were plenty of bad signs at midnight, but he went to bed sure that Harris Terry was just enjoying his turn as the prophet of doom."

"Did Peter display any grace in victory?"

"I didn't see him until an hour ago. He came by looking a trifle the worse for wear. He asked for two aspirin and a cup of coffee, and then he gave Margaret a ride to school. 'Constituent service,' he called it. She remembered she needed to be in early for rehearsal."

"Can it really be over?" Anne asked. As yet she no more believed in the upset than Jack did.

Carol pointed to the radio, which was only murmuring. "It will be," she said, "if 'the Buckeye State' declares it so. They keep trying to find new ways to refer to Ohio since it became the center of the universe. It's gotten on my nerves so much I had to turn down the volume."

"What are we all going to do? Here in town, I mean."

"Die of embarrassment, I suppose. All of us but Al Jackson. He'll be on to something else, bless his heart."

Anne played with her teaspoon against the oilcloth.

"Why aren't you looking happier?" Carol asked. "You're the only Truman voter between here and Jack's."

"You're not counting the colonel," Anne replied. But she saw the point of Carol's question. Why *wasn't* she happier? Had she started rooting for Dewey? For the town's sake? Was she that fond of the unbuilt Walk? In the last few hours, had the candidate's preening, pint-sized perfection metamorphosed into an underdog's lovable scruffiness? Or did she just somehow fear seeing what wasn't supposed to happen, happen?

She snapped out of her perplexity. "Are you ready for the *local* news?"

"What's that?" asked Carol.

"Mrs. Wagner had a call from Frank Sherwood this morning. He's in New York."

"No!"

"She gave no details, acted very privileged and mysterious, but she says he's all right and—"

"Excuse me." Carol went to answer the telephone.

"Margaret? What's all that noise? Are they building sets?"

"No, Mother, that's traffic."

"Where are you?"

Carol could hear Margaret cupping her hand to get that information from whomever she was with, before she relayed the answer: "At a big intersection in Perry. Outside a diner. Now, Mother, you've got to listen carefully. I'm with *Tim.* He's *alive.*"

Anne could see the knuckles of Carol's hand, the one with the receiver, squeezing themselves white.

"He's alive and well, Mother, but so skinny! It's an amazing, terrible story, but he's come back. To all of us. To me especially. And I need to be with him. We have to—"

"Don't leave the line!" shouted Carol, handing off the phone to Anne. "Harold!" she cried, rushing up the stairs. "Harold! Wake up!"

"Margaret, it's Anne. What's going on?"

"It's Tim. He's back! And I need to be with him for a while. Anne, it's a miracle! Tell them not to spoil it by worrying. I'll explain everything later, but now—"

Amidst the dozen questions forming in her mind, Anne had the distinct impression that Margaret's voice, coming through the wires, sounded more alive, closer and more fully present, than it had the last time she'd been face-to-face with the girl.

"Margaret, how did you get where you are? Who took you to Tim?"

"I drove out in Arnie's Chevrolet. It started up like it had been driven the day before! The keys were in the ignition, just where Tim left them in August."

"Does Mrs. Herrick know he's all right?"

"She must have been fast asleep when I backed the car out of the garage. There wasn't *time* to tell her, Anne. I had to get here. And Tim needs to talk to me first. I'm the one he trusts. He can't have her and the police and everybody else sweeping down on him yet. I just wanted to tell Mother and Father not to worry. We'll—"

"Slow down, Margaret. Tell *me* something. Who let you know where to find him?"

"Peter," she said, as if the name carried unspoken adjectives for everything that was brave and noble and all for love. "He never intended to take me to school. He gave me the news on the way to Mrs. Herrick's garage. Once we got there, he told me to follow him to Perry in Arnie's car."

Lucy Cox on Monday night: "There's something on his mind, and I can't figure out what it is."

"Margaret, how did he know about Tim?"

"I'm still not sure," said Margaret. "He hasn't told me everything. He's been up all night with—"

"Does anyone else know Tim is safe?"

"I'm sure I'm the only one besides Peter. Anne, I've got to go. The operator's going to—"

Anne could hear the Fellers coming down the stairs.

"Margaret," Anne insisted, "put Peter on. *Please let me talk to him.*"

"What does Peter have to do with this?" Carol shouted.

"Yes," yelled Harold into the receiver he took from Anne's hand. "What does Peter Cox have to do with all this?"

Anne retreated toward the kitchen counter with the radio, which was suddenly louder, though its volume hadn't been raised. The announcer in Flint had begun to shout, as loud as Harold Feller, like a man begging to be let out of the box in which he was sealed. "That's right, ladies and gentlemen! Let me repeat it! The Buckeye State of Ohio has just

put its twenty-five electoral votes into the Democratic col-
umn! It's 9:30 A.M., eastern standard time, this Wednesday,
November the third, nineteen hundred and forty-eight, and
Harry Truman has just been re-elected President of the
United States!"

NINETY MINUTES LATER, HORACE SINCLAIR WAS STILL
listening to WOAP. He had switched to it from the Flint station for the pleasure of hearing the Owosso narrator rip and
read such wire-service statistics as the one he was now struggling through: "Preliminary figures indicate that Governor
Dewey actually carried a smaller percentage of the popular
vote this time than he did in 1944 against the late Franklin
D. Roosevelt."

But these sentences from the radio were just grace notes
to the glorious piece of music he held in his hand, the letter
he'd found pushed through the mail slot when he came
downstairs from his bedroom at five-thirty this morning.

4:45 A.M.

Colonel—

Jonathan Adams Darrell is back where he spent the
last half century. When the billboard comes down, the spot
will look just as it did for all those years and for the next
fifty to come. If the GOP is dumb enough to nominate
Dewey a third time in 1952, I doubt even Mr. Jackson will
try to revive the Walk.

The Herrick boy is okay. He won't say anything; I've
seen to that by providing him with his heart's desire.

I'm glad you had *your* heart's desire, Colonel. I refer,
of course, to the late Mrs. Sinclair. We don't all get ours,

and it's too bad J.A.D. never had his. (As you must know by now, I read the papers in the box while you were mixing me a drink.)

Do *not* save this note for fifty years. Better yet: Throw your whole damned box away, along with these things I took out of the casket.

Well, I got 58 percent instead of 65. Next time, when I'm not being squashed by the top of the ticket, I'll do better.

Peter Cox

P.S. Your lantern and shovel are back in the garage.
P.P.S. I borrowed your monkey wrench.

Horace opened the blinds, and Mrs. Sinclair's tea service caught the light that poured in. It was a fine day. Leaving *The Lady of the Lake* on the floor, where she'd fallen from his lap last night, he went out to the garage, clutching Peter's note and the little silver container of incriminating pledges left on the porch. He put it, along with the new note, into the buckram box that had been sitting out on the workbench the past few weeks. It was almost cool enough to make a fire, and that's what he would do once he went back inside the house. He'd consign the whole secret to the ashes and the air, and then he'd go out for a walk.

He'd go to the library for a mystery, and he'd take the long way there—not to gloat his way past the neighbors; only to enjoy the freedom from fear. He wouldn't even scoff when he crossed the Main Street bridge and saw Mr. Jackson's billboard. He'd just look down to the spot where Jon used to be and was again—but with a difference. Jon had been up and around for a while, refreshed, released forever from his grim end, its morbid tokens taken off his chest and destroyed.

Horace turned the handle of the Reginaphone. Its celestial tinklings would be a better hymn of thanksgiving than any mutterings he might make on his arthritic knees. The music came out with the same utter clarity it had had in the days of President Harrison, every note springing from the same slots of metal that had once served the ears of Mrs. Sinclair, before the Victrola and radio began their siren songs of infinite variation.

The old music swam around Horace's head in liquid perfection until a single thump against the garage door made him raise his eyelids. He got up to open the door and caught sight of the rear wheel of the schoolbound Billy Grimes' substitute, a mile wide with his throw of the *Argus*. The paper had come early today, the edition something between the regular afternoon one and the Extra they'd hoped to have on the street last night. Horace bent down as gingerly as he could to pick it up. He peeled off the rubber band and opened it up to the black banner headline whose 108-point characters seemed to be cringing at their own size, but doing their duty, conveying what everyone up and down Oliver Street knew by now: TRUMAN DEFEATS DEWEY.

WHEN ANNE ARRIVED AT THE BOOKSHOP, LEO ABNER WAS REmoving the picture of Thomas E. Dewey from the window. All over downtown, where she'd been walking in circles for nearly an hour, the candidate's visage was disappearing in a furtive frenzy. Leo had decided to keep his indoor spotlit bunting and provide it with a new focal point, a stiff cardboard notice that read:

GENERAL EISENHOWER TELLS HIS OWN STORY!
CRUSADE IN EUROPE
AVAILABLE NEXT MONTH
RESERVE YOUR COPY NOW!

"Late again," she said. "Sorry."

"That's all right," replied Leo. "I don't think too many people are going to be showing their faces today."

She was about to tell him the news of Tim Herrick, but made a snap decision not to. Until she knew the whole story herself, telling Leo any of it might put Peter at risk over whatever foolish thing he'd gone and done.

"Maybe I'll take one of these home for myself," mused Leo, picking up a copy of the '44 campaign biography. "I'm lucky I sold you yours two nights ago. I don't think I could give them away this morning."

He waited for her to say something, with no result. "I thought you'd be crowing this morning. Are you saving it all for Jack? Oh, that reminds me. He called." Leo handed her a slip of paper with the number of a bar in Flint near Walt Carroll's house.

"Okay," she said. "I'll call him. I'll bet they're drinking an Ohio brand of beer. But before that I'll take these to the basement." She scooped up the three remaining Dewey books. "The sight of them will only depress anyone who does come in. I'll do a little straightening up while I'm down there."

"Fine with me."

Once downstairs, she took a seat on the stool, lit a Lucky and began to cry. *Dudley,* she thought, until she could hear only "Peter," the way it had been pronounced by Margaret Feller's revitalized voice, the way she'd been hearing it in her head for an hour.

It could not turn out this way. Like all writers, Anne suspected, she saw two movies for every book she read, and every movie she could think of and every book she could remember told her it couldn't end like this. The romantic thing, which was to say the right thing, was to go off with the underdog. But what if the impossible overdog was really the prodigal romantic, and the underdog merely decent and loving and wonderful in bed? She had the definite feeling that Peter Cox would turn out to be pretty bad in that department, not so bad as the grad student in Ann Arbor, but nothing to write home about, if one wrote home about such things and if she'd had enough comparative experience to make the writing worthwhile.

Jack was the comparative experience she'd have in her memory for as long as she lived, and if her suspicions about Peter turned out to be right, those memories would always be her punishment, though they wouldn't be punishment enough.

Jack called. Call him at FL 6790. Granger's Bar.

She looked at the slip of paper and then closed her eyes, knowing she had to do the worst thing she would ever do.

"Anne?" It was Leo at the top of the stairs. "I've got to go home and check on Mrs. Abner. I'll be back after lunchtime. Do you mind bringing your sandwich back here?"

"No, Leo. Tell Martha I hope she's feeling better."

In the year 2000, Jack would bring her cups of tea and massage her swollen ankles. Peter? She couldn't get any picture of him, probably because he'd have been gone for years, after their divorce. She strained to put him onto the screen of her imagination, but all that came was the vision she'd had at the City Club a week and a half ago, just before Jack made Peter see stars: the turn of the century, the next century, with Owosso as the fixed center of a swirling, galactic vortex.

She heard Leo close the door upstairs. Now she could go from sniffles to tears. She could cry over her own awfulness. What was she going to do?

There was only one thing she *could* do. She was going to go upstairs and call Flint and shout into the receiver how wonderful it was that Harry would still be in the White House seven years from now, when Junior's little brother was going off to kindergarten.

But once back at the cash register she did nothing, and before she knew it, it was 11:45, and the day's apparent first customer was really a breathless Harris Terry, who couldn't bring himself to speak the name he needed to. He just pointed through Leo's window, back across the street to Feller, Terry & Nast, and asked Anne: "Have you seen him?"

"No," she replied. "Honest."

"Harold and Carol are in pursuit of Margaret. And I'm supposed to be in pursuit of Peter. I'm on my way to the hotel to see if he's with his mother. If he's not, maybe she knows something. Can you go over to the Matthews Building and see if he's holed up in his headquarters? I don't know what would possess him to come back here at all, let alone do whatever he's done, but it's all I can think of."

They left the shop together, after Anne flipped the BACK
IN A MINUTE sign behind the door blind. At the corner, they
wished each other luck and split up. Harris Terry entered
the Hotel Owosso, and Anne headed west on Main, noticing
as she went how the street once more looked like a sensible
brown parcel, the curled ribbon of bunting having disappeared along with most of the governor's pictures. To the
traveler passing through, the Dewey story would soon be like
that of the tornado, a piece of old-timers' lore, something to
be acquired through a little interested questioning, while
Owosso remained the perfectly ordinary place it had so recently celebrated itself for being. She walked slowly, trying to
remember the street as it had been two Saturdays ago, during the town's brief enchanted hour on a dateline that traveled coast to coast, and as she went she crossed her fingers
and even prayed that Peter was at the hotel with Mrs. Cox.

It was 1:05 when she climbed the stairs of the Matthews
Building. The door to COX FOR SENATOR was ajar, so she entered. The litter from last night's celebration remained: the
champagne bottle Harold Feller had drained, a napkin with
the co-ed's lipstick, the giant check mark on the blackboard.

"Mrs. Bruce?" she called, but got no answer.

A radio was playing in the small back room; its door,
too, was open several inches. Through the crack Anne could
hear, for what she realized would be the last time ever, the
voice of Thomas E. Dewey, conceding the election from New
York: *"Our task now, as I said in my telegram to the President, is to
get together and support the administration in the interest of the
peace of the world."* She approached the second doorway and
found what she was still telling herself she hoped not to.

"Everyone's looking for you, Peter."

His hair was uncombed and he hadn't shaven. He was in yesterday's shirt, still wearing his own campaign button.

"Maybe I'll go hide in Curwood Castle. It's a great spot for that."

"Is that where Tim was?" she asked, sitting down on the edge of the desk.

"Only part of the time."

"I don't care how you found him, I—"

"You don't know the half."

"I only want to know why you sent Margaret to him."

Peter drank the last gulp of flat champagne from a bottle in front of him. "So she could get her heart broken. Instead of just slowed down until it stops. You know, in the Cox family tradition."

"Is she coming back with him?"

"I don't know."

"What happened to the plane? Does he still have it? Suppose he takes off with her in it."

"Can't happen," said Peter, tossing Monday's newspapers into the wastebasket and then collapsing back into his chair from the effort. "I threw a monkey wrench into the engine. Literally."

"Has it occurred to you," cried Anne, "that Harold and Carol will go to the police with what happened? Margaret may come home, but what if your part in everything gets into the *Argus*? What are you going to do then?"

"Gee, Anne, I don't know." His expression mocked her prudence, told her it disgusted him. "I guess I'll resign my seat."

"Even if the Fellers forgive you, how long do you think this will stay a secret?"

"I don't know. Fifty years? Yeah. If people can keep *dark* secrets that long, I ought to be able to hold a pleasant little one like this down."

"You're exhausted. What are you talking about?"

"The other half of the story."

The '44 campaign biography that she'd brought him the other night was still on the blotter. They stared at it until Peter broke the silence.

"You said everybody's looking for me. Does everybody include you?"

She continued staring at the book. "Harris Terry asked me to come."

Peter grabbed the telephone receiver and pushed it into her hand. "Hear the operator? It's still connected. Mrs. Bruce paid the bill through the fifth of the month. Most people would have tried *calling* first."

She said nothing. He slammed the receiver back into its cradle, and then got up out of his chair to take her by the shoulders. "You're in love with me, Anne. It's not a political or a literary decision you get to make. It's the simple truth. I'm not an idea, and it's not my fault that I'm richer and better-looking than Jack."

"And what am I supposed to do about *him?*"

"We'll fix him up with Harvey P. Angell's wife's cousin."

She smacked his face. "That's exactly the kind of heartless thing he'd never say."

"And one of the reasons you're in love with me is it's just the kind of thing I would."

She knew she mustn't let the air hang silent, but she waited too long and the radio got the next word. The CBS man was reporting that "Governor Dewey has just left the room, telling members of the press, 'It's been grand fun, boys and girls.' "

"Game's over, Anne."

"I could never stay in this town! Not with Jack here."

"Well, now you won't have to."

"But I *love* this place!"

"Then pay a price! Why should *you* not have to give anything up?" She saw him shaking, more with fatigue than anger, and she knew that somewhere, in the place it most counted, she was stronger than Peter, too, stronger and harder than both Peter and Jack, and of all the things she hated about herself right now, she hated this one the most.

"Goddammit, Anne." He was crying. "I've been up all night, doing more heavy lifting than you can guess. And now I've got this Rotary Club posse bearing down on me. They're going to be here any—"

She finally took his hand. "There's only one problem," she whispered to him, as he let his head collapse onto her shoulder, and as the other part of her mind silently asked forgiveness for doing what she knew, at last, was the right thing.

"What is it?" he asked.

"Wherever we go, I'm still going to be a Democrat."

He kissed her long neck. "At least I know the worst."

SIX HUNDRED AND FIFTY MILES TO THE SOUTHWEST, IN INDEpendence, Missouri, sirens crowed and schoolchildren, dismissed for the day, ran home laughing. In downtown Owosso there was hardly a sound. Kay Schmidt wiped an empty countertop in the hotel coffee shop; inside the Argus building the bale of papers reserved for Billy Grimes lay unclaimed; and across the street at the post office, the extra clerk who'd been put on for lunchtime customers wanting November 3, 1948, cancellations stepped out for a sandwich at the Great Lakes.

At Gute's drugstore, Jane Herrick took the third copy of the *Argus* from the bottom of the stack and headed toward Main Street. She was on her way to the library to reconfirm the exact position of the Twelfth Army Group on November 3, 1944, which also happened to be the birthdate of Private Fred Mitchell of Durand, who had died the year before that in the Solomons. This was the job she had assigned herself an hour before Frank Sherwood's phone call. And yet, as she looked at her note in today's box on one of the calendars she bought at Abner's, the task seemed pointless. She recognized her own hand, but the urgent pencil pressure seemed to have been applied by someone else.

On the steps of City Hall, Al Jackson's cutout of Thomas E. Dewey stood by itself. The edges of its paper suit were frayed from four months of mute campaigning, but no arm was draped across it now. Jane mounted the steps and sat down next to it, her hand covering her mouth while she rested for a moment and thought about New York City. She and Arnie and eight-year-old Tim, persuaded by her cousin in New Jersey to pay a visit, had stood on the observation deck of the Empire State Building on the cold, clear morning of February 10, 1939. The boys had spent most of their time looking miles eastward, down to the spikes and globules of the nearly finished World's Fair. It looked just like the future it advertised itself to be, and she promised the two of them they would all come back after it opened. Through the binoculars, Arnie showed his brother each of the pavilions whose shapes were already familar from the magazines. She spent the time looking north, making sure her eyes, like fingers running over a venetian blind, touched each one of the streets as far as they could see. That way she would know that she had visited them all, even if they never got back to New York, which they didn't.

She must have seen Fifty-seventh Street, and the one with the planetarium, and she knew for sure that she and the boys had passed Lord & Taylor on the ground. Last night, as the Times Square beacon waved unexpectedly southward, it must have raked the observation deck on which she and her sons—how clearly she could see them now!—had stood that morning. Right this minute, November 3, 1948, here at 84°W/43°N, the sun was glinting off the name of Pfc. Arnold Herrick on the honor roll, a drop of reflected light looking as bright as Jupiter had the night Frank Sherwood showed it to her through his telescope.

She took the photograph out of her pocket and tilted it into the light, allowing it to catch the ray leading from the memorial back to the sun and out to Jupiter itself, wherever that planet was hiding in the brightness of midday. Frank Sherwood had loved her son. Frank Sherwood, the only man she had kissed—on the cheek at the Grand Trunk depot— since Arnie left her house on October 2, 1943.

She rose to her feet and stood face-to-face with Thomas E. Dewey, and she burst out laughing. If he didn't have one already, she would have drawn a mustache on him. As it was, she just started down the steps, at twice the speed she'd gone up them. Heading west, toward the Main Street bridge, she went on tiptoe at the moment ten sudden explosions filled the air. Some high-school boys, not dismissed for the day, only at their lunchtime recess, had found the fireworks behind Al Jackson's billboard on the riverbank and shot them off. You couldn't see the sprays of light, for they were lost in the kind of sky so bright it looked more silver than gold, but they were there.

Jane stepped onto the bridge just ahead of the deserted Dewey birthplace. The sound of the rockets prevented her from hearing Chief Rice's deputy a hundred feet behind. He was shouting "Mrs. Herrick! Mrs. Herrick!", trying to tell her what the police had just learned. The noise of the fireworks died, and their ashes fell on the roof of Curwood Castle, and he kept calling her name, but still she couldn't hear him. She was dancing across the bridge in the arms of a young man in a private's uniform. You couldn't see him, but he was there.

Author's Note and Acknowledgments

In doing research for this book, I received help from the staff of Owosso's public library and a number of its citizens, including Ivan Conger, Phil Welch, and Bruce and Elizabeth Wilson. Thomas E. Dewey's biographer, Richard Norton Smith, and Karl Kabelac of the University of Rochester, where the Dewey papers are housed, generously answered queries, and Michael Barone provided political lore and confidence. My thanks to all.

No one was, or could have been, more helpful than Helen Harrelson, Owosso's splendid historian, whose exactitude equals her love for her subject. I thank her for hundreds of facts, and for indulging my deviations from some of them.

In an afterword to my previous novel, I wrote: "Nouns always trump adjectives, and in the phrase 'historical fiction' it is important to remember which of the two words is which." This applies in spades to *Dewey Defeats Truman*, where I have taken a number of liberties with both local and national history.

I owe real debts to my editor, Dan Frank; my agent, Mary Evans; my good friends and readers Frances Kiernan and Lucy Kaylin; to Sallie Motsch; and, as always, to Bill Bodenschatz.

I first visited Owosso several years ago on a tip from my colleague at Vassar College, the author Nancy Willard. Had I never written a word about the place, I would still want to thank her for leading me to it.

Westport, Connecticut
April 12, 1996